KT-153-592

'She understands a woman's secret fantasies . . .
Johanna Lindsey creates fairy tales that come true'
Romantic Times

'Lindsey has mastered her craft, she creates fantasy
. . . You want romance – you got it!'
Inside Books

'High-quality entertainment . . . The charm and
appeal of her characters are infectious'
Publishers Weekly

'First-rate romance'
New York Daily News

'I have never been disappointed in her stories . . . A
constant high level of quality'
Affaire de Coeur

'Spirited characters, contrasting settings and intense
conflicts of the heart . . . Johanna Lindsey has a sure
touch where historical romance is concerned'
Newport News Daily Press

A LOVING
SCOUNDREL

Johanna Lindsey

CORGI BOOKS

A LOVING SCOUNDREL
A CORGI BOOK : 0 552 15131 9

First publication in Great Britain

PRINTING HISTORY
Corgi edition published 2004

1 3 5 7 9 10 8 6 4 2

Set in 11/13pt Plantin by
Kestrel Data, Exeter, Devon.

Corgi Books are published by Transworld Publishers,
61–63 Uxbridge Road, London W5 5SA,
a division of The Random House Group Ltd,
in Australia by Random House Australia (Pty) Ltd,
20 Alfred Street, Milsons Point, Sydney, NSW 2061, Australia,
in New Zealand by Random House New Zealand Ltd,
18 Poland Road, Glenfield, Auckland 10, New Zealand
and in South Africa by Random House (Pty) Ltd,
Endulini, 5a Jubilee Road, Parktown 2193, South Africa.

Printed and bound in Great Britain by
Cox & Wyman Ltd, Reading, Berkshire.

Papers used by Transworld Publishers are natural, recyclable
products made from wood grown in sustainable forests. The
manufacturing processes conform to the environmental
regulations of the country of origin.

A Loving
Scoundrel

Prologue

The rain didn't wash away the stench or lessen the heat. It seemed to make them both worse. Trash was piled high in the alley – boxes, rotten food, crates, broken dishes, all manner of discarded things no one wanted anymore. The woman and child had crawled into one of the larger crates on the edge of the pile of trash – to hide. The child didn't know why they needed to hide, but she'd felt the woman's fear.

It had been a constant thing, that fear, in the woman's expression, in her voice, in the trembling hand that held the child's and dragged them from alley to alley at night, never during the day when they might come across other people.

Miss Jane, the woman had said to call her. The child thought she should have known that name, but she didn't. She didn't know her own name either, though the woman called her Danny lass, so that must be it.

Miss Jane wasn't her mother. Danny had asked

and been told, 'No, I'm your nurse.' She never thought to ask what a nurse was, though, because it sounded like something she should know. Miss Jane had been with her from the start, the start of her memories, that is, which were actually only a few days old. She'd awakened lying beside the woman in an alley much like this one, both of them covered in blood, and they had been running and hiding in more alleys ever since.

Most of the blood had come from Miss Jane. She'd had a knife stuck in her chest and had other assorted wounds from where she'd been stabbed more than once. She'd managed to pull the knife out herself, when she woke up. But she hadn't tended to those wounds. Her only concern had been the child and stopping the blood still seeping from the back of Danny's head – and getting them away from that place where they'd woken up.

'Why are we hiding?' Danny had asked at one point, when it became obvious what they were doing.

'So he doesn't find you.'

'Who?'

'I don't know, child. I thought he was just a thief who went on a rampage of mayhem in order to leave no witnesses behind. But I'm not so sure now. He had too much purpose and was too intent on finding you. But I got you safely away and I'll keep you safe. He won't hurt you again, I promise you that.'

'I don't remember being hurt.'

'Your memories will come back, Danny lass, don't you fret none about that, though we can hope not too soon. It's a blessing, truly, that they're gone for now.'

Danny wasn't upset that she could remember nothing prior to the blood. She was too young to worry about what might happen next. Her concerns were only immediate, hunger and discomfort, and that Miss Jane hadn't woken up from their last sleep.

Her nurse had seemed to think they'd find something useful in the trash piled around them, but she'd been too weak to look yet. They'd crawled into the crate in the middle of the night, and Miss Jane had slept through the day.

It was night again and she was still sleeping. Danny had shaken her, but Miss Jane didn't stir. She was cold and stiff. Danny didn't know that meant she was dead and was what accounted for the worst of the stench.

Danny finally crawled outside the crate to take advantage of the rain while it lasted, to let it wash away some of the dried blood on her. She didn't like being dirty and so concluded she must not be used to it. It was confusing though, knowing simple things like that, yet having no memory to support it.

She supposed she could search through the trash as Miss Jane had intended to do, though she wasn't sure what to look for, what could be termed 'useful.' She ended up gathering a few things she found interesting, a filthy rag doll that was missing one arm, a man's hat that would keep the rain out of her eyes, a chipped plate that they could eat on – the missing arm from the doll.

Miss Jane had bargained a ring she'd been wearing yesterday for some food. It was the only time she'd ventured out during the day, wrapped up in her shawl to cover the worst of the bloodstains.

Danny wasn't sure if she had more rings to bargain with, she hadn't thought to look. But that was the last time she'd eaten. There was rotten food in the trash, but although she was hungry, she wouldn't touch it. Not because she knew better, but because she had no concept of being desperate and the smell of it was offensive to her.

She would probably eventually have died of starvation, huddled in the crate next to the body of Miss Jane, waiting patiently for Miss Jane to wake up. But she investigated the sounds of someone else searching through the trash that night and came upon a young woman. She was a girl of no more than twelve, actually, but being so much bigger than herself, Danny put her in the category of adult at first.

Thus her tone was respectful, if a bit hesitant, when she said, 'Good evening, ma'am.'

She'd startled the girl. 'What are ye doing out in this rain, lass?'

'How did you know my name?'

'Eh?'

'That is my name. Dannilass.'

A chuckle. 'More'n likely only half o' that, dearie. You live near 'ere?'

'No, I do not think so.'

'Where's yer mum, then?'

'I do not think I have one anymore,' Danny was forced to admit.

'Yer folks? Yer people? Yer too pretty to 'ave been let loose on yer own. Who are ye with?'

'Miss Jane.'

'Ah, there ye go,' the girl said brightly. 'And where's she gone off to?'

Danny pointed to the crate behind her, causing the girl to frown doubtfully. She took a look though, then a closer look, crawling inside the crate. Danny preferred not to go in it again herself, so didn't. It smelled much nicer out with the trash.

When the girl returned, she took a deep breath and shuddered. She then bent down to Danny's level and gave her a weak smile.

'Ye poor thing, was she all ye 'ad?'

'She was with me when I woke up. We were both hurt. She said the hurt on my head took my memories, but I would get them back someday. We have been hiding ever since, so the man who hurt us wouldn't find us.'

'Well, now, that's a bleedin' shame. I s'pose I could take ye 'ome wi' me, though it's not really a 'ome, just a lot o' children like ye, wi'out folks to care for 'em. We make do as best we can though. We all earn our keep, even the youngest like you. The boys pick pockets, so do the girls for that

11

matter, till they're old enough to earn their coins on their backs, which is wot I'll be doing soon if that bastard Dagger 'as 'is way.'

The last was spit out in disgust, causing Danny to ask, 'That is a bad job?'

'The very worst, dearie, sure to get ye the pox and a young death, but wot does Dagger care, long as the coins are comin' in.'

'I do not want that job then. I will stay here, thank you.'

'You can't—' the girl began, then amended, 'Listen, I've an idea. I wish I could've done it for m'self, but I didn't know then wot I do now. It's too late for me, but not for ye – not if they think yer a lad.'

'But I am a girl.'

'Sure ye are, lass, but we can get ye some pants, chop off yer 'air, and—' The girl chuckled. 'We won't even need to tell 'em wot ye are. They'll see ye in pants and think yer a boy right off. It will be like a game o' pretend. It will be fun, ye'll see. And it will let ye decide for yerself what job ye'll be wanting to do when ye get older, 'stead o' being told there's only one job for ye, 'cause yer a girl. So how's that sound, eh? Want to give it a try?'

'I do not think I have ever played pretend before, but I am willing to learn, ma'am.'

The girl rolled her eyes. 'Ye talk too fine, Danny. D'ye know no other way to talk?'

Danny started to offer yet another 'I do not think so,' but shook her head instead, embarrassed.

'Then don't talk at all, eh, till ye can talk like me. We don't want yer speech drawing eyes to ye. I'll be teaching ye, never ye fear.'

'Will Miss Jane be able to come with us, when she is feeling better?'

The girl sighed. 'She's dead. Too many wounds, it looked like, that never dried up. I covered 'er wi' that big shawl – now don't cry. Ye've got me to look after ye now.'

1

Jeremy Malory had been in some unsavory taverns before, but this one was likely the worst of the lot. Not surprising, since it was located on the edge of what was quite possibly the worst of London's slums, a neighborhood given over to thieves and cut-throats, prostitutes and wild packs of urchin orphans who were no doubt being groomed into London's next generation of criminals.

He didn't actually dare to enter the heart of that area. To do so would probably be the last his family would ever see of him. But this tavern, on the very edge of that den of thieves, was there for the unsuspecting to stumble upon, have a few drinks, and get their pockets picked, or if they were stupid enough to let a room there for the night, to get completely robbed, clothes and all.

Jeremy had paid for a room. Not only that, he'd spread his coins around freely, buying a round of drinks for the few customers in the tavern and giving a good performance of being quite foxed. He had deliberately set the stage for a robbery – his own. But then that's why he and his friend Percy were there – to catch a thief.

Amazingly, Percy Alden was keeping his mouth shut for once. He was a chatterbox by nature, and quite scatterbrained on top of that. Percy's keeping mostly quiet on this unusual outing attested to his nervousness. Understandable. Whereas Jeremy might feel right at home in this element, having been born and raised in a tavern before his father stumbled across him when he was sixteen, Percy was a member of the ton.

Jeremy had more or less inherited Percy when Percy's two best friends, Nicholas Eden and Jeremy's own cousin Derek Malory, had gone the domesticated route and got leg-shackled. And since Derek had taken Jeremy under his wing when Jeremy and his father, James, had returned to London after James's long estrangement from his family ended, it was quite natural that Percy would now consider Jeremy his closest cohort for entertainments of the nondomesticated sort.

Jeremy didn't mind. He was rather fond of Percy after chumming about with him for the last eight years. If he weren't, he certainly wouldn't have volunteered to extricate Percy from his latest folly – getting royally fleeced by one of Lord Crandle's gambler friends at a house party last weekend. He'd lost three thousand pounds, his coach, and not one but two family heirlooms. He'd been so bloody foxed, he didn't even remember it, until one of the guests commiserated with him the next day and told him all about it.

Percy had been quite done in, and rightly so. Losing the money and coach were no more than he deserved for being so gullible, but the two rings were a different matter entirely. One was so old it was the family signet ring, and the other, quite valuable because of its gemstones, had been passed down in Percy's family for five generations now. Percy would *never* have thought to use them as betting tender. He had to have been coerced, goaded, or otherwise duped into putting them in the pot.

All of it now belonged to Lord John Heddings, and Percy had been beside himself when Heddings refused to sell the rings back to him. Money the lord didn't need. The coach he didn't need. The rings he must have considered trophies, a testament to his gambling skill. More likely a testament to his cheating skill, but Jeremy could hardly prove it when he hadn't been there to witness it.

Had Heddings been a decent sort, he would have sent Percy off to bed, instead of plying him further with drink and accepting the rings into the pot. Had he been a decent sort, he would have let Percy redeem them for their value. Percy had even been willing to pay more than they were worth. He wasn't poor, after all, as he had already come into his inheritance when his father died.

But Heddings wasn't interested in doing what was decent. Instead he'd gotten annoyed at Percy's

17

insistence and downright nasty in the end, threatening Percy with bodily harm if he didn't stop bothering him. Which is what had annoyed Jeremy enough to suggest this alternative. Percy was quite convinced, after all, that his mother was going to disown him over this. He'd been avoiding her ever since, so she wouldn't notice the rings were missing from his fingers.

Since they'd retired to the tavern's upstairs room several hours ago, there had been three attempts to rob them. Bungled attempts each, and after the last, Percy was beginning to despair of finding a thief to carry out their mission. Jeremy was more confident. Three attempts in two hours meant there would be many more before the night was over.

The door opened again. There was no light in the room. There was no light out in the corridor either. If this new thief was any good, he wouldn't need light, he would have waited long enough for his eyes to adjust to the dark. Footsteps, a bit too loud. A match flicked.

Jeremy sighed and, in one fluid movement, left the chair near the door where he was keeping vigil. He was quieter about it than the thief had been upon entering the room and was suddenly there blocking his path, a mountain of a man, well, in comparison to the short thief, but big enough to scare the daylights out of the urchin, who immediately bolted back the way he'd come.

Jeremy slamnmed the door shut behind the

fellow. He still wasn't disheartened. The night was young. The thieves hadn't gotten desperate yet. And if it came down to it, he'd just keep one of them until they agreed to bring him their best.

Percy, however, was fast giving up hope. He was sitting up on the bed now, his back resting against the wall – he'd been appalled at the thought of getting under *those* sheets. But Jeremy had insisted he lie on the bed, to at least give the impression of being asleep. He'd done so on top of the covers, thank you very much.

'There must be an easier way to go about hiring a thief,' Percy complained. 'Don't they have an agency for this sort of thing?'

Jeremy managed not to laugh. 'Patience, old boy. I warned you this would likely take all night.'

'Should have brought this to your father's attention,' Percy mumbled.

'What was that?'

'Nothing, dear boy, nothing a'tall.'

Jeremy shook his head, but said nothing more. Percy couldn't really be faulted for wondering if Jeremy was capable of handling this mess on his own. Jeremy *was* nine years his junior, after all, and Percy, scatterbrain that he was and quite incapable of keeping a secret, had never been apprised of Jeremy's real upbringing.

Living and working in a tavern for the first sixteen years of his life had left Jeremy with a few unexpected talents. A tolerance for hard spirits that had reached the point that he could drink his friends so far under the table that they'd be passed out cold while he'd still be mostly sober. A way of fighting that could be quite underhanded if called for. And a keen ability to recognize a real threat as opposed to a mere nuisance.

His unorthodox education hadn't ended there, though, when his father discovered his existence and took him in. No, at that particular time, James Malory was still estranged from his large family and living the carefree life of a pirate in the Caribbean, or, *gentleman* pirate, as he preferred to be called. And James's motley crew had taken Jeremy in hand and taught him still more things a boy his age should never have learned.

But Percy knew none of this. All he'd ever been allowed to see was what was on the surface, the charming scamp, not so scampish anymore at twenty-five, but still charming, and so handsome that Jeremy couldn't walk into a room without every woman in it falling a little bit in love with him. Aside from the women in his family, of course. They merely adored him.

Jeremy had taken after his uncle Anthony in his looks; in fact, anyone who met him for the first time would swear he was Tony's son, rather than James's. Like his uncle he was tall with wide shoulders, a narrow waist, lean hips, and long legs. They both had a wide mouth and a strong, arrogant jaw, as well as an aquiline, proud nose, darkly tanned skin, and thick ebony hair.

But the eyes were the most telling, a mark of only

20

a few Malorys, purest blue, heavy-lidded, with the barest suggestion of an exotic slant, framed by black lashes and slashing brows. Gypsy eyes, it used to be rumored, inherited from Jeremy's great-grandmother Anastasia Stephanoff, whom the family had just last year discovered had really been half Gypsy. She'd so captivated Christopher Malory, the 1st Marquis of Haverston, that he'd married her the second day of their acquaintance. But that was a tale only the family would ever know about.

It was quite understandable why Percy had wanted to get Jeremy's father involved instead. Hadn't his best friend, Derek, gone straight to James when he'd had problems of the unsavory sort? Percy might not know of James's pirating days, but who didn't know that James Malory had been one of London's most notorious rakes prior to his taking to the seas, that it was the rare fellow indeed who dared stand up to James, then or now, whether in the ring or on the dueling field?

Percy had settled back down on the bed for his 'impression' of sleeping. After a few more mumbles, some tossing and turning, he was then mostly quiet in anticipation of their next intrusion.

Jeremy wondered if he should mention that taking this particular matter to his father wouldn't get it settled anytime soon, that James had hied off to Haverston to visit his brother Jason the very day after Jeremy had been presented with his new town house. He was quite certain his father had gone to the country for a week or two out of fear that Jeremy would drag him about furniture shopping.

Jeremy almost missed the shadow moving stealthily across the room toward the bed. He hadn't heard the door open this time, hadn't heard it close either, hadn't heard a bloody thing for that matter. If the occupants of the room really had been asleep, as was to be expected, they certainly wouldn't have been awakened by this intruder.

Jeremy smiled to himself just before he lit a match of his own and moved it over the candle on the table he'd placed next to his chair. The thief's eyes had been drawn to him instantly. Jeremy hadn't moved otherwise, was sitting there quite relaxed. The thief wouldn't know how quickly he could move to prevent his escape if he had to. But the thief wasn't moving either yet, as he was apparently frozen in his surprise at being caught.

'Oh, I say.' Percy raised his head. 'Did we finally get lucky?'

'I'd say so,' Jeremy replied. 'Didn't hear him a'tall. He's our man, or boy as the case may be.'

The thief was starting to shake off his surprise and probably didn't like what he was hearing, to go by the narrowed, suspicious look Jeremy was now getting. Jeremy ignored it. He looked for a weapon first, but didn't see the thief carrying one. Of course, Jeremy had his own hidden in his coat pockets, a pistol in each, so just because he didn't see one didn't mean the lad didn't have one.

Much taller than the previous miscreants who'd tried their hand at robbing them, and lanky besides, this thief was probably no more than fifteen or sixteen, to go by those smooth cheeks. Ash blond hair so light it was more white than blond, naturally curly, worn short. A misshapen black hat several centuries out of fashion. He wore a gentleman's coat of dark green velvet, stolen no doubt, and quite grubby-looking now, as if it got slept in a lot. A discolored white shirt was under it with a few ruffles at the neck, black trousers of the long variety, and no shoes. Smart fellow, no wonder he hadn't made a single sound yet.

Very flamboyant looking for a thief, but probably because he was such a handsome young lad. And he was definitely recovered from his surprise. Jeremy knew to the second when he would bolt and was there at the door before him, leaning back against it, crossing his arms across his chest.

He offered a lazy smile. 'You don't want to leave yet, dear boy. You haven't heard our proposal.'

The thief was gaping again. It could have been Jeremy's smile, but was more likely his speed in getting to the door first. But Percy noticed it this time and complained, 'Damn me, he's staring at you the way the wenches do. It's a man we're in need of, not a child.'

'Age is irrelevent, old man,' Jeremy replied. 'It's skill we're in need of, so the package it comes in doesn't matter all that much.'

The lad, blushing now, was insulted, apparently,

and with a glower toward Percy spoke for the first time. 'Ain't never seen a nabob so pretty is all.'

The word *pretty* started Percy laughing. Jeremy was no longer amused. The last man who'd called him pretty had lost a few teeth because of it.

'Look who's talking, when you've got the face of a girl,' Jeremy said.

'He does, don't he?' Percy agreed. 'You should grow some hair on those cheeks, at least until your voice drops an octave or two.'

Yet another blush from the boy and a distinct grumble: 'It won't grow – yet. I'm only fifteen – I think. Just tall for m'age, I am.'

Jeremy might have felt sorry for the lad because of that 'I think,' which implied he wasn't sure what year he'd been born, which was usually the case with orphans. But he'd noted two things simultaneously. The boy's voice had started out high-pitched, then lowered before he'd finished his speech, as if he were going through that awkward time in a boy's life when his voice started changing to the deeper tones of manhood. And yet, Jeremy didn't think it was a natural slip, it had sounded much too contrived.

But the second thing he noticed upon closer examination was the lad wasn't just handsome, he was downright beautiful. Now, the same thing might have been said about Jeremy at that age, except Jeremy's handsomeness was decidedly male, while this lad's handsomeness was decidedly female. The soft cheeks, the lush lips, the pert little nose – yet there was much more. The chin was too weak, the neck too narrow, even the stance was a dead giveaway, at least to a man who knew women as well as Jeremy did.

Still, Jeremy might not have drawn the conclusion he did, at least not quite so soon, if his own stepmother hadn't used the same sort of disguise when she'd first met his father. She'd been desperate to get back to America, and signing on as James's cabin boy had seemed to be her only option. Of course, James had known from the start that she wasn't a lad, and to hear him tell it, he'd had a great deal of fun pretending to believe she was a boy.

Jeremy could be wrong in this case. There was that slim possibility. And yet he was rarely wrong where women were concerned.

But there was no need to expose her. Whatever reason she had for hiding her gender was her business. He might be curious, but he'd learned long ago that patience reaped the best rewards. And besides, they only needed one thing from her – her talent.

'What do they call you, youngun?' Jeremy asked.

'None o' yer bleedin' business.'

'I don't think he's figured out yet that we're going to do him a good turn,' Percy remarked.

'Ye set a trap—'

'No, no, think of it as an opportunity for employment,' Percy corrected.

'A *trap*,' their thief insisted. 'And I don't need wotever it is yer offering.'

Jeremy raised a black brow. 'You aren't even a little curious?'

'No,' said the thief most stubbornly.

'Too bad. The nice thing about traps is – you don't get out of them unless you get let out. Do we look like we're letting you out of this one?'

'Ye look like ye've bleedin' well lost yer minds. Ye don't think I'm alone, d'ye? They'll be coming for me if I don't return when I'm expected to.'

'They?'

The question just got Jeremy another glower. He shrugged, unperturbed. He wouldn't doubt she ran with a pack of thieves, the very bunch that had systematically been sending their numbers in, one at a time, to rob the unsuspecting gentry who had blundered into their territory. But he doubted they'd come looking for her. They'd be more interested in obtaining the expected fat purse first, before they thought of any rescuing. If anything, they'd assume this attempt had failed, that she'd been apprehended, knocked out, or killed, and would be sending in the next thief soon.

Which meant they should wrap this up and be on their way, now that they had their quarry in hand, so Jeremy said congenially, 'Sit down, youngun, and I'll explain what you've volunteered for.'

'I didn't vol—'

'But you did. When you came through that door, you most surely did volunteer.'

'Wrong room,' their thief tried to assert. 'Ye've never walked into the wrong room by mistake?'

'Assuredly, though usually with my shoes on,' Jeremy said dryly.

She blushed again and swore a blue streak.

Jeremy yawned. Much as he'd enjoyed the cat-and-mouse bantering, he didn't want this taking *all* night. And they still had a good distance to travel to reach Heddings's house in the country.

He injected a note of sternness in his tone when he ordered, 'Sit down, or I will physically put you in that chair—'

Jeremy didn't have to finish. She ran to the chair, practically dove into it. She definitely didn't want to risk his touching her. He forced back another smile as he moved away from the door to stand in front of her.

Percy, amazingly, injected a bit of logic into the proceedings: 'I say, we could explain this on the way, couldn't we? We've got our man. Is there any reason to remain in these god-awful accommodations a moment longer?'

'Quite right. Find me something for binding.'

'Eh?'

'To tie him up with. Or haven't you noticed that our thief isn't being the least bit cooperative – yet?'

At which point their thief desperately bolted for the door.

2

Jeremy had known it was coming, one more effort to escape them before it was too late. He'd seen it in her eyes just before she flew past him. He was at the door before she could get it open, though, and rather than just lean his weight against it to keep her inside, he decided to find out conclusively whether he was right about her sex and put his arms around her instead. He'd been right. Those were definitely female breasts under his forearms, packed down flatly, but unmistakable to his touch.

She didn't just stand still there and let him discover that. She turned around, and good God, that was even better, since he wasn't letting go of her yet. The very last thing he'd expected to find that night was a pretty wench wiggling about in his arms. Now that he was positive she was a wench, he was quite enjoying himself.

'I suppose I should check you for weapons,' Jeremy said, his voice lowered to a husky note. 'Yes, indeed, I really should.'

'I ain't got—' she started to claim, but ended on a gasp as his hands slid over her derriere and stayed there.

Rather than pat her pockets as his suggestion had implied, he gave each rounded cheek a gentle squeeze. Supple, soft she was, and suddenly he felt an urge to do more than just feel her with his hands; he wanted to press her loins firmly to his, pull down those ridiculous trousers she was wearing, run his fingers over her bare skin, and enter her wet warmth. He couldn't have been in a better position to do so, his hands cupping her luscious bottom. But he was already rising to the occasion, as it were, and didn't want her to know the effect she was having on him.

'Will these do?' Percy asked, reminding Jeremy that he wasn't alone with the girl.

With a sigh, Jeremy got back to the matter at hand and toted their thief back to the chair and shoved her into it. He leaned over her, his hands on the arms of the chair, and whispered, 'Stay there, unless you like having my hands all over you.'

He almost laughed, she went so motionless. But the glare she gave him promised retribution. Not that he thought she was capable of anything of the sort, but she probably did.

He glanced back to see that Percy had ripped up the bedsheet, having found a good use for it after all, and was dangling a number of strips from his hand.

'Those will do nicely, bring them here,' Jeremy said.

He should have had Percy take over from there, but he didn't. And he tried not to touch the girl more than he had to, really he did, but he was a man who loved women and he just couldn't help himself. He held both her hands in one of his while he wound the strip of cloth about her wrists. Her hands were warm, moist with fear. She had no way of knowing that they meant her no harm, so her fear was natural. He could have eased her mind, but Percy was right, they needed to vacate the place before the next thief showed up, so the explanations could wait.

The gag was next, and he didn't mind at all leaning close to her to get it tied behind her neck. He should probably have tied her hands behind her back instead, but he didn't have the heart to make her any more uncomfortable than he had to. The fisted punch he got to his gut when he leaned over her wasn't expected, but didn't annoy him all that much since there wasn't much strength behind the punch from her current position.

Her legs he didn't trust a'tall, though. Squatting down to get the cloth around her ankles would have put him in a prime position to get knocked on his arse, so he sat on the arm of the chair instead and brought both her legs over his lap. She shrieked under the gag once, but then was quiet and still again. She had long pants and socks on, so there was no bare skin he could touch. But still, just having her legs across his lap affected him profoundly, much more than it should have. He glanced down at her when he was done, and there was such heat in his eyes, she would have had no doubt that he saw through her disguise – if she'd been looking at him to catch it. She wasn't. She was trying to work her wrists loose from the binding and had nearly succeeded.

He put his hand over hers again and said, 'Don't, or instead of my friend toting you out of here, I'll do it.'

'Eh? Why me?' Percy complained. 'You're the stronger by far. Don't mind admitting it. No indeed, specially when it's so bloody obvious.'

Much as Jeremy would love to carry the wench, he had to be sensible for the moment. 'Because one of us has to make sure there are no objections to our leaving with this chap in tow. And while you might be up to the task, old man, I doubt you'd enjoy it quite as much as I will.'

'Objections?' Percy said uneasily.

'We aren't exactly walking out arm in arm, the three of us.'

Understanding now, Percy said abruptly, 'Quite right. Don't know what I was thinking. You're better at bashing heads by far.'

Jeremy managed not to laugh, since Percy had probably never bashed a head in his life.

They didn't run into much opposition. Only the bartender was still around downstairs, a huge, ugly

31

fellow who would likely give most men pause if he even glanced their way.

''Ere, now ye ain't leaving 'ere wi' that baggage,' he growled.

'The "baggage" tried to rob us,' Jeremy cut in, attempting for the moment to be peaceable about the matter.

'So? Then kill 'im or leave 'im, but ye ain't taking 'im to the watchmen. Ain't 'aving no law come sticking their noses round 'ere.'

Jeremy gave it one last try. 'We have no intention of visiting the authorities over this matter, my good fellow. And this *baggage* will be returned by morning, none the worse for wear.'

The big man began lumbering his way around the bar with the intention of blocking their exit. 'We've rules round 'ere, gov'nor. Wot's 'ere stays 'ere, if ye catch my meaning.'

'Oh, I'm very good at catching. And we've rules where I come from as well. Sometimes, they don't need explaining – if you catch *my* meaning.'

Jeremy didn't think any head bashing would work on a head that big, so he simply lifted one of his pistols and shoved it in the chap's face. That worked very well. The man spread his arms wide and started backing off.

'Smart fellow,' Jeremy continued. 'Now you can have your thief back—'

''E ain't mine,' the burly bartender thought it prudent to mention.

'Whatever,' Jeremy replied on his way out the

door. 'He'll be returned just as soon as we've concluded our business with him.'

There was no other attempt to stop them from leaving the area. And the only other person they came across at that late hour of the night was an old drunken woman who still had enough of her wits to cross to the other side of the street to get out of their way when she saw them.

But Percy was definitely out of breath after traversing four blocks with the bound thief over his shoulder. They hadn't left the coach near the tavern for obvious reasons, mainly being that it probably wouldn't have been there when they were ready to leave. Four blocks away in a safer, well-lit area had seemed a reasonable spot, but was a bit far to tote their thief. So it wasn't surprising that Percy simply dumped his package on the floor of the coach and none too gently, too worn-out to do more'n that.

Climbing in behind Percy, Jeremy saw there was no help for it, he was going to have to touch the wench again after all, to get her up on the seat. He'd been trying to avoid temptation by letting Percy carry her. It wasn't as if he couldn't have carried her *and* seen to any interference along the way. But he'd given the chore to Percy because he'd already discovered what touching her did to him. Looking was one thing. It had no effect on a man who overindulged in women. Touching, however, was much too intimate, and Jeremy reacted to intimacy on a purely prurient level.

And the simple fact was, he didn't want to want this wench. She was beautiful, yes, but she was a thief, probably raised in the gutter or worse. Her personal habits were more than likely so far below his standards that they weren't worth contemplating.

There was no help for it. Percy, poor fellow, was no doubt as exhausted as he presently looked. But before Jeremy actually put his hands on the girl, he realized that enough time had passed while contemplating his dilemma that the coach was on its way, the outskirts of the city were in sight, and it would be a simple matter to keep their prize from escaping now. So he could simply untie her and she could make herself comfortable on the seat.

He did that now, first her feet – damned dainty they were. Then her hands. He didn't touch the gag. She was able to remove it now herself and she did that most quickly. Quick, too, was the punch she threw at him as she came up off the floor.

It was the one thing he hadn't expected, though he should have, since she'd tried to punch him earlier. Ranting and raving could be expected, yes, more vulgar swearing, certainly, but for her to do what a man might do . . .

She missed, of course. Jeremy was no slouch in his reactions. And although he did get his jaw out of the way, which she'd aimed for, her fist still slid along his cheek and clipped his ear, which was now stinging.

But before he dealt with that as it deserved, Percy said in an excessively dry tone, 'If you're going to beat him to a pulp, dear boy, do it quietly, please. I'm going to nap until we get there.'

And that had their thief turning toward the door. Jeremy reached out and caught the back of her collar and yanked her onto his lap instead. 'Try that again and you can spend the next several hours right here,' he said, wrapping his arms around her so tightly she couldn't move.

She couldn't get loose, but that didn't mean she was going to stop trying. Wiggling about in his lap, however, was probably the worst thing she could have done. The position was much too sensual, producing lascivious thoughts of what he'd like to do – no, *would* do if they were alone. Stripping her clothes off slowly, finding out how she was concealing her breasts, nibbling on her shoulder as he drove into her. *Bloody hell.* If she continued to bounce on him like that, he might just kick Percy out of the coach for a while.

She must have realized her efforts were useless about the same time he realized he couldn't stand the wiggling and bouncing of her bottom on his thighs and loins anymore without becoming quite obvious in what she was stirring up. She groaned, yet to him it sounded more passionate than frustrated and had him dropping her as if he'd just been burned. Good God, she shouldn't be affecting him this strongly. He had to get it under control.

She'd fallen to the floor again, but immediately scrambled up on the seat opposite them, jerking down her coat lapels, dusting off her grubby pants, and avoiding eye contact as best she could, all the while watching for the counterattack that Percy's remark had suggested might be coming.

Jeremy waited a full five minutes, about the time it took for him to get his desire in check and hope his voice wouldn't reflect it. Finally he stretched out his legs, crossed them, leaned back and crossed his arms as well, and said, 'Relax, youngun. We'd as soon not hurt you. You're going to do us a favor, and in the process make yourself rich. What could be more agreeable than that, eh?'

'For ye to take me back.'

'That isn't an option. We went to a lot of trouble to obtain you.'

'Ye should've obtained me bleedin' consent first – *m'lord*.'

The title was added as an afterthought, and with a large heaping of contempt.

She was glowering at him again, now that she was relatively sure he wasn't going to throttle her. He'd tried not to examine her eyes too closely, hoping the dim light of the candle in the tavern room had misled him. But the brighter coach lamp and close proximity were his undoing. Her eyes were simply incredible and added tenfold to her beauty. Violet they were, dark, rich violet, and such a startling contrast to her white-gold mop of curls. Her eyelashes were long, but not overly dark. The brows, too, weren't very dark, merely a few shades more golden.

He tried, he really did, to find some masculinity in the face across from him, but it just wasn't there. How anyone could mistake her for a boy boggled his mind. And yet Percy had no trouble seeing a lad, albeit a 'pretty' one. Her height, he supposed, was the deciding factor. It was rare, after all, to find a female who was bloody well as tall as his father was. Anyone that tall would naturally be assumed to be male.

He'd also tried, truly, not to react to her as he would any other beautiful woman he came across. But those eyes . . . He gave up the fight. He would have her in his bed, and before the night was done. It would happen. He had no doubt whatsoever.

Having given in to his prurient nature, the change in Jeremy was immediate. Some might call it charm, but it was in fact pure sensuality, and to look at him when his thoughts were carnal was to know he promised pleasures untold.

The wench reacted immediately to the way he was now looking at her, casting her eyes away from him, but not before she blushed. Jeremy smiled. He'd known she wouldn't be an easy conquest, yet that blush spoke volumes. She was no more immune to him than other women were. But he wasn't going to give away her little secret. He'd let her play her manly role for now – at least until he got her alone.

For the moment, he addressed her remark,

wondering aloud, 'Should you have obtained our consent before you robbed us?' That got him another blush, so he merely concluded, 'No, I didn't think that was your habit. So let me just explain what's needed and why, before you get back to refusing out of hand. My friend here got himself robbed, you see, but in a legal way.'

'If ye insist on explaining,' she injected, 'ye could at least make sense.'

A mere grumble. Encouraging. Apparently she was going to listen to him.

'The "legal" way I mention was gambling.'

A snort. 'That ain't being robbed, that's being stupid. A big difference there, mate.'

Jeremy grinned, and the wench became obviously flustered by it, which only made his grin turn knowing. He then explained that John Heddings was the culprit who chose not to play fair and that she was going to exact retribution for them.

'We're taking you to Heddings's house in the country,' Jeremy continued. 'It's rather big, will be filled with servants, and thus, they'll be confident that no thief in his right mind would ever consider robbing them, and rightly so. Which is to your benefit, lad.'

''Ow's that?'

'The doors might be locked, but the windows will pro'bly be open this time of the year. The fact that they don't expect to be robbed means they won't be on their guard for it. And it's past midnight, so the servants should be asleep and out of the way until morning. So you should have no difficulty entering the house.'

'And then wot?'

'You will need to enter the master bedroom undetected. Chances are Heddings will be in it when you do, but you're quite used to that I'm sure. Like the servants, he should be fast asleep this time of night. Then proceed to do what you do best. Rob the man.'

'Wot makes ye think 'e won't 'ave his valuables locked away in a safe?'

'Because he doesn't live in London. The gentry feel much more secure on their country estates.'

'Wot do these 'eirlooms look like then, that I'm s'pose to be nabbing?'

'Two rings, both very old.'

'I'm still needing a description, gent, if I'm to pick them out o' the pot.'

Jeremy shook his head at her. 'It doesn't matter, since you can't just take Percy's two rings. That would leave Heddings knowing right where to point the finger. Your job, dear boy, is no different than you're accustomed to, to take everything of value you find. Your gain is that you may keep all the rest for yourself, thousands of pounds' worth of jewelry, I'm sure.'

'Thousands!' she said, gaping at him.

He nodded with a chuckle. 'Now aren't you glad we insisted you come along?'

Those lovely violet eyes narrowed abruptly on him. 'Yer a bleedin' idiot if ye think any trinkets, no matter how costly, makes up for the trouble I'll be in for not getting permission to do this first.'

Jeremy frowned, but not over the name-calling. 'You're on that tight a leash?'

'I've rules to abide by, aye, and ye've made me break most o' them.'

His sigh was long and drawn out. 'You *could* have mentioned this sooner.'

'I figured the barkeep would've stopped ye. Didn't take 'im for no coward, big as 'e is.'

'No one likes to get a bullet in their face, lad,' Jeremy said in the barkeep's defense. 'But he can attest that you weren't given a choice in the matter. So what, really, is the problem?'

'It's none o' yer concern—'

'Beg to differ, you've just made it my concern.'

'Like 'ell. Figure it out real quick, mate, that ye've interfered in m'life too much as is. Drop it, or we're done talking about *any*thing.'

A long moment passed before Jeremy nodded – for now. But causing their thief extended grief had not been part of tonight's agenda. He'd have to accompany the girl home now, when they were done, to get whatever trouble he'd caused her set right.

There shouldn't have been any trouble, though, and that's where this situation was getting most odd. They were offering a thief a golden opportunity. Any *normal* cutpurse would have jumped on it and been grateful to have such a golden egg dropped in his lap. But no, they had to get the one exception, a thief from a gang that was apparently so bogged down in rules that they couldn't even do odd jobs without getting permission first. Which defied reason. What bloody difference could it make when, where, or what, as long as the fat purse got brought home?

The coach stopped. Percy said with a sigh, 'Finally.' Then: 'Good luck, youngun. Not that you'll need it. We've every confidence in you, 'deed we do. And can't tell you how much this is appreciated. It's deuced hard hiding from your own mother, specially when you live with her.'

Jeremy opened the coach door and ushered the girl out before Percy's dissertation turned into his usual long-winded sort. They were parked in the woods near Heddings's estate. He took her arm and led her through the trees until the house was in sight.

'I'd wish you luck as well, but you aren't likely to need it,' he said in parting. 'I've seen how capable you are at what you do.'

'Wot makes ye think I won't be bolting for home soon as I'm out o' yer sight?'

Jeremy smiled, though she probably couldn't see it. 'Because you have absolutely no idea where you are. Because it's the middle of the night. Because we can get you back to London much, much sooner than if you try to find it yourself. Because you'd rather return home with your pockets full of dazzling gems than empty. Because—'

'That were enough becauses, mate,' she interrupted in a low grumble.

'Quite right. But one last assurance. If for some inexplicable reason you are apprehended, don't panic. I'm not sending you to the wolves, dear boy. I *will* see to your release no matter what it takes. You may depend upon it.'

3

I'm not sending you to the wolves. Who did he think he was kidding? He was the bleeding wolf. But she could breathe normally again, now that he was no longer near her and looking at her with those penetrating blue eyes.

She'd nearly given herself away, with all those blushes, and that had frightened her, too, that she'd been unable to control what that gent made her feel. She usually dealt well with men, she was 'one' of them, after all. But then she'd never come so close to one of Malory's caliber. Just looking at him flustered her, she found him so attractive!

Danny had never been so distraught in her entire life, with possibly one exception. But she'd been too young to realize the danger she had been in then, hadn't known that if she'd stayed where she was she'd surely die, only knew that she was completely alone in the world, with no one to turn to for help.

She wasn't alone anymore, but she might as well

be. She'd been living on a tightrope of anxiety for several years now because she was getting too old to hide that she'd never fill out with manly proportions like the rest of the boys eventually did. Sooner or later, someone was going to realize and reveal that she'd deceived everyone from the very beginning.

It had been easy, keeping that secret over the years, much easier than she could have hoped for, and all because Lucy had been right. Bringing her home to the pack in ragged knee breeches, a shirt too big, a coat too small, that old hat she'd found to keep the rain out of her eyes, and with her long hair chopped off to the neck had left a lasting impression that had never altered.

She quickly became 'one of the boys.' She'd learned to steal with them, learned to fight with them, learned everything they did – well, except when they went looking for female companionship of the type Danny didn't want to know about.

There were fourteen of them at present, and they lived in a dilapidated house that Dagger paid the rent on. There had been many houses like it over the years, even a few abandoned tenement buildings when there wasn't enough money to pay for rent.

Dagger never stayed in one place long. The current house had four rooms: a kitchen, two bedrooms, and a large living area. Dagger had one of the bedrooms for himself. The girls got the other bedroom to sleep in, or work in, if they were old enough to start whoring. Everyone else slept in the large living area, Danny included.

There was a small backyard. Though no grass grew in it, it was still nice for the younger children to play in. Danny had enjoyed backyards herself, once she got over her aversion to being dirty. Bathing wasn't an option for her, at least not in the communal tubs set up once a week in the kitchen. She snuck off to the river instead, when she could manage to. And the rain became her friend.

Lucy was her only confidante. Lucy didn't get the pox as she'd feared, but she did end up selling her body at Dagger's insistence. Danny understood his logic, even if she didn't like it. Being a comely woman, Lucy would have gained too much notice from the victims she intended to rob. A pickpocket had to be almost invisible to his target. Lucy couldn't be that, and how else was she to earn her keep then?

Dagger had been the oldest among them back then and he still was, so he was their leader by default. There'd only been a few rules to start with, nothing anyone could really mind. But Dagger seemed to think if he didn't add more rules every so often, then he wasn't doing his job.

Danny never argued with him. She did what she was told to do without complaint. His was the only keen eye she really worried about because, aside from Lucy, he was the only one left who had been there the day she'd arrived with Lucy, and eventually it was going to occur to him to count up the years – and wonder why a twenty-year-old man still had the face of a twelve-year-old boy.

He was thirty himself now or thereabouts, thirty and still running a pack of orphans. He could have moved on. Most of them did when they reached their high teens, wanting more than the pack offered, wanting to be able to keep what they stole, rather than turning it all over to Dagger to buy the food and pay the rent and bring home the occasional trinket to make one of them smile. Dagger could have moved on himself to more lucrative crimes, but he hadn't.

He meant well, even if he was abrasive. Danny had concluded years ago that he had a kind heart hidden somewhere in his scrawny chest. As leader, he probably thought he had to be hard and un-bending. But she guesed he didn't see himself just as their leader, but also as their father. And that's why he hadn't moved on with the rest. More orphans joined them, more left. Their numbers never really got higher than twenty or so, but they never got lower than ten either. There was always someone who needed looking out for.

The number one rule of the pack was never, ever, rob the gentry in their own homes. That was the surest, quickest way to get them up in arms to have the authorities come sweeping through the slums in search of the culprits. Finding a house full of orphans who weren't official orphans would be a dead giveaway. And the horror stories that Dagger told about real orphanages were enough to enforce that rule. He knew firsthand, since he'd escaped from one years ago. Danny was breaking that rule tonight.

Not that the gentry were off-limits, no indeed. But they were only to be robbed when they were found out and about, on the streets, in taverns, at market or otherwise shopping, where they might not even notice a few coins missing, and if they did, might think they'd merely dropped them by accident or spent them without remembering.

The second rule that served them well was that they were to stick to their own areas and never go off to steal in places they weren't familiar with. Dagger assigned each an area and changed it weekly, so the normal residents in those neighborhoods wouldn't start to recognize any of them. Danny was breaking that rule, too.

Another rule pertained only to her and a few others, since their age and height marked them as no longer children. The logic was, the taller they were, the harder time they'd have reaching their hand into a pocket. So when they reached a certain height, they graduated into the 'specific jobs only' class, which meant they did no stealing on their own, only jobs that Dagger sent them to do. Danny was definitely breaking that rule.

Dagger had arrangements for these jobs with three taverns and one inn. And because Danny was very recognizable due to the color of her hair and eyes, Dagger no longer let her do any job other than 'sleepers.' She'd never failed before, but then, she'd never walked into a deliberate trap before either.

The trouble she was in pertained only to her though. If one of the others boys had been captured instead, she had no doubt Dagger would have called it an exception and been glad of the unexpected riches that would tide them over for quite a while. There would be pats on the back and a celebration. But because *she* was the one captured and forced to break the rules, Dagger's attitude was going to be just the opposite – because he'd been looking for a reason to give her the boot.

For over two years now, nearly three, she'd been on the outs with Dagger. Whereas they used to get along just fine, used to joke and laugh a lot, now it seemed that he despised her. He singled her out for reprimands every chance he got. He criticized her constantly, deserved or not. He couldn't be more obvious that he wanted her gone, but she'd given him no reason to kick her out. Until now.

She didn't even know why he'd turned against her, but it had started about the time she'd surpassed him in height. It could just be that as leader, he figured he should be the tallest. But he wasn't a tall man to begin with, only about five feet seven inches. And she was flamboyant in her dress, whereas Dagger was nondescript. This impressed the children. Many of them modeled themselves after her and came to her when they needed something.

She supposed Dagger might be fearful that she

wanted to take his place. She didn't. She didn't even like to steal herself, so she certainly didn't want the responsibility of sending out others to do the same. She felt it was wrong, an ingrained feeling that she'd never been able to shake. But she hadn't had much choice in the matter, living among thieves. However, she'd tried to subtly reassure Dagger that his position didn't appeal to her, without actually discussing it, but it hadn't seemed to help.

She could lie to Dagger, say they'd carted her out of the tavern to take her to jail, but she'd managed to escape, that it just took her a long while to find her way back home. Dagger couldn't kick her out just because she'd walked into a trap. She had to settle for that hope.

Her distress stemmed not just from knowing what she'd have to face when she got home. It was also him, that Lord Malory. He'd disturbed her so much she couldn't think, couldn't even breathe. But not only that, he frightened her to her core because he mesmerized her.

Danny had never in her life imagined anyone could look like him. He wasn't just handsome. His looks were so far beyond handsome, she simply couldn't find a word to describe them. The closest she could come was *beautiful*, yet in a masculine way, which was a combination that was utterly amazing – and mesmerizing.

It was a wonder she'd been able to talk to him at all, he so flustered her. And she knew exactly what it was that turned her senses to much and stole her breath when she looked at him. He appealed to her sexually, something she'd never really had to deal with before. Other men had caught her interest over the years, but none had made her wish she could actually do something about it. Playing the role of a man meant she had to ignore such things and that had been easy enough to do. Not this time. And that's what frightened her the most about Lord Malory.

She'd spent fifteen years, her entire life, actually – at least all that she could remember of it – avoiding Lucy's fate. And she had done it only for one reason: to not end up a whore. Nor had she ever changed her opinion about it. Lucy might have settled into the job, might not have complained as much after the fact as she had beforehand, but Danny still saw it as the worst sort of degradation.

For her, it would be the end of her life, and not just metaphorically, because she would rather starve to death in some alley than suffer strangers paying for the use of her body. But here was a man who could make her jump willingly into that role. Worse, he'd looked at her as if he knew her secret, as if he could see right through to her core – as if he wanted to touch her. Surely her imagination was playing tricks on her, yet she couldn't shake the feeling that he knew, especially when his look turned so sensual, it nearly melted her on the spot.

He'd be a *lover*. Lucy's term. Lucy had put all men into one category or another, depending on how they wanted to use her and for how long. The names she gave them were mostly derogatory, and some were explicit, like the *grapplers* and the *beasts*. *Good-bye Henrys* she liked the best since they didn't take up much of her time, in and out in under five minutes, not there long enough to say hello to, just good-bye. Lovers, she claimed, were rare, a man who actually wanted to give pleasure as well as receive it.

A definite danger, Lord Malory was. A danger to Danny's senses, her peace of mind, her secret. The sooner she saw the last of him – well, it couldn't happen soon enough.

4

The job those young lords sent her on was so simple in comparison to her troubled thoughts that Danny did it almost without thinking about it. Just about every window in the large mansion was open. She climbed through one on the side of the house, made her way to the hall, then up the carpeted stairs.

No lamps had been left burning, but with all those opened windows, a good deal of moonlight filtered in. Not that Danny needed light, as she was used to working in pitch-dark. But even the upstairs hall had a window opened at the end of it.

A lot of closed doors were up there. It was a really big house, larger than anything she'd ever been in before. One side of the hall had more doors than the other, however, so she started on the side with less, thinking those led to larger rooms, the master bedroom in particular.

She was correct. It was the second door she opened. The sheer size of that room gave it away, as well as the lump in the bed. Heddings was sleeping soundly, his loud snoring making an uncommon racket. That was annoying. Danny prided herself on her catlike movements, never making a sound, but she didn't need to be extracautious with all the noise that Heddings was making.

She moved straight to the tall bureau first. The second drawer held the jewelry chest. A large chest, it nearly filled the drawer. It wasn't locked, didn't even have any means of locking it. Too trusting by half, Lord Heddings was.

She lifted the lid and was dazzled for a moment at how much glitter spread across the bottom of that chest, not just rings, but bracelets, brooches, even necklaces. In fact, most of the jewelry it contained was feminine. More gambling winnings? Danny couldn't care less.

She decided not to take the chest. It was too big and she wasn't even sure she could lift it out of the drawer, so she stuffed her coat pockets instead. She ran her hand across the bottom of the velvet-lined chest before she finished, just to make sure she hadn't missed a dull piece of jewelry. She did *not* want to have to do this again if Percy's two heirlooms weren't in this stash.

With that thought in mind, she even did a quick search through the other drawers, but found nothing else of interest. She also checked the desk, but it contained only papers. Lastly she moved over to the vanity table where she discovered a fat wad of money, a gold watch fob, and another ring that

53

had rolled back among the cologne bottles, as if it had just been tossed on the table. She swiped those up as well, stuffing the money in her pants pocket, since her coat pockets were full.

There was nothing else to look through. The night tables next to the bed didn't have drawers, and she discounted the bookcase, reasoning that a man who left a fortune in jewelry unlocked in his bureau wasn't likely to hide things in hollowed-out books.

Relieved to be almost done, she headed toward the door, but stopped cold when Heddings started a fit of coughing. She ducked down at the foot of his bed. The coughing was harsh enough that it could wake him. He might even get up for a drink of water from the pitcher across the room. She was prepared to slip under the bed if he did.

The coughing got much worse. It even sounded as if he were choking. The horrid thought came to her that he could die, and a vision flashed across her mind of her being accused of murder, standing before a judge, being sentenced to hang. Her palms broke out in a cold sweat. For a moment she wondered if she should try to help him. For a moment she was paralyzed with fear and couldn't move to help him even if she was temporarily that stupid.

It took still another moment to realize he was peacefully snoring again, the sweetest sound she'd ever heard. Well, actually, it quickly became an annoying sound again now that the crisis was over, and she wasted no more time in getting the hell out of there.

All was still quiet downstairs. She quickly slipped back into the room she'd first entered and was immediately yanked back against a hard chest, a hand clamping over her mouth to keep her from screaming. She had no wits to scream with her heart in her throat. She nearly fainted . . .

And then she heard hissed in her ear, 'What took you so bloody long?'

Him! and her relief lasted about a second before fury took over. She jerked about, snarled, albeit in a whisper, ''Ave ye lost yer flippin' mind? Wot are ye doing in 'ere?'

'I was worried about you,' he replied somewhat contritely.

She snorted to herself. What a whopper. Worried that she was going to take off with their precious rings was more like it.

'The next time ye want to scare someone 'alf to death, pick yerself. I'm done 'ere.'

'You got the rings?'

'This ain't the place to discuss it,' she shot back. 'I am so gone from 'ere I left yesterday.'

'Quite right,' she heard behind her as she headed to the window – and tripped over a rug on the way.

Falling took her by surprise. She wasn't the least bit clumsy, and that rug had been nice and smooth when she'd walked over it on her way in. No doubt Malory had bunched it up. She reached for something to prevent the fall, but the only thing nearby was a tall pedestal with a bust on it. The pedestal was heavy and did stop her from falling, but she knocked the bust off it in doing so. It hit the floor with a loud thud.

She groaned inwardly. In the still of the night, that noise had been loud enough to wake the dead, or at the least, one of the servants sleeping on the same floor. She turned back to tell Malory to get out immediately and saw the man standing in the doorway with a gun pointed at the nabob.

Danny went so still she stopped breathing. The man was fully dresed, obviously already up and nearby even before the bust had crashed to the floor. Maybe Malory had made some noise on his way in and roused the man to investigate.

He was within his rights to just shoot them and figure out what they were doing there later. That's what she would have done if she caught a pair of men sneaking around her house in the middle of the night.

Malory's back was to the door. He'd leapt forward to try to prevent her fall, but had stopped when she'd managed it on her own. He was still looking at her, but in good light now, since the man had a lamp in his other hand. She wasn't even sure if it had dawned on Malory yet that someone was there holding that lamp.

'Don't turn around,' she whispered as quietly as she could. 'If ye get recognized, yer in bigger trouble than if 'e shoots ye.'

Gathering her wits about her, she moved around

him to block him from view somewhat and told the man holding the pistol, 'There's no need for guns, mate. We were just looking for a place to wait out the night. Our coach broke down in the woods nearby. M'lord ere thought 'e recognized yer 'ouse. 'E's foxed to the gills, so if 'e were wrong, I wouldn't be surprised none. And we did knock. Bleedin' lord wouldn't give up though when we didn't get an answer, insisted on coming inside and sleeping in the parlor. 'E said that 'Eddings wouldn't mind. Were 'e wrong? This ain't 'Eddings place?'

The man's tense expression altered immediately. His pistol lowered as well, though not completely. So Danny laid it on a bit thicker.

''E tried to blame that wheel fallin' off on me, 'e did, when I warned 'im just last month that 'e needed new wheels on that old coach o' 'is. Course 'e'd rather spend all 'is blunt on fancy women and gamblin', so 'e didn't pay me any mind as usual.'

The man coughed. 'Should you be mentioning this in front of him?'

She managed a laugh. ''E's so foxed, 'e won't remember. Don't know 'ow 'e's still standin', I don't.'

'Who is he?'

Danny hadn't been expecting to come up with any names, but considering how she ended up being there herself, one came easily to mind. 'Lord Carryway o' London town.'

'Why didn't you just let him sleep it off in your coach then?' the man asked next.

'Would 'ave, but I saw some movement in those woods we were passing through near 'ere. Could 'ave just been some animal, but could 'ave been some bleedin' highwaymen, too, I was thinking. Didn't want 'im adding getting robbed to the tally against me. I'd prefer to be keepin' me job, even though it means puttin' up with a lord who's foxed more often than 'e's not.'

There was a long pause where Danny was sure the fellow was going to call her bluff and laugh in her face. She was calculating which way she should run, or if she should just dive at his legs and try to take him by surprise.

'Bring him along then,' the man said. 'We have several empty guest rooms upstairs. There's a comfortable couch in one you can use yourself.'

Danny hadn't really expected the man to believe her. He must be no more than a servant himself, probably the butler, and so he couldn't bring himself to kick a member of the nobility back out into the woods. He could have thought to lock them up until the morning, when what she'd told him could be verified. But he must not be a suspicious sort, to have believed her outright.

A good opportunity to bolt through the window presented itself as soon as the man turned his back on them to lead the way upstairs. But he hadn't put his pistol away yet. And with that weapon still in his hand, Danny preferred to play out the charade and not risk a bullet or two flying her way. Besides, there were two of them to get out that window, and no way they could both manage it before one of them got shot for trying.

The nabob hadn't said a single word, thank God. He could have spoiled the whole story if the servant realized he wasn't foxed at all. He was either smart enough to play the part she'd set up for him or nervous enough to keep his mouth shut.

No, she doubted he was nervous, at least not as much as she was. He'd handled that barkeep tonight too easily for him to be bothered by the mere possibility of flying bullets. Stupidly brave was probably what he was, and a high-handed blackguard for getting her into this mess.

She grabbed his arm now and dragged it over her shoulder so it would look as if she were holding him up, then blanched to see the pistol in his hand. He'd had it trained on the man the whole while, just hidden behind her back. Bleedin' nabob could have gotten them both killed!

She snatched it out of his hand and stuffed it back in his pocket, only to hear him chuckle at her for doing so. God protect her from half-wits!

She hissed at him now, 'I 'ope ye know 'ow to play the drunkard, mate, and 'ang yer 'ead so 'e don't get a good look at ye.'

It was easy to get him upstairs. She was too nervous to take note of the closeness of their bodies, and he only rested his weight on her when the servant glanced back at them; otherwise, he was mostly getting up the stairs on his own, was in fact leading her instead of the other way around.

'In here,' the servant said, opening a door. 'We should be able to find someone to fix your coach in the morning so you can be on your way.'

''Preciate it, mate.'

He'd followed them in, lit a lamp for them, then headed toward the door. He still hadn't relinquished the hold on his pistol other than for a moment to light the lamp. Danny began to wonder if he'd believed her tale after all. And as soon as the door closed behind him, she threw off Malory's arm and hurried to the door to hear if the fellow was actually leaving. What she heard instead was the soft click of the lock on the door.

5

Locked in to await . . . what?

Danny lost what little color she had left in her cheeks. Had the man not believed their story, or was he simply being cautious?

She hoped he was just being cautious. After all, they were strangers until his employer verified otherwise. But if he was going to stand out there and guard their door the rest of the night, then this mess was just going to get worse.

She turned back to Malory to see him watching her curiously, one brow raised in question. She rushed back to him to whisper, ''E's locked us in.'

'Bloody hell,' he growled low.

'Ye got that right, mate. So go stick yer 'ead in a pillow and start snoring, eh, and loudly. 'E needs to think we're sleeping so 'e'll go back to bed 'imself.'

Having said that, she didn't wait to see if he'd comply. She moved back to the door and lay down in front of it to look under the crack. Sure enough, there were shoes right on the other side of the door. The servant was still standing out there, probably trying to listen through the door himself.

When she didn't hear any snoring starting up yet, she turned around and glared at Malory. He rolled his eyes toward the ceiling, his lips twisted in disgust, as if her suggestion was quite beneath him. And he didn't move directly to the bed but went to the window instead, to see how much trouble it would be to leave that way. He must have decided that wasn't an option because he sighed then and moved to sit on the bed, bounced on it actually, then tested out a few snoring sounds till he got one he was satisfied with and started making a lot of racket with it.

Danny almost grinned. He looked so disgruntled to be doing something so simple as snoring. Too bad. They wouldn't be locked in an upstairs bedroom if he hadn't come in the house to begin with. She would have been out of there without a hitch, instead of lying on the floor hoping a suspicious servant would get tired and go back to bed.

It didn't look as if he would. It was starting to look as if he was going to stand 'guard' out there in the hall all night. She could almost hear the prison door slamming shut on her and she was getting a queasy, sick feeling in her belly.

With desperation creeping up on her, she went to look out the window for herself. Malory's sigh had been accurate. It was not an avenue for easy departure, not without a rope. No tree nearby to jump to, no ledges of any sort to use to climb down with.

They could rip up the sheets to make their own rope, which she wouldn't even have thought of if the nabobs hadn't done that earlier in the evening, but a glance about the room showed nothing heavy enough to use as an anchor to support Malory's weight. Hers maybe, but not his. The bed might work, but it was just a small one for a single guest and had a wooden frame that could break. They'd probably make too much noise trying to move it next to the window anyway.

When it finally dawned on her that the servant might be waiting for the lamp to go out, Danny could have kicked herself. Her drunk 'employer' might not worry about the lamp, but why would the sober 'driver' want to leave the light on to sleep, unless he wasn't planning on sleeping? She hoped that was what the servant was thinking, and sure enough, about ten minutes after the light went out, he moved off down the hall and back down the stairs.

All the while, Malory had been trying out a wide assortment of snoring sounds that would have caused Danny to bust a gut laughing if she hadn't convinced herself they were going to be stuck there all night. The servant definitely distrusted them, or else he wouldn't have stood outside their room so long. But it could have been worse. He could have gone to wake his employer, they could have checked to see if anything was missing from their house, and there'd be no talking her way out of having her pockets filled with Heddings's jewels.

She moved over and told the nabob, 'He's finally gone. We'll give him a few minutes to go back to bed.'

'Then what?'

'Then I pick that lock open and we get the 'ell out o' 'ere.'

'You know how to do that?'

She snorted. 'Course I do, and I carry m'own picker.'

She pulled a thick pin out of her hat and went to work on the door. Piece of cake. Bedroom doors usually were.

Within seconds she was saying, 'Come on. And we'll use the front door. Since they already know we've been 'ere, leaving it unlocked won't matter.'

She didn't wait to see if he was going to follow her. The moment she was outside she took off at a run and didn't look back or stop once until she reached the trees. Only then did she pause, but merely to catch her breath and her bearings. It took a moment to spot the coach lamps through the thick foliage. Malory caught up to her then.

He took her arm to lead her the rest of the way to the coach. She tried to jerk it away but that effort just made him put his arm around her shoulder. He obviously didn't trust her to turn over the jewels now that they were safely out of Heddings's house.

Without the danger of having a servant holding a gun nearby, she couldn't handle being this close to

Malory. She'd put his arm around her earlier when they'd walked up Heddings's staircase and had felt nothing but her fear. This was nowhere near the same thing. Now she was feeling the length of him pressed to her side, his muscular thigh, his hip and his hard chest, feeling how perfectly she fit under his arm, feeling the heat coming off him – or was it her heat? She was remembering just how bleeding handsome he was, even though she couldn't see his face in the dark of the woods. She was remembering those sexy blue eyes moving over her in the coach, as if he could see right through her disguise.

If he stopped right then and there and turned her toward him, she would have been mush for whatever he had in mind. He stopped. Her heart began to pound so loudly it throbbed in her ears. He was going to do it, lower his mouth to hers. Her first kiss, and from the most handsome man she'd ever encountered. It would be sublime. She knew it and held her breath, trembling in anticipation.

He pushed her into the coach. They'd only stopped so he could open the door.

Deflated more than she wanted to admit, Danny sat back on her seat in a huff, then glared at Malory as soon as he took the seat across from her. More than half of that glare was because of what had just happened, or hadn't happened – all in her own mind, of course. But that didn't stop her from feeling disgruntled. Malory wouldn't know that though. He would attribute her look only to the topic she introduced.

'That were the most stupid thing I ever saw,' she told him. 'D'ye realize gettin' caught in there were yer fault! If ye were going to enter that 'ouse, ye could 'ave stolen the rings yerself. Wot did ye need me for then, eh?'

'What happened?' Percy asked, but was ignored.

'You were gone longer than necessary,' Malory pointed out stiffly. 'Or I wouldn't have gone inside.'

'I weren't gone even ten minutes!'

'So it was an inordinately *long* ten minutes. All of which is irrelevant now.'

'You could 'ave got us killed! I wouldn't be callin' that irrelevant, mate.'

'*What* happened?' Percy asked again.

'Nothing the youngun here wasn't adept at handling,' Malory conceded. Then to Danny, as if he hadn't just pumped up her pride with that casual compliment, he added, 'Let's have a look at your findings to see if all that trouble was worth it.'

'Get this coach moving first,' she said, mollified somewhat that he'd just admitted she'd saved his arse. 'We ain't safe till we're nowhere near 'ere.'

'Good point,' Percy agreed, and tapped on the roof of the coach, which signaled the driver to head back to town. 'Now, please, keep me on tenterhooks no longer.'

As long as Lord Malory wasn't doing the insisting, Danny saw no reason to deny his friend. She started emptying her pockets on the seat next

66

to her, including the wad of money, then scooped up the whole pile and dumped it on the seat between the two nabobs. She even turned her pockets inside out to show them she wasn't keeping anything back.

Percy immediately pounced on one old-looking ring with the exclamation 'Good God, yes!' He brought the antique to his lips to kiss it, then with unseemly haste, stuck it back on his finger where it apparently belonged. 'Can't thank you enough, dear boy! You have my—' His appreciation was cut short when his eye was caught by the jewelry again. 'Oh my, there's the other!' he exclaimed, and spread the jewelry wider to snatch the second ring out of the pile.

'You have our thanks, lad,' Lord Malory finished Percy's thought.

'Eternal thanks,' Percy added, beaming at Danny.

'I wouldn't go *that* far,' Malory rejoined.

'Speak for yourself, old chap. You weren't the one hiding from your own mother.'

'I don't have a mother.'

'From George then.'

'Point taken,' Malory conceded with a grin.

'George?' Danny asked.

'My stepmother.'

'Is named *George*?' she gasped.

When the young lord laughed, his cobalt eyes fairly sparkled. 'It's Georgina actually, but m'father cut that short just to be contrary. Habit of his, don't you know.'

She didn't know and didn't want to. She'd done what they'd asked – insisted – she do. And successfully, so there was no question about doing it again. She just wanted to get home now and face Dagger – and find out if she still had a home.

Reminded of that, her expression turned gloomy. They didn't notice. They were still glancing down at the pile of glitter.

Percy tapped a large oval-shaped pendant surrounded by emeralds and diamonds. 'Looks familiar, don't it?' he said to his friend.

'Indeed. I admired Lady Katherine's bosom more'n once when it graced her chest.'

'Didn't take her for a gambler, least not the sort to part with something like that.'

'She isn't. Heard it was stolen several months ago while she was vacationing in Scotland.'

'You pulling my leg, old man?'

Malory was frowning by then. 'No, and this bracelet looks rather familiar as well. I'd swear my cousin Diana was wearing it just last Christmas. Don't recall her mentioning it was stolen, but I know *she* doesn't gamble a'tall.'

'Oh, I say, are you suggesting Lord Heddings is a thief?'

'Looks that way, don't it?'

'But that's splendid news. Can't tell you how much guilt I was trying to ignore over this distasteful business.'

Malory caught Danny rolling her eyes over that remark. She could tell he had to work really hard not to grin at her. Percy wasn't finished, however, and his next question sobered the young lord.

'But what are we going to do about it?'

'There's nothing we *can* do about it, without implicating ourselves and our young friend here.'

'Well, that's too bad. Hate to see a thief go about his merry way without paying a price for . . . it . . .' Percy intercepted Danny's pointed stare and coughed. 'Present company excluded, naturally.'

'Let's not forget yerselves,' Danny sneered. 'Stealing that glitter weren't *my* idea.'

'Quite right,' Percy said with a blush.

But Lord Malory noted with displeasure, 'No, *your* idea was to empty *our* pockets, so there's no need to be pointing fingers here.'

The heat from the multiple blushes she felt just then could have lit the coach brazier. Danny hated having the tables turned on her, she really did. But under the circumstances, she was fresh out of rejoinders.

He was quick, that one, and suspicious, or he wouldn't have followed her into the house to make sure she did the job. Astute, too, and clever. She didn't doubt coming here had been his idea.

It was too bad he wasn't a half-wit like his friend. She might have called him that in her mind earlier, but she knew it wasn't so. She could probably have talked her way out of her involvement if he was. She still probably could have – if he weren't so bleedin' handsome. But she had trouble putting two thoughts together when he turned those cobalt eyes on her. Her cunning and wits had gone right out the door, leaving behind a brainless ninny, hopelessly out of her element.

6

It seemed to take much longer getting back to the city than it had taken getting to Heddings's house. Danny didn't have a watch, but she wouldn't have been surprised if the sun had soon made an appearance. She was tired, exhausted really, from so many emotions she wasn't used to experiencing. She was starting to get hungry, too. And she still had a lot to deal with when she finally got home.

Actually, she hoped Dagger would be asleep so she could get some sleep herself. It would be much easier to offer explanations, or lies for that matter, with a clear mind that wasn't muddled with exhaustion.

Percy was napping again, smart man. Danny wished she could do the same, but with Lord Malory still wide-awake, she didn't dare. Not that she thought he'd do anything to her while she slept. She just needed to be alert to watch for an opportunity to escape in an area she recognized.

She didn't doubt they were going to let her go,

now that she'd done what they wanted, but she doubted they'd take her back where they'd found her. Why would they go out of their way, late as it was? And dropping her off in *their* end of town would mean she'd be hopelessly lost and wasting hours more trying to find her way home. She might have grown up in London, but it was a big town and she was only familiar with her small section of it.

She knew to the second when his eyes were back on her. Glancing at him confirmed it. He had something on his mind. The look he was giving her was much too thoughtful.

'By the by, where'd you leave your shoes?'

The question surprised her. It certainly wasn't what she'd expected to hear, considering his pensive frown. And actually, she was surprised he hadn't mentioned it sooner, since he'd had her march through the woods in her stockings. And he'd tied up her ankles earlier. He would have had to be blind not to notice she wasn't wearing normal footwear.

'These are me shoes,' she replied, and lifted one foot so he could see the soft sole of leather on the bottom of her wool stocking.

'Ingenious.'

She blushed slightly, but only because she was rather proud of her improvised footwear. She'd made them herself. She had a pair of normal shoes, since running around in what looked like her stockings would draw too much comment during the day. These she wore only when she worked.

'Mind if I have a closer look?' he asked.

Quickly she tucked her feet under the seat, as far away from him as she could and gave him a mutinous stare. He merely shrugged.

Then he amazed her when he added, 'You're much smarter than I would have thought. That was quite a tale you told back there on the spur of the moment. Lord Carryway?' As soon as he said it, he chuckled.

Danny merely shrugged. 'It fit.'

'I suppose,' he allowed, but his curiosity was still present. 'Do you often get caught and have to talk your way out of it?'

'No. Never been nabbed, not once – until to-night. Twice in one night, and both times because o' ye.'

He coughed slightly. But to avoid tossing around blame again, he instead introduced what was *really* on his mind.

He tapped the necklace and bracelet on the seat next to him that had been under discussion earlier and said, 'Would like to return these two pieces to their rightful owners, anonymously, of course.' He cleared his throat and looked distinctly uncomfortable as he added, 'Would you mind, youngun?'

'Why would I mind?'

'Because this pile is yours.'

She snorted. She'd already decided she wanted no part of that glitter. The vision of her being caught and hanged was still too fresh in her mind.

But knowing the jewelry was twice stolen made it even more risky and she said so.

'It's one thing to get rid o' stuff like that when it's first stolen, just a matter o' being quick about it. But trying to dump stolen goods that were already stolen goods is just askin' to get caught. Some o' that suff, if not all, is already being looked for. I'd as soon toss it out the window as touch it again.'

He shook his head. 'This won't do. You were promised a fortune in—'

'Get over it, mate. If I want anything from ye, ye'll know it.'

Oh, God, his look suddenly turned sensual again, heating her thoughts, turning her innards to mush. If she said anything else just then, it would be utter gibberish. How could he *do* that with just a look? And what had she said to change his expression like that? The mention of 'want'? That would mean he knew she was a woman, but he *couldn't* know. No one knew. And he couldn't have guessed. She didn't even know *how* to act like a female anymore, she'd played her male role so long, and she'd made no mistakes to give herself away.

He let her off the hook by cooling his carnal stare. Was it the squirming she'd done? He picked up the wad of money, thumbed through it briefly, then tossed it on her seat.

'Not quite a hundred pounds there, but it will do for the moment I suppose.'

Why did he make it sound as if they weren't done with each other? 'That's more'n I've ever seen at one time, or two, or more,' she quickly assured him. 'That will do me fine.'

He merely smiled. She went back to staring out the window. Her eyes widened to see London on the other side now.

She didn't recognize anything, but she still said, her tone somewhat desperate, 'Ye can let me out 'ere, mate. I can find m'way—'

'Not a chance, lad. I'll take you to your door and do any explaining that's needed, to get you out of the trouble you mentioned. We'll just drop Percy off first. Won't take long a'tall.'

And then be alone with him and his bleedin' eyes that undressed her? Not a chance was right.

'I exaggerated,' she lied. 'This money will more'n make up for the time I've been missing.'

'I insist,' he said, not buying her lie. 'Wouldn't be able to sleep if I thought this nasty business had repercussions for you.'

'Like I care if ye can sleep?' she snapped churlishly. 'Yer idea o' favors is my idea o' getting buried, so don't do me any more. I'd be in even more trouble if I showed ye where me friends live. Waking up in an alley beat nigh to death would be lucky.'

'You expect a beating for—'

'Not me,' she cut in pointedly.

He chuckled. 'All right, I get the picture. But I'll escort you back to that tavern. Very least I can do.'

She didn't think he'd settle for that once he got that far, so she had no choice but to say, 'No.'

'Wasn't asking for permission, dear boy.'

Danny opened her mouth to snarl something really nasty, but since it wouldn't accomplish anything, she decided to save her energy for what was about to come next.

7

Danny had to wait until the nabob took his eyes off her before she made her move. When he finally did, she didn't spare another thought on it, just shot toward the coach door, jumped out, and took off at a run down the block.

Too easy, just as she'd figured it would be, though she'd underestimated how much ducking she should have done to get through the door. Not being a frequent rider in coaches, never in one so fine as his, she hadn't taken her above-average height into account when leaping out that coach door. She was lucky she'd only knocked her hat off and hadn't knocked herself unconscious.

She'd miss the hat. She was right fond of that hat, had won it in a fight down the block last year. It gave her a certain 'flair' that she loved, probably because it appealed to her feminine vanity. But it was gone now, left on the floor of the nabob's coach, and it would be a sorry day before she'd risk running into that young lord again to retrieve it.

She didn't slow her pace, didn't need to as she wasn't winded yet. But a block away she figured she better stop running before she did wear herself out. She started to, then finally heard someone running behind her. A glance back and she shot forward at full speed.

She simply couldn't believe it. The bleedin' nabob was chasing her! And not just a short distance either. He should have given up after the first block, but he was still at it.

It made no sense, since they were done with each other. She'd done what they'd wanted and they had gotten her back to London. Why in the bleedin' hell would he go out of his way just to get her closer to home when she obviously didn't want him taking her any farther?

Three bleedin' blocks now and he still wasn't stopping! She was getting winded now. His legs were longer. He was slowly catching up to her. She almost stopped and gave up, but she rounded a corner and found a passing hack just approaching it. While she was out of Malory's line of view for those few seconds, she dove under the hack, grabbed hold of the frame to lift herself off the ground, anchored her feet to it as well to help hold herself up as close to the frame as possible, and waited until she saw his legs run by.

Pressed close to the underbelly of the coach, she was out of Malory's sight. He kept on running, in the oppoisite direction from her now, which allowed her to drop back to the ground when the hack turned another corner.

She was still somewhat winded, heart still racing, even more hungry now, and close to toppling over from pure exhaustion. If she didn't think it would make matters much worse to delay getting home, she'd find a nice alley to curl up in and sleep the day away.

She was lost, of course, in an area of the city she'd never been in before. And she was drawing too much attention. Without her hat to hide the white-gold of her hair, her mop of curls was like a beacon, especially in contrast to her dark green velvet jacket. She was drawing attention wherever she passed, making her more uncomfortable than she cared to admit.

It took another hour to find a landmark she actually recognized so she could stop walking around in circles as she'd been doing and start heading in the right direction from there. It took yet another hour and a half to finally reach home at the slow pace she could manage, as tired and sore as she was by then.

And she still had the feeling someone was following her. She knew bloody well she'd lost Malory, so it wasn't him. But every time she glanced behind her, she merely saw other people going about their business. There were too many alleys along the way though that someone intent on following her could slip into and just peek out of to keep sight of her. She finally concluded she was being silly, that her exhaustion and overactive imagination were just playing tricks on her.

And she was worried. That was probably the main reason why she was getting jumpy and imagining things. It was getting worse and worse, the closer she got to home, because she wasn't sure if she'd have a home after today.

Tyrus Dyer had been unable to believe his eyes. He was either losing his mind, because he knew the woman couldn't have regressed in years to look that young again, or he was seeing the girl who was supposed to be dead. It was one or the other, had to be, and he'd rather not think he was losing his mind, so obviously the girl wasn't dead. And she'd grown up to look just like her mother.

Tyrus was the one who'd been hired to kill her – her and her father. Getting rid of the man had been no problem. The child should have been even less trouble. But she'd had a nurse guarding her, and that woman had fought like a banshee. Though he was sure he'd mortally wounded her, she'd even managed to knock him out with his own club! He wasn't out long, just long enough for the nurse to drag the girl out of the house and hide her somewhere.

When he'd been unable to find her, he thought she'd curled up in a hole somewhere to die, her body just never discovered. That had *not* satisifed his employer, however. Money was involved, a lot of it, and the fellow had been so livid over Tyrus's incompetence, he hadn't just refused to pay him, he'd tried to shoot him. But Tyrus had seen it coming and had managed to dodge the bullets and make his escape.

Tyrus had been livid himself for quite a few years after. He'd done half the job. But after that his luck had turned so rotten, it was as if that unfinished job had jinxed him. No matter what he did, he bungled it now. As a result, he'd been fired so many times he'd lost count.

But his bad luck had just showed up. It wasn't illusive anymore. It was tangible. And he'd just been given the means to actually get rid of it. This required some thought. He didn't want to be hasty and mess up again. But he knew where she lived. Hiding in the slums all these years, who would have figured! He'd be back . . .

8

It was too much to hope Dagger wouldn't be awake. The sun had been up for a while now. And he was sitting at the kitchen table, drinking a cup of tea Nan had made him. Six of the children were in the main room, not counting a couple still sleeping there. They all took one look at Dagger staring at her through the arched opening to the kitchen and started vacating the house.

Danny entered the kitchen and dropped down in the seat across from Dagger.

He was a plain-looking man, but the long scar on his chin and the short one under his left eye gave him a mean look. His long brown hair was mussed, his eyes bloodshot. He looked haggard at the moment. Actually, he looked about as tired as she was. She guessed then that he hadn't slept at all, that he'd stayed up waiting for her to get home. It wouldn't be because he'd worried about her. No, when she hadn't returned when she should have, he would have realized she'd given him the excuse he'd been looking for to get rid of her. He wasn't a stupid man. She could have talked circles around him if he was.

She was too tired to lie about what had happened. She'd trip herself up if she tried. Before he said a word though, she took out the wad of money from her pocket and tossed it on the table between them. None of them had ever brought home so much. A hundred pounds was a bleedin' fortune to them. She was hoping it might make a difference. It didn't. He barely glanced at it. And too late she realized it made her look as if she'd willingly broken the rules.

'Will ye 'ear me out, Dagger?' she asked. 'I've not 'ad many choices since leaving 'ere last night.'

'I know ye were caught, but I also know ye weren't taken to jail.'

'It was still a trap. They wanted a thief to do some stealing for them.'

'Ye know better, so why didn't ye refuse?'

'Why do ye think I was carted out o' there tied up?' she countered.

'But ye didn't stay tied up, did ye?' he said with a pointed glance at the money on the table. 'Ye could 'ave escaped them sooner.'

That was true. Tiredly she explained, 'That would've stranded me in the countryside wi' no telling when I would've found me way back to London.'

'Ye left London!'

She flinched at the shout. 'That's *why* I didn't try

to escape sooner. I've never been out o' London before. It probably would've taken me a week to get 'ome. But they swore they'd bring me back soon as I robbed the lord for them.'

'A *lord*!' That shout was even louder than the last one. 'I s'pose in 'is own bleedin' 'ouse, too?'

She could have lied at that point, should have. That was the number one rule, after all. But she knew, could tell by the very questions he'd been asking, that her answer wasn't going to make a bit of difference.

'Pack up yer things and get out. Ye've broken the last rule ye'll be breaking 'ere.'

Danny didn't move a muscle. She'd *known* she was going to hear that, that no matter what she said, she was going to hear it. But still she wasn't prepared for the tightness filling her chest or the emotion clogging up her throat. Dagger had been 'family' to her for fifteen years. That he *wanted* her gone was what hurt the most.

She wasn't going to cry. She wasn't supposed to be a female who would. She was no longer a child who would. She was supposed to be a man who wouldn't, so she couldn't. It wasn't something she could stop though, so she stumbled quickly away from the table before Dagger could notice the moisture filling her eyes.

She went straight to her pallet on the floor in the main room. It was hers. She'd roll it up and take it with her, though she couldn't imagine where she'd lay it down next. Her sack of clothes was beside it, not a very big sack. The outfit she was wearing was her favorite so she wore it daily, changed to her only other outfit just to wash it. Her pet was there in his little box. She managed to stuff it into the sack for ease of carrying.

The two children who had still been sleeping were sitting up on their pallets now openly crying. She stopped by each to give them a hug. Ordinarily she would have tried to cheer them, but she still couldn't get any words out past the lump in her throat, so she didn't try.

Opening the door, though, she found the rest of the children lined up outside it, most of them crying, too. They'd listened at the door, knew they wouldn't be seeing her again. It was breaking her heart. She'd been their hero for the longest time. They'd probably follow her if she gave the word. But she couldn't do that to Dagger, despite how callously he'd treated her. They were all Dagger had. She tore herself away from them and headed down the street.

Ironically, she'd wanted to leave for years, to find a real job, a respectable job, so she'd never have to steal again. Dagger was just forcing her to realize that dream sooner than she'd expected. She hoped she could be grateful to him someday for that, that the hurt wouldn't last too long.

Reminding herself that this was something she had wanted to achieve wasn't helping to ease the pain. She'd wanted to leave on good terms, to be able to come back and visit, to maybe help the other children find respectable jobs, too.

'Danny!'

She swung around with a gasp, saw Dagger marching determinedly down the street toward her. The hurt eased up immediately. She'd known, deep down, that he couldn't do this to her. He'd only wanted to scare her is all, so she'd stop breaking the rules and set a good example for the other children.

He reached her and she saw that his expression wasn't conciliatory at all. Her brief burst of hope was dashed. He was still angry. In fact, she'd never seen him quite this angry before.

'Ye want to know why, Danny?' he hissed at her. 'Yer too bleedin' pretty for a man. I've found m'self wanting ye, and that makes me so disgusted wi m'self I can't think sometimes. But I'd as soon kill ye as touch ye, so the better choice was to get rid o' ye, now weren't it? Ye'll make do. I've no doubt o' that. I taught ye well. But ye'll make do somewhere else. Now be gone wi' ye 'fore I change me mind and we both end up regrettin' it.'

She could have told him right then that he didn't need to be disgusted with himself for wanting her. She was a girl after all. But that confession would probably produce a serious rage the likes of which she'd never seen, because she'd deliberately deceived them all these years. And besides, he'd just admitted he wanted her. If he knew she really was a woman, he'd want her in his bed for a time, then probably set her to whoring – or both. And why had she hidden her sex for fifteen years if not to avoid that very fate?

She turned away and walked on before she said something that *she* would regret – and ran into Lucy around the next corner.

'Cor, where've ye been, Danny? I've been look-ing every— wot's wrong?'

It was her undoing. The tears started rolling down her cheeks. She could have controlled it, gotten away without having it all ripped out of her, if she hadn't run into Lucy. Anyone but dear Lucy, her sister, her mother, her only true friend . . .

'He did it, didn't 'e?' Lucy guessed immediately. 'Kicked ye out?' At Danny's nod, she added, 'Ah, luv, don't take it so 'ard. This is yer chance, ye know, to do something wi' yer life that 'as some meaning. Ye talked o' gettin' yerself a husband, raisin' some kids, teachin' them proper. Ye've wanted to do that, but ye couldn't begin while ye were still 'ere.'

'I know,' Danny replied, barely able to get the words out past the lump in her throat.

'Then buck up, eh?' Even as she said it, Lucy's own tears were starting. She turned her back on Danny, as if that could hide the emotion welling up in her.

'I'll send word, once I'm settled,' Danny prom-ised.

'Ye better. I'll worry m'self sick till you do. Now go. This is a good day for ye, luv. Ye 'ave to believe that.'

Danny tried, she really did, to dredge up that optimism, but she couldn't. She started to hurry past Lucy. This good-bye was much more painful than she could have imagined. But the other woman's hand caught her shoulder, stopped her for one last minute.

'Be yerself, Danny lass,' Lucy whispered through her tears, as she put her arms around Danny and hugged her tightly. 'It's finally time. Just be yerself, and it will all turn out right for ye.'

9

'I've a package to deliver to a Lord Malory. Would ye 'appen to know where 'e might be found?'

'Heard tell there's a Malory family lives over in Grosvenor Square.'

'And where would that be?'

'New to town, are ye?'

'It's that obvious?'

A chuckle. 'You'll find Grosvenor north o' here. Head down the block, then turn right and just keep going that way till you come to the rich houses.'

An address would have helped, but then again, probably not. Danny would need a map for that and didn't know where to get one, wouldn't be able to read one either, for that matter. An address would have helped only if she could afford to hire a hack, which she couldn't.

She was so out of her element it was beyond pathetic. She was keenly feeling the disadvantage of her lack of education, too. She would have given up by now if her anger weren't goading her on.

She had found a nice quiet alley to sleep the day away in, but didn't actually sleep that long. Her hunger woke her much sooner than she would have liked, and the headache it was causing lent desperation to her situation.

She had to find a job fast. If she had to resort to stealing just to eat, then she'd be no better off than she had been. This was an opportunity to *better* herself, not slip back into the gutter and old habits. But it wasn't going to be easy. She knew, because she'd tried before.

Lucy used to cover for her absence when Danny would go out to look for a respectable job. The problem had always been her appearance, and her lack of even a basic education. To apply for a man's job that didn't require being able to read and write did require muscle, which she couldn't muster. To apply for a woman's job she'd need some female clothes first, which she didn't own. And no matter what job she could talk her way into getting, she'd need a roof over her head and some coins in her pocket to last her till her first pay.

She'd thought she'd had that solved at one point. The job of a maid often came with room and board, which was ideal for someone starting out completely broke. She'd borrowed one of Lucy's dresses for the interview and had been so thrilled to get hired – for all of two hours. The butler had given her the job, and only because he'd been fascinated by her looks. As soon as she met the housekeeper though, she was fired. They were a middle-class household trying to move up the social ladder, which meant they wanted only a better class of servant, at least none that sounded like gutter trash or looked like whores.

Danny had been so disappointed and discouraged by that experience, she'd stopped looking for decent work for a long time. Then when she did start looking again, she simply had no luck.

Recalling her many failures, she got angry. The fact was, she'd hunted for a job sporadically, maybe four or five times a year. She'd never done it daily because she hadn't really been ready to go out on her own. To be alone. But she had no choice now, and she didn't have the luxury of taking her time about it. She needed to find a job immediately, that very day. And she needed to find some food even sooner. Calling herself ten kinds of a fool for not holding back at least a few of the pound notes Malory had given her, instead of giving the whole wad to Dagger, wasn't going to feed her.

She didn't like being on her own. She was finding that out firsthand, but she'd known she wouldn't. She'd grown up with a houseful of children around her. She wanted that back, but she wanted them to be *her* children, so she could have a say in raising them proper. She needed a husband to help with that, though, a good man, and one with a respectable job. That had been a goal of hers for a long time, she'd just never been able to get serious about it while she was still living the life of a boy.

She wasn't going to find a husband around the next corner though. And food was a necessity, which meant a job of her own came first. Then she could start looking for a husband to start raising a family with.

She got lucky with the food. She found that one of the rings from Heddings's stash had fallen through the little hole in her coat pocket to the lining underneath. She couldn't sell it by normal means, since it might be one of the stolen pieces being looked for. But she remembered Miss Jane selling a ring all those years ago to buy food.

She hadn't thought of Miss Jane in years, not since the nightmares had stopped. She wasn't sure why they had stopped. They'd plagued her from as far back as she could remember – which was the short time she'd spent with Miss Jane. And they'd usually been the same, filled with blood and screams, until a club fell on her head to end it.

One dream she had far too infrequently was very nice and left her feeling warm and comfortable. It was a dream of a young woman, one she'd never met, but the lady had white-gold hair just like hers, though arranged in one of those fancy styles she'd only seen ladies wear. A beautiful woman, dressed elegantly, like an angel she was, walking in a field of flowers.

Lucy had figured the angel dream really was an angel calling to her because she was supposed to have died all those years ago but didn't. Of course Lucy had been fanciful. But Danny had been even more fanciful, figuring the beautiful lady was herself, something she could aspire to. The dream gave her hope.

She needed hope now, and a lot more. The ring had fetched her less than a pound note. Very disappointing, but then the best she could get from a total stranger who'd only looked as if he could afford a good deal.

Her predicament was entirely that young lord's fault. If he hadn't been so high-handed, if he'd just accepted her refusal and instead found himself someone who would have been thrilled to do what he wanted, she wouldn't be worrying about where her next meal was going to come from.

He owed her. And he could bleedin' well pay up, or she'd let Lord Heddings know where his stash of stolen jewelry had trotted off to. Well, she wouldn't *really* go that far, but Malory would get the idea.

She finished the meal she'd bought in a nice restaurant and thanked the waiter for the food and his directions. She didn't see his frown. If she had, she wouldn't have realized it was because she didn't know to leave a tip for him. Ignorance was sometimes bliss, or it could have been.

In this case, the waiter was annoyed enough that he wasn't going to let her remain ignorant. He followed her outside to shout at her, 'Cheap bastard! And after I gave you directions, too, which I didn't have to do!'

Danny swung around, realized he was yelling at

her, though she couldn't imagine why. 'Wot are ye talking about, eh? I paid for the bleedin' meal.'

'Shows how dumb you are! You think service is free? I should have known better than to let your kind through the door.'

Her kind? That stung and made her cheeks bloom with color. She'd picked the first restaurant she'd come across, hadn't really noted that it was in an affluent business district, with well-dressed people everywhere she looked. A crowd was gathering because of the waiter's shouts. And she heard other angry murmurs now.

'A thief, no doubt.'

'Better check your pockets if he's been working this area today.'

'Better check *his* pockets.'

'All I wanted was some food,' Danny said quickly to the waiter. 'Which I paid for. If I didn't pay enough, ye could 'ave just said so. Ye didn't 'ave to insult me.'

The fellow looked as if he realized he had over-reacted. But too many of his regular customers were about now for him to back down and apologize.

'Just get out of here and don't come back,' he warned. 'This is a respectable district. Go back to the slums where you belong.'

10

Danny walked away from that restaurant trying to hold her head high, though it took every ounce of will she had to accomplish it. She wanted to run instead, had an overwhelming urge to do so, but she had no doubt someone would try to detain her, because running would make her look guilty. They wouldn't consider that she just wanted to find a deep hole that she could crawl into and cry, she was so heartsick and embarrassed.

She'd experienced that kind of snobbery before, when she'd looked for jobs in the past. She shouldn't have let it crush her as it did. It merely pointed out just how hard it was going to be to find a decent job.

It took a while to push the hurt aside. When she finally did, it was replaced with unease, because for the second time in two days, she felt that someone was watching her, following her. This time it was probably just someone who'd been in that crowd, making sure she left their neighborhood.

But turning to look, she saw nothing out of the ordinary, at least, not close to her. A lordly type entering an office building. A delivery boy. A lady with a maid following behind her bogged down with packages, a few couples walking along arm in arm, and dozens of other people going about their business. For the next two blocks, the feeling just wouldn't go away, but every time she looked over her shoulder, she couldn't imagine who it might be. There were just too many people on the street in this part of town.

She finally ducked into a shop, then got yelled at when she kept on going, running through the back, which was restricted to employees only, and out the back door. For the next ten minutes she ran, backtracked, passed through other buildings, and finally, the feeling went away. If someone had been following her, she was satisfied she'd lost them.

It was a long walk to Grosvenor Square. Night arrived before she got there. And there was a definite lack of nice alleys in the areas she'd been passing through. There were parks, though, lots of them, some so big she worried that she'd wandered out of the city by accident. She finally curled up in some bushes to wait for morning so she could get her bearings again.

Dawn brought the hunger again, and even more anger because of it. But that was pushed aside when she actually looked around her and *recognized* the park she was in, though she'd never been in that part of town before to her recollection. She'd barely seen any of the park last night, it was so dark. But this morning, the benches along the pathway, the giant old oak shading them, the child running through a flock of pigeons to scatter them, laughing in delight. She blinked, and the child was gone, had never been there. A memory!

Danny sat back down, shaken to her core. It was the first memory of her past that had ever come back to her, and it had come to her because it was the first time she'd ever been to a place that she must have visited as a child. Had her parents lived in this part of London, or had they only been visiting? There had been a hotel on one side of that park, along with a middle-class neighborhood, though she found more fancy houses on the other side when she left in that direction.

She tried to remember more, to recognize other things, but nothing else stirred any memories, and it was giving her a headache to try. No, the hunger was doing that again. So she hurried now, had to question a few more strangers for directions, and finally arrived at the Malory house around mid-morning.

It was a bleedin' mansion! It stood by itself, was fenced in, even had grass all around it, and nice flowers and shrubs, hardly what she'd been expecting. She was too intimidated to approach a house like that, especially after what had happened at that restaurant yesterday, so more time was wasted while she waited around for someone who looked like a servant to leave the house. A young woman finally did, dressed in a maid's uniform – well, not so much a uniform, but not a fancy lady's dress, so Danny took a chance and hailed her.

'G'day, ma'am. The 'andsome Malory live 'ere?'

'That's rich, dearie,' the woman replied in a good-natured tone. 'They're all handsome.'

''Ow many Lord Malorys are there?'

'In this household, three.'

'With black 'air and—'

'No, the earl lives here, with his two sons, none with black hair. You must mean his brother Sir Anthony. His house is over on Piccadilly. Or you could mean his nephew Jeremy. Those two lords both have black hair.'

'I've this package to deliver,' Danny said, tapping her pet's box, the best excuse she could come up with to gain access to Malory. 'It were a young lord that placed the order, around twenty-five 'e was.'

'That'd be Jeremy Malory then. Lives with his father in Berkeley Square.'

Danny blushed, forced to lie again to get directions. 'I'm new to the city. Could ye point me to Berkeley?'

The woman did, and it didn't take all that long to find the square, which was crowded at that time of the morning with pedestrians and carriage drivers pulled up to the curb, waiting on their passengers to leave their fancy houses. So she easily got pointed again to the house she needed. It wasn't quite as imposing as the other one.

She knew enough to go around to the servants' entrance from all her job hunting.

But it just wasn't her day for luck, she was beginning to fear. Jeremy didn't live there anymore, had moved out just last week to his own residence over on Park Lane, near his cousin's house. As if Danny gave a flipping hoot for all the extra information the friendly cook's helper passed on as she tried her best to flirt with Danny.

More directions, more walking. Tarnation! She'd never walked so bleedin' far in her life. It was a nice street though, that she finally reached, at least she thought it was, because one side of it bordered a park in full summer bloom. But even getting there in good time, another hour was wasted before she found someone who pointed her to the right house. Since Malory had only just moved in, most of the passing servants on the street didn't know which house was his.

Now after all that running around, she didn't expect to find Malory at home. At the rate her luck had been going, tomorrow would be more like it, or even the day after. Which meant another night or two sleeping in parks. But at least one was near to hand. And as long as she kept her expectations low, she could keep her anger to just simmering. But that young lord *was* in for a ripping earful, when – if – she ever clapped eyes on him again.

11

He was home! Not only that, Danny was actually let in the front door!

A young girl around her own age did so. Slightly plump of frame, with lackluster brown hair, she barely glanced at Danny, said merely, 'Wait here, and don't touch anything if you know what's good for you.' Then she disappeared up some nearby stairs.

Danny stood there tensely, still amazed that she'd gotten in the door. She ran her hand through her mop of curls to make sure they were orderly. Lucy always saw to her hair when they were alone, keeping it trimmed short. Lucy wasn't very good with scissors though, so the chopping she did was usually uneven. But Danny wasn't vain about her hair, and besides, not much of it could be seen when she was wearing her hat, which she missed keenly at the moment.

She wasn't going to touch anything. She didn't want to even *look* at anything, she was suddenly so

nervous. This was a bad idea. Hadn't she concluded, when she was still in his company, that
Malory was too dangerous to deal with? Her anger
had made her forget that, but she recalled it now in
her nervousness.

She turned to leave, the *smart* thing to do. But
she was arrested by the mirror on the wall next to
the door. Not very big, it hung over a narrow table
that held only a plate with two small cards on it.
The sight of herself had stopped her – and fascinated her.

Rarely did she ever get to look in a mirror. The
houses Dagger rented never had them. The rooms
she robbed in that old inn didn't have them, at
least none that she'd ever noticed in the dark. This
one showed her from the waist up, and without the
debonair, manly hat, it pointed out just how pretty
she really was. Amazing that anyone could still
mistake her for a boy. Amazing what a pair of pants
did for first and lasting impressions. Well, the
flatness of her chest probably helped some with
those impressions.

That had been one of her old fears, that she'd
develop really huge breasts like some women did
and be unable to hide them. But she was lucky.
Her breasts were a modest handful, medium-sized,
and thanks to Lucy, easily contained.

The easy part was because one of Lucy's rare
well-to-do customers had left behind a corset.
They'd laughed a bit, that men would wear them,
but then Lucy got the idea that it might come in

handy for Danny in a few years, and it had indeed. Instead of wearing it around her waist where it was designed to go, she was thin enough that she could wear it around her chest. She just laced it up the front instead of the back, so she could manage it herself.

It was a stiff contraption for the most part, but of a fine quality, the material that encased it so soft, she barely noticed anymore that she was wearing it. Yet it flattened her bumps nicely. That, and the slightly slouched posture she affected, was all she'd needed to look as flat-chested as any male.

The sound of footsteps coming down the stairs reminded Danny that she had decided she didn't want to be here after all, and she'd dawdled too long, ogling herself in the mirror. She didn't turn around to see who it was though. She quickly reached for the door handle again.

'Leaving?' the girl said. 'Good. He can't see you now anyway. He's entertaining a lady friend. I hadn't heard them come in, but then I don't come in this part of the house often. We're short of staff, or I wouldn't have answered the door at all.'

Danny swung around. She hadn't needed to hear all that, figured the girl just needed someone to complain to. Her tone had been distinctly grumbling.

'You're the maid?'

'No, we don't have a maid yet, not even a footman to open the doors, much less a butler. I work in the kitchen. And you'd best run along.

Come back later today. His lady friend should be gone by then.'

Danny was about to take that advice when her belly growled. Roam around starving for several hours while Malory whiled away his time in bed with some lady? Not bleedin' likely.

'I'll wait here if it's all the same to you. It's important I see him as soon as possible.'

'Suit yourself. You might as well go into the parlor then, it's through there. Though don't expect to find anything to sit on. This house hasn't been completely furnished yet.'

The girl walked away toward the back of the house. Danny didn't move, was still amazed at the speech that had come out of her own mouth. It was the way she used to talk! The way Lucy had insisted she forget if she was going to survive with the pack. And she'd learned Lucy's way of speaking, learned it so well, she hadn't spoken any other way in all these years.

It no longer seemed natural to talk like that. She wasn't even sure why she had just done so. Being in a fine house? Listening to a servant complain – with good speech? But it had obviously put the girl at ease with her, enough to leave her alone in their house.

As for Malory, she'd give him exactly ten minutes to get his lovemaking over with. She'd experienced too much hunger in the last couple of days to wait any longer than that on that high-handed young lord.

12

'I was pleasantly surprised to run into you this early in the morning,' Mary Cull said as she lazed back in the overstuffed chair by Jeremy's bed. 'So unexpected. I was sure all you young rakehells were in the habit of sleeping the day away, since you stay up to all hours of the night searching for your entertainments.'

Jeremy smiled at the lady as he knelt by her feet, removing her shoes. Mary was a rather young widow, the youngest he'd ever seduced. Old Lord Cull had died on their wedding night. Too strenuous an enterprise for the old boy to undertake was the consensus.

Mary was no beauty, but she was rather pretty with her round blue eyes and dark blond hair. And she had taken to lovemaking so well, she entertained a number of gentlemen in her home now regularly. Jeremy wasn't one of her 'regulars,' though he'd been invited three times now and had enjoyed himself each time. Today when he had run into her, they had been closer to his house than hers, and it being so new, he had the ready excuse of wanting to show it off to her. Of course they hadn't stopped to see much of the house; they had come straight upstairs to his room instead.

'I had some business to attend to with my uncle Edward this morning,' Jeremy replied.

'Something to do with your family?'

'No, actually, I've been managing several of the family's investments, including one of my own.'

She was surprised. 'You? Involved in business? You must be joking.'

'Not a'tall. I've found that I rather enjoy the managerial aspect. Wouldn't dream of trying my hand at *finding* investments. We leave that to my uncle, who has a knack for only picking winners.'

'You amaze me, Jeremy. You are quite frankly the most handsome man in the city, *and* you know it. Your family is extremely wealthy. Like many of your peers, you don't need to work. Why on earth would you?'

'Bite your tongue, m'dear. I don't see it as "work," but as something I enjoy doing. Big difference there, don't you think?'

'Not really.' She grinned at him. 'But whatever suits your fancy—'

It was the wrong thing to say to a rakehell like Jeremy Malory if conversation was on your mind. His expression turned immediately sensual, his hands started rising up her skirt. Mary's heart fluttered. But when she glanced over at his bed, which was their intended destination, she frowned.

'This room is entirely too – bachelorish. Is that even a word, darling? Never mind.' A sigh. 'I really wish you had come home with me. I'd feel much more comfortable in my own bedroom.'

Her skirt rose up her thighs as his hands continued their path and pulled her hips closer to him so she was almost lying in the chair, her legs straddling his waist. 'Pretend it's your bed.'

She laughed. 'It doesn't look anything like mine and you know it. Where are the satin sheets, the fluffy pillows, the things that make you want to *stay* in bed? That's a bachelor bed if I've ever seen one.'

'But you won't know how nice it is until you get in it, will you? I promise you, you'll find no complaints with my bed.'

It was said so huskily, Mary couldn't resist clasping his head to draw it to her bosom. And that's when the pounding started on the door and someone shouted, 'Get decent, mate, I'm coming in.'

Danny bristled on the other side of the door. She'd given Malory his ten minutes, more like twenty, though she didn't have a watch to confirm it. She was afraid he was one of those 'lover' types that Lucy praised, that he'd be taking all day with the wench he had in there with him, and she wasn't about to wait that long. So she'd finally marched upstairs and put her ear to each door she passed until she heard voices behind one.

It didn't take long, though, for the door to get

106

yanked open after she'd pounded on it. Malory was standing there, impatience turning immediately to surprise when he recognized her.

'You?'

'Ye got that right,' she snapped, her street slang coming back in her anger.

Her tone brought back his frown. 'What the deuce are *you* doing here?'

'Get rid o' the wench, then we'll talk.'

It looked as if he'd momentarily forgotten about the lady behind him, and she'd taken offense at the word *wench*, was stiffly adjusting her skirts as she looked about for her reticule. Finding it, she snatched it up and marched to the door.

Jeremy quickly told her, 'You don't have to leave, Mary. This will only take a moment.'

'That's quite all right, darling,' she stopped long enough to say, and patted his cheek to assure him she wasn't that upset to have their tryst end so abruptly. 'Come and visit me later today, where we *won't* be interrupted.'

With one last glare in Danny's direction, the lady left. The nabob ran a hand through his black hair in frustration and turned back into the room, heading toward the mantel over the fireplace, and a bottle of brandy and two glasses kept there. Danny followed him in, then stopped cold when she saw the bed. Where was her sense? She should never have barged into his bedroom of all places.

'I'll wait for ye downstairs,' she said uneasily, and turned back for the door.

'The devil you will.' When that didn't stop her, he added, 'Don't make me tackle you. I might like it.'

That definitely stopped her. She could have been made of stone for all the movement she was capable of at that moment. Could she outrun him again?

As if he could read her thoughts, he added the warning, 'I'd have you in my grasp before you could reach the hall. You may depend upon it. So you might as well close the door and tell me what you're doing here.'

She wasn't about to close the door, but she did turn around to face him again. It was galling, though, to find him not even close to her; in fact, he was leaning against the wall next to the mantel, arms crossed, ankles crossed, in that damned relaxed posture he'd used at the inn. Deceptive. He'd been no more relaxed that night than he was now.

He lifted a black brow at her. 'Well? I doubt you've come to rob me. You wouldn't have knocked. Or would you? D'you think you're that good?'

She felt a blush coming, but with it, some of her anger returned, too, which bolstered her enough to say, 'I've retired from robbing. Got kicked out, thanks to ye and yer bleedin' high-handedness.'

'Did you? Well, now, that's too bad. Indeed it is.'

Not a speck of sympathy was showing in his

expression to support his remark. He even smiled! And that smile hit her in the gut, started her pulse leaping, had her eyes so mesmerized her thoughts scattered. How was she going to blister him with a piece of her mind if her mind wouldn't function in his presence?

'Should have let me escort you home to do the explaining,' he added in a slightly scolding tone.

'Wouldn't 'ave 'elped,' she grumbled. ''Is mind was made up to get rid o' me long ago. Ye just gave 'im the excuse 'e needed.'

'He? Your boss?'

'Something like that.'

'So you were expecting this ousting?'

'Not this soon, and not without a job lined up nor a penny in me pocket,' she snarled.

'What happened to the money you earned that night?' he asked with only mild curiosity.

Another blush. 'I turned it over, 'oping it would change 'is mind. It didn't.'

'So you're looking for a new band of thieves to join up with? Good God, you didn't think you'd find one here, did you?'

Her eyes snapped up to find his expression as appalled as his tone had been. She should say yes and give him several reasons why he fit the role of thief, at least in her opinion. After all, it hadn't been *her* idea to rob Lord Heddings. But she'd rather just get to the point.

'I told ye I've retired from thieving. Never liked

it and 'ope to never 'ave to do it again. It's a real job I'm looking for.'

There was avid curiosity in his expression now. 'What sort of job?'

'I'm not particular,' she replied with a shrug. 'Anything decent that will let me afford a roof over me 'ead and food on the table. I've been sleeping under the stars since I got kicked out. And being that's yer bleedin' fault, I figure ye owe me some.'

'I find it rather admirable that you'd prefer to sleep in some alley than do what you do so well.'

A third blush, but this one had her snarling. 'Don't. Ye were the preferred option, since ye *do* owe me, and I would've been 'ere sooner to collect if it didn't take me so bleedin' long to find ye.'

He chuckled. 'Since you are determined to blame me for your dire straits, I'm not going to send you off with your pockets full and never find out if that exonerates me in your mind. And, no, before you think to mention it, I wouldn't trust you to come visiting from time to time to let me know how you're getting on.'

Her back stiffened. 'I were going to ask for money, but the wench downstairs says yer short o' staff here. I've decided I'll be taking a job from ye instead.'

'*You've* decided?' He burst out laughing. 'What would you prefer, footman or maid?'

She glared at him. He wasn't taking her seriously. That was easy to tell. And then it dawned on her what he'd just said, bowled her over actually. He knew! He wouldn't have mentioned the maid's job otherwise.

There was no point in denying it. She asked baldly, 'When did ye guess?'

He left his position, strolled casually toward her – more like a wolf stalking his prey, she thought nervously. He stopped in front of her, raised a hand, was going to touch her cheek. She leaned back, even though he stopped just short of touching her.

He was smiling as he said, 'There was no guessing, m'dear. I've an eye for beautiful women, no matter what they're wearing. Though truth to tell, I do prefer them naked.'

Nervously she took a step back from him. 'Ye won't be seeing me naked.'

His brow rose. 'No? Well, that's a shame and leaves us nothing further to discuss, does it?'

'The devil it don't. We're discussing the job yer going to be giving me.'

He sighed. 'We just did, and you turned it down without giving it the least bit of thought.'

'Getting naked?' She gasped indignantly. 'Ye call that a job?'

He laughed. 'More or less. I'm willing to take you on as my mistress. I find you quite amusing. Don't mind admitting it. So I'm sure we'd both enjoy it for a while.'

Danny's cheeks bloomed red, not with embarrassment this time, but with anger. 'Forget it, mate. It's a decent job I'm wanting, and ye *will* give me one, or I'll be paying a visit to Lord 'Eddings. I'm sure '*e'd* give me a job in exchange for the information I can supply 'im with, o' where 'is jewels ran off to.'

The nabob was flushing with some angry color himself now. 'This is preposterous. You don't know the first thing about propriety or how a household like this is run. And you talk like a guttersnipe,' he said contemptuously.

'I can speak properly,' Danny replied slowly.

She *did* have to think it out though, since she wasn't quite familiar with it yet. And it wasn't going to be easy, especially when she was angry or even nervous, which seemed to be the perpetual case around Malory. After fifteen years, she was much more used to the slang.

She'd managed to surprise him, but only for a moment. 'So you can mimic your betters? But you don't know how to behave like them, do you? How d'you expect to get on here without embarrassing yourself as well as this entire household?'

'By learning. Yes, you heard me right. I will learn the job as well as how to conduct myself.'

'Why?' he demanded in exasperation. 'Why go to all that trouble when you're much more suited to—'

She took a swing at him. He ducked, but he probably got the point, that she was sick and tired of being insulted today. Just to make sure, she snarled, 'Because I'm getting m'self a respectable husband and then lots of children. Those are me goals, mate. A good job, a husband, then to get started on a big family, in *that* order. And ye'll be 'elping me with the first goal or there will be 'ell to pay.'

'Bloody hell,' he snarled back, then sneered. 'What's it to be then? Footman I suppose?'

The nabob was trying to insult her again and doing a good job of it. Or was he just stressing how difficult the task that she'd set for herself was going to be? Could she really fit into this handsome aristocrat's world, even if only as his maid?

13

Jeremy was so furious he was having a hard time containing it. It was so unusual for him to be angry at a woman, but blackmail! Bloody hell, that would get a saint furious.

It boggled his mind that she had resorted to that, but he should have expected it. She was smart, after all. He wouldn't have expected that either from someone who came from the slums, but she'd proved it the night of the robbery, when she'd extricated them from a sticky, even somewhat dangerous, situation.

Remembering that he did owe her for that took a small chunk out of his anger, though only a small chunk.

This was absurd. He knew how to handle women. Where was his bloody finesse with this one? He ought to be looking on the bright side. Now that she was going to be living under his roof, he didn't doubt he'd get her into his bed eventually.

He was nothing if not confident where women were concerned. And this one was rather unique, adorable in her manly togs, amazing in her height, incredibly lovely with those big violet eyes, and not the least bit susceptible to his charms – yet.

She was attracted to him, though. He bloody well knew when a woman was attracted to him. But she gave every indication that it didn't matter. 'Don't touch me, don't even get near me' was the subtle message she exuded. Was that partly responsible for his anger? Another first for him. No, he simply didn't like being blackmailed, and by a wench he'd prefer to be making love to. Bloody hell.

He sighed. The sound brought her out of her pensive state and had her informing him, 'I'll take the maid's job.'

'Too bad. It would have been amusing watching you bungle your way through as a footman.'

She glared at him. He raised a brow. 'You don't think so? And by the by, you don't scowl at your employer. You "Yes, sir," "No, sir," "Very good, sir," and with a smile or no expression a'tall. When you're my mistress, you can scowl at me all you like.'

She started to snap something at him but turned her back on him instead. A stiff posture, full of indignation and ire.

'Counting to ten, are we?' Jeremy said dryly.

She turned back around, gave him a tight little smile, and gritted out, 'Yes, sir.'

He burst out laughing. He simply couldn't help it. And it removed the rest of his anger for the moment. It was going to prove amusing, after all, her attempt to 'better' herself. He supposed he could tolerate being blackmailed as long as the blackmailer was going to end up as his mistress.

Still grinning, he said, 'Let's get you settled then. Shall we start with your name?'

She unbent enough to answer, 'It's Danny.'

'No, I meant your *real* name. If you were sincere about turning over a new leaf, as it were, then you'll want to start with a clean slate.'

'That *is* my real name,' she replied with a stony stare.

'Truly? It's not short for Danielle or—?'

'It's the only name I 'ave any memory of. If I were given another at birth, it ain't one I'll ever be knowing.'

Jeremy found himself slightly embarrassed. Of course an orphan might not know her real name, and this one apparently didn't even have a surname. Deuced odd, to go through life without a last name.

He asked hesitantly, 'Would you mind if I called you Danielle?'

'I would mind. I ain't no Danielle. My friends call me Danny. Since you ain't one o' them, *you* can call me Dan.'

She was delightfully amusing in her stubborn adherence to being standoffish. Wouldn't give an inch, he was guessing. Habit, he was sure. But he supposed she would have had to be defensive, growing up where she did.

'But we *are* going to be friends, dear girl, so I suppose I will get used to Danny. Actually, it's a nice name, has a nice ring to it.'

'Get over it, mate,' she grouched, then at his raised brow, added, 'Sir.'

He grinned. 'Very well. On to the next subject then. Have you any dresses in that sack you're guarding with your life?'

She shook her head. 'Just my pet and one change o' clothes.'

'More pants, I presume?'

'Course more pants,' she said tersely. 'I've been a boy for fifteen years.'

'Good God, really?'

She was blushing now, profusely.

'Well, you do realize that you picked the job that will require feminine togs? My father might thumb his nose at convention, but I'm not my father. I don't expect uniforms, though,' he assured her. 'No indeed. This is a bachelor residence, and as such, I expect my servants to enjoy working here. No worrying about collars not being stiff enough or wrinkled skirts or the like.'

'I was expecting to wear a dress,' she said stiffly. 'Did I mention I 'ave no money?'

'You did, didn't you?' He grinned again. 'Not to worry. My housekeeper will be able to help in that regard and to get you otherwise situated and instructed. Come along. Much as I enjoy your company, I suppose I should turn you over to her now.'

She followed him, but stopped when they reached the bottom of the stairs, told him, 'You'll let her know you hired me? That she can't fire me? The last time I tried to be a maid, soon as I met the 'ousekeeper I got fired. She didn't like the way I talked, or looked.'

'I can imagine,' he said dryly.

'No, ye can't,' she snorted. 'Ye've never tried to be a maid b'fore.'

'Well, no, I don't suppose I have.'

'Don't be laughing at me again, Malory. I won't tolerate it. And that was in a lower-class 'ousehold, not one up 'ere on the bleedin' rich end o' town.'

He wiped the grin off his face. 'So you *have* tried honest work before?'

'Never got a chance to. Either got fired quick or couldn't get 'ired. Can't read, ye know, which don't give me many choices for jobs.'

'Would you like to be able to read?' he asked curiously.

'Sure I would, but I'm too bleedin' old for any schooling now.'

'But you're never too old to learn. Regardless, you needn't worry about anyone firing you here. You didn't exactly get hired under normal means, now did you?'

He was surprised that she actually looked embarrassed by that reminder. She wasn't going to be easy to deal with. Stepping on eggshells around her came to mind. It was that defensive stance of hers, ingrained, that so easily took offense. And she didn't have a deferential bone in her body. Cocky guttersnipe was what she was. But that was to be expected from someone who'd never had to deal with their betters before – except to rob them.

'Come along,' Jeremy suggested. 'Mrs Robertson is probably in the back of the house somewhere. You'll like her. Motherly sort. She—'

He got no further before the front door opened and his cousin Regina barged in. Bad habit, Reggie had, of not knocking. Of course, she did live just down the street, and she did know that he'd yet to find a butler.

She was startled by his presence there in the hall. 'Goodness, didn't expect to find you this quickly. Were you on your way out?'

'No, just getting my new servant situated.'

She looked at Danny then and tossed her a brief smile, but to Jeremy she said, 'Well, that settles that.'

He raised a brow at her. 'Dare I ask what?'

Reggie sighed. 'I came to offer you one of my footmen. Billings returned from his leave of absence. Have to have him back, of course. He's like family. But that new man who took his place has worked out splendidly, too. But I don't *need* three footmen, only two, so I was hoping you could take the new man. But you don't need two, one will do you fine. And—'

119

'Hell's bells, Reggie, don't write a book about it. Spit it out.'

She gave him a reproachful look. 'I was getting to the point. This fellow here is too young to be a butler, so it's obvious you've just hired your footman. Which is perfectly—'

Danny interrupted her this time. 'I've taken the maid's job, ma'am. Decided footman would be too easy.'

Reggie blinked at her, then rolled her eyes at Jeremy. 'Very funny. I see why you've hired him. He'll amuse you endlessly with drollery like that. Now I must run. I've hundreds of things to do today. And don't forget you're coming to dinner.'

'I am?'

'You *did* forget!' she said, appalled.

He grinned at her. 'No, I'd say you did. This is the first I'm hearing about it.'

'But Nicholas was going to stop by to – famous, I suppose *he* forgot. Well, never mind. Now you do know, so don't be late. Uncle Tony and Ros will be there. And Drew. Derek and Kelsey, too. I've even invited Percy.'

'Drew is back in town?' Jeremy asked in surprise.

She nodded. 'His ship docked this morning. And since your father and George are visiting Uncle Jason at Haverston, I imagine Drew will be at loose ends. Though I also expect George will be rushing back to London as soon as she knows her brother is here.'

'So you thought to entertain him?'

'Of course. Your father might still hate his brothers-in-law, but the rest of us like them well enough.'

Jeremy chuckled. 'You know he doesn't hate them. He just – well, doesn't *like* them. Principle, don't you know.'

'Yes, just like he doesn't *like* my husband,' she grouched.

Jeremy laughed. 'Well, old Nick did try to get him hanged.'

'So did George's brothers, but who's counting,' she huffed on her way out the door.

Jeremy almost felt out of breath after that brief visit. But Reggie was like that, a whirlwind of chatter. He glanced back at Danny to find her looking a bit dazed as well. He imagined all that rapid chatter hadn't made a bit of sense to her.

Considering the conclusion Reggie had drawn, Percy as well, for that matter, Jeremy asked her curiously, 'Am I the only one who sees the woman in you?'

Her lips twisted in disgust. 'Aye, you are. It's the pants. They usually serve me well, but didn't fool you none.'

He took a step closer, but he only had to glance down a few inches to meet her eyes. 'No, I'd guess it's the height. You're taller than many men. That's very rare.'

She broadened the space between them again before she spat out, 'Like I can bleedin' well 'elp that.'

'Don't get defensive. It's not a bad thing to be tall. Though come to think of it, Mrs Robertson will probably have trouble finding you any ready-made clothes. Having you making the beds wearing your—'

He stopped that thought abruptly. Thinking of her near a bed quite undid him.

'Was that yer sister?'

A safe subject, thank God. 'No, m'cousin Regina Eden. She and her husband, Nicholas, have a town house just down the street from here, though they are more often at Silverley, his country estate.'

'It were easy to tell ye were related. Yer whole family like that?'

'No, most of the Malorys are big and blond like m'father. There's just a few of us who took after my great-grandmother's side, m'self included. Why, I look so much like my uncle Tony that most people who meet us think he's m'father.'

'Ye look like ye find that amusing.'

'But it is.'

'I'll bet yer father don't think so.'

He chuckled. 'Course not, but then that's why it's amusing.'

14

Dinner was relaxed that night. It usually was when it was just family and close friends. Anthony had to get in a few digs at Reggie's husband, Nicholas, of course. It was the one thing that James and Anthony Malory were in complete agreement on, that Nicholas Eden, former rakehell, just wasn't good enough for their favorite niece and never would be. That the brothers had both been notorious rakes themselves before they married didn't make a bit of difference.

Reggie was special to them. All four Malory brothers had had a hand in raising her after their only sister died. And despite that Reggie so obviously adored her husband, James and Anthony weren't going to let Nick forget that he'd be dealing with them if he ever hurt her.

But Anthony's digs tonight were more good-natured than derogatory, and after his wife, Roslynn, kicked him under the table as a gentle reminder to behave, he turned his attention to Jeremy instead.

'So how's the new residence shaping up? All staffed and furnished and ready for a grand party?'

Jeremy coughed. 'Half-staffed, barely furnished, and as for parties, perhaps by the winter season.'

'You have your own place now, Jeremy?' Drew Anderson, his stepmother's brother, asked in surprise.

Jeremy grinned. 'Just. Uncle Tony and m'father decided it was time for me to experience true bachelorhood.'

Anthony coughed now. 'Bloody hell, makes it sound like we bought him a license to debauch.'

'I believe he does that very well without a license,' Reggie replied with an impish grin.

'Don't encourage him, puss,' Anthony scolded. 'Charming scamp that he is, the idea was to introduce him to property management in running his own household, to become his own man, as it were.'

'Well, he didn't need help with that,' Reggie disagreed. 'He's been acting the man since he was twelve.'

'I didn't mean *that* sort of manly endeavors.'

'Och, Tony, you're falling for her teasing,' Roslynn chimed in with her soft, Scottish brogue. 'We know your intentions were good ones.' Then she teased a bit herself, 'Though you do need to leave management out of your excuse, since he's been helping your brother manage our investments for quite a few years now.'

Jeremy came to Anthony's rescue this time. 'Inspecting rentals, seeing to repairs, and keeping agents honest is quite different from dealing with a household staff.'

'And good servants are so hard to come by, especially those you want to keep,' Reggie added. 'By the by, Jeremy, how's your new footman working out?'

'Actually, I'll take your man,' Jeremy replied. 'Send him round tomorrow.'

'Splendid. But I hope you didn't let that handsome young lad go just because I offered—'

'No, no, nothing like that.'

Jeremy didn't bother correcting his cousin about the sex of his new servant. He'd installed Danny as an upstairs maid, so there wasn't much chance of Reggie coming across her again. And truthfully, he didn't want to talk about her or explain why he'd hired an ex-thief – well, *hopefully* an ex-thief – to work for him.

Thankfully, the conversation turned in other directions after that, because having been reminded of her Jeremy became quite distracted with thoughts of his new maid. It was a novel experience, having to deal with two such opposing emotions where she was concerned, anger and desire. The anger he could control, the desire he wasn't so sure of. The anger should have canceled the desire. But it didn't, not even a little.

Being distracted around his family had its disadvantages as Jeremy found when he realized Drew Anderson was coming home with him. He wasn't sure how he got elected to put Drew up until his father and his stepmother returned to town, though it was probably because the whole family knew he and Drew had hit it off well, and now that Jeremy had his own bachelor residence, they figured Jeremy would enjoy the company. Which was true enough.

He liked Drew Anderson. They got along famously, enjoyed the same things, which was women and more women. They'd had some rousing good times together since the Anderson brothers had started coming to London, after their only sister, Georgina, had married into the Malory family. But now was *not* a good time to have a houseguest, and in particular, one as handsome as Drew was.

George had said of her brother once that Drew had a sweetheart in every port he'd ever sailed into, and that was probably true. The second youngest of the five Anderson brothers, Drew was the most devil-may-care of the lot, and at thirty-four, still a fun-loving rogue with no intention of ever limiting himself to just one woman, so matrimony was absolutely out of the question for him. Even seeing how nicely his older brother Warren, confirmed bachelor that he'd been, had settled into marriage with Amy Malory and had never been happier wouldn't change Drew's mind. Like Jeremy, he was of the firm opinion that variety was the spice of life, and the more of it the better.

Above average in height at six feet four inches, in prime shape from captaining his own ship for so many years, Drew was definitely a man the ladies cast their eyes toward. With a golden brown mane of curls and eyes so dark it was impossible to guess if they were anything other than black, he was an extremely handsome man – which was why Jeremy *wouldn't* have invited him to move in, no matter how temporarily, at least not now when a female was under Jeremy's roof that he had designs on himself.

Which had Jeremy saying as they walked the short distance to his house, 'Are you sure you wouldn't prefer a hotel for a few days, Drew? My house is barely furnished yet. Beds for every bedroom are about all I've bought so far. The other rooms are still empty. I've even been eating in the kitchen m'self.'

That room at least was filling up nicely, now that he had a cook and had given her carte blanche to get whatever she needed. And his own bedroom was fully furnished, thanks to George's insisting he take everything from his old room.

Drew chuckled. 'A bed is all I need.'

'It's too early for bed,' Percy added. His house was just a few blocks away, so he was walking with them. 'Aren't we going—'

'Not tonight, Percy,' Drew cut in. 'It's been a busy day for me. Docking is always a headache here with so many ships waiting in line for it. And I also spent a good portion of the day at the Skylark Shipping office and have to return there in the morning.'

'You pulling my leg, old man? Thought all you sailors were eager for some female company after being at sea.'

Drew grinned. 'Absolutely, but I'd prefer to seek that sort of entertainment when I'm fresh and thinking of beds as other than objects to sleep in. Tomorrow night?'

'Certainly. Looking forward to it. Jeremy? Are you up for—'

Jeremy decided to interrupt before he was tempted. 'I'm due for a good night's sleep m'self, Percy. Still haven't caught up from coming home at dawn the other night.'

Mention of their trip out of London to Heddings's house had Percy agreeing. 'Quite right. Now you mention it, bed does sound rather appealing, don't it?'

Jeremy didn't go directly to bed himself. As soon as he showed Drew to his room, he went to his own and yanked on the bellpull connected to the servants' quarters. He hoped his housekeeper had explained to Danny what the bell's ringing in her room signified. He doubted she'd be asleep this early, then again, she could be.

Actually, it might work to his advantage if she was and the bell woke her. Danny, soft and drowsy, had him thinking of things other than showing her what a lazy employer could be like. Waiting on him hand and foot had been the plan, but not if she was susceptible to his charms instead. He'd have to play it by ear, retribution or some immense pleasure.

She must have been awake because she arrived soon enough to indicate she hadn't needed to dress first. He'd been undressing down to just his shirt and pants when she rapped loudly on the door. He opened it quickly and yanked her inside before Drew investigated the noise.

''Ere now,' she objected, and jerked her arm out of his grasp.

'Keep it down. I have company across the hall.'

She raised a brow, indicating she wasn't quite buying that excuse. 'Wot are ye wanting then?'

Apparently having secured a job, a roof over her head, and food just down the hall hadn't improved her disposition any. But she appeared to regret her choice of words immediately because she broadened the distance between them.

Jeremy knew well that to say what he really wanted would be a serious mistake at this point. She wasn't ready to hear it. His expression said it though, something he couldn't seem to control when he was near her.

But to put her at ease for the moment, he quickly replied, 'I need a new bottle of brandy. You'll find a stock of them in the pantry.'

'Ye called me up 'ere for that?' she asked

incredulously. 'When ye could've fetched it yerself?'

His eyes widened innocently. 'Why ever would I do that, when I have a maid now?'

She started to snarl something, but snapped her mouth shut and left to get the brandy. Jeremy had a hard time keeping the grin off his face, but managed it before she returned a few minutes later, brandy in hand.

He'd made himself comfortable in one of the chairs by the fireplace. She approached and shoved the bottle toward him. He merely nodded toward the mantel where the empty bottle sat.

'Pour me a glass while you're there,' Jeremy said, then continued derisively. 'And I hope I don't need to add, bring it to me?'

She made a sound of impatience rather loudly and dumped nearly a third of the bottle in the snifter, much more than was needed. It was a large snifter. She obviously didn't know any better.

He sighed, showing some impatience of his own with her ineptitude, and instructed, 'No more'n an inch next time.'

Her back stiffened as she turned with the snifter in hand. It was a wonder the brandy didn't slosh all over him, she thrust it at him so forcefully. Too bad. He would have had her clean it up. The thought of her leaning close and dabbing a cloth over his chest was quite delectable.

'You might as well turn the bed down while you're here,' he suggested. 'Mrs Robertson did explain your duties to you, didn't she?'

'Not yet, though I doubt bed turning is one o' them.'

'Of course it is, and I'll expect to find it done each evening. You'll catch on soon enough, I'm sure. By the by, how did it go with Mrs Robertson after I left you in her care? Any trouble? You did seem to have some fears in that regard.'

She seemed to relax slightly with the new subject and, with a shrug, headed toward the bed to yank down the covers. 'She's a nice old bird, she is. She had me repeating m'self a few times until she got used to my speech, but she didn't seem to mind it.'

'Danny, Danny,' he sighed. 'Look at the mess you've made. Turning down the bed is done neatly, not as if you're changing the bedding. I expect to slip under the sheets, not fight to find them.'

She blushed over the scolding, but she didn't balk at trying again. That surprised him. She'd blackmailed her way into the job, so she didn't really have to take it seriously. Apparently she was going to though, which opened up numerous possibilities that he would find enjoyable, but she probably wouldn't.

'Don't forget to fluff the pillow, too,' he ordered.

She stiffened again just before she slammed a fist down in the center of his pillow. Jeremy had to bite back a laugh. Retribution was *so* sweet.

'My boots now.'

She glanced at him with a nervous frown and slipped back into her slang. 'Wot about them?'

'Come help me get them off.'

131

She didn't move, sounded quite nervous again when she asked, 'Don't ye 'ave a man for that? Wot's the position called?'

'A valet. And, no, don't need one. I have you – to see to such minor details.'

She closed her eyes. He thought he even heard a groan, though he wasn't quite sure. Was it the pause? Was he actually getting to her, despite her disagreeable mood? His own blood was warming. Seeing her next to his bed made him want to see her *in* it.

'Come here,' he said, his voice turning sensual.

Her eyes opened wide, but she still wouldn't approach him. He supposed he'd made her too nervous.

To alleviate her fears for the moment, he glanced at his feet and reminded her, 'My boots? I'd like to get to bed *some*time tonight and without them.' She *still* didn't move, so he said tersely, 'Need I remind you that you wanted, *insisted*, on having this job?'

That got her moving. She fairly flew across the room to grab hold of one of his boots and started yanking on it. It wasn't coming off that way, of course. She tugged and yanked some more. It still wasn't budging from his foot.

He finally said dryly, 'I suppose you don't know how to do this either?'

'I do,' she said in her own defense. 'I was just hoping you nabobs wore boots that came off easy.'

'Well, no need to be squeamish about straddling my leg, dear girl. Just get to it.'

She did, presenting him with her back and waiting for him to plant his other foot on her backside for the shove needed to get the boot off. But this time Jeremy was frozen. She'd come upstairs without her coat, wearing only her shirt, pants, and socks, so nothing was covering the shapely derriere that was suddenly in front of him and quite within his reach. It was probably one of the harder things he ever did, not taking advantage of that and instead putting his foot to her derriere instead of his hands.

Annoyed that she was making him want her again, he shoved a bit harder than necessary. She stumbled several feet away as the boot came off, but she didn't seem to think anything was amiss in that and she came right back to tackle the other one.

In an attempt to cool his ardor, he remarked casually, 'I notice you're still wearing your thiefly garb. Couldn't Mrs Robertson find you any suitable clothes?'

She glanced around to give him a cross look for the term he'd used, but there was no inflection in her tone. 'She did. She took me to her sister's seamstress. Said it would be a waste of time to look for that new ready-made clothing to fit me. Didn't want my ankles showing, she said.'

'Well, that's too bad. Showing ankles sounds interesting.'

She snorted at his grin. 'The first dress will be sent over sometime tomorrow, the other one by the next day.'

'Only two? That won't do a'tall.'

'I don't need more'n that and told her so.'

'Of course you do. Can't have you washing your clothes every day. Pure waste of time, that. I'll let her know to increase the order. And how d'you like the room? Finding it satisfactory?'

The second boot came off, in time for her to turn and lift a brow at him. 'And you'd be changing it if it weren't?'

He stood up and leaned close to her to say in a conspiratorial whisper, 'My room is available for sharing if you'd prefer. I know *I* would.'

Her back stiffened. 'Not bleedin' likely, mate.'

He straightened and sighed at her tone. 'You need to stop being so defensive, Danny, over such harmless flirtation. Really, I don't bite, you know – well, only if it gives pleasure, which is usually does. Like nibbling on your neck.' His tone got husky. 'And your ear – and this might be a good time for you to leave.'

Bloody hell, she did.

15

Danny hurried down the hall to the kitchen. She'd overslept and had had to be wakened, which wasn't a good way to start her new job. And it was such a nice job. She still couldn't believe she'd be living and working in such a fine house. Even the hall in the servants' wing was carpeted! But even needing a maid, Malory wouldn't have hired her if she hadn't blackmailed him. She felt bad about that. She'd make up for it though, vowed to be a better maid than he could have found by normal means.

Thinking about him brought on a twinge of excitement that she quickly tamped down. It wasn't going to be easy ignoring her attraction to him, but she would, because a man like that would be her downfall otherwise.

Danny reached the kitchen. The cook was there, Mrs Appleton. She was a jovial middle-aged woman, short but hefty. She liked to sing while she was cooking and got very loud at it, too.

She'd laughed yesterday when Mrs Robertson

had introduced Danny as the new upstairs maid, laughed for nearly ten minutes, off and on, every time she glanced at Danny. It was the clothes, at least Danny hoped that was all that was causing the woman such amusement. She'd probably never seen a woman wearing pants before.

Her helper, Claire, was in the kitchen now, too, the grumpy girl who'd let Danny in the house yesterday. She was quick to point out when Danny walked into the room. 'You're late.'

'I know. I'm sorry.'

'The food is cold now.'

It was said as if that were Danny's fault. Claire was definitely a glum sort. Dumpy of shape, shoulders stooped, she seemed to wear a perpetual frown – at least Danny had yet to see any other expression cross her face. Or maybe it just seemed so in contrast to the happy cook.

'I 'aven't time to eat it now,' Danny explained with a wistful sigh as she stared at the wide assortment of dishes that had been prepared. She was hungry.

'Why not?' Claire demanded. 'Where else are you going then? It's the food you're late for.'

'Oh. But ain't I late for work?'

Claire snorted. 'I work early, you don't. You have to wait until the master vacates his room so you can clean it. There's to be no noise upstairs that might wake him sooner than he planned to wake.'

'But wot if 'e sleeps all day?'

136

'Then you'll be working at night, won't you. And work on your speech as well,' Claire added in disgust. 'Cor, you sound like a street urchin. Where do you come from?'

Danny didn't answer, was too busy blushing. She could have spoken better just then, but it would have required concentration, and it was hard to do that when she was nervous. And besides, just because she'd recalled that she did used to talk much differently didn't mean it was all going to come back naturally. The way she talked now was natural to her, had been ingrained in her for fifteen years.

The cook tsked at her helper and said to Danny, 'Don't worry about it, dear. Mrs Robertson will train you well in what needs doing and when. Just follow her instruction and you'll do fine.'

The lady in question came through the doorway then, spotted Danny, and said, 'There you are. All done eating? Follow me.'

So she wasn't to be scolded? She had only been late for breakfast? Danny's relief was immense, but so was her hunger.

With a last glance at the wide assortment of food spread out on the table, she quickly swiped up two rolls and stuffed them in her pockets, then hurried after the housekeeper. The cook had seen what she'd done and her laughter followed Danny out the door.

Mrs Robertson took her upstairs and into one of the unoccupied rooms to explain in exact detail what her duties would be. Even though the room was pretty much empty at the moment, it wouldn't stay that way, and so Mrs Robertson explained what Danny would have to do when it was fully furnished.

There was never to be a speck of dust in the house. That was Mrs Robertson's first rule. Danny would have dirty laundry to fetch and return cleaned. Floors, windows, just about everything upstairs, fell to her to keep spotless.

The upstairs would be her domain, Mrs Robertson had stressed. Danny rather liked the sound of that. But in the meantime, at least until the downstairs maid was hired, she'd have to help in keeping those rooms clean as well. Claire took care of the kitchen. And at the moment, most of the other downstairs rooms were empty, so keeping them dust-free wouldn't take up much time at all.

'You will wait until Master Jeremy leaves his room before you enter it to clean it, unless he needs something, in which case he'll likely call for you. If he has guests, again, wait until they go downstairs before you enter their rooms. Do not, in any case, disturb any occupants upstairs if they are sleeping. Currently a member of his family is staying with us, so two of these rooms are occupied. You do not need to do your chores in any exact order, just make sure they are all done by the end of the day.'

Mrs Robertson had a *lot* more to say, and Danny

managed to retain it all, but it still didn't seem like enough work to keep her busy all day. She pointed that out.

'Wot if I finish up early each day?'

'You will need to keep yourself available if Master Jeremy is at home, in case he requires something. Otherwise you will be free to do as you like, rest, read, go out, visit friends, whatever suits you. You will have Sundays off after you make the beds and make sure everything on your floor is in its proper place. You might also wish to spend some time each day working on your diction.'

'Eh?'

'Exactly. The proper response would have been, "What is wrong with my diction?" or "What is diction?" or even "I like my diction the way it is, thank you."'

'But – that's wot I said, I just tossed it all into one word.'

The woman actually laughed. 'Danny, lass, this is nothing personal. Frankly, I find your speech quaint. It reminds me of my younger years. I didn't always work for the nobility, you know. But you'll find that improving your speech can only be a benefit to you. Unless you like being embarrassed when you have difficulty conveying your thoughts?'

Danny was jarred by what the housekeeper had called her, *Danny lass*. It brought back a vague memory of being surrounded by a room full of toys, someone holding her hand and telling her, 'Make a choice, Danny lass. Your father said you could have any toy that strikes your fancy for this birthday.'

Had her life really been that nice before someone had ripped her from it by trying to hurt her? Or was that just some dream she'd once had? Her head started aching, trying to remember more, but nothing else would come to her to prove that it had been a dream – or a real memory. And Mrs Robertson was waiting on an answer from her.

'I – I might know 'ow to talk better,' she said hesitantly. 'It's just been so long, I've mostly forgotten. My friend Lucy, she wanted me to talk as I do now. She worked 'ard at it, making sure I did.'

'How odd. But at any rate, I don't mind correcting you, if you won't mind being corrected. Master Jeremy also mentioned that he would try to assist you in that regard.'

''E did?'

'Yes, he's apparently taken quite an interest in you. This is an upper-crust household. If you were employed by tradespeople, it wouldn't matter that much. But servants of the nobility can be quite as snobbish as their employers, and you do want to fit in, don't you?'

Danny thought about that for a moment, then said, 'I don't think I'm wanting to be a snob, no.'

Mrs Robertson burst out laughing again. 'You're priceless, child. I haven't laughed this much in years. I wasn't suggesting turning *you* into a snob. Good heavens, no. I don't believe I'm one myself,

140

and Master Jeremy certainly isn't. But, you will meet other servants on this street, I'm sure. And we have yet to finish staffing this house. My point was, you are likely to come across such people, and while you might look down your nose at them, just as they will at you, you don't want to stand out for ridicule if you don't have to, do you? No, of course not. No one enjoys ridicule.'

Danny hadn't been expecting this type of instruction. But since it did fit right in with her desire to improve herself, she was quite grateful that the woman suggested it and said so.

'Thank ye, ma'am. I'd be beholden for the teaching.'

'Splendid. Shall we devote a half hour each evening to it for a while? We'll get those *h*'s and *u*'s back into your speech in no time!'

Danny grinned. 'There's fifteen years to correct. It may take more'n a while.'

'Possibly. But, you aren't going anywhere, are you? So we've plenty of time to work on it.'

Not going anywhere? Some of the weight just lifted from Danny's shoulders. Now if Malory would just get off them as well . . .

16

'Hullo! Where is everyone?'

Danny heard the women's loud call and poked her head around the upstairs corner to glance down the stairs where the noise was coming from. Three women were in the entry hall, decked out in high fashion, beauties all of them. She recognized one – Malory's cousin Regina Eden, who'd barged in on him yesterday. Which explained how they got in when no one was around to let them in.

Danny had no intention of answering the lady's question. Her duties were fresh in her mind and they didn't include answering doors or dealing with guests. She was aware that there was no butler or footman yet to do that, but Claire was around somewhere and had managed to answer the door just fine yesterday.

Danny quickly leaned back out of sight again, but not soon enough. 'You there! Come here, please.'

Danny didn't move. Just because it seemed as if

the woman was talking to her didn't mean she was. Claire could have appeared. *Someone* should have by now, with all that yelling going on.

'I know you heard me, so don't run off. Come down here, please.'

Danny stuck her head around the corner again. Sure enough, Regina Eden was looking directly at her and beckoned her forward with a wave of her hand. There was no help for it. Rudeness wasn't part of her job.

She bounded down the stairs in her usual get-to-it-quickly pace, then nearly landed on her arse on the marble floor as she slid a few feet. Bleedin' slippery floor. Her blush didn't last long though as she was boggled by the three women, now that she was closer and could see them better. They weren't just beauties, they were raving beauties.

One of them had flaming red-gold hair and gray-green eyes. She was petite, a good five inches shorter than Danny, and looked to be in her early thirties. The other new one was younger, perhaps twenty-five, with black hair that looked naturally curly and soft gray eyes. She was a bit shorter, too, making Danny feel positively huge standing next to the three of them.

Malory was related to Regina Eden, but these other two women? He'd said the rest of his family were blond, so they weren't family of his. And if he had beauties like these visiting him, maybe he wasn't out to get her in his bed after all. Maybe he had only been toying with her. She was nothing compared to these elegant ladies, and they were definitely ladies. Nobility was written all over them.

'How are you liking your new job, lad?' Regina was asking her. 'My footman will be over later today. I'm sure you'll get along with him splendidly. He's such a nice fellow. But in the meantime, it looks like you're the only one available to fetch Jeremy for us. I imagine he and Drew made a late night of it after they left my house last night, not that Jeremy is known to be an early riser in any case. He's still sleeping?'

The hour was still early, barely ten in the morning. Danny could truthfully say he was still in his room, since she'd been keeping a close eye and ear on his door, to make sure she'd be behind some other door when he left his room. Running into Malory in the hall upstairs was *not* going to be part of her daily routine.

'I 'aven't seen 'im today, so, aye, 'e's probably still abed.'

That should have been their clue to leave, but, no, Regina said, 'Well, run along and wake him. And do tell him to hurry. We have a great many shops and warehouses to stop in today if we're going to get this house furnished.'

'Yer taking 'im shopping?'

'Indeed. Waiting for him to muddle through the process on his own will never get this place up to scratch. He has entertaining to do, but he can't do it if there isn't a sofa to sit on.'

Danny wondered if Jeremy knew he had

entertaining to do. She was smirking as she headed back upstairs. His cousin seemed so pushy, Danny wouldn't be surprised if the entertaining was her idea, not his.

She stopped short in the hall before his door, realizing suddenly that *she* was supposed to wake him. She'd been hoping she wouldn't have to see him today. She'd been hoping to get used to her job before she had to deal with him again. After what he'd said last night . . . she caught her breath, thinking of it, and remembering the way he'd looked at her.

She went ahead and pounded on his door, shouting, 'Get up, mate! Ye 'ave company.'

Then she took off down the hall to hide in an empty bedroom. Not soon enough though. The door across from his opened and a blond giant of a man stepped out to growl at her, 'If that's the way you wake people, make sure you send a maid to my door, or you'll end up being tossed down the stairs in short order.'

Danny could have cried at that point. Just when she'd begun to feel comfortable, she had to blow it again and get a member of his family annoyed enough to send her tossing. She turned about, ready to apologize, and forgot what she was going to say. Big, blond, and gorgeous. And he was as surprised as she was, now that he got a look at her.

'I'll be damned, if you aren't a woman, I'll eat my ship plank by plank.'

'A gut full o' splinters don't sound too appetizing,' she said by way of acknowledgment.

He grinned. 'I take it you *are* the maid? Or rather, let me rephrase that. I *hope* you are the maid and not one of Jeremy's ladyloves.'

'I ain't no one's ladylove.'

'Then it's my lucky day.'

'Eh?'

'Means you're available, sweetheart.'

Danny snorted. 'Don't mean any such thing.'

'Don't devastate me this early in the morning. I may not recover.'

Since he didn't look the least bit devastated, looked nothing but confident and full of mirth, she replied simply, 'Get over it, mate.'

Danny turned to leave again. She wasn't used to men flirting with her. Women, yes, all the time and everywhere she went. She was very used to that, but then they saw a handsome lad when they looked at her. And she'd developed trite phrases that didn't insult, but let them know she wasn't interested. But men . . . and how the devil had another one seen through her disguise so easily?

Bleedin' hell, she'd been right to worry that she couldn't go on much longer playing the man. Twice in a matter of days she'd been figured out.

She'd gotten no more than a step away when she heard Jeremy say in a less-than-friendly tone, 'My servants are off-limits, Drew – just so you know.'

'So, it's like that, is it? I'm not surprised. A face like that is worth giving up the sea for.'

'Which you have no intention of ever doing.'

A chuckle. 'Not a chance.'

One of the doors closed, Danny couldn't tell which. She took the chance of glancing back, hoping it was Jeremy who'd gone back in his room. It wasn't. He stood there looking at her, and he wasn't completely dressed. He only had his pants on.

She couldn't move, she even forgot to breathe for a moment, she was so mesmerized. He was more muscular than his clothes indicated, and rock-firm. Even his tan extended down his chest, implying it was his natural skin tone. And his hair was mussed from sleeping, giving him an irresistible sexy appeal that was so strong, she was almost drawn forward like a moth to a flame . . .

Oh, God! Looking for a door, any door, to dash behind, she found the closest, opened it, and stepped inside. Bleedin' hell, she was in the closet where the clean bedding was kept, along with a supply of cleaning materials! It was dark with barely any room between the door and the shelves behind her. But she wasn't going back out there to see that man half-naked again.

He rapped on the door. She groaned inwardly. 'Go away. Ye ain't dressed.'

'You could get used to it.'

'Not bleedin' likely.'

She heard his chuckle. She gritted her teeth.

'Was there a reason you nearly broke my door down waking me?'

147

She blushed. Hearing it put that way, she probably shouldn't have been so loud about it. Having to wake him at all, well, she supposed that task was going to fall to her occasionally and be the hardest part of her new job. She'd have to find a way to avoid it, maybe make a deal with the new footman when he arrived. She felt better already, until she recalled that Jeremy was on the other side of the door waiting for her answer. And half-naked.

'A good reason. Ye've a gaggle of females downstairs . . .'

Her words trailed off. He'd opened the door. He leaned against the frame of it, too, crossing his arms over his bare chest. It was a wide chest, tapered down to a lean waist. Broad shoulders and sculpted muscles went with it. He was put together too fine, he really was. That's probably why he always seemed so confident. He bleedin' well knew he was a prime piece to look at.

At the moment he was perfectly relaxed – and amused. She stared at his blue eyes to keep from looking at his chest.

'Having a conversation through a door is rather silly, don't you think?' he asked.

''Aving a conversation at all is silly, when ye've got guests waiting on ye.'

'Who?'

'Yer cousin and two other ladies.'

'I suppose they aren't stopping by just to say hello?' he asked hopefully.

She shook her head and, for the life of her,

couldn't figure out why a smirk was in her tone when she replied, 'They mean to drag ye shopping.' Probably because it was obvious that he didn't particularly like to shop, or he'd have finished furnishing his house on his own.

And his sigh wasn't happy. 'Bloody hell, I wish Reggie would give some warning when she makes plans for me. Course, then she wouldn't be our sweet Reggie. Be a love and fetch me a couple of pastries while I dress. My cousin won't want to wait while I eat a decent breakfast.'

Anything to get out of his presence!

But he didn't move! She had to squeeze past him and didn't quite manage it without brushing against his arm. That arm shot out across her waist to stop her.

'The next time you want to hide in a closet' – he leaned closer to whisper by her ear – 'you might consider some company. You'd be surprised what delights can be found in cozy spots like this.'

Danny didn't answer, wouldn't have been able to utter a word even if she'd thought of one. She pushed past him and bolted down the stairs. The last thing she'd heard from Jeremy was his sigh. The only surprise she had was that she made it to the kitchen without falling apart from having been that close to him.

17

'I don't see how you're going to manage it. He's a confirmed bachelor, a rakehell even. He only comes to these affairs to please his family.'

Emily Bascomb listened to her friend with only half an ear as she watched Jeremy Malory across the room. He would have stood out in any crowd, as tall as he was, but he was also so sinfully handsome, every single woman in the room had become aware of him the moment he arrived. His black evening togs fit him to perfection. His hair, which fell in thick black waves about his ears and neck, might be worn a trifle longer than was fashionable, but that just gave him a rakish air.

Both girls were debutantes that season, though Emily had been stealing all the attention with her unparalleled beauty. Jennifer was used to that, having grown up in the same shire. With blond hair and light blue eyes, petite, exquisite Emily was a smashing success and basked in so much adoring attention.

But from the moment Emily had clapped eyes on Jeremy Malory last week, she had become entranced with him and had determined he would be hers. She hadn't expected to have to work at winning him, though, was quite annoyed that he'd barely glanced at her during their too-brief introduction last week, and now that she was finally seeing him again, he was ignoring her completely, as if they hadn't even met.

It was intolerable. She had every young lord that season in the palm of her hand as she'd known she would, all except for Malory. And she had no interest at all in any of the others now – because of him.

For years she'd been hearing rumors about how handsome he was, but living in the country with her family, and rarely ever getting to London, she'd never had an opportunity to meet him to find out if the rumors were true. They were. His looks were positively mesmerizing.

Her friend Jennifer was still warning her, 'And the only women he pays any attention to a'tall are' – she paused to add in a whisper – 'those he knows he can take to his bed without risk of losing his bachelor standing.'

'Jen, you don't get it,' Emily replied impatiently. 'I *will* marry him, even if I have to sleep with him first to accomplish it. One way or another, he's going to be mine.'

'Emily Bascomb, you wouldn't dare!' Jennifer gasped.

Emily made a moue with her pretty lips and pulled her friend off to the side to whisper, 'Of course not, but it wouldn't be the first time that the rumor of an indiscretion has brought a fellow to the altar, now would it?'

'What rumor?'

'Give me a few moments and I'll think of one. But I'll give him one last chance to redeem himself first. Come along. Let's remind him that he's met us.'

'I haven't met him,' Jennifer pointed out, not liking in the least being dragged in on her friend's scheme.

'Then I'll introduce you.'

'You can't be so bold!' Jennifer complained, hanging back. 'You've barely met him yourself.'

Emily tsked and let go of her friend. 'How do you expect to get what you want out of life if you play the coward?' Then she sighed, 'Suit yourself then, I'll go alone. It's perfectly appropriate to approach the man you're going to marry.'

'But you . . . aren't . . .'

Jennifer closed her mouth, embarrassed that she was talking to no one, since Emily had gone on without her. Much too bold, her friend was, but that's what came of being the prettiest woman in all of England. It lent confidence on a par with royalty.

Jeremy saw her coming, turned around abruptly, looking for the nearest exit, but got caught by Drew, who was coming to join him. 'This wasn't exactly what I had in mind for this evening,' Drew was saying. 'I'm much better at socializing after I've bedded a few wenches.'

'Aren't we all.' Jeremy grinned and took Drew's arm to steer him toward the door. 'Shall we then? This ball was Percy's idea, since he'd promised he'd make an appearance. But we've done that, so—'

'Jeremy, you can't possibly be leaving so soon. We haven't danced yet.'

He could pretend he hadn't heard her, should do just that, but he simply wasn't that rude. With an inward sigh, he turned around.

'Lady Emily, how nice to see you again,' Jeremy said politely if in a somewhat bored tone, hoping she'd take the hint that he wasn't interested in her.

She didn't. She beamed at him. Positively stunning when she smiled like that, with her light blue eyes sparkling, Jeremy thought. She was quite the sensation this season. And looking for a husband, which put her off-limits to him.

'And you as well,' she said to him demurely. 'We had so little time to talk when we met last week.'

'I was late for an appointment. And I'm afraid you've caught me late for another one. We were just—'

Drew jabbed him in the ribs, said, 'Aren't you going to introduce me?'

Jeremy sighed. 'Lady Emily Bascomb, meet Drew Anderson, my uncle by marriage.'

'Make me feel positively ancient, why don't

you,' Drew complained, taking the hand Emily had offered Jeremy and shaking it gently. Nor did he let go immediately. 'The pleasure is entirely mine, especially if you've come here without your husband.'

'Husband? I'm not married – yet.'

Drew coughed, realizing his mistake, though it was understandable. Even an American knew that young, unmarried debutantes, either on this side of the ocean or his own, didn't approach bachelors without an escort in tow.

'I'm sorry to hear that,' Drew replied, baffling the young lady.

Jeremy almost laughed. Drew had been quite interested until hearing that she was a young innocent.

Jeremy saved him having to explain that remark by saying, 'Sorry, old chap, but you'll have to find some other time to further your acquaintance with the lady. We really need to be off. We're already quite late.'

'Such a shame,' Drew replied. 'But if we must . . .' And this time he did the dragging to get them out of there.

Despite her pleasure with the new furnishings that had arrived that day, a glum mood had settled on Danny and was still present when she went to bed, keeping her from sleeping. She couldn't figure out what was causing it. She should have been filled with euphoria. She'd gotten through her first day of working at a decent job and hadn't been fired. She could be proud that she was firmly planted on the straight and narrow. The job was easy. The other servants were nice. The house-keeper was even willing to teach her to talk better. And she had a wonderful room all to herself. She should bleedin' well be ecstatic.

Her new clothes had also arrived that day. They were plain and serviceable and comfortable to work in, the white blouse long-sleeved with small ruffles at the cuff, high-necked, but not tight enough to choke her. The skirt was unadorned black. A short white apron had come in her package to wear over it. It was trimmed with a tiny ruffle, but otherwise was definitely a maid's apron, with deep pockets on both sides, even a long, tube-shaped one that looked as if it would hold her feather duster.

She'd spent quite a while admiring herself in a mirror. After tucking her curls back behind her ears so they were a little more contained, she'd been amazed at how pretty she looked. No, she was more than pretty, she was every bit as beautiful as those women who'd fetched Malory. Is that what he'd seen all along when he looked at her?

The new footman had shown up around noon, about the time all the new furniture started arriving. Carlton was the new man's name. He was young, probably only a few years older than Danny, plain looking, though he had some pretty doe-brown eyes. A talkative sort, he seemed good-natured. Danny had paid close attention to him when he was introduced to the staff, a bit too close probably, since it caused him a few blushes. She wasn't exactly attracted to him, but she realized he was definitely the sort of fellow who would make a respectable husband, so she determined to get to know him better when she got the chance.

She still couldn't sleep. Finally she got back up and went to make sure everything was still in its proper place upstairs. It was, except for the occupants. The two young nabobs were still out on the town, probably prowling about looking for wenches to bed. That's what rich young men did. Was that what was bothering her? That Malory was out trying to find a skirt to toss because she'd put him off? That should please her. It would mean he might leave her alone. The thought didn't please her at all.

She went back downstairs, just as glum. She'd made it around the corner at the back of the hall when she heard the front door open and the tail end of an ensuing conversation.

'Then what are you waiting for? She's just a wench,' Drew was saying.

'No, she's not,' Jeremy replied. 'And I don't want to talk about her.'

'So it's like that, is it? And what about that pretty little Emily Bascomb who fairly drooled all over you tonight at that ball. Don't tell me she didn't prick your interest at all?'

'Did I seem interested?'

'Not a bit, which was my question. Why not?'

'Same reason you backed off as soon as you heard she wasn't married. In that we're quite alike, old man. I avoid debutantes having their first season, second season, or any bloody season. Emily was rather obvious that she's set her cap for me, but all she's interested in is marriage, which I'm not. I'm sure you know how that goes.'

'Yes, marriage or nothing.' Drew sighed. 'That's too bad. Pretty little thing. And she did seem like she'd offer you a lot more.'

There was a shrug in Jeremy's tone. 'I don't doubt she would. Some of them don't mind putting the cart before the horse, but only because they're confident they'll get what they want in the end. I've seen more'n one lord get leg-shackled over mistakes like that.'

'Eh?' A long pause. 'Oh, you mean married. Well, damn, that's depressing. Think I'll stick with tavern maids and parlor maids.'

'Did anyone ever tell you that you talk too much when you're foxed?'

'I'm not foxed. Might be a little drunk though. And why don't you English *talk* English? Need a blasted dictionary to understand you sometimes.'

A chuckle. 'Accents can get pretty strong in some quarters of the country, but you're probably referring to *cant*. Just a passing phase, old man. Could be gone from the vocabulary in a year or two.'

'And get replaced by something just as un-decipherable?' Drew complained.

'And you Americans have no slang?'

'Nothing that isn't perfectly understandable,' Drew said with a smirk in his tone.

'Understandable by *you*, old boy, but it would be foreign to me, now wouldn't it?'

'Try not to be logical when I'm drunk, Jeremy, it gives me a headache.'

Jeremy laughed. Danny even caught herself about to chuckle, which was a good cue for her to take herself off to bed before she was discovered there in the hall. And she went to sleep immediately now that Malory was home.

18

'There's going to be a dinner party tonight,' Mrs Appleton announced to Danny and Claire the next morning. 'Mrs Robertson will tell you all about it and what you need to do. I was given warning only last night. Barely enough time to plan the menu and shop for it!'

'This soon?' Danny asked as she started filling a plate. She wasn't going to miss a full breakfast today. 'Doesn't it take time to send out invitations for parties?'

'Usually,' Mrs Appleton agreed. 'But not when it's just family coming.'

'Oh,' Danny replied, not all that interested. 'Well, I'll be sure to stay out of the way.'

'No, you won't. You and Claire will both be serving. So will Carlton.'

Danny had been doing just fine with her speech until she heard that. 'Serving wot?'

'The food and drinks, of course.'

'That ain't me job,' Danny pointed out reasonably.

'It is when we're short on staff,' the cook countered, much to Danny's dismay. 'Every hand will be needed with some fifteen to twenty guests expected.

'So it's not just 'is family?'

'It is. The Malorys are a *big* family. But not all of them are in London at the moment. The Marquis of Haverston, head of the family, rarely comes to town, I'm told. And the earl's two daughters aren't in town either; they're on their country estates with their husbands. One is married to a duke, you know.'

Royalty, Danny thought. The bleedin' nabob was related to royalty! And Mrs Appleton was sounding so proud, to be able to mention it.

'I'm feeling sick,' Danny said.

'The devil you are,' the cook snorted. 'This will be a good test of your resourcefulness, my dear. With a little instruction, you'll do just fine.'

That was doubtful, but Danny said no more on the subject. The breakfast didn't sit well with her, going down on a nervous stomach, which she now had, so she didn't eat her fill after all and headed upstairs to start her routine. Maybe if she avoided the housekeeper for the rest of the day, the woman would forget about giving her new instructions and Danny wouldn't be forced to serve royalty that night.

In her nervous state, she managed to clean the

entire upper floor by noon – except for Jeremy's room. He was still in it, so she wasn't going near it.

By midmorning, Mrs Robertson had found her and took her to the large dining room for that promised instruction. There really wasn't that much to learn, just whom to serve first, how to pour wine without gaining notice, to watch the glasses and refill them as needed. The men would apparently serve themselves drinks prior to dinner. She'd only have to fetch a tea tray if the ladies requested it. She was to stay on hand, though, in the parlor, in case there were any other requests. She just had to stay unobtrusive and not draw any attention to herself.

'And look your neatest,' Mrs Robertson had warned before she sent Danny back to her cleaning.

Danny blushed. Claire had snidely mentioned her wrinkles that morning, too. She was going to have to give up her habit of sleeping in her clothes, obviously.

'Danny, come here, please.'

She sighed mentally. So much for avoiding Malory. He was the only one left upstairs, and he *still* hadn't left his room. But obviously, he was no longer sleeping in it. He'd opened his door to call her and had left it open.

She peeked her head around the corner of the doorframe. He was still abed, lying on it, his arms crossed behind his head, looking so damned comfortable and relaxed. He wasn't fully dressed. He was wearing just a white lawn shirt, fastened only halfway up his chest, and buff-colored breeches. No shoes or stockings.

Lazing the day away, that's what she used to do before she got a *real* job. Bleedin' nabobs. And how was she supposed to clean his room if he wouldn't leave it?

She was making excuses for her annoyance when, the truth was, seeing him lying in bed set her pulses racing. God, she wished he wasn't so damned handsome that her fingers itched to touch him.

'Don't you have something to do during the day that would take you elsewhere?' she said more sharply than she should have.

Her voice drew his attention to her and his cobalt eyes widened in surprise. He even sat up on the edge of the bed. 'Good God, you're beautiful!' he exclaimed.

Danny would have been pleased to hear Carlton say so, but Malory's flattery didn't impress her, since she knew his motives. Besides, she wasn't at her best, so she snorted. 'You're a bleedin' liar. I've been told twice already today that I'm wrinkled beyond salvation.'

'Wrinkles can't hide potential, dear girl. What you wear doesn't detract from your amazing bone structure, doesn't change the unique color of your hair, doesn't alter the violet clarity of your eyes. But since I was already familiar with all that, what I probably should have said was, "Good God, you've got nice breasts!"'

162

Her face went up in flames. But she couldn't call him a liar this time, not when she'd spent ten of those thirty minutes yesterday in front of his mirror admiring just how nicely she filled out her new blouse.

She scowled at him though, flustered enough to slip back into her street talk. 'Mentioning me breasts ain't proper, is it?'

He grinned unrepentantly and assured her, 'Only in mixed company.'

Her lips flattened out. 'Then ye talk to all yer servants like ye do to me, eh?'

'No, just those I hope to get extremely intimate with. By the by, this is a comfortable bed. Would you like to try it sooner rather than later – like now?'

She should have known better than to ask questions that would encourage him to be more outlandish. 'The only thing I'll be doing with that bed is fixing the covers on it after ye get out o' it.'

'I'm wounded.' He sighed.

'Yer lazy. Go do something so I can clean yer room.'

'But I am doing something. I'm recuperating from last night's entertainment, and resting up for tonight. And besides, your job doesn't require a room to be unoccupied. You can clean around me.' He turned on his side, bent his elbow to rest his head on one hand, and grinned at her again. 'Just pretend I'm not here.'

Right. As if that were even remotely possible.

But she could try not to look at him. Bleedin' hell, that wouldn't work, because she'd know he was watching her. And even if he wasn't, she'd think he was and be glancing at him to find out, and . . .

'I'll wait.'

'You can't,' he seemed happy to tell her. 'I'll be resting here until dinner.'

She gritted her teeth, ripped the duster out of her apron pocket, and turned toward his small writing desk with the intention of attacking it with her feathers. She gasped instead, seeing the hat lying on it. It hadn't been there yesterday.

'Me 'at! Why do ye still 'ave it?'

There was a shrug in his tone. 'I kept it as a keepsake of an – interesting experience.'

'I've missed it.'

'Too bad. Belongs to me now.'

She glanced back at him curiously. 'Why? You wouldn't be caught dead wearing it.'

'Don't intend to wear it. Don't intend to give it up either. So if I find it missing, I'll know where to look, won't I?'

'I've given up stealing.'

'Glad to hear it. Then I'll consider my hat safe.' That got him a glare, to which he only chuckled. 'Cheer up, luv. It really doesn't go with skirts, you know. Frilly bonnets are what you need now.'

She snorted. 'I'll wear these bleedin' skirts, but those silly lady hats aren't for me.'

He tsked. 'You're thinking like a man again.'

'So shoot me.'

She went on to attack the desk as she'd intended, but it was rather deflating to find no dust on it yet that she could scatter about the room. She was careful not to touch her – *his* hat. She had a feeling he was silently laughing at her for having gotten into such a rotten mood over a hat. As if she cared.

When she took a moment to really look at the room, she was glad to see she'd done such a good job on it yesterday that there was barely anything to do to it today other than pick up a few clothes he'd dropped here and there. She gathered those and started to leave with them, keeping her gaze well away from the bed.

'Hell's bells, Danny, you aren't thinking of depriving me of your delightful company already, are you?'

He truly sounded disappointed. A ruse, no doubt. Still, she found herself stopping at the door to say, 'You have guests coming tonight. There's a lot of work that needs to be done before they get here.'

He sighed. 'Ah, yes, my first foray into entertaining on the home front.' Then he added somewhat snidely, 'Mimicking your betters again, are you?'

She stiffened, realizing he was referring to her speech. 'No, actually, Mrs Robertson has been coaching me.'

'Good God! And you caught on that quickly? Amazing.'

He was being derisive, so she didn't bother to tell

him that the way she used to talk was coming back to her more and more. She still had too many lapses when she got nervous or angry for him to believe her, so she changed the subject instead.

'I'm surprised you're having a party this soon. I've barely gotten all the dust and grime off the new furniture.'

'I assure you it wasn't my idea.'

She lifted a brow. 'Let me guess: your cousin?'

'Of course.'

Since he sounded annoyed at the moment, Danny's mood improved a lot. She even flashed him a cheeky grin. 'Cheer up, mate. I was told it's just your family coming. No need to impress family, eh?'

'On the contrary. I could care less about impressing mere acquaintances. It's my family that needs to think I'm getting along fine or they'll join forces to find out why not and proceed to correct the matter.'

'You're a grown man. Why don't they let you muddle through on your own?'

'Because they love me, of course.'

19

Because they love me, of course. Danny couldn't get those words out of her mind. Must be nice to have that kind of family. Her 'family' had never really felt like family. Members joined Dagger's band between the ages of five and ten, so there was no birth bond to generate a feeling of true closeness, and they usually left between the ages of fourteen and seventeen, to set off on their own. Rarely did any that left come back to visit. Once gone, gone for good.

Danny had enjoyed helping the younger children and had even had a few favorites over the years, but still, none that felt like brothers or sisters to her. Lucy was the only one she'd really developed a closeness to. Lucy was like a sister. But once Lucy had started whoring, she didn't have much time to spare for Danny.

But she was going to start a family of her own. That thought had been in the back of her mind now for quite a few years, though never seriously until now, since her masquerade had restricted her options in that regard. Hard to go looking for a husband if you looked like a husband yourself. She was herself now, though, or trying to be, so there was nothing to stop her from getting married as soon as the right man came along. And then finally, she'd have a real family.

The Malorys didn't arrive all at once; they trickled in over several hours prior to dinner. Regina Eden and her husband, Nicholas, were the first to arrive, probably because they lived only a few houses away.

Regina stopped short when she saw Danny in her dark blue skirt and white blouse, a light blue apron this time giving her even more color. She said only, 'Famous. My eyesight must be going. I can usually recognize my own sex, no matter what they're wearing.'

'Was pro'bly my hair, ma'am. The rakish male style, you know.'

'I suppose.' Regina sighed. 'Just feels deuced awkward, having made such a colossal mistake.'

'Beautiful chit,' Danny heard Nicholas Eden remark to his wife as they moved off to join Drew on the other side of the large parlor.

'*You* weren't supposed to notice,' Regina chided him, though in an amused tone. 'But I'm sure Jeremy did.'

More and more Malorys arrived after that. Carlton was letting them in. Danny did have to fetch a tea tray, and still another as the evening wore on. She caught their names in snippets of conversations that she overheard. She also caught many of them looking her way curiously.

The two ladies who had joined in the shopping expedition yesterday turned out to be Jeremy's cousin and his aunt by marriage. The dark-haired cousin was Kelsey, married to Derek, one of the big, blond, handsome Malory men. Derek's father, Jason, was the marquis who rarely came to town.

The copper-haired beauty was Roslynn, married to Jeremy's uncle Anthony. This chap bowled Danny over when she first saw him. Anthony looked so much like Jeremy it was uncanny, just an older version. It must be odd, though, knowing exactly what you will look like when you get older. But then the older version was so bleeding handsome, it was no wonder Jeremy fairly reeked with confidence. He knew he had many, many years of the amazing sexual appeal he possessed to look forward to.

Another uncle arrived, the earl Mrs Appleton had mentioned. Edward Malory was a jovial sort from the blond side of the family. About ten years or so older than his brother Anthony, Edward had a large family of his own. His wife, Charlotte, was present, and their two grown sons, Travis and Marshall. They had three daughters, too, apparently, all married, and none expected tonight. Two of the girls lived in the country, but the youngest, Amy, had sailed to America with her husband, Warren, who was one of Drew Anderson's brothers. They were expected home sometime that summer, but no one knew for certain when.

Because it was only going to be family and close friends, Anthony and Roslynn's young daughter, Judith, had been allowed to come to dinner. With such handsome parents, it was small wonder that Judy, as she was called, was such a beautiful child. She had her mother's red-gold hair and those amazing cobalt blue eyes that her father, Regina, and Jeremy possessed. She was precocious, too, and quite frank in her remarks, as children tended to be.

She came over to Danny before dinner was served and after staring up at her for a few moments said candidly, 'You're very pretty.'

'So are you.'

'I know.' But the girl sighed as she said it, as if she wasn't pleased by it. 'I'm told it will give m'father grief when I grow up.'

'Why?'

'Because of all the suitors I'll have.'

'So many?' Danny asked.

'Yes, hundreds and hundreds. Uncle James doesn't think m'father will be able to deal with it very well. Thinks he'll make a' – she paused to lean forward and whisper – 'bloody arse of himself.'

Danny choked back a laugh. 'But what d'you think?'

'I think Uncle James might be right.'

Danny couldn't help but laugh and wished she had better restraint. She ended up drawing every eye in the room to her. She could have withstood that, despite the embarrassment it caused, except that she'd drawn Jeremy's eyes, too.

He'd been making the rounds, chatting with each of his family as he or she arrived, and doing a good job of ignoring Danny at her station next to the door. But he wasn't ignoring her now and his eyes were fairly eating her. And they were all talking about her now. She knew it, sensed it, even caught a snippet of conversation here and there, though not enough to figure out what they were saying about her. It was highly embarrassing to know she had temporarily become the center of attention.

Across the room, Anthony whispered to Jeremy, 'Get her set up in her own place. It will cause dissent among your servants when it's found out that you're bedding her. Jason might have gotten away with it for over twenty-five years, bedding his housekeeper, but he had a secret entrance to Molly's room. Doubt this house has it set up so conveniently.'

'I'm not, bedding her that is.'

'What a whopper,' Anthony chuckled. 'You wouldn't pass up a prime article like her.'

'Don't intend to,' Jeremy grumbled. 'It just ain't happened yet.'

Anthony lifted a black brow. 'Losing your finesse, dear boy?'

Jeremy frowned. 'I'm beginning to think so. I have to constantly remind m'self that she's unique.'

'Uniquely beautiful, I couldn't agree more. But that isn't what you meant, is it?'

'No. As it happens, there isn't a bloody thing about her that can be called typical. Her background, her habits, everything about her isn't what you'd expect.'

'She can't be that far off the mark, youngun,' Anthony disagreed.

'You'd be surprised. Yesterday she talked like a street urchin. Today I caught her talking like an English tutor! And she thinks like a man. In fact, until a few days ago, she wore pants for most of her life. But as soon as she gets into skirt, she wants a husband,' Jeremy added on a mumble.

Anthony coughed. 'You?'

'No, she knows I'm a confirmed bachelor, which is why she'll have nothing to do with me. She wants a *respectable* husband.'

Anthony laughed. 'Well, the pants part convinced me, but now we're back to typical. Most women do want respectable husbands.'

Jeremy raised a brow. 'When she's not the least bit respectable herself?'

'Ah, I see. Trying to move up in the world, is she? Well, if you really don't stand a chance of winning her over, then perhaps you should consider getting rid of her, to avoid temptation as it were.'

Jeremy finally grinned. 'Malorys don't give up that easily.'

In another corner, Edward asked his wife, 'Does the maid look familiar to you?'

'Can't say that she does,' Charlotte replied.

Edward's brow knitted. 'Can't place her, yet it seems I *should* know her.'

'So you've probably seen her in passing, perhaps on the street or in one of the shops. Pretty gel like that would make an impression.'

'I suppose.' He sighed. 'Though it's going to nag me now until I recall where I've seen her before.'

By the fireplace, Travis remarked to his brother with a sigh very like his father's, 'I suppose Jeremy's already staked his claim.'

Marshall chuckled. 'Course he has. Damned if I'd make her play the part of maid, though.'

'Maybe she likes being a maid.'

'More likely she hasn't realized yet that she don't need to lift a finger to do anything other than keep our cousin happy. That lucky dog. *Where* does he find all these beauties? I never see him at a gathering that the prettiest gel there isn't trying to gain his attention. Emily Bascomb has set her cap for him, of course, and she bowled me over, she did,' Marshall confessed. 'Was considering courting her, even had her interest – until our cousin showed up and caught her eye.'

'I know what you mean,' Travis said. 'Wish Jeremy would get married already. Deuced hard to get anywhere with the ladies, with him around. Had the same problem with Derek before he married.'

'We'll be old and gray before Jeremy ever considers marriage. Damned if I would either if I

173

looked like him and had women throwing themselves at me all the time.'

And in the center of the room, sitting on one of the two new sofas, Regina said to Kelsey, 'Can't imagine what Jeremy is thinking, to install her in his house. I think Uncle James is going to have to have a talk with him, about flouting convention.'

'It *is* a bachelor residence, m'dear.'

'Yes, I know, and if he wants to keep his mistress here, I doubt the servants would raise a brow. And as long as he's discreet about it, it won't make the gossip mills. But he's hired her to his staff, so there will be problems in the lower quarters. *He* might not have to deal with that, but the poor girl will.'

Kelsey patted Regina's hand. 'I think you should let him muddle through this one on his own. He's never had his own servants before. He'll get the hang of it. His father and uncle certainly did. Notorious rakes that they were, I'm sure they ran smooth households.'

If Danny knew that every Malory in the room thought that she was Jeremy's mistress, she wouldn't have been embarrassed, she would have been furious – and caused a scene guaranteed to get her fired, blackmail or not. But she was blissfully unaware of the conclusions that the Malorys had reached about her. And although she *did* guess that she was being talked about, which embarrassed her, Percy's arrival took her mind off it.

He stopped by her as he entered the room, frowned for a moment, then said. 'Ah, I have it!

Twins. Met your brother. First-rate chap. Did me a good turn, for which I shall be eternally grateful.'

Danny wasn't sure what to say to that. Correct the mistake he'd just made and risk having him blurt out that she'd been wearing pants a few days ago?

Jeremy saved her from having to answer at all. He knew what Percy was capable of spilling and obviously didn't want it spilled in front of his family.

'You're late, old chap. Barely enough time for a drink before dinner. Come along and we'll fix that.'

'Don't need a drink,' Percy replied. 'Looking forward to finding out if you got lucky with a cook, though. But by the by, *where* did you find the twin sister of our little cutpurse? Don't tell me you went even deeper into that den of thieves than the tavern we found that night?'

Since Jeremy had already led Percy halfway into the room, there weren't many who didn't hear what he'd just said. Jeremy put his hands over his eyes with a groan.

Danny decided it was a good time to go see if dinner was ready to be served.

20

Tyrus Dyer's luck was improving already. He'd given the matter a good deal of thought, several days' worth, and had decided if he was going to kill the wench proper he ought to get paid for it proper this time. He wasn't going to be greedy about it. Getting his luck back was the better reward. But as long as he was going to kill her anyway, why not get paid for it as well, he'd reasoned.

So he went to find the lord who'd wanted her dead. He remembered where he lived. He hadn't been sure he would, as he had only been there twice before. But he recognized the house. And the lord was at home.

That's where his luck was improving, because the chatty servant who let him in told him that his master lived in the country now and rarely came to London anymore, perhaps only once or twice a year. That he'd just arrived a few days ago for a brief stay to conduct some business left Tyrus incredulous that he could get so lucky. In fact, the lord was due to return to the country in the morning. Another day of debating and Tyrus would have missed him completely.

Of course, the nabob might not see him when he heard his name. They had parted association with bad feelings, after all, because of Tyrus's failure. The man might even try to kill him again. But Tyrus reasoned that incident had been spawned by anger, and the lord had had fifteen years to calm down about it.

He was made to wait though, for nearly three hours. Deliberate he didn't doubt. But he wasn't leaving, if that was what the lord was hoping he'd do. He was going to demand a lot of money to finish the job he'd been hired to do all those years ago. That was worth a little wait.

The hour was approaching midnight when the servant finally came to take him to his master. He was in an officelike room toward the back of the house, sitting behind a desk. Standing on either side of him were two men who looked like street thugs. Tyrus's palms began to sweat.

He had to wonder now if he'd been fooling himself. Perhaps he wasn't as lucky to find the lord at home as he'd first thought. Had he been kept waiting so those thugs could be summoned to kill him?

Before the lord could give an order to have him removed, permanently, Tyrus blurted out, 'Wouldn't 'ave come 'ere if I didn't think you'd want to 'ear wot I 'ave to say.'

177

'Sit down, Mr Dyer.'

Tyrus let out a sigh of relief and grinned cockily as he took the seat across from the desk. The two thugs, though they kept their eyes on him, were expressionless. 'You remember me, do you?'

'Unfortunately, I do, at least your name. I must admit I wouldn't have recognized you. Your appearance has changed drastically, hasn't it?'

Tyrus's lips twisted in annoyance. The nabob was referring to his hair, of course. Forty-two years old, not a wrinkle on his face, yet his hair had turned pure gray a number of years ago. While the nabob hadn't changed much at all. He must be nearly fifty now himself, yet looked much younger.

'Runs in the family,' Tyrus lied. 'You've fared well, m'lord?'

'Extremely well – no thanks to you.'

Tyrus wasn't sure if he should be relieved to hear that. If the nabob wasn't desperate anymore to get rid of the girl, then he wouldn't be paying for it. But on the other hand, if his pockets were pleasantly plump these days, then he might just pay even more than Tyrus had planned to demand, to get the job finished.

'The hour is late,' the lord said tiredly. 'State your business, Mr Dyer.'

Tyrus nodded. 'I've found the girl, the one that got away. She's still alive.'

'Yes, I know.'

Tyrus's hopes just plummeted. 'You know?'

'There was a commotion on the street the other day near my bank. I was close enough to see what the trouble was. Couldn't quite believe my eyes to find the girl the cause of it.'

'I know wot you mean. Doubted m'sight, too.'

'I'd almost forgotten about her. I would have had her declared dead all those years ago when she never surfaced, but I got – convinced – that wouldn't be a good idea.'

'You didn't follow 'er?'

'Certainly I did, but I lost sight of her a few blocks away.'

'I didn't. I know where she lives.'

The lord had been sitting back, giving the impression he wasn't all that interested in the subject. He sat forward abruptly now, causing Tyrus's hopes to soar again.

'Where?'

Tyrus chuckled. 'You don't think I'll be giving you that sort o' information for free, d'you?'

The lord sat back again, gestured at his two companions, who immediately started moving around the desk. Tyrus nearly knocked his chair over in his haste to get out of it. He nearly fell, but recovered nicely and came up with a pistol in his hand. The thugs stopped immediately as he waved the gun between them. They weren't expressionless now, they were looking quite angry.

Nervously, Tyrus demanded, 'If you still want 'er dead, I'll be doing it, and you'll be paying me twice wot you promised before, 'alf now and 'alf

179

when I tell you where the body is. I ain't taking no chances wi' you this time, m'lord.'

The man laughed. 'Not a penny without results. You've already proved how incompetent you are, Mr Dyer. You'll have your payment, but only if you succeed this time.'

Tyrus was happy to settle for that. Aye, his luck was definitely improving.

21

Mrs Appleton was so happy that her first dinner party was such a success that she poured herself a glass of wine to celebrate – and poured one for Danny and Claire, too. Claire declined. She was still washing dishes. But Danny only had to check the dining room and parlor once more, to make sure they were back to looking orderly before she retired, so she chugged down her glass.

The cook shook her head at Danny in disgust. 'Now that was purely a waste I hope to never see again. That used to drinking, are you? Or do you just not know that good wine should be savored?'

Danny didn't blush – well, not much. But she did regret having drunk the wine that quickly, tasting it after the fact, as it were. She was used to cheap wine, not this fine stuff with such a heady flavor.

'Can I 'ave another taste then? Missed it the first go-round, I did.'

Mrs Appleton laughed. 'Yes, I suppose you've

earned it. You did good tonight, lass, very good indeed. Didn't spill or drop anything. The mark of a good maid is, she's never noticed. Of course, you'll never aspire to that with the way you look, but you can still manage to be the best maid on the block if you work at it.'

'And wot's wrong with the way I look? Mrs Robertson picked out these togs, ye know.'

'Bless you, child, you must know how pretty you are. That face of yours will always draw attention to you. There's simply no help for that. But as long as you do your job well, you can overcome that flaw. Now run along. You've earned some rest and morning will come around quick enough.'

Danny left the kitchen with a grin on her face. Who but a domestic would consider a pretty face to be a flaw?

The last guest had departed the house quite a while ago, so Danny had been able to collect all the dishes from the dining room in peace. She didn't expect to find anyone there when she passed through it to give it one last quick inspection, but there was Jeremy back at the table, a decanter of wine in front of him and a half-empty glass in his hand. He didn't look happy. He looked quite miserable and didn't even notice that she'd entered the room.

Danny was torn between wanting to ask him what was wrong and wanting to slip back out of the room before he noticed her. She chose the smarter option and turned to leave.

'Don't want to join me?'

'No.'

'Too blunt,' he tsk-tsked. 'Shouldn't be blunt with a man in the doldrums, you know. Any excuse, even a lame one, would have sufficed.'

Danny tried to concentrate so she'd be able to answer him properly, but the wine she'd drunk herself made it too difficult. 'Ye want to be lied to then?'

He thought about that for a moment, then said, 'Well, no, 'spose not. But excuses aren't considered lies, they are considered polite whoppers.'

'Are ye foxed, Malory?'

He blinked at her, then staggered to his feet to pose in an offended manner. 'Course not. Never been foxed a day in m'life.'

Danny snorted. 'That's wot they all say. So wot excuse d'ye 'ave, eh? Yer party was a success. Ye should be pleased, not drowning in yer cups.'

'Would be pleased if I didn't know that at least three members of m'family, possibly four, and I know exactly which ones, are going to go straight to m'father and chew his ear off that I'm failing miserably at my first foray into property ownership.'

'Ye 'ave a smashing party and think yer failing? Aye, yer foxed to the gills.'

Jeremy finished off his wine, set the glass down hard on the table, and admitted, 'Isn't about the party, dear girl. It's Percy and his bloody big mouth. And if you knew m'father, you wouldn't want him annoyed with you.'

'Ye 'ave a nice family. Even I could see that. Yer father can't be worse than the rest o' them.'

He laughed. She waited, but that was apparently his answer.

She shook her head at him. 'Go to bed and sleep it off, mate.'

He scowled for a moment. 'I would, except I can't seem to find my bed.'

'Eh?'

'I tried, really I did. But I kept finding beds that weren't mine. I'd recognize m'own bed, you know. So there was nothing for it but to come back here and find a chair instead.'

Danny rolled her eyes, marched over to him, grabbed his arm, and pulled him out of the room and toward the stairs. He got harder to pull though when she started up them. She glanced back to see him frowning.

'Don't think I can manage those again,' he confided. 'Not without help.'

'And wot d'ye think I'm doing, eh?'

'But if you should let go for some reason, I could lose m'balance. Course, a broken neck would probably make m'father go easy on me.'

Danny was starting to get amused. When Jeremy Malory was drunk, he was pretty funny. And harmless. The sensual glances that always undid her were missing. The nervousness she always felt when she was around him went away completely. She didn't even mind touching him at the moment.

'You want to sleep on the couch then?'

'When I've a perfectly good bed upstairs?' he said indignantly. 'No, perhaps if you let me hold on to you, that would work?'

Her violet eyes narrowed suspiciously. 'Hold on to what?'

'Your shoulder, of course. What the deuce did you think I meant?'

She blushed slightly, grabbed his waist, and pulled his arm over her shoulder. 'This better?'

'Much.'

They made it up the stairs with no mishaps. He *was* leaning on her a bit hard, but despite her narrow frame, she was strong and could support him well. He didn't let go of her when they reached the upstairs hall, though, even seemed to be leading her down it. She decided it would be quicker to get him to his room if she said nothing and just got him there. But he still didn't let go of her at his room and apparently wanted assistance right to his bed.

Danny's suspicions returned, particularly when he got clumsy right next to his bed and fell onto it, dragging her down with him. That she ended up beneath him didn't help her to extricate herself quickly. Jeremy at a dead weight was quite heavy. She still shoved and bucked to push him off her, but it was wasted effort.

'You better not have fallen asleep, mate,' she growled. 'Let me up now or—'

'Be still,' he admonished with a groan. 'I think I'm going to puke.'

Danny went very still. She'd forgotten for a moment that he was drunk. She felt bad now, for her suspicions – for all of five seconds. He'd turned his head toward her when he'd spoken, lifted it slightly now, and put his lips right on top of hers.

Danny turned her head aside. She was going to give him the benefit of the doubt, that he hadn't meant to do that. But his lips grazed her neck now, sending shivers up her spine, and she heard, 'You must know that I want you. I've made no pretense about it. There is such pleasure awaiting us, luv. Don't fight it anymore.'

Before she succumbed to it – desperately now, because his words had such a weakening effect on her – she turned her head back to tell him what he could do with his offered pleasure and got trapped again. She tried to resist, she really did, but all she could do was forget every single reason why she shouldn't be kissing him. She'd always wondered what it would be like. Lucy had told her about sloppy kisses, wet ones, drunk ones, and the right ones, those rare instances when a kiss could stimulate her sexual urges.

Danny knew well the latter was happening to her. She even knew why. This was Malory, after all, and she was already attracted to him more than she'd ever been to any man before. And he might be drunk, but his kiss didn't reflect that at all, far from it. In fact, she wouldn't be a bit surprised if this first kiss of hers was the most fantastic kiss she'd ever get, that she'd never find another one as powerful or sensual again.

She should have ended what he was doing instantly, before she got a good taste of him. It was going to spoil her for all time, she was sure, because how could any man compete with the best, and she was being shown the best. But ending it was the last thing she wanted to do at the moment. She just couldn't muster the willpower to do so, when her every sense was being manipulated so expertly, when all she wanted to do was wrap her arms around him and never let go.

And she had the odd thought that if this was how he kissed when he was drunk, heaven help her when he wasn't.

'God, you taste good!'

She'd been thinking the same thing. His lips were so velvety soft. Or maybe it was because hers were soft and the combination of the two meeting made for a perfect meld. His breath wasn't fumed with alcohol at all, was rather heady in scent. His taste was exotic, beyond her capability to describe. And she was feeling things other than the kiss, delightful sensations, all new to her, all highly pleasant.

One of his legs had slipped between hers. The pressure there was exquisite because he wasn't keeping his leg still; he was moving it against her loins in the most erotic way. And he'd gathered her so close, holding her to him as if he weren't already pressed fully to her, one hand behind her back, the other cupping her bottom, actually pressing her even harder against his thigh. Heat was swirling madly there, about to explode . . .

'Hell and tarnation, Jeremy,' Drew complained out in the hall, his tone as disgruntled as his words. 'You could at least close the blasted door.'

Drew's door was then slammed shut. And Danny had no trouble getting off the bed now. She didn't just shove this time, she balled her fingers into a fist and knocked it hard against Jeremy's ear. He howled and moved off her right quickly.

She shot off the bed and didn't bother to look back, just hissed on her way out the door, 'Ye'll be getting no 'elp from me the next time yer foxed, mate. Ye can bleedin' well sleep on the floor.'

22

The next morning, as Danny was on her way downstairs to clean the lower rooms because nothing was left to clean upstairs until the two slugabeds rose for the day, a knock came at the front door. Carlton wasn't around to answer it. She knew that he'd left the house with Mrs Robertson earlier to help her with a few errands, and it didn't look as if they'd returned yet. She still didn't approach the door immediately. In her current mood, she wouldn't make a courteous butler.

She wasn't angry at Jeremy over what had happened last night. Drunks were drunks, after all, and did stupid things while they were at it. But she was angry at herself. *She* had no excuse for what she had let happen. She could think of any number of ways she could have extricated herself immediately from that kiss last night, but she hadn't used them simply because she didn't really want to. And that's what infuriated her. Knowing better hadn't counted. Knowing what that kiss would have led to hadn't counted. Nothing had counted but the pleasure Jeremy Malory was capable of handing out.

Claire wasn't showing up to answer the front door. And the pounding got a lot louder, indicating the impatience of the caller.

With an annoyed sigh, Danny finally yanked it open and snapped, 'They're all sleeping, come back later.'

'I beg your pardon?' the man said in a sardonic tone that implied he wasn't doing any such thing.

Danny's palms began to sweat. The large fellow standing there on the doorstep was quite likely the most intimidating man she'd ever seen.

He was big, solid big, with hefty arms and an extremely wide chest of hard muscle, but he wasn't much taller than she was, probably just short of six feet. Somewhere in his midforties she would guess. And it was impossible to tell if he was an aristocrat or not. His bone structure indicated he was, but he was dressed too casually: no cravat, a white lawn shirt opened at the neck, a black coat, buff trousers, and black riding boots. His blond hair was much too long, though, for him to be a member of the ton, who prided themselves on being fashionable. It was so long it rested on his shoulders in thick waves, giving him the air of a pirate. His expression, though, said clearly this was not a man to cross. He fairly reeked of danger, which was probably why she was suddenly so nervous. She'd never encountered anyone who

190

exuded such an aura, didn't doubt for a moment that he could be utterly ruthless if provoked – and deadly.

She was tempted to close the door on him and lock it. She might have, too, if he hadn't brushed past her into the entryway, where he now stood with his arms crossed.

She cringed since she was forced to put him off. 'They really are still sleeping. Which one o' them did ye want to see?'

'Jeremy.'

'It's doubtful that one will be up anytime soon. 'E got foxed to the gills last night and is sleeping it off.'

A golden brow rose quite high. 'What utter rubbish. Jeremy foxed? That's an impossibility. He was weaned on strong spirits. The youngun is quite incapable of overimbibing, I do assure you. So go wake him and tell him to get his arse down here.'

Danny ran up the stairs, forgot to hike her skirt and tripped a bit, hiked her skirt high, and continued running till she was out of sight. She wasn't running to get to Jeremy, just to get away from that fellow. But upstairs in the hall, after a long sigh of relief, it sank in what the man had said.

Malory was incapable of getting drunk? So all that nonsense last night had just been a ruse to get her upstairs and into his bed? That bleeding bastard! How dare he trick her like that?

She didn't knock on his door, she was too angry for that. She marched in and found him on the bed,

191

wide-awake, just lying there looking smug and self-satisfied. He was surprised by her unannounced entrance, though, and sat up. His expression even turned wary when he noted hers.

She stopped in front of him, her hands on her hips, and shouted, 'Ye son of a bitch! Ye ever try tricks again to get under me skirt and I'll gullet ye. And I don't care if I get fired for it!'

'What tricks?'

'Being foxed. Ye weren't drunk last night. Yer incapable o' being drunk!'

He actually grinned. 'I did mention that, didn't I? Definitely recall doing so.'

'And that ye couldn't find yer bleedin' bed on yer own? D'ye recall mentioning that, too!'

He chuckled. 'Danny, luv, you leave a man few choices. So I was getting desperate enough to take advantage of the conclusion you drew. A few minor fibs, but it was well worth it to finally taste you.'

'Was it?' she snarled just before her fist cracked against his cheek.

She'd expected him to move out of the way. He'd done that easily enough before. She didn't expect to have her knuckles throbbing now. But it was very satisfying that they were.

'D'ye still think so?' she asked him smugly. 'And that's letting ye off lightly, mate. Keep yer kisses to yerself from now on!'

She marched back out of the room and ran straight into a brick wall. Well, that's what it felt like. The intimidating chap she'd left in the entry hall had come upstairs, his patience gone, apparently.

'Run along, wench,' he told her. 'I'll be taking over where you left off, you may depend upon it.'

That sounded too ominous by half. Malory was about to get more than a black eye, she'd wager. Couldn't happen to a more deserving scoundrel.

23

Jeremy dropped back on his bed with a groan, recognizing that voice outside his room. He'd thought he would have another day or two before his father returned to town. But George had no doubt dragged him back as soon as she'd gotten word that her brother's ship was in. And to go by what James had just said, Jeremy had been right last night in thinking his wonderful relatives were too concerned about his behavior to keep it to themselves. Either Percy's remark had been relayed to James, or he'd been told that Jeremy was bedding his upstairs maid. Probably both. Though how the deuce they'd gotten to James this quickly boggled him.

'Hiding behind a black eye, puppy?'

Jeremy sat up and pointed to his upper cheek. 'Take a look. Her fist landed here, but my eye does smart a little. Think it will turn black?'

'What I think,' his father said, 'is you've bloody well lost your mind, tangling with a wench who throws punches instead of slaps.'

Jeremy grinned. 'You don't think any such thing. You saw her. You know exactly why I'd want to tangle with her, no matter what she throws.'

'Beside the point,' James said, but he still came over to the bed, took hold of Jeremy's chin to tilt his head at a different angle, and examined the rapidly bruising area on his upper cheek. 'Won't be a full shiner, but you might have enough bruise there to put off Albert Bascomb's girl, so she'll tilt her cap elsewhere.'

Jeremy flinched and exclaimed, 'Hell's bells, you even heard about *her*?'

James moved his large frame over to one of the two stuffed chairs in the room and got comfortable. 'Let me tell you about my morning, dear boy. I manage to get to the family home by midmorning, much to George's delight, only to find Eddy boy burning a hole in the carpet of my study with his impatience to see me. Thirty minutes later the elder marches off, unsatisfied with my replies, of course.'

'Naturally,' Jeremy grinned.

His father was unique to the Malory clan, always had been, going his own way and breaking convention as he pleased, the black sheep of the family, as it were. He'd been disowned by his brothers for over ten years when he took to pirating on the high seas. He was back in the fold now, but he still bucked convention.

James simply enjoyed being different. Even names had to be different for him. Most of the family called Regina 'Reggie,' but James insisted on calling her Regan, much to his brothers' annoyance. Even his own daughter, Jacqueline, he called Jack, much to *her* uncles' displeasure.

'Then Tony shows up with the prediction that your staff will soon be abandoning ship because you're bedding one of them,' James continued.

'I would have thought at least *he'd* understand,' Jeremy said.

'Oh, he was quite amusing for the most part. My brother took to fatherhood rather well and now *thinks* like a father, don't you know.'

'Which means he's forgotten what it's like to be young and unshackled?'

'Exactly.'

'But you haven't—'

'We'll get to that, puppy,' James cut in. 'And then Regan, the dear puss, walks in before Tony's finished and proceeds to add yet a new subject, said Lady Bascomb to be exact, to this growing list of concerns.'

'How the deuce did she find out about that chit? I only mentioned it to Drew and Percy – never mind. Percy and his bloody big mouth.'

'Actually, the Bascomb girl is spreading the rumor herself that she'll be married to you before the end of the year. But as it happens, Regan overheard her telling a friend that she was going to have you – one way or another.'

'One way or another?' Jeremy frowned. 'And what the devil does that mean?'

'Exactly what you think it means. There will always be a few rotten apples in the bunch who will lie and manipulate to get what they want. *Are* you pursuing the lady?'

'She's a debutante, her first season out. I avoid them like the plague.'

'I thought as much. I'd advise you to keep your distance from her then, a very far distance, though even that might not help. False rumors tend to condemn a man just as easily as the truth does.'

'I can keep away from the social scene for a while, until she starts casting her eyes elsewhere. The young husband-hunters aren't known for their patience, seem to think they *have* to get married their first season out, which doesn't really give them much time to work their wiles for the most part. And now that George is back in the city, she can see to dragging her brother about to those fancy affairs that all the debutantes flock to.'

'Bite your tongue, puppy. That means I'd get dragged to them, too.'

Jeremy chuckled. If there was one thing his father detested above all else, it was London's social whirl. 'Fortunately, Drew's preferred form of entertainments are more in line with mine, places where he can be guaranteed a wench for the night. He'll make his excuses to George as he always does.'

'That's *after* she gets her way a few times. My dear wife always does, you know. But never mind, I've already got my own excuses lined up to avoid joining my wife and brother-in-law. Now—'

There was enough of a pause that Jeremy groaned inwardly, knowing what was coming. 'What in the bloody hell were you doing entering the very bowels of this city's criminal element?'

'I didn't,' Jeremy was quick to assure him. 'Well, only the edges, but that was for a very good cause.' He quickly explained the problem Percy had had and how he'd elected to solve it.

When he finished, James grinned. 'Stole them back, eh? Don't think I'd have thought of that.'

'No, you would have invited Heddings into the ring for a round or two.'

James shrugged. 'Does work wonders, don't you know. I don't think I like the fact that he had one of Diana's trinkets, though. Stealing from m'niece feels like he stole from me, damn me if it doesn't.'

'Well, we cleaned him out, or rather, our thief did. I managed to return those pieces we recognized to their rightful owners and had the rest delivered to our nearest magistrate. Hopefully, he can figure out what belongs to whom and get it back to them.'

'Didn't want to just turn Heddings over to them?' James asked.

'Couldn't do that without admitting we'd found the jewels in his house while robbing him.'

James coughed. 'Quite right. I suppose they *would* require proof of where you found the stolen baubles. Well, maybe he'll see the error of his ways and steal no more, now that he knows someone is onto him.'

'But he doesn't. He probably just thinks he got robbed by a common thief and nothing will come of it. Very unlikely that he'd think the thief might recognize any of the pieces, or even know he was stealing already stolen property.'

James sighed. 'I suppose I'll just have to kill the fellow then, to make sure he doesn't rob any members of my family again.'

Jeremy coughed now. 'You really don't need to get involved. I intend to keep an eye on the chap. I was going to find out his haunts and start frequenting them m'self. I'm not sure how he's stealing, but I plan to catch him at it. No trouble a'tall then, turning him in.'

James was silent for a moment. His next remark indicated he'd let it go for now. 'By the by, how'd you manage to hire your thief's sister if you didn't go back into that den of thieves?'

Jeremy wished he could lie to his father for once, he really did, but he never had and he wasn't going to start now. 'My new maid *is* our thief. And I didn't have to find her again, she came to me, since I was responsible for her getting kicked out of her gang.'

James raised a brow. 'I take it your chum Percy don't know that?'

'No. She masqueraded as a male, has done so apparently for most of her life. Percy never saw the woman in her, so when he saw her again last night, he concluded it was her twin brother he'd met before.'

'I see. Bloody hell – no, I don't. You've hired a common thief to your staff?'

Jeremy flinched at the raised tone. 'There's nothing common about that wench. Did you really look at her face? She's got such fine bones she could be a princess! She talks like a guttersnipe, but she would, since that's where she was raised. But she's an orphan. She has no idea where she came from or even what name she was born with. But she wants to better herself. I've no doubt she can, because she's smart as a whip. Her speech has even improved in just the few days she's been here. She sought me out merely because she blames me for losing her home.'

'*Was* that your fault?'

'Apparently. I didn't exactly give her a choice about coming along with us that night. Her little band of pickpockets had their rules to abide by, and she ended up breaking a number of them by helping us.'

'So you hired her because you feel you owe her?' James asked.

'Course not,' Jeremy said, and with a blush added, 'I hired her because she gave me no choice in the matter. She threatened to go to Heddings and tell him all.'

James frowned. 'Let me get this straight. Instead of extorting money from you to keep silent, she demands you put her to *work*? I thought you said she was smart?'

'She is. A good job is part of her plan to better herself.'

'Money would have done that,' James pointed out dryly.

'I know. Deuced odd that she didn't go that route instead. But then I'm beginning to think it was just a bluff.'

'Probably. If she's as smart as you say, then she must know that confessing to Heddings would implicate herself as well.'

'Exactly. But she's working out rather well as a maid. Didn't think she would, but she is, and besides, I still mean to bed her.'

'Then why the devil don't you do so and then send her on her way?'

'Because I doubt once will be enough, and well, she isn't interested in a pleasant tumble.'

'Good God, don't tell me a thief and blackmailer is holding out for marriage!'

'No, she just wants nothing to do with me.'

James rolled his eyes. 'What an odd statement. I'm sure you believe it to have said it, but you'll never get anyone else to believe it.'

'It's true. I just haven't found out why yet.'

'Did you think to ask her why?'

'That's putting too many cards on the table, ain't it?'

James snorted. 'To go by why she socked you, I'd say you've already tossed the whole deck on the table. Ask her, deal with it, bed her, then get her out of this house. Aside from the fact that she'll probably rob you blind if you keep her here long enough—'

'She's given up stealing.'

'Sure she has,' James replied dryly.

'No, really, she claims to hate it, and come to think of it, that's probably why she didn't demand money from me. She'd see that as stealing.'

'Regardless, set her up elsewhere if you want to enjoy her for a while, but get her off your staff. You can even install her here if you must, but do it right. Keeping her as a maid and bedding her as well is going to make for a very unhappy household.'

'Is that *your* thought on the matter, or what got whispered in your ear this morning?'

James chuckled. 'Malorys don't whisper complaints, youngun. But you're right, doesn't matter to me if you want to muck up the hearth and home with contention. What I *do* object to is having the elders breathing down my neck about it, Jason in particular. So satisfy the rest of the family that you're not bucking convention and managing your household splendidly, then they won't go running to Jason about it, and I won't have to listen to any more of his rants.'

Jeremy sighed. 'Reggie's the only one who comes by so often. I wonder if I could bar her from my house. D'you think a butler could stand up to her and keep her out?'

James laughed. 'Not a chance, not that you'd really want to. The little darling does her fair share of manipulating and matchmaking, but always with the best intentions, and she's usually right on the mark. Bloody shame she had to marry a bounder like Eden.'

Jeremy grinned. His father got along well enough with Nicholas Eden these days, as long as he always won their verbal skirmishes, which he usually did. Those two went way back, to the high seas actually. Jeremy had been injured in the sea battle between the two men, which was why James had given up pirating. Nick had sailed away unscathed *and* thumbed his nose at them, which you just didn't do to James Malory.

James finally got even, trouncing Nick soundly – right before his wedding to Reggie, which he almost missed because of it. Nick in turn landed James in jail for it, which turned out for the best, actually, since James was able to arrange the 'death' of the pirate Captain Hawke, the name he was known by on the seas, when he escaped, allowing him to come back to England for good.

'Speaking of butlers,' James said as he got up to leave, 'how would you like to borrow one of mine?'

'Hell's bells.' Jeremy grinned in delight. 'I've been hoping you'd suggest that.'

'Borrow, puppy, not keep, so you're still to look for a permanent man. Artie suggested it, actually. Since he and Henry share the job at my house, it really doesn't give them both enough to do.'

'Which one do I get?'

James laughed. 'Both of them, of course. They'll take turns here as they do at home. Those two old sea dogs have been sharing the job for so long, I wouldn't doubt they think that's the normal way it's done.'

24

Jeremy found Danny in the parlor, dusting one of the tables, over and over, so deep in thought she didn't hear him enter the room. He wondered if her thoughts were about him. He wondered if she was still furious. He wondered if she would blacken his other eye if he turned her around and kissed her again.

He coughed instead to drew her notice. She spun around and seemed more surprised than she should have been to see him there.

Her question indicated why. 'You're still alive?'

Jeremy mulled that over for a moment. 'Expired from a black eye? No, don't think I've heard of that one.'

'Weren't referring to wot I did,' she mumbled. 'And your eye ain't black.'

'Yet,' he corrected cheerfully, causing her to scowl at him. He chuckled. 'Very well, I give up. Spit it out, wench. Why were you expecting my demise?'

'That visitor ye 'ad,' she almost whispered in her nervousness. 'I hid in the kitchen till 'e finally left. Scared the bejesus out o' me, 'e did. Was easy to tell 'e'd slit yer throat without batting an eye. There's not many men who are that ruthless, but 'e 'ad that look about 'im, if ye know wot I mean. And 'e was mad at ye.'

Jeremy started laughing. Danny was back to scowling. 'Wot d'ye find so funny, eh?' she demanded indignantly.

'You're talking about my father, dear girl.'

'Sure I am,' she scoffed. 'Wot a clacker. 'E looked nothing like ye.'

'No, he doesn't, but he *is* my father. James Malory, Viscount Ryding, fourth born of the elder Malorys, ex-rake, ex-pir – er, never mind, but he's now a devoted husband, and father of four with more on the way.'

She believed him finally, even commiserated, 'You poor man. I'd 'ate to 'ave a father that frightening.'

He grinned. 'He's not, really, well, not once you get to know him.'

She humphed. 'Well, obviously 'e didn't rip ye to pieces as I figured 'e were 'ankering to do – more's the pity, if ye ask me.'

That easily her own anger was back in place. Jeremy coughed. 'Let's have a chat, Danny.'

'Let's not.'

'You haven't figured out yet that you need to humor your employer at all times?'

'Not bleedin' likely when my employer is a randy buck only interested in getting under my skirts.'

'Devil take it, you have to work on this bluntness of yours, really you do.'

'Why?'

'Because—'

He stopped short. She was right. It was one of the things about her that was unique and he didn't want to change her in that regard. Besides, right now he was after frankness from her, and he wouldn't get that if she started prevaricating as most women tended to do when they were asked pointed questions. And he intended to ask a few of those.

'So you have brothers and sisters, do you?'

Jeremy's hopes soared high. She hadn't waited for him to answer her question, and her curiosity was an excellent indication that she was more interested in him than she pretended to be.

'Twin brothers and a sister, actually,' he told her. 'All quite young still.'

'Why weren't they at your party? Or your father for that matter?'

'They were visiting my uncle Jason in the country. He's head of the family and doesn't come to town very often. So if we want to see him, we go to the family estate at Haverston. But children that young aren't usually allowed at adult gatherings anyway.'

'Not even when the gathering is all your own family?' she asked.

Jeremy grinned. 'We've tried that. There are a *lot* of youngsters in m'family now. It's quite like a battlefield when they all get together.'

She chuckled for a moment. 'I've been in a few o' those m'self.'

'Have you? There were a lot of children in your band of misfits?'

'Mostly all children, and all o' them orphans like me. Dagger supplied the roof and food and taught us how to make do.'

'You mean, how to steal.'

'That, too.'

'He was your elected leader, I take it? The one who kicked you out?'

She nodded curtly and turned away, going back to her dusting – with a vengeance. A touchy subject, apparently. It was probably still too soon after her ousting from that band for her to want to discuss it. He was surprised she'd said as much as she did, when she'd refused to talk about any of it before.

'Have a seat, Danny,' he suggested agreeably. 'There are a few more things I'd like to ask you. Might as well get comfortable.'

He'd indicated the sofa. She stared at it a moment then shook her head. 'Wouldn't be proper, would it? You have a seat. I'm fine right 'ere.'

'What I'm going to ask you is rather – intimate. Really, sitting down would be most appropriate.'

'So ye can sit next to me and try yer tricks again? I'm onto you now, mate. You might as well give up.'

'Not a chance, luv.'

It wasn't intentional, but Jeremy's look turned so sensual, Danny actually gasped and quickly glanced away. She even started fanning her face with her duster, apparently not realizing she was doing it. When she did, she made another sound, close to a groan.

And Jeremy was met with a dilemma. Should he take advantage of having just aroused her or proceed with his plan to get to know her better? Much as it went against his instincts, he was forced to opt for the latter. He simply wanted more from her than immediate gratification. And he was afraid that even if she succumbed fully, she'd later see it as his taking advantage of the moment and be so furious with him, this time, that she'd quit her job and leave.

A moment later she said rather breathlessly, 'I'll sit. But you sit somewhere else, eh.'

Jeremy grinned. Progress, definite progress. But when she moved to sit on the sofa, she sat on the end farthest away from him. He sighed and moved to the other sofa across from her.

'This won't take long, will it?' she asked, sounding somewhat annoyed now that she'd given in. 'I've more work that needs doing.'

'It could, but it probably won't. And don't worry about your work when I detain you. If you don't finish today, I'll accept the blame.'

'Wot do you want to know then?'

'Let's start with your age?'

'Thought I'd already mentioned that.'

'Fifteen, was it?'

'Ten actually. Just tall for my age.'

He burst out laughing. She didn't share his humor so he tried to curb it quickly and asked, 'So you were orphaned when you were what? Two or three?'

'I'm guessing closer to four or five, might even 'ave been six.'

'So you're closer to twenty? Might even be twenty-one?'

She nodded. It was curt though. She still wouldn't relax and he wasn't sure how to fix that when he was the one making her nervous. He'd been hoping she'd open up and forget that she'd rather be anywhere other than having a conversation with him.

He tried a different route. 'Was Dagger the one who taught you to steal?'

'It were Lucy. She were the one who found me and took me in.'

Two *weres* that close together reminded him that he'd meant to help her with her vocabulary. '*Was* instead of *were*.'

'Eh?'

'You used the word *were* twice. The correct—'

She cut him off indignantly, 'I know I don't talk good enough to be a maid in a fancy house like this. Mrs Robertson is trying to help, but she gets distracted easy and goes off on some other subject.'

'I'll teach you.'

For some reason that garnered a scowl. 'Teach me wot?'

He chuckled over her overly suspicious mind. 'Anything you like, dear girl, but what I was referring to was your speech. It *can* be corrected, you know. Had to have m'own corrected as well. That doesn't surprise you? Oh, I see, you don't believe me.'

'And wot did ye talk like?' she asked, her tone scoffing. 'Me?'

'Not quite.' He grinned. 'But close.'

She snorted. Apparently, she still wasn't buying it. 'Were ye stolen then as a babe? Raised amongst thieves?'

'I was raised in a tavern on the docks, Danny, and if you snort again, I'll come over there and squeeze your nose shut. It was where my mother worked for many years and where I stayed after she died. I'm a bastard, don't you know,' he added cheerfully.

'Ye aren't joking, are ye?'

'Not a'tall. And roll that *u* off your tongue, m'dear.'

She blushed, but only slightly. 'When did ye-ur father take you in then?'

'I was sixteen when he found me, or rather, I found him. He didn't know I existed.'

'Then how'd you know who he was?'

'Because my mother was so taken with him that she talked about him at least once every single day and described him so perfectly, I knew him the moment I saw him. Bowled him over, of course, when I told him I was his son.'

'And he believed you?'

Jeremy chuckled. 'Well, there were a few moments of doubt, extreme doubts actually, not that I wasn't related to him, but that I was his. He *knew* I was related, couldn't miss that, when I look just like his brother Tony. But after I told him about my mother, he actually remembered her, and the time he'd spent with her.'

'So wot you're saying is, you didn't become a nabob till you were sixteen?' she asked incredulously.

'Indeed.'

'But you act like one so bleedin' perfectly.'

He laughed. 'Quite acquired, dear girl. All of which proves my point, don't it?'

'That I can learn to talk like you?'

'Exactly.'

'I used to,' she admitted.

'Eh?'

She laughed now. It was such a delightful sound Jeremy caught his breath. And she didn't keep him in suspense, adding, 'Talk like you.'

'Really?'

'A few times it's come back naturally to me, but most times I have to think about it first, and when I'm nervous or angry, I forget about even trying. It was so long ago that I talked proper that it just doesn't seem familiar to me now.'

'Sure, you're ancient, I know.'

She grinned but said no more, which drove his curiosity through the roof. 'So you weren't born in the slums?'

She shrugged. 'I don't know where I was born. I lost my memory when I was young. Lucy found me, like I mentioned, and took me home with her. She weren't more'n twelve or so herself. It's hard to remember that long ago, but I recall she said I talked too fine, that I wouldn't fit in unless I talked like her, so she fixed that – probably like you've been doing,' Danny ended with a grin.

'Where were you when she found you?'

'In an alley.'

'You don't remember how you got there?'

'Sure I do. Miss Jane brought me there. She died though, the same day Lucy found me.'

'Who was Miss Jane? Your mother?'

'She said she weren't, that she was a nurse. She w-was with me after the blood. I think she took me away from it.'

Jeremy sat forward abruptly, exclaiming, 'Good God, *what* blood?'

Danny frowned. 'That part o' my memory ain't clear, and I remember nothing from before then. I had a nasty gash on the back of my head. Lucy said it was bad enough to leave a scar. I've never seen it m'self.'

'So you have no memory a'tall of your parents?'

'None. I have dreams though. One is nice, of a pretty lady. She's so pretty and dressed so fine, she's like an angel. I told Lucy about it, and she figured she were an angel, that I were dreaming that I should have died and the angel were looking for me.'

'*Was*,' he corrected almost automatically. 'Did she look like you, the angel?'

Danny blinked. 'How'd you know? I never told Lucy that. But she did look like me some, at least, her face did. And her hair was white, but done up real fancy. She wasn't old, though, not a'tall.'

'She's probably your mother, Danny.'

She snorted. 'Sure she is. She was dressed too fine for that. My thoughts on the matter are more likely. She's what I want to be.'

He gave that some thought, then had to concede, 'Possibly.' He grinned. 'And not an unreasonable goal either. I wonder what you'd look like in silk and with your hair in an elegant coiffure – God, never mind. I can imagine, and you'd have me groveling on the floor kissing your feet and promising you the world.'

She laughed. Again, he caught his breath. Her violet eyes fairly sparkled when she did that. Her whole face changed, glowed, making her even more beautiful than she was, and he hadn't thought that was possible, she was already so lovely it hurt.

'I am appalled at the notion m'self, so why are you laughing?' he demanded with mock sternness.

'Because when you're silly, you're *really* silly, mate. Kissing my feet, eh? Will I need to remove my boots first?'

He blinked, looked down at her feet. 'Well,

damn me, you *are* still wearing boots. Did Mrs Robertson forget about that part of your new wardrobe? You should have some comfortable house shoes, m'dear. After all, your job requires you to be on your feet for most of the day. Although, come to think of it, I'd much prefer you be flat on your back all day. Care to switch jobs?'

'Not bleedin' likely.' She was back to snorting.

He raised a brow. 'You're not even curious what the other job entails?'

'Being one 'o the "boys" for fifteen years means I know how you gents think.' She stood up stiffly as she said it and added as she marched out of the room, 'Keep that in mind, mate, 'fore you insult me again.'

'Now wait – I didn't—'

Jeremy gave up. She was already gone. Blister it, how the devil had he erred so quickly? She'd been laughing only a moment before.

He sighed, then a grin came slowly to his lips. Their talk might have ended on a distinctly sour note, but he'd made great progress nonetheless. He'd gotten her to relax with him a little, *and* he'd made her laugh. The next step would be joking, teasing, more laughter. Then he could progress to some legitimate stolen kisses – well, perhaps he should wait until his bruises healed. After all, she was a woman who threw punches instead of slaps.

25

Lucy!' Danny gasped when she got to the door after being told she had a visitor. She threw her arms around Lucy, gave her a big hug, but one look at her friend's expression when she stepped back had her adding, 'What's wrong?'

'Let's go for a walk, eh? I don't feel right, being in a place like this.'

Danny understood. Lucy wasn't just a whore, she dressed like one and was so out of place in this neighborhood. She was surprised Lucy had made it this far without someone trying to run her off.

'Let's go over to the park,' Danny suggested, taking Lucy's arm and leading her across the street. 'How'd you manage to get here?'

Lucy grinned at that point. 'Found a hack. The driver were so pleased to do me, 'e were more'n willing to bring me up 'ere. In fact' – she turned to blow a kiss to the hack driver, who was waiting just down the block – ''e's going to wait and take me 'ome, too.'

'I didn't expect a visit this soon. I haven't even been gone a week yet.'

Danny had used some of the coins Mrs Robertson had given her to hire a chimney sweep, to take Lucy her new address. Mrs Appleton had written it out for her, and the lad had been more'n pleased to run the errand, since he didn't get as much work in the summer as he did in the winter.

'It's wonderful to see you though,' Danny said as they sat down on a bench, the street still in sight.

'I were worried that ye wouldn't find a job soon, with all the trouble ye 'ad before when ye went looking. But it appears ye landed a right nice one. Look at ye. I barely recognized ye in yer fancy clothes. And it bowled me over it did when the driver pointed me to that 'ouse. Ye like it 'ere? Cor, 'ow could ye not!'

'It takes getting used to, but the people are very nice and helpful. They're even teaching me to talk better.'

'I noticed, and not better. Ye used to talk so fine, it 'urt me ears.'

Danny chuckled. 'No, it didn't. You were forever pinching me when I'd slip up, when you were teaching me.'

'I never pinched 'ard, just didn't want ye getting kicked out 'cause ye didn't fit in. Though truth to tell, I always figured ye wouldn't be with us long, that yer family would find ye and take ye away from us.'

'Did you really?'

Danny had hoped for the same thing. For many years, she had cried herself to sleep for parents she couldn't even remember. But when she was old enough to think about it logically, she had to conclude she had no family left, other than the one Lucy had brought her to. If there had been anyone, even a distant relative, wouldn't Miss Jane have mentioned it and tried to get to them?

Reminded that she'd gotten kicked out of the gang anyway, just years later, had sobered them both. 'It were time ye go on yer own, Danny, and look 'ow well it turned out.'

'I know, but I still miss all of you.'

'Ye can visit from time to time. Be good to rub it in Dagger's nose, 'ow well ye've done on yer own. Speaking o' 'is nose, 'e got it broke.'

Danny blinked. 'Well, good for him. I've no sympathy a'tall for him at the moment. But you didn't come all this way just to tell me that.'

'Actually, I did,' Lucy said, uneasy now. 'I weren't there when it 'appened, so didn't get a look at the man who broke it, but 'e slapped Dagger around good, to get 'im to tell where ye went.'

'Me?'

'Aye, course Dagger couldn't tell 'im wot 'e didn't know. That boy who brung me yer address found me on the street, so Dagger didn't know I 'ad it.'

'But the man was looking for *me*?'

Lucy nodded. ''E didn't give a name, or why 'e was searching for ye. 'E scared Dagger, though, and ye know Dagger don't get scared by much. And that scared me, 'cause if 'e could 'urt Dagger just to get to ye, then 'e likely means to 'arm ye, too. And Dagger knows now.'

'What?'

'That yer a woman. The man called ye "the white-'aired wench."'

Danny flinched. 'Was he very angry?'

''E were too busy moving us to a new place, so that bloke don't find us again, and nursing his nose and other bruises. Were 'ard to tell if 'e were angry over wot happened or over yer deception.'

'You think it's someone I've robbed?'

'I can't think o' any other reason. But ye were always so careful not to be seen.'

'I know, but—' Danny broke off as it occurred to her who it might be.

'Wot?'

'That lord I robbed that night, his servant got a good look at me. And although I talked my way out of there, he would've known the next day that I was the thief, when the lord's jewelry came up missing. Turns out he were a thief himself, that lord, so he'd probably know how to go about hiring some street thug to track me down.'

'That don't sound good,' Lucy said nervously.

'No, it don't.'

26

Giving it more thought after she left Lucy, Danny had to doubt the person looking for her had been hired by Lord Heddings. He'd asked for a female, but Heddings's servant that night had given no indication at all that he'd seen through her male disguise. So they'd be looking for a white-haired man, not a woman.

And besides, she remembered having the feeling that someone was following her home that morning. They must have lost her, asked around, and finally found where she lived. She'd passed through some nice areas getting home that day. So it could have been no more than some nabob who'd recently been robbed. Seeing her passing through his neighborhood, he could have decided she was the culprit and followed her for some payback. She'd lost her hat by then, and it was much easier to tell she was a woman when she wasn't wearing her hat. Or he could have followed her all the way home, but seeing where she lived, decided not to confront her himself but to hire some tough to teach her a lesson instead.

That made more sense and wasn't really worth worrying over. The gent would never find her where she was living now. So she got back to cleaning the upstairs and didn't give it another thought.

Lucy's unexpected, though welcome, visit had thrown Danny off schedule a bit. It was late in the afternoon when she finally got around to cleaning the downstairs rooms. Thinking it was empty, she entered the parlor, but did an about-face upon seeing Jeremy and his cousin Regina Eden sitting on the sofa. She didn't get back out quickly enough, though.

'Come in, Danny. You can clean around us,' Jeremy told her.

'It can wait,' Danny assured him.

'At this late hour? Don't be silly. Go ahead and finish up, then you'll be done for the day.'

She would be, too. The parlor was her last room to see to. And it didn't need much cleaning today, hadn't been used since she'd sat on that same sofa yesterday.

This was the first time she'd come across Jeremy since then. He'd gone out last night, went out again early this morning, and had only just returned. Oddly, the house didn't seem the same when he wasn't in it. She couldn't exactly tell why, but it was definitely noticeable, by her anyway. Maybe because she couldn't completely relax when she knew he was around. No, that *should* be why, but it was the opposite. She couldn't seem to relax when he wasn't there.

She was still slightly annoyed with herself for letting her guard down with him yesterday. The trick he'd pulled on her the other night was clue enough that she could never do that again. And yet yesterday all they'd done was talk. She'd learned a few interesting things about him.

He was a bastard. Imagine that. Who would have thought, with him living in a grand house like this, and in the nabob part of town – and with such a huge family, all of whom had obviously accepted him without question.

Born and raised in a tavern. It still boggled her mind. It brought him down to her level, it did. His mother had been no different from what her parents had probably been. And why had he told her that? You'd think it would be something he'd want kept secret.

'You still have her dusting?' Regina said to Jeremy as Danny crossed the room to clean the mantel above the cold fireplace. 'Or does she just love to dust?'

'Don't start—' Jeremy began, only to get cut off.

'I swear, Jeremy, I would have thought you of all people would know how to treat a mistress properly.'

Danny glanced over her shoulder in time to see Jeremy kick his cousin and glare at her. The lady merely tsked and changed the subject, which seemed to be back to what they'd been discussing before Danny'd arrived.

'You can't avoid this ball, Jeremy, really you can't. And it's a perfect opportunity for you to set matters straight. Emily started a new rumor last night, that she actually had a lovers' rendezvous with you. You *do* know what that means, don't you?'

'Means she's a bloody liar.'

'No, *we* know that, but no one else does. It means she's already moving on to the last resort, and the season's barely begun!'

'Hell's bells, I've barely even looked at the chit!' Jeremy complained. 'I don't understand why she's picked me, when I haven't given her even two minutes of my time, let alone indicated I'd like to know her better.'

'What dealings *have* you had with her?'

'None worth mentioning. She had someone introduce us, as I recall, don't even remember who, but I was already leaving that party, so I didn't say more'n a few words to her. And she approached Drew and me the other night, but again, I barely even glanced at her. You'd bloody well think she'd want *some* clue that I was interested, before she started this campaign to get me leg-shackled.'

'Famous! Denial doesn't help us here, Jeremy. You know very well that there isn't a young unmarried female in this whole town who wouldn't jump at the chance to catch you. Emily Bascomb is just *doing* something about it, whereas the others just wait around hoping to gain your notice.'

Danny glanced back again, in time to see Jeremy blushing. Fascinated by their conversation, she knew she should move on to a different piece of furniture, but she didn't want to remind them that she was there.

'If you know so much, puss, tell me why the rush?' he complained. 'I only clapped eyes on the lady for the first time last week. D'you think she has to get married? Already enceinte?'

Regina frowned, then shook her head. 'No, highly doubtful. I think she just fell head over heels for you and has decided no one else will do for her now. And her impatience stems from being spoiled. I *have* learned that much about her. Found an old chap who's known the Bascombs for many years. He mentioned that she's an only child, so her father spoiled her beyond redemption.'

'But to blacken her own name in this campaign? That's a bit much, ain't it?'

'Well, that can only be for one reason,' Regina said. 'She wants her father to hear about it and take matters into his own hands. Now do you see why you need to attend this ball tomorrow night?'

'No. My attending if she is there is just going to—'

'No, no, you won't be going there alone. I ran into an old friend of our cousin's last night.'

'Which cousin?'

Regina tsked impatiently, 'Diana, not that it

matters. The point is that her friend's younger sister is also having her first season.'

'Do I know her?'

'No, don't think so.'

'Then what are you getting at?'

'I'm sure she would agree to have you escort her to this ball if we present the plan to her. And if you devote the entire evening to her, it will prove without a doubt that your romantic inclinations are directed elsewhere. Particularly if you ignore Emily completely in the process.'

'Easy enough to do, but the chit isn't going to get her own hopes up, is she?'

'No – well, probably. They all do, if you just happen to glance at them. But we *would* explain fully that she'd merely be helping you out of this horrid situation which is escalating far too quickly. And she would benefit from your attention. It will quite raise her on the ladder, as it were, since it will draw her to the attention of every other young buck. They'll want to know what *you* find so fascinating about her.'

Jeremy chuckled. 'You overstate the effect I have, puss.'

'Rubbish. We both know that your appearance at any social gathering quite stirs up the pot. Mostly everyone wonders if you've taken after your father and uncle. Those two rakes did leave their mark, notoriously, before they quit the social scene. You, however, have managed to avoid any scandals thus far, so no one knows what to make of you yet.'

'I do try.' Jeremy grinned.

'We know you do,' Regina said, patting his hand. 'I suppose you learned from Derek's example, to keep your affairs strictly private. Of course it helps that you choose your women from the ones who don't feel a need to brag about it to anyone who will listen. And don't you dare mention my Nick's bad luck in that regard.'

Jeremy hooted with laughter. 'Never entered my mind, old girl. Although, come to think of it, his bad luck with Lady Eddington turned out to be your good luck. Doubt you would have met him otherwise, or been forced to marry him, if Lady E hadn't crowed to her friends that he'd meant to abduct her, but abducted you instead.'

Regina scowled. 'Thank you for *not* mentioning it. Now *as* I was saying, if you show up tomorrow night with this young debutante and spend the entire evening devoted to her, it will hit all the gossip mills that you're courting her and should quite undo the gossip Emily is spreading. And Emily will be forced to back off—'

'That is if she believes it,' Jeremy cut in. 'This sister of Diana's friend, she's prettier than Emily?'

Regina frowned. 'Well, no, actually. Famous! All my brilliant thoughts on the matter wasted. You're quite right, it won't work. Emily will easily see it for the ploy it is. It won't put her off a'tall, will more'n likely double her own efforts.'

'Well, it would work if you can find me a chit

who is prettier than Emily. No easy task, I know. The lady is quite stunning.'

Regina sighed. 'Devil take it, Jeremy, if you think so, then *why* aren't you interested in her? *She's* probably wondered the same thing, *and* thinks you're just playing hard to get. She could think she's merely doing you a favor, to hurry things along with these lies she's spreading.'

'One simple answer, puss. Give it just the tiniest bit of thought and you'll come up with it.'

Raising a black brow, Regina said in a droll tone, 'Because you've decided to spend your life without a wife?'

'Exactly. So I keep my eyes and hands off debutantes, and any other young misses on the marriage mart. There are quite enough women to enjoy without risking my bachelorhood.'

'Spare me the details, please,' Regina said, rolling her eyes now. 'And we can forget about my brilliant idea. There simply are no other young hopefuls this go-round who can even come close to Emily Bascomb in rank and looks. The lady is hands down the reigning belle of the season.'

Jeremy did some hand-patting now. 'I'm sure you'll think of something else, puss. You always do.'

Regina sighed. 'But we're running out of time. She's already claimed you've had a lovers' rendezvous, when you haven't. But that little on-dit is going to reach her father eventually, then he'll be calling on *your* father, and you know how that goes.'

Jeremy grinned at her. 'My father will laugh in his face and tell him to go buy her a husband elsewhere, that I ain't for sale.'

'Then he'll just move on to Uncle Jason, and you know very well Jason won't laugh over the matter.'

Jeremy cringed now. 'Very well, we are down to desperate measures. Your plan was a good one. Just think of some other chit to play the part who is at least somewhat comparable to Emily.'

Regina shook her head again. 'I hate to say it, but we just don't have a sterling crop of young hopefuls this year. The only other girl who even comes close is already engaged. In fact, I can't think of a single unmarried woman in all of London who – well, hmmm.'

'What?'

'I should rephrase that. There is one, and I'm looking at her.'

Danny swung around to see whom Regina was talking about and found the pair on the sofa staring at her now. She started blushing. She'd been following their conversation avidly. She didn't need to ask what Regina Eden meant. She'd just been given an amazing compliment and was still absorbing how nice it felt.

Jeremy glanced back at his cousin and with a frown said flatly, 'No.'

'But she's perfect!' Regina exclaimed. 'She quite outshines Emily Bascomb by far.'

'No.'

'And why not? Yes, yes, I know, she'd have to keep her mouth shut, of course.'

'It's not that—'

'Course it is,' Regina interrupted. 'For her to speak at all would quite give away the ruse. Can you keep your mouth shut, Danny?' Danny said nothing, prompting Regina to add triumphantly, 'There, you see, she can.'

'Reggie, I love you, but you've gone half-baked on this idea now. She can talk well enough when she's not nervous, b—'

'She can?' Regina interrupted again in surprise.

'Yes, though there's no guarantee she wouldn't slip up. But she doesn't have attire for a ball, and there's no way a gown of that sort could be done up between now and tomorrow night.'

'So I'll lend her one of mine.'

He lifted a brow. 'Did you grow an extra seven inches last night?'

'So we'll add a hem. Stop being so negative, Jeremy, you know this will work, especially if she can mimic her betters.'

'It won't. She can't dance. She—'

'How d'you know I can't dance, eh?' Danny cut in now. 'Maybe I've attended those masked balls in convent gardens. Maybe I'm a right fine dancer.'

'For a man,' Jeremy countered impatiently. 'Ever try it as a woman?'

Danny blushed again. Actually, she'd never danced in her life, but she resented him taking that for granted. And this idea was starting to sound like fun. Attend a fancy high-class ball? Something she'd never dreamed possible. And what a perfect opportunity to meet a man who might fall in love with her and want to marry her! Not a lord, of course. She knew she couldn't aspire that high. But surely it wouldn't be just lords at such a gathering. Other well-to-do, respectable men would be invited, men without titles who weren't as restricted in whom they married.

And she *had* attended a masked ball before at the gardens – well, not actually attended, but looked on from a distance wishing she could. The people at it seemed to be having such a rousing good time. And those balls weren't just for the nabobs, far from it. Anyone could go to those and pretend for a night that they were someone other than who they were.

'So she won't dance,' Regina was saying to counter Jeremy's last objection. 'Sprained ankle and all that.'

'So she can't talk, can barely walk. Sounds like she should be in a sickbed, not showing up at a ball.'

Regina scowled at him as she insisted, 'She lost her voice on a particularly exciting fox hunt in the country earlier this week. She's recovering nicely, but still pampering the vocal chords. Twisted her ankle at the same hunt, don't you know. She *would* have declined this ball, but she didn't want to disappoint you, when you were *so* looking forward to showing her off tomorrow night. And since she's only in town for the weekend—'

'I catch the drift, Reggie. And just who are you going to pass her off as being?'

'Perhaps she can be distantly related to Kelsey. Kelsey does come from all sorts of titles, though they rarely get mentioned since she married our cousin Derek. But I'm sure she wouldn't mind claiming Danny as a relative.'

'Related to a duke is a bit much, don't you think?' Jeremy said.

'No, no, one of the lesser titles, of course. And very distantly. Perhaps her parents moved to America and she grew up there – no, I know, Cornwall! Just in case her thick accent gets noticed. This *is* going to work, and splendidly. No one, and I mean no one, is going to doubt that you've been courting this lovely girl for the last several months, so you couldn't possibly have been rendezvousing with Emily Bascomb. Must have been some other lucky chap.'

Jeremy shook his head at his cousin, but he did so in amazement. 'How do you do it, Cousin? You simply boggle me, 'deed you do.'

'Rubbish,' Regina scoffed. 'And I'll be taking her home with me to get her ready. Come round with a carriage tomorrow night to pick us up at precisely nine p.m. We only want to be fashionably late, nothing more.'

'Us?'

'I'll be going with you, of course. She must have a chaperone.'

'When did you become my guardian angel, puss?'

'When Amy asked me to keep an eye on you while she was gone.'

He rolled his eyes. Amy wasn't just their cousin but his best friend, and she worried about him far more than was necessary.

'Far be it for me to put a damper on your amazing scheme, but don't you think you should ask Danny if she's willing to rescue me from Emily's clutches?'

'Oh, dear,' Regina sighed. 'Yes, I suppose.' And to Danny: 'Are you up to the task at hand, m'dear? Jeremy here really does need rescuing, or he'll be dragged to the altar through no effort of his own.'

Danny grinned. 'I'm right handy at masquerading.'

Regina blinked. 'Why, yes, you are, aren't you? Well, come along then. We've a lot to accomplish in very little time.'

27

Regina Eden was simply amazing. She was a whirl-wind of activity, instructions, and nonstop chatter. She did drag Danny out of Jeremy's house and down the street to hers and took her straight up to her bedchamber, not giving her any time to gape at the magnificent town house they were rushing through. Regina immediately summoned her maid, Tess, told her what was required, and between them, they pulled out from Regina's wardrobe countless gowns of the like Danny had never before seen. When they finally settled on one, Danny barely got a look at it before Tess sent another maid off to work on it.

The next order of business was shoes, but those that matched the gown simply wouldn't fit Danny's feet no matter how they tried to stretch them, and there was no time to have a pair made. So Regina sent a footman around to her relatives'. Danny wasn't sure whose white satin slippers showed up before dinner, but they were only slightly short at the heels and her toes weren't nearly as scrunched as they had been when trying on Regina's shoes.

There was no break for dinner. Regina had trays brought up to her room, and Danny got to eat from hers while Tess tried to figure out what could be done with her hair. No easy task. In fact, this turned out to be the toughest of their problems. Such short curls simply didn't want to be tamed. And a good number of them had to be cut even shorter, to even out the butchering Lucy had done.

Regina finally produced a tiara and Tess exclaimed, 'This will do it! I can divide the curls now and control them like this. It's as close as we'll get to a contained look.'

'Famous! I knew you could do it, Tess. I'll want it looking just so tomorrow.'

Danny didn't get a chance to see it herself before the tiara was removed and she was shown to a guest bedroom, where Regina told her to get right to sleep. They had a *lot* more work to do tomorrow, and she'd be woken early.

A guest bedroom! She couldn't believe it, couldn't believe either that Lady Regina was going to such bother to save her cousin from marriage to a beautiful heiress. If someone like that didn't tempt him to put the shackle on, then Jeremy obviously hadn't been exaggerating when he'd said he was going to remain a bachelor the rest of his life. Which was too bad, she thought with a pang of sadness. For him to go to such lengths to avoid marriage just proved he wasn't the man for her.

She was excited, though, at the prospect of his seeing her transformation into a lady tomorrow. She'd be attending a ball with him! He was even going to pretend to be courting her. For a short while reality would be suspended and she could do some pretending of her own – that the whole glorious evening was for real . . .

She was awakened earlier than she expected the next morning. It seemed as if she'd barely gotten to sleep when a maid was knocking on her door and coming in with a platter of breakfast. She'd only eaten half of it when Regina walked in complaining, 'Not done yet? Well, do hurry. You shouldn't need to dance tonight, but just in case something goes wrong and you end up having to, I've decided we have enough time for a little instruction in that regard.'

'You're going to teach me to dance?'

'Not me, dear girl, Jeremy is. I've already sent for him.'

Danny couldn't help snorting. 'You won't get him out of bed this early.'

'Yes, I know.' Regina sighed. 'But he will be roused, since I've mentioned it's an emergency.'

'Is it?'

'Course not, but that will get him here in quick order. Now, I suppose I should tell you a little bit about this ball. Lady Aitchison is having it, and that means it is going to be the premier ball of the season, because her parties are all the rage, yet she only has them every four years or so.'

'That means there will be a lot of people there?'

'Yes, it will be an immense crush, with the very cream of London society in attendance. All the young debutantes this season, all the young men who *do* want to get married, their mamas and papas and other assorted escorts, and a few scoundrels like our sweet Jeremy whom you should avoid.'

'He's not a scoundrel,' Danny said, though she'd thought the same thing herself more'n once.

'Course he is, though a lovable one. Why look what he's doing to you? He makes you his mistress, but still has you cleaning his house!'

'I'm *not* his mistress, nor will I ever be!'

Regina blinked at the vehement tone as well as the words. 'Really? Oh my, I do apologize then. I thought, well, the whole family thought, well, blister it, it's rather obvious he wants you to be, and Jeremy has never failed to obtain a woman he wants.'

Danny was blushing by then, because she'd come close to succumbing to his seduction herself and had to constantly remind herself of her goals and that Jeremy Malory wasn't one of them. But Regina didn't notice the blush and, as usual, went from one subject to the next seamlessly.

'Come along, then. I've already had the parlor cleared so we'll have room to work.'

The work wasn't just dancing. As soon as they got downstairs, Regina told her, 'Now, let me see how you walk. No, no, you aren't wearing britches anymore. Take small steps. That's better, but, no, don't walk with your whole body, just your legs. We want it to look like you're gliding across the room without really moving a'tall.'

Danny slowed down and took smaller steps. 'Perfect!' Regina exclaimed.

Danny grinned. 'Do *you* walk like this?'

Regina chuckled. 'Well, I do try, really I do. But truth be known, I used to be a bit of a tomboy. I was raised with my cousin Derek after my mother died, and I enjoyed the freedom that boys have. Course, you must know what I mean. Isn't that why you wore britches?'

'No, where I come from, girls work on their backs, and at young ages. I didn't want to be forced into that line o' work, so I lived the life of a boy.'

'Oh my.' Regina was blushing now. 'No one knew?'

'Only my friend Lucy.'

'Reggie, where are you?' Jeremy suddenly called from the hall.

'In here!'

He appeared in the doorway, his expression quite disgruntled and turned on his cousin. 'D'you know what time it is?'

'Yes, and half the morning is already wasted. You're going to teach Danny to dance.'

'I am?' He crossed his arms and leaned against the doorframe. 'I thought she was going to have a sprained ankle?'

'She is, but it's mostly recovered, merely a bit tender. We're not making her limp, after all. And this is just a precaution. What if King George shows up and asks her to dance?'

Jeremy rolled his eyes. 'That's stretching it, Reggie, 'deed it is.'

'That was merely an example of why she needs to learn to dance. Don't be difficult. This is your ankle we're saving from the shackle.'

He glanced at Danny and his eyes widened slightly. 'Cut your hair, did they? Looks very nice.'

Danny blushed becomingly. 'It will be fancied up for tonight.'

'Heaven help me if you get even more beautiful.' Then he grinned and said to his cousin, 'Damn me, I don't suppose you'd leave us alone for this instruction, Reggie?'

'Not a chance. This isn't an excuse for you to manhandle her, so behave!'

He sighed. 'Don't we need music for this?'

'I'm going to hum, and if you laugh about my humming, I'll box your ears, see if I don't.'

He crossed over to Danny and extended his hand. 'Are you ready to be taught, luv?'

He said it in such a way that she humphed. 'To dance and nothing else.'

'More's the pity,' he whispered as he drew her a bit closer and began to waltz with her about the room.

She keenly felt his hand on her back, his other warm against her palm. The room was large. Regina was on the far side of it, so she couldn't hear Jeremy when he began to fluster Danny with his whispered comments.

'I love touching you. D'you think she'll notice if I put my hand on your derriere?'

'*I'll* notice,' Danny gasped.

He chuckled. 'But you'd like it, wouldn't you?'

'No. And don't you dare! We're supposed to be dancing.'

'But I can make love and dance at the same time,' Jeremy whispered. 'I promise you.'

Danny sucked in her breath and was barely able to reply, 'What a whopper. Now stop it!'

But, of course, he didn't. Leaning slightly closer he whispered, 'Shall I tell you how it can be done? You only need to hold on tight and wrap your legs about my hips. We'd both have to be naked, of course.'

She tripped, was surprised she hadn't done so sooner when she suddenly couldn't concentrate on anything but him and the images he was drawing in her mind. He gathered her closer till she regained her balance, which *didn't* help, only made her distraction worse.

Regina had stopped humming. Danny became aware of that when she noticed a servant had come in to speak to the lady. Jeremy must have noticed as well that his cousin wasn't paying attention to them because his mouth was suddenly on Danny's neck, kissing her hotly, then moving over her ear where his tongue laved deeply. Oh, God, the feeling was amazing. Her knees went weak, but she didn't need the strength to stand. Jeremy was holding her so close her feet were off the floor! And she was clinging to him. She couldn't help it. The feelings he aroused in her made her want to get even closer . . .

Regina's loud throat-clearing drew them apart again, but slowly. Her feet back on the floor, Danny tried to regain her composure. Noticing Jeremy's grin helped in that regard. That scoundrel! He knew exactly what he'd just done to her senses and was puffed-up pleased about it.

Jeremy took pity on her and got serious after that, told her to follow his lead, and she actually learned a thing or two about dancing before he was done.

Danny had thought they would continue after lunch, but she got sent back to bed instead, with Regina warning her to sleep, not just rest, because they would be up until the wee hours of the morning. Danny was sure that she was too excited by that point to actually fall asleep in the middle of the day, but all the information and instructions that had been thrown at her had quite worn her out, and she was asleep within moments of lying down.

28

Danny slept so soundly she was disoriented when she awoke and keenly disappointed. She assumed that she must have been dreaming that she was going to a ball. But then the knock came at the door and she opened her eyes to find she really was in Regina Eden's house, really was going to a ball.

A bath was drawn for her after her nap, and then it was time to get ready. She was led to Regina's room again and set before the vanity so this time she could watch Tess work her wonders with her hair. Regina was being dressed as well by another maid, yet all the while she was giving last-minute instructions that Danny barely heard, she was so fascinated by what was happening to her appearance.

Tess was using a jeweled tiara with a large amethyst at its center to tame her curls. With the tiara as a dividing point, the short curls left at her temples were twisted to look like ringlets, and the rest was combed in such a way that it resembled a short style many women had favored a few years back. Then in quick order, they were tossing petticoats over her head and draping her in the most exquisite ball gown.

The dress was basically a pale lavender silk. It had two layers of tulle lace ruffles toward the hem. To the second layer the maid had attached another border in white silk, over which violet lace was added. Once the same violet lace was added to the short puff sleeves, a narrow layer to the low, wide décolletage, and a half inch to the top edge of the long white gloves that she was also to wear, the entire effect was as if the ball gown had been created just so to begin with.

They had had to cut the shoulders, since the waist had been a bit high for Danny to begin with, Regina having a shorter torso than hers. But with the insertion of more white silk and violet lace that blended in with what had been added to the sleeves, it now fit her snugly about the waist as it should.

The entire ensemble was so fancy, Danny was reminded of the dream she'd had of the beautiful angelic woman. It had come true. For one night, she would be that incredibly beautiful woman. Danny simply couldn't stop staring at herself. Regina had to literally drag her away from the mirror to go downstairs when they were done.

'Close your mouth, Jeremy, do,' Regina complained when they found Jeremy waiting in the foyer for them.

He didn't, and he wouldn't stop staring either. Danny started blushing. She had a feeling he hadn't even heard his cousin's admonishment. Deep down, though, she was so pleased she could barely contain it.

He looked splendid himself in his formal black togs. His coat was open, the frilly white cravat tied loosely, giving him a rakish look. His raven black hair had been combed back, but it wouldn't stay. It fell over his temples and about his neck. His expression thrilled her.

He was shocked by her appearance, no doubt about it. She'd been shocked as well, so she understood why he could do nothing but stare.

Regina had to nudge Jeremy several times. When he finally paid attention to her, he dug in his feet and said adamantly, 'She ain't leaving this house looking like that.'

'And what's wrong with the way she looks? I'll have you know—'

'She's too bloody beautiful and you know it, Reggie.'

She stared at him wide-eyed. 'Well, that was the point, you daft boy.'

'Not even close. Didn't expect her to look like this. She'll cause a sensation the likes this town has never seen. She stays home, and that's my last word on it.'

Regina tsked at him in annoyance. '*You* stay home. *She's* going to the ball. Come to think of it, you don't really need to be there to accomplish what we're after. I can spread the word quite easily without your attendance. She has to be there, though. The rumor won't fly without the proof staring them in the face.'

'You aren't listening, Reggie.'

'No, *you* aren't. This is quite out of your hands now. I'm going to save you despite yourself. Come along, Danny, and get in the coach.'

Jeremy followed them, of course. And continued his objections all the way to the Aitchisons' home, which wasn't all that far. The ball was taking place in one of the mansions near the first Malory house Danny had visited.

Regina had stopped listening to Jeremy as she was quite annoyed with him now. Danny did, too, for that matter. She was disappointed that he was making such a fuss and didn't quite understand his reasoning. She was too pretty? Was going to cause a commotion because of it? She'd thought that had been the idea, to dispute the false rumors that Emily Bascomb was spreading.

Riding with Jeremy in a coach again also brought back memories of the night she'd met him. Jeremy must have guessed what she was thinking from her expression because he whispered to her, 'Quite the change from the last time we rode together, eh? You're rather good at bolting from coaches. Feel free to do so anytime now.'

She gave a soft snort at his suggestion. The man was determined to be in a rotten mood and predict dire consequences for tonight's agenda.

But reminded of what they'd done that night, she whispered back, 'D'you think he'll be there?'

Without having to ask whom she meant, he said with a shrug, 'Wouldn't matter if he is. It's his servant that would recognize us, not him.'

Regina stopped Jeremy once more, just before they entered the Aitchison mansion. With a finger poked in his chest, she snarled, 'If you don't stop with the doom and gloom, I'll never speak to you again.'

'Do you promise?' he asked.

She ignored that and added, 'And if you *are* going in there with us, then do your part and act appropriately smitten, or this entire farce will be pointless. Now get hold of yourself, Jeremy. The performance is about to begin.'

The moment was at hand and Danny was finally hit with a large dose of apprehension. Regina had drilled her with a long list of dos and don'ts while they were working on her gown. She was afraid she was going to forget every one of them now. And then she was simply struck dumb by the sight of a high-fashion ball in full swing. The lights, the colors, the most exquisite ball gowns twirling about the huge room. She'd never seen anything like it in her life.

Her mouth must have dropped open, because Jeremy hissed in her ear, 'Stop looking like you've never seen anything like this. You are supposedly gentry tonight and accustomed to such entertainments.'

'Yes, but I 'ave' – she paused to cough, then continued – '*have* done very little socializing, *hav*ing only just finished my schooling.'

'Reggie feed you that line?'

She blushed. 'Yes, and a lot more.'

'Why?' he groaned. 'You aren't supposed to be talking at all.'

Danny shrugged. 'I suppose she figured I'd make a mistake or two.'

'Or three or four. This was *such* a bad idea. I've simply lost my mind, no other answer for my agreeing to this. And it's your fault, you know.'

She swung around, wondering how the devil he could blame any of this on her. 'How's that, mate?'

'I want you so much, I simply can't think at all clearly anymore.'

Danny's mouth dropped open again, to the accompaniment of a vivid blush. Her knees had gone weak, giddiness swirled in her stomach, and an image of them twirling about the dance floor without a stitch of clothing on popped into her mind . . .

Why did he have to say things like that, that got her all mushy inside? And now, of all times, when she was on display to half the ton?

Regina moved closer to whisper, 'Don't upset her now, Jeremy. Let her have her moment of glory. She's quite brought the house down.'

Danny swung back around. Sure enough, the music was still playing, but the dancers had all

246

halted, every single one of them staring her way. Her blush deepened. So did Jeremy's groan.

'I warned you she'd cause a sensation,' he told his cousin in disapproval.

'And I'm pleased you were right. If you haven't noticed, Emily *is* here, and at this precise moment she's looking daggers at our Danny.'

'Our Danny? When did she get to be *our* Danny?'

'I take credit when it's due. *You* might have found her, but *I* helped to make her shine, dear boy. Now stop looking like you're annoyed with her. You're supposed to be in love. Do your part. Or do I need to instruct you how it's done?'

He rolled his eyes at her, but he did start grinning. And he warned Danny, 'We're about to be overwhelmed. Remember, no talking if you can help it. "Yes," "No," "Nice to meet you," "Good-bye." That should do you fine. Do a lot of head nodding, goes a long way in a conversation.'

He wasn't joking about being overwhelmed. It had only taken two people whose curiosity simply wouldn't allow them to wait before approaching them, then twenty more followed suit right behind them. Regina Eden proved once again how amazing she was. She fielded all the questions, made the statement about the lost voice and sore ankle as she'd planned to, and kept Danny from having to do any more than smile and extend her hand in greetings, at least for the most part. A few people were persistent and managed to get a word or two out of her, but it seemed more like a competition on their part, so they could tell their friends, 'Well, she spoke to *me*!'

She didn't try to keep track of any of the names she was hearing in the introductions, didn't expect to see any of these people ever again. She was playing the part of a young miss fresh out of the schoolroom who just happened to have caught Jeremy Malory's eye and was making him seriously consider giving up his bachelorhood. She was Danielle Langton, with repeated mentions that she was distantly related to Kelsey's family.

Of course *that* became a source of conversation as it was remembered that Kelsey came from The Tragedy. Apparently her mother had shot her father over his gambling debts, then killed herself, both being an accident. She hadn't meant to shoot him or fall out the window afterward, but then that's why it had been termed The Tragedy.

Nothing was stated as fact, but the ton ended up assuming Danny was a Langton from Kelsey's side of the family, assuming she was engaged to Jeremy already, assuming she belonged among them. That several older gentlemen swore she looked familiar to them, Regina explained as a phenomenon known as 'if they hear it enough times, they believe it and begin to think they always knew it.'

Jeremy had also relaxed and stopped complaining, after watching how smoothly Regina handled all the questions. One handsome young man came back though and must have missed the part about the sore ankle. Danny had been introduced to him she was sure, but she couldn't remember his name.

He flashed her an engaging grin. 'I intend to shoot m'self if you won't allow me the first dance, Lady Danielle.'

Jeremy didn't give her a chance to reply to such an outlandish statement. 'You won't have to do that, Fawler,' he told the fellow. 'I'll be happy to oblige in that regard. She won't be dancing with anyone but me. Now move along.'

The expression on Jeremy's face was so unnerving, the fellow didn't say another word; he simply backed off rather quickly.

Even after the last person moved on and she was finally standing there alone with Jeremy, the room was still buzzing about her. She'd played her part well, though, and was feeling mighty triumphant about it.

'Would you like to try dancing?' he asked her when they had a few minutes with no one else nearby.

'And muck up a good performance?'

'I didn't spend an hour twirling you about Reggie's parlor for you not to at least try it while you're here. If you trip a time or two, your sore ankle will be blamed. You know there's not much to it. You just need to follow my lead again.'

She did want to try. It looked like such fun. So she nodded and let him lead her out to the dance floor. And for a short while, she forgot about where she was and all the people watching her.

His grip was firm, his palm against hers warm, the skin slightly rough. Was the rest of his skin like that, too? she wondered. Her hands almost itched to find out. And that image was back in her mind, of the two of them twirling around the dance floor, her legs wrapped tightly around him, both of them naked, the music filling her, him filling her, oh, God . . .

'What's wrong?' Jeremy questioned, hearing her gasp.

'Nothing,' Danny lied, and desperate to get her mind off lovemaking, she asked, 'That chap wasn't serious, was he, about shooting himself?'

'Course not. I'm sure he tells all the young misses that. Flattery of that degree is bound to work for him occasionally. I prefer to stick to the truth, so what I would have said would have been, if you don't make love with me soon, I'm going to shoot m'self.'

She blinked at him, then burst out laughing. 'You call that the truth?'

'Well, stretched a little, but the sentiment was apt. I *am* getting desperate, dear girl.'

She caught her breath. It was there in his eyes, not so much desperation, but passion hot enough to burn. She glanced away, was desperate herself to bank those fires of his before she succumbed to them.

To get him thinking along other lines she asked, 'Who taught you to dance?'

'My father's first mate.'

She looked back at him in amazement. 'He had a woman for a first mate?'

'No, his nickname might have been Connie, but Conrad Sharpe is a six-foot-tall, red-haired Scot, and if you could have seen him pretending to be a female for an hour to teach me how to lead in a dance, you would have laughed your arse off.'

She chuckled. 'I can imagine.'

'But I know he didn't have as much fun teaching me as I had teaching you.'

She blushed. 'Behave, Jeremy.'

'Never!' he whispered in her ear.

He continued to tease her and make her laugh. He was such a good dancer, and he was so handsome tonight – cor, he was always handsome – but tonight in his black, fancy togs, exceptionally so. He made her feel special, dancing with him, made her feel as if she really did belong there. She couldn't remember when she'd had such a good time. And she couldn't deny it anymore. Jeremy might be pretending tonight to be in love with her, but she was beginning to suspect that she wasn't pretending on her part at all.

29

Jeremy might have relaxed enough to do his part as the evening progressed, but he still wasn't liking it. The only thing palatable about the evening was that Danny seemed to be having such a good time. He didn't begrudge her that at all. He simply hated sharing her.

She was his was the way he saw it, and every time another man got near her he felt the most primitive urge to protect what belonged to him. Which was insane. She wasn't his a'tall, she was his maid! He'd *like* for her to be more than that, but she wasn't cooperating in the least.

He went to fetch Regina and Danny some champagne. They'd had to twist his arm. He had *not* wanted to leave Danny alone for even a minute. Unfortunately, his glance passed over Emily on the way and he noticed her casting sad eyes at him. Good God, was she going to play the wounded lover now? And still insist he'd bedded her when he hadn't?

'I do believe you are quite ready for bedlam,' a voice he knew all too well said behind him.

Jeremy cringed. His father. He hadn't noticed James's arrival, hadn't noticed much of anything all evening other than Danny.

'I know.'

'What the devil could you have been thinking, to bring her here?'

'It wasn't my idea. Think I wanted to share her with the ton and have every randy buck around ogling her? Not bloody likely.'

'Who then? Or do I even need to ask?'

'You don't. Reggie, of course.'

'My dear niece has come up with some very odd manipulations during the course of her interfering-in-every-little-thing career, but I can't fathom the reason for this one.'

'Pro'bly because only a woman would think of it. She figured the only way to get Emily to back off was to show her that I was interested in someone else, and she couldn't think of anyone who could outshine Emily other than—'

'I get the idea, but wouldn't a "Get lost, wench" have sufficed for this troublesome young lady?'

'Reggie didn't think so, didn't think anything would make Emily find a new target. But this farce is more for the gossip mills, since Emily has been spreading the tale now that I've bedded her.'

'Bloody hell!'

'Exactly. But there will be an opposite view now.

After all, why would I pursue a mere daisy when I've been courting a rare white rose.'

'Courting?' James choked.

'Just for effect,' Jeremy assured him. 'And we won't have to repeat this performance. Danny has made such a smashing impression, the ton will be talking about nothing else for weeks. Now what are *you* doing here? I could have sworn you said you had your excuses already prepared to escape being dragged along to these things?'

'Changed my mind. Wanted to have a look at this conniving chit who is trying to maneuver you to the altar. By the by, which one is she?'

Jeremy looked to where he'd last seen Emily. She wasn't there. He then glanced back to see that his stepmother, George, had Regina's attention for the moment, which left Danny unobserved by either of them, and alarm bells went off when he saw who'd taken advantage of that.

'Good God, Emily is confronting Danny.'

James raised a brow as he looked in the same direction. 'This should prove interesting. Don't think I've ever watched two women throwing punches, and considering where your Danny comes from, that's a distinct possibility.'

Danny's hackles rose when the lady pinched her arm to gain her attention. She was beautiful. Blond hair arranged elaborately in a perfect coiffure, a stunning white ball gown, which seemed to be the favored color for young debutantes, this one trimmed in powder blue to match the lady's azure eyes. Those eyes were narrowed in a baleful scowl though. In fact, so much hate was pouring out of them, Danny was stunned for a moment.

'I don't know who you are, but if you think you're going to steal him from me, you are sadly mistaken,' the young woman told her.

It clicked then, who the lady was. Regina should really have pointed her out to give Danny some warning. Not that she could have avoided this, when she hadn't noticed the lady approaching her.

After that unnecessary pinch, though, she didn't pull any punches when she replied, 'Ah, you must be Emily of the many lies.'

'I beg your pardon?'

'You're making a fool of yourself, lady. He's onto you, his family is onto you, and after tonight, the entire town will be onto you. Your lies will only serve to bury you in your own shame.'

Emily gasped, a high blush rising up her ivory cheeks. 'I don't think you quite understand. He *is* going to marry me. My father will see to that.'

Danny raised a brow. 'Based on a lie?'

'I see you've been misinformed. I'm not a liar. He is, though, if he's trying to deny that he trifled with me.'

'Is that what you call having a few words of conversation?' Danny asked innocently.

'Is *that* what he claims?' Emily looked incredulous, and it didn't seem the least bit contrived. And then she added with a sigh, 'I should have known he couldn't be trusted to keep his promises. After all, his father was the most notorious rake this town has ever seen, his uncle Anthony a close second, and obviously, Jeremy is endeavoring to follow in those same footsteps.'

Danny had no comment for that. She wouldn't be a bit surprised if some of it was true. She knew Jeremy had no intention of getting married, had heard him say it. And obviously he took his pleasure where he could find it. His trying to get under her own skirts was proof of that. She didn't think he was that callous though, to make promises he had no intention of keeping. He could have seduced the lady, yes, but Danny doubted he'd done it with anything more than a quick tumble in mind.

Danny hadn't expected the lady to seem so sincere either. She was quite believable. Either she was very, very good at lying, or she was telling the truth.

Danny pointed that out. 'If he's as despicable as you say, why do you even want him?'

'I don't anymore,' Emily insisted. 'But I have no choice in the matter now.' Then she explained in a whisper, 'I suspect I'm enceinte.'

'How can you know that already? He only met you last week!'

'I said suspect,' Emily hissed in annoyance. 'I won't know for certain for another week or two. And I hope I'm wrong, I really do, but unfortunately, I doubt it. So you can see now why you're wasting your time and are headed for nothing but disappointment.'

Danny shook her head. 'No, what I see is you're deluding yourself. Buck up and accept your loss. Getting your father involved will just add to your own shame. And for what? He still won't marry you.'

'What a dense twit you are! You don't know how these things are handled. When the heir to a fortune is involved, it goes beyond personal preferences. Believe me, Jeremy will have no more say in it than I will. It will be quite out of our hands.'

Danny didn't even know this lady and she was beginning to seriously dislike her. 'Go away, wench. You've given me a bleedin' headache.'

Emily gasped in outrage. 'Well, I never!'

Danny nodded in agreement. 'Likely the first truth out of your mouth.'

Emily opened her mouth for a rejoinder, but changed her mind and quickly hurried off. Danny found out why when Jeremy said behind her, 'Are you all right?'

She turned to give him a sour look. 'That were tough work, mate, keeping all them *h*'s and *u*'s in line for that much talking. Give me a bleedin' headache, she did.'

'Here, this will help,' he said, handing her one of the champagne glasses he was holding. 'I'm sorry you had to deal with that. I'm amazed she had the nerve to approach you. She wasn't spiteful, was she?'

'She was very believable, was what she was.'

'Your appearance with me at your side hasn't made her change her mind a'tall?'

'Not a chance. I'd wager this has merely forced her hand. She's likely to move up her time schedule now.'

'Bloody hell.'

'Buck up, mate,' Danny said cheekily. 'You can always move to Africa.'

He burst out laughing, then wound down enough to say 'I rather like it here. And at least Reggie's plan was half successful. The tongues will be wagging in a different direction now. Shall we further that along and dance some more? Might as well enjoy the rest of the evening, as long as we're here.'

She humphed, though she was grinning at him. 'I'm onto you, mate. You just want an excuse to put yer hands on me again.'

'Never think so,' he protested, but his own grin said, Absolutely! She might have given him the idea, or he might have already had it, but they didn't remain long on the dance floor. A few twirls around and then he was dancing her off to the side of the room where plants and potted trees had been arranged to resemble a small garden.

He was giving the impression of trying to be discreet, but he just couldn't contain his ardor any longer. The foliage only concealed them from half the room. The other half got a full view of Jeremy being most indiscreet.

'This should do it,' he said, just before he kissed her.

Danny was taken by surprise. A man and a woman didn't kiss in public unless a wedding date had been announced, and even then it wasn't considered acceptable behavior. Only a scoundrel like Jeremy would ignore such rules. His remark meant this was part of the plan and she should go along with it. Danny might have argued the point, but she wasn't given a chance and besides, she'd been too close to Jeremy all evening, had felt his hands on her, had been seduced by the sensual promise in his eyes.

Just a few moments, she told herself just a few ... Oh, God, she didn't want this kiss to end. Heat spread along every nerve of her body, steamed up between them so swiftly, if she'd been wearing spectacles they would have completely fogged over. The fluttering in her belly spread, too, lower to the juncture of her thighs when it throbbed deliciously.

She was at the point of wanting to rip his shirt off and press her mouth to his warm, muscular chest, to unbutton his trousers and feel his heated flesh, but she had just the tiniest measure of sense left. If she didn't stop him now she never would.

She gasped out, 'Stop!'

'Must I?'

He said it so simply. She was trembling with passion while he didn't sound the least bit affected by what had just passed between them. But then she met his eyes, and it was there, the promise of what could have been, and what could be, if she'd just let it happen.

30

It was hands down the nicest time Danny had ever had in her life. She'd never thought she would go to a ball, let alone the grandest one imaginable. She was still bubbling over with pleasure and champagne on the way home. She knew she'd drunk too much. She'd felt light-headed after two glasses, but then she'd gone on to have two more. It just wasn't the same as that fine wine she'd had the other night. Champagne went down too easily and its potency snuck up on her.

But that was all right. She'd soon be in bed to sleep it off. And she was sure her intoxication hadn't caused her to slip up on her performance tonight. Jeremy would have said something if she had, and after Emily Bascomb's visit he hadn't left her side for the rest of the night. Well, he had let her dance once with one other gentleman, though she wished he hadn't. All other men he'd chased away, but this one he couldn't.

She had *not* enjoyed dancing with James Malory.

That fellow still scared the pants off her, though he did try to put her at ease with a few droll remarks designed to make her laugh. He hadn't succeeded.

She pitied his wife, Georgina, whom she got to meet briefly. George they called her. Nice lady for an American, and very pretty.

Jeremy helped her out of the coach. His hand lingered on her waist as he led her into his house. She thought nothing of it. She was still floating in contentment, still savoring how much fun the evening had been. She vaguely noted that she was climbing the stairs. That was all right, she worked up there. No, actually . . .

She stopped in the upstairs corridor. 'I'm thinking I made a wrong turn.'

'Not a'tall,' he disagreed, pointing out, 'you're going to need help getting out of that gown. It's fastened rather tightly up your back.'

It was, too. She remembered Regina's saying she'd have to get one of the servants to help her out of it. But they were all asleep at this hour.

'Would you lend me a 'and then, mate?'

'Certainly, as soon as I light a lamp so I can see what needs undoing. You'll need one to get to your room as well.'

'One what?'

'Lamp, m'dear. Didn't look like any had been left burning downstairs other than in the foyer.'

Danny nodded. Jeremy led her into his room. She waited while he lit a lamp, then turned her back to him so he could loosen her gown enough for her to slip out of it. She sighed dreamily while he worked at it and shivered in turns, as his fingers brushed against her skin.

'So you enjoyed yourself tonight?'

'Too much, I'm thinking,' she admitted with a grin. 'I like dancing.'

'So do I – with you.'

She giggled. 'Don't be using any o' those seducer lines on me, mate. Remember, I'm onto you.'

'That was no line, Danny. I can't remember ever enjoying dancing so much as I did tonight.'

She wished she could believe him. It still warmed her to hear it.

Glancing over her shoulder at him, she said sincerely, 'Thank you for teaching me.'

'It was my pleasure, but the lessons for the day aren't over.'

The gown was loosened. He'd helped her out of it while they talked, so it didn't occur to her yet that she shouldn't be dropping it in his room, but hers. She was simply having trouble concentrating on two things at once, three, actually. He'd kept touching her as he'd worked the gown off her, and she'd managed to notice every single brush of his fingers against her bare skin.

But she shouldn't have glanced back at him. She'd been doing fine until she met his eyes and got lost in the deep, pure blue of them. And in those eyes as well was his expression, everything he was feeling, passion so hot she felt the heat of it wash over her. Or was that her own heat that was swiftly rising?

He turned her toward him. He placed one hand on her neck, his thumb tilting her chin up. This breathless moment ended in an exquisitely tender kiss. One kiss. What could it hurt? And it felt so bleeding nice.

She didn't notice his other hand on her back until it pressed her closer to him, and still closer, until she was so close she could barely breathe. Yet that felt exquisite, too. Deceptive, that tender kiss. He didn't need to be overwhelming her with his passion when her own was doing a right handy job of it.

But now he kissed her again. By slow degrees this kiss became much more erotic, his tongue delving into her mouth, finding hers, capturing it, sucking it forward until she groaned into his mouth. She had to grip his shoulders, her knees turned so weak. And his hands moved, one sliding through her curls to cup the back of her head, keeping her mouth under his control, while the other slid down her back to caress her derriere. Then abruptly both his hands were on her bottom as he lifted her to his loins.

Oh, God, there was no help for it after that. Too much heat was escalating between them. And Danny was tired of trying to fight it. What he made her feel was so wonderful, she couldn't recall why she wasn't supposed to enjoy it.

Somehow he got them on the bed without breaking that kiss. Danny became a little more dizzy, lying down, but after a few moments, she no longer noticed. She noticed Jeremy's hand on her breasts though, squeezing them gently, teasing her nipples, which had already hardened under his manipulation. She'd never paid much attention to her breasts, other than regretting when they got so plump, which made it harder to keep them flattened. She had no idea they could tingle at a touch or cause fascinating sensations elsewhere. And the kissing never stopped. It got so hot, there should have been smoke in the room.

Danny was approaching an erotic state of no return and she didn't care anymore. She'd lost her chemise and petticoats. She had a vague memory of them sliding off her to the floor soon after Jeremy had started kissing her, probably because he had unfastened them at the same time he'd done her gown. Something else she hadn't noticed. Or that he'd taken his own coat and shirt off. She simply had no idea when or how he'd done that, but she became instantly aware of it when he hugged her closer at one point and she was scorched by the heat of his bare skin on hers.

He removed her drawers now, by slow, agonizing degrees. Was he afraid she'd stop him? Not a chance, when she had such an amazing urge to feel his naked body against hers. But that removal was one long caress, his hand hot on her thigh, her calf as he bent her knee, her ankle, the drawers merely hooked on the back of his wrist as he explored her long limbs.

She didn't know what to do with her own hands other than to hold on to his hair, because she really didn't want him to stop kissing her. The trouble was, she didn't know *what* she wanted, but she wanted it now.

Jeremy must have known. He didn't make her agonize much longer with the primitive urges that had been overwhelming her from the start.

He put her arms around his neck and told her, 'Hold me tight, luv, tighter.'

She did just that, squeezing for all she was worth as he covered her body completely with his just as she'd been dying for him to do. And then she felt the sharpest pain.

Danny screamed, yanking his hair until he raised his head. 'What in the bleedin' 'ell did you do that for?'

Jeremy was staring down at her as if she'd lost her mind, but then he smiled gently. 'Danny . . . luv,' he started to explain, but broke off to kiss her instead, deeply, with the same passion he'd bestowed on her earlier.

Did he think that would mollify her? Well, it *did* distract her.

'That wasn't part of lovemaking, other than the first time,' he continued. 'An initiation as it were. But it's never going to hurt you again. Really it isn't.' And then he sobered and demanded, 'And how is it that you were still a virgin?'

'What was I supposed to be, when I've been a lad all these years?'

'Well, I thought – never mind.' His expression turned infinitely tender. 'I'm rather glad you were.'

'Am,' she corrected.

'*Were*,' he stressed with a slight cringe, as if expecting another clobbering.

And she did explode, eyes wide. 'You bleedin' bastard, you've turned me into a whore!'

'Good God, where'd you get that ridiculous notion? You can't be a whore if you only make love with one man. That's about as far from whoredom as you can get – well, other than remaining a virgin, which is moot now.'

'Then what am I?'

'M'dear, you are the sweetest thing this side of creation.' He bent to lick her nipple. 'Beautiful beyond compare,' he added before he went on to lick and suck her other nipple. 'And the only thing you should be worrying about is how often we can do this.'

He leaned up and grinned at her again. Danny had drawn in her breath, fighting the urge to pull him back to her breast. He didn't understand what he'd done to her. He figured it was a trifling thing, this initiation as he called it. For him it was. For her it was utterly earth-shattering.

'Ye don't get it, mate, but I wouldn't expect ye to. Now let me up.'

He didn't move other than to caress her cheek with his finger. 'You know you've loved everything we've been doing. *Why* would you want to deny yourself such pleasure. It gets better, you know. You may depend upon it.'

'I don't doubt that a'tall,' she replied with a sigh. 'But I might be able to salvage this if I *don't* find out just how much better.'

'You have *got* to be joking. The damage is done, Danny. Let me prove it to you, that it was more'n worth it. You could be wrong, you know. Whatever it is you're thinking, you could be absolutely wrong. And then you will have missed out on this.'

He moved inside her, showing her what 'this' was. Oh, God, the heat came back so swiftly, it spread clear to her toes. No trace of pain was left, just the deepest, most delicious pleasure. He continued to move in her, must have thought she didn't get the point. She'd stop him in a moment, just another moment. But before she knew it she was moving with him, and then it was too late. It came upon her suddenly, bloomed up, had her gripping him to her for dear life, then oh, God, the most sublime feeling burst and spread, lingering deliciously as he continued to drive his point home.

She didn't want to let him go. Even when it seemed that he'd found his own pleasure, she didn't want to lose the least bit of contact with him. He answered her wish in his own way, moving off her, but pulling her back into his arms.

Wisely, he didn't say a word, didn't gloat that he'd been right, didn't do anything but hold her close and caress her back gently. He did sigh in contentment. She couldn't miss that. Then he fell asleep.

She wished she could do the same. She wished he hadn't been right. But more than that, she wished she hadn't been right either.

31

Danny woke by slow degrees, a luxury she hadn't experienced for quite a while. She was probably late for work. She wondered if Claire had been looking for her when she'd gotten no response from her room. Did the rest of the staff know where she'd spent the last night? Maybe not. Maybe they assumed she'd spent the night at the Eden household again, since they hadn't seen her since she went off with Regina.

She was holding at bay what she felt about last night. It wasn't easy when she was still in Jeremy's bed. He'd probably sleep the morning away. He usually did. It wouldn't be that hard to sneak out of there without waking him.

But she didn't move yet. She felt more relaxed than she'd ever been, with the oddest feeling of contentment, which she wanted to savor just a little while more. Which was crazy. Her world had been turned upside down. She should be frantic, at the very least furious. She was neither.

She couldn't blame Jeremy for what had happened. He'd been trying to get her in his bed since she'd started working for him. He'd made no pretense about it. She couldn't blame the champagne, either, when the pain he'd dealt her had sobered her quickly. She could blame herself, but for what? Wanting him so much that she just didn't want to fight it anymore?

And, oh, God, making love with him had been so nice, even nicer than she'd imagined it would be. She'd worried that it would be added to her small list of cravings. She'd been absolutely right. It was going to be an irresistible craving now – with him.

Ah, well. She wasn't one to cry over her lot or endlessly bemoan her mistakes. She'd have to find another job, though. Jeremy would only have to look at her now and she'd probably lead him to the nearest bed.

'You aren't pretending to be asleep, are you, when I know you're not?'

Danny opened her eyes to find that he was lying on his side next to her, elbow bent, head resting on his hand, grinning at her. She hadn't felt him move into that position and realized he must have been watching her before she woke.

She wished she'd thought of that. Staring at him at her leisure would have been quite pleasant. Just looking at him now was rather thrilling, considering he was still naked and covered only to his waist. She knew now that his skin was smooth and tight over thick muscles. His hair was mussed – God, he was so damn sexy when it was. One lock had fallen half over his eye, making her want to push it back.

'A bit early for you to have your eyes open, ain't it, mate?'

'When I knew, at least hoped, that you'd still be here? Barely slept a wink.'

She laughed. She loved his humor. And there was no longer any reason to restrain her own. He seemed surprised, though, by her agreeable mood.

His grin widened. He even said, 'No wonder you got away with a boy's disguise so long. You snore!'

She blinked at him and then snorted. 'What a rotten thing to say.'

'You think so? I thought it was better than mentioning how much I loved making love to you. Wasn't sure you wanted to hear that just yet.'

'I don't,' she agreed, then added lightly, 'I should sock you.'

'Yes, I suppose you should.' He sighed. 'I'd let you again, too, if you feel you must.'

'Let me?' she asked incredulously as she sat up.

He grinned again, but she had the feeling he hadn't been joking. And his gaze had moved down to her breasts when she sat up. It didn't cause her to blush, but it did remind her that she should be getting dressed and out of there.

With that thought in mind, she left the bed. He didn't try to stop her, probably because he was too busy staring at her body. She found her underclothes where he'd dropped them and began putting them on, then the beautiful ball gown. She wasn't going to have him fasten it, when she'd just need someone else to undo it again when she got downstairs. So she went into his dressing room and grabbed one of his coats.

'I'll be borrowing this long enough to get down to my room,' she said as she came back out, stuffing her arms in the sleeves.

Amazing how big that coat was on her. Jeremy didn't seem *that* big, yet obviously he was. And glancing at him now, with his bare chest above the cover, she could see that he really was broader of chest than he seemed when dressed. It shouldn't have surprised her. She was used to having clothes conceal her own shape.

He was also looking damn pleased with himself. Well, why not? He'd gotten what he'd been after. And it hadn't changed *his* life any. It appeared that the woman got the short end of the deal, in the matter of 'first times.' Not bleeding fair, she was thinking.

Which was why she gave him a sour look when she asked, 'Did you get me foxed last night just so you could bed me?'

'No, you managed that on your own if you'll recall, though if I *had* thought of it, I probably would have. By the by, you don't have to work anymore. You can stay here, do as you like, spend your time as you please – as long as you spend some of it with me. Or if you'd prefer to have your own residence, that will work just as well. Some-place close by where I can visit.'

'And you'd pay for it?'

'Of course.'

'What would you prefer?'

'I'd prefer you never leave this bed.'

She had a feeling he was serious. And he was talking about making her a mistress. She should be pleased. Lucy would jump at a chance like that and worship the bloke who offered it. She would be thrilled to service one man exclusively. But Danny didn't see it that way, found it about as distasteful as going out and selling her body for coins on the street.

She didn't tell Jeremy that. She wasn't even going to tell him she was leaving. Just pack up her things, grab her pet, and take off was the smartest way to go about it. She didn't want to have to explain why or risk the chance that he would talk her out of it. She didn't really want to go, after all, now that she craved him. She was going to be miserable, working somewhere else.

She moved over to the bed, nudged it with her knee. 'Never leaving this is unrealistic, mate.'

'Not a'tall!' he disagreed, then frowned a bit suspiciously as he pointed out, 'You're being awful calm about this, after the fuss you made about it previously. Realized the objections you had, what-ever they were, were silly, did you?'

'Not silly. But I understand why you don't get it.'

273

'Then why don't you explain it to me.'

'I'd rather not. You wouldn't understand, when you can't even figure out how you've turned me into a whore.'

He sighed. 'There's that word again. Do I need to find you a dictionary?'

'That I can't read? Sure, that would be real helpful.'

He grinned at her sarcasm. 'Why do I get the feeling that you equate *whore* with *prostitution*? Yet neither would apply to you. We made love. It was the most incredible experience of my life, I don't mind telling you. A whore spreads herself around, mainly, because she enjoys the variety.'

'Sort o' like you?'

He coughed. 'If you insist, though there's another word for it when it applies to a man. But in either case, no money exchanges hands. Now come here.' He patted the bed next to him. 'Let's greet the morning properly.'

She almost laughed. It took every ounce of will she had not to crawl back into bed with him just then, to shake her head instead.

'Why not?' he asked simply.

Why not? Because to do so would be to completely give in and not have any will left of her own. But she wasn't going to admit that she craved him as much as she did. With him looking so damned sensual lying there, she wanted to be kissing him, not arguing with him. She liked him too much, that was the problem. But the damage was done so why couldn't she enjoy him for just a little while? Not for long, a few weeks, maybe a month, at least until he lost interest in her.

'I was going to leave,' she told him. 'I still should. Playing with temptation once was one time too many. But I'll stay for now. Just don't be tempting me every time I turn around. And I'll be keeping m'job, thank you. Doing nothing means you're paying my way, which means you're paying for bedding me. Don't try to deny it. I don't pay you for it and you don't pay me for it. Got that, mate?'

On her way out the door, she realized that Jeremy hadn't had to talk her into staying. She'd done that just fine on her own.

32

Danny was cleaning the parlor when Jason Malory, the Marquis of Haverston and the head of the entire Malory clan, arrived later that week. She shouldn't have been there to run into him. A downstairs maid had finally been hired yesterday who *should* have been there. But the new girl had been insulted by the new butler Henry and had quit in a huff barely four hours after she started.

Henry was actually one of two new butlers at the house. A Frenchman who tried to speak English, he was really quite funny. But the new maid hadn't thought so. He swore he'd only tried to compliment her. She must not have understood English with a French accent.

Henry had shown up first, then the very next day, his friend Artie had arrived to do the butlering. They were actually going to share the job, had apparently been sharing it for years at James Malory's house. They were both old sea dogs who used to sail under James when he captained his own ship. When he gave up sailing, they elected to stay with him. But since he didn't have enough jobs to go around, they'd agreed to share the butler's job.

What they hadn't done was actually learn how to properly butler. They figured they did just fine at it, but Claire had been complaining about their rudeness, and even Mrs Robertson had been heard to mumble a bit under her breath about their unorthodox approach to the job.

Danny didn't mind the loss of the new maid. She still didn't really have enough to do to keep herself busy for the entire day. Even with the downstairs added to her list of duties, she was finished long before dinner. And with Drew moving over to his sister's house for the duration of his visit, all but one of the upstairs bedrooms was empty, which meant less work for Danny up there.

Then there was Jeremy. If *he* had his way, she'd be spending most of each day in his room. If she had her druthers, she would, too. But she had to draw the line somewhere, and lazing the day away in his bed didn't get her work done. As it was, if he found her upstairs when he awoke, he usually got his way. She was a pushover when it came to his style of persuasion. That sexy voice of his lowered to a deep timbre when he was aroused, and his expression promised such wicked delights. Hell, just looking at him was all the persuasion she needed, he was so bleeding handsome. So although she had determined not to make love with him every single day, she was doing just that, and one day, more'n once.

He wanted her to sleep with him each night, too, but she managed to dredge up enough willpower to find her own bed each night. Actually, it was more like escape to her room before she ran into him again. And even then, he came down to her one night and spent the night in her bed. She hadn't really had the least desire to kick him out. But she *had* insisted he not do that again. And much to her own frustration, he didn't.

She'd had to do some serious thinking about staying. Doing so meant she'd have to put her goals aside for the time being. That wasn't going to be easy, when she wanted them so bad. But she'd reasoned a month wouldn't be too long a delay, and during that time she'd be saving her pay, so when she did leave, she could afford to let a flat while she looked for a new job.

When she did leave – God, that was going to be so hard. Never see Jeremy again? The thought nearly brought tears to her eyes now, how much worse would it be a month from now? But what if he fell in love with her during that month? It wasn't an impossible notion. She could fit into his world, she'd proved that the night of the ball. He might even defy convention and marry her then. And that was the deciding factor that convinced her to stay for now. That slim hope, that Jeremy could be more than just a temporary diversion, that he could be the man for her.

Jason Malory wasn't alone when he arrived. Jeremy's father was with him. The two brothers looked very much alike. The elder was a few inches taller, but they were both big, blond, handsome men. Jason was a little narrower of build, whereas James's arms and chest were more muscular, reminding Danny of some of the brutes she'd watched in street fights.

James Malory still frightened her, more than any other man ever had, and for no good reason that she could think of. The overall feeling she got in his presence was that he'd as soon kill you as talk to you. Which was why Danny kept her back to them both after a single glance.

Fortunately, she'd learned the phenomenon of being 'invisible' to the nobles. Mrs Robertson tried to explain it to her one night. The upper crust, living in houses full of servants, tended go about their daily lives without 'seeing' the underlings who worked around them all day, every day. Unless, of course, one of the nobles wanted something, then every single servant in the house would become visible to them again.

It was the case with these two Malorys – she hoped. And it seemed to be when she heard the elder ask as they entered the parlor, 'By the by, who is this relative of Kelsey's that I've been hearing so much about since I got to town? Didn't think she had any that I didn't know about. Is Jeremy really courting her?'

Danny sucked in her breath. That she was the subject of their conversation appalled her. She'd never get out of there unnoticed now. And the Marquis of Haverston wasn't likely to take lightly the scam they'd pulled off. He'd probably be furious with them all for duping the ton like that. Nor did James try to avoid answering.

'No, she's just one of Regan's inventions, conjured up to try to counter the Bascomb rumors.'

'Blister it, James, must you—'

'Give over, old man,' James cut in dryly. 'It's just a bloody habit, calling her that. Wouldn't hurt for you to accept the fact that she's Regina, Reggie, *and* Regan.'

'You forgot Eden.'

'Intentionally, I do assure you.'

Jason sighed. 'And that's another thing. It's high time you and Tony let up on Nick already. He's made her an exemplary husband.'

'Course he has. We'd kill him otherwise.'

Danny's blood turned cold, but Jason was apparently going to ignore that remark altogether and asked again, 'So there is no such relative?'

'No,' James replied. 'Just a wench our niece found who's much prettier than the Bascomb chit. She didn't have very far to look.'

'Prettier? I was told Emily Bascomb is a raving beauty. That was the excuse I've been hearing for why Jeremy couldn't keep his hands off her.'

'My son picks his women well, which is why you haven't heard of any more scandals from him since he finished school. I already told you he ain't touched her. You didn't need to hear it from him.'

Danny held her breath, though it still seemed as if they hadn't really noticed her. But at least James hadn't stated that the 'wench' who had been found was a mere maid. Now if she could just slowly work her way to the door and disappear for real. She started inching in that direction, still keeping her back to them.

'So her father actually went all the way to Haverston to pay you a visit?' James asked next.

'Yes, and I don't mind telling you, that was a very embarrassing conversation, particularly since I had no prior warning about these scandalous rumors that have been making the rounds.'

'Rumors the lady started herself, and all lies,' James assured him.

'Be that as it may, you know very well the damage a few rumors can do, lies or not. The girl's reputation is quite ruined now.'

James actually laughed at that point. 'When she ruined it, and deliberately, mind you? Since when do we dig strangers out of the holes they dig for themselves? This is her father's problem, not yours, not mine, and certainly not Jeremy's, who's barely even spoken two words to the chit.'

'It became our problem when it's simply her word against his.'

'Then why don't you let me see to this?' James suggested mildly.

'How? By shooting the chap?'

'Think you have me pigeonholed, do you?'

'I'm sorry. That was uncalled for.'

James nodded, accepting the apology. Danny caught that as she moved a few more inches toward the door. But then Jeremy burst into the room, having been fetched by Henry. He managed to notice her first with no difficulty and even gave her a smile that she *hoped* his relatives didn't notice.

But then he said, 'Hell's bells, I hope this visit ain't what it looks like, Uncle Jason.'

Jason Malory cleared his throat. 'Albert Bascomb came to Haverston yesterday.'

Jeremy groaned and dropped down on the nearest sofa. 'Whatever he told you, it's all lies.'

'So your father has informed me,' Jason replied.

James added for Jeremy's benefit, 'The chit has played her last card and painted the foulest picture of you, younggun, that you seduced her, promised her marriage, then tossed her aside as soon as you got what you wanted from her – and that she's now pregnant with your child.'

'I knew she was already hinting at that. But if she is pregnant, it ain't mine. I never touched the wench, never even *thought* about touching her. Not that it matters, when she's obviously convinced her father.'

'I see you already understand the gravity of the

282

situation,' Jason replied. 'And to make matters worse, Albert Bascomb was a school chum of mine. Wasn't well liked. Full of himself, if you know what I mean. He made a remarkable marriage, though. Courted a beauty in his neighborhood before she had a chance for a London season and got her to marry him. They had only the one child.'

'And spoiled her rotten. I already know most of that. Reggie's good at ferreting out that sort of information and passing it on.'

'Well, what you may not know is Bascomb, through his wife, has some very high connections.'

'So what you're saying is I'll have to marry the wench?' Jeremy said.

'As a temporary measure. After it's proven that she isn't pregnant, we'll get it annulled, of course. So you will have to "continue" to keep your hands off of her.'

Considering the turn the conversation had taken, Danny couldn't help but turn and stare at Jeremy. He looked despondent, as if he had already accepted his fate. She looked despondent as well, though she didn't know it. Jeremy married was Jeremy out of her reach, and she hadn't gotten nearly enough of him yet to satisfy her craving. Whether it was a marriage in name only or not, it still meant he'd be off-limits to her. And she wasn't about to stick around and deal with his wife, either.

James Malory didn't look despondent, he looked like hell warmed over. 'You really should have mentioned these were your thoughts on the matter before we got here, Jason. You know bloody well I won't allow my son to be thrown to the wolves, as it were. Bascomb never should have gone to you in the first place. You ain't the boy's father.'

'He probably came to me because of our prior association. And he knows your reputation. Frankly, the idea of his bringing this matter to you probably scared him to death.'

James snorted. Jeremy sighed and said, 'The problem is that Lord Bascomb is quite convinced I'm the culprit here. And he's convinced because he believes his daughter. Which is understandable. Why wouldn't he, after all?'

Danny took the moment of silence that followed that remark to blurt out, 'Then he'll just have to be unconvinced, won't he?'

'How?' Jeremy asked her, having no trouble including her in the conversation as if she'd been in it from the start. 'I've already disputed it. Fat lot of good that did.'

'The lady has based her scheme on a lie, so why don't you counter it with some lies o' your own, eh?' Danny suggested logically.

As if he'd also known she was there all along, James replied, 'How's that going to help? It's still her word against Jeremy's.'

Danny was even more nervous, having to speak to James directly, particularly since he was still frowning. But for Jeremy's sake, she got out, 'Weren't thinking o' having Jeremy do the countering. No, that wouldn't do a'tall. It's her lie against his truth, after all. But what if it were her one lie against two others – hmmm, no, make that three others for good measure?'

'What the deuce is she talking about?' Jason demanded of no one in particular.

Danny had no trouble answering the elder Malory. 'Well, it's a matter of a child now, aye? She says it's his. You know it ain't. But I'm guessing there's no child a'tall. There's no way to prove that though, is there, least not for four or five months down the road, and she wouldn't be waiting for the wedding that long, would she now? And she could always lie again later and say she'd lost the babe – after she's married to Jeremy, of course.'

'So where do these other "three" come into play?' Jason asked.

'Three other men who claim they've bedded her. She'll deny it, but even she will see that three to one ain't good odds. Can you think of three men who would lie for you, mate?' she asked Jeremy directly.

'Certainly, but – damn me, that just might work,' he said with a wide grin.

James started chuckling. 'Indeed, dear boy, especially if all three confront her at the same time, with her father present to hear it. Brilliant solution, indeed it is. Surprised I didn't think of it m'self.'

'I believe I shouldn't be hearing any of this,' Jason said with a stern look, but then gave his younger brother a barely discernible nod of approval and added, 'I'll leave it in your capable hands, James.'

'Thought you might.' James grinned.

Jason prepared to leave, but he stopped by Danny on the way out. He studied her face for a few moments, a frown growing on his brow.

He couldn't have helped notice the duster in her hand, yet he said to her, 'You are familiar to me, though I can't seem to figure out why. Have we met before?'

'Not that I recall, m'lord.'

'Worked at Edward's house, did you? Or Reggie's? Is that where I've seen you?'

'No, this is m'first time working as a maid, anywhere.'

'Odd. It's going to bother me now, till I recall where I've seen you.'

Danny was starting to get uncomfortable. She hoped she'd never robbed the bloke, but it was possible. She doubted it, though. When she used to pick pockets, she'd rarely picked men of his size, who would have had an easy time keeping up with her if she'd had to flee. And he had a presence she wasn't likely to forget.

James must have been having the same thoughts because as soon as Jason left, he said to her, and in a most derogatory manner, 'Lightened his pocket at some point in your previous career, did you?'

She blushed. Jeremy came quickly to her defense though. 'Don't start in on her. She just saved me from a marriage made in hell. I'm bloody well pleased with her at the moment.'

James rolled his eyes toward the ceiling. 'You've been bloody well pleased with her since you found her. Be that as it may, her contribution to saving your arse does deserve some praise, but you ain't saved yet. So round up your three liars and bring them to me. I'll drill them on what they're to say, and what will happen if they muck it up.' And then on his way out the door: 'But for God's sake, don't pick Percy for one of them.'

Danny was able to relax immediately after James left, even grinned at Jeremy. 'Does your whole family distrust your friend Percy?'

'Not a'tall. They love Percy, 'deed they do, they just *know* him. I've no doubt had he been at the ball last week, he would have blurted out, "Good God, Jeremy, what's your maid doing here!" '

She giggled. 'He wouldn't have.'

'Oh, he would, you may depend upon it. So we were damned lucky he was off in Cornwall for a couple of days buying new horseflesh and missed that ball.'

'Not that our performance that night did much good,' she reminded him with a sigh.

He shrugged, but he also grinned. 'Don't worry about it, luv. We might not have accomplished the original goal, but we had fun trying.'

And a lot more fun afterward, but she didn't point that out because he was already looking as if he had some of that fun on his mind now, when he should only be thinking about collecting some friends who were willing to lie for him. She hoped her suggestion would work, she really did. Jeremy would end up getting married if it didn't work. And she'd be looking for a new job.

33

Danny waited anxiously to find out how Jeremy's search had gone. When he came home that day, he didn't look discouraged, but he hadn't had much luck in rounding up three friends, at least, not on the spur of the moment. Most of his old school chums apparently didn't live in London and didn't visit often either. And he'd had only one thing to say about the young rakehells that he and Percy chummed about with who did live in London.

'Wouldn't trust a single one of them to keep his mouth shut about this matter after it's resolved.'

And that would ruin the entire scheme if Lord Bascomb heard about it later. Which was why Danny suggested, 'Then maybe you shouldn't be looking for friends, but some men who lie for a living.'

'I hope you don't mean of the criminal variety?'

She gave him a disgusted look that he'd think of that before anything else. 'No, I meant actors, of course. It's their job to be convincing in the roles they play, ain't it? So they're good at lying – well, that is, if they're any good at acting.'

'Damn me, they are, aren't they? Think I'll pay a visit to the theater district. And we should celebrate tonight, maybe a night on the town. I owe you for all these splendid ideas you've been coming up with, luv, 'deed I do.'

'I don't know about that,' she replied doubtfully, but he was already back out the door, so she wasn't sure if he'd heard her or not.

A night on the town? She had no idea exactly what that entailed, but she had a good idea she wouldn't have the proper clothes for going out with a nabob. The ball gown had been returned to Regina, only to have it returned back to her since it no longer fit the petite lady. But still, that was an outfit for only a grand occasion, not for a night of gallivanting around London.

She finished her work early that day. Nervous anticipation helped to speed her along. With nothing else to do, she offered to help Claire with her chores in the kitchen. She hoped it would improve the girl's attitude as well, since Claire had been decidedly frosty to her lately. Not that she'd ever been chummy, but still, there'd been a noticeable difference. It didn't help, though she did finally find out why Claire was displaying such dislike for her now.

As soon as Mrs Appleton left the room for a short break, after she got dinner started, Claire hissed at Danny, 'You're such a slut. I knew you'd end up in his bed. You're just too pretty.'

Danny was stunned, but only for a moment. She was too pretty? She gave Claire a critical look and finally replied, 'You're not a slouch yourself, Claire. Well, you are, but I think you try to be. Why is that?'

Not surprisingly, Claire took offense and slammed down the knife she'd been paring the potatoes with. 'None of your damn business.'

Danny shrugged and continued cutting her share of the potatoes. 'Course it ain't, but neither is what I do your business, so why'd you remark on it, eh?'

'It's wicked what you're doing.'

Danny laughed. 'In whose opinion? So I've been having a little fun with the nabob. In *my* opinion that ain't wicked as long as it's only with him. Might 'ave took me a while to figure that out, but I finally did. And it's only my opinion that counts. 'Sides, he ain't married. I ain't married. So who's getting hurt by it?'

'You will,' Claire said simply.

That sobered Danny real quick. She'd already figured out that much for herself. He'd get tired of her eventually. She hoped she'd get tired of him about the same time, but the way she felt about him, she seriously doubted she would. But she *was* going to leave in a few months, to get on with her life and to find a man who would want to marry her, not one who never wanted to get married at all.

With a sigh she said, 'I pro'bly will. But that's my concern, not yers.'

'Yours,' Claire corrected.

Danny stiffened. She'd made so many mistakes with her speech in the parlor today that having it mentioned now had been bound to set her off. 'Is every bleedin' person in this house going to correct me now?'

Claire assumed an offended stance again. 'I thought you wanted to learn proper?'

'I do, but it ain't easy, thinking every word out o' my head, you know.'

'Which is why reminders are necessary, so it becomes habit, rather than a chore.'

The logic of that was too accurate to dispute. Danny even vaguely recalled Lucy doing the same thing when she'd taught her to talk like her all those years ago. Danny just wished she didn't mess up when she got nervous or upset, but Lucy had done a good job of drumming that 'fancy talk,' as she'd called it, out of her.

'I'm sorry,' Claire added. 'I didn't mean to change the subject.'

Danny couldn't help laughing at that, considering the subject that had been changed had been what Claire called Danny's 'wicked' behavior. 'You should try being so wicked. It improves the disposition greatly.'

She'd been joking, to show there were no hard feelings, but Claire amazed her with the reply 'I did.'

'And?'

Such a long silence followed, Danny was sure Claire wasn't going to explain. But then she said, 'I got to know my last employer well, too well. It led to the worst grief imaginable.'

Danny wasn't sure what to say. Worst grief imaginable was an odd way to describe a broken heart, so maybe . . .

'Did he die?' she asked hesitantly.

Claire snorted at that. 'Don't I wish.'

Danny frowned. 'So you hate him now?'

'No, I can't really say that I do. I'm not even surprised by what he did. If I want to be completely unselfish, then I can't even say I'm sorry for what he did.'

'Blimy, what'd he do?'

Another long silence followed. Claire seemed to be fighting with herself, on whether to say any more. And the subject was obviously painful to her. Moisture had gathered in her eyes.

Danny was about to say forget it when Claire said, 'It was just one time. A mistake. It shouldn't have happened. I didn't even like it – well, not all of it. And I shouldn't have got a child from *just one time*, but I did.'

Good God, she'd had a baby and it died. No wonder she'd mentioned grief.

'Claire, you don't need to—'

'I was happy about the child,' Claire continued, as if Danny hadn't spoken. 'I didn't think I would be, but my life was an endless round of work and sleep, with nothing out of the ordinary ever happening to me. The child could have changed that, would have, too, if – if—'

Claire was crying in earnest now, though silently, large tears rolling down her cheeks. Danny didn't know whether to try to hug her, when they weren't close at all, or leave for now, so Claire could work on composing herself. Her urge was to hug her when so much grief was just pouring out of her.

Danny started to, then thought better of it again. They *really* weren't close, and Claire might take it the wrong way, might be completely offended if Danny offered sympathy. After all, the girl had given every indication of disliking her from the very beginning.

She opted instead to press more, thinking Claire might feel better if she talked about it. Maybe she'd never had anyone to grieve with her, to help her share her loss. It did seem as if she'd kept all this grief to herself.

'How did it die?' Danny finally asked.

Claire blinked and stared at her, a frown forming. 'Die? He didn't die. They stole him from me.'

Danny stared now. 'Eh?'

'His lordship didn't believe the child was his, at first. He'd scoffed and said some really nasty things that boiled down to "one time doesn't make babies." That's what I'd thought, too, but I'd found out differently firsthand. But I wasn't going to try to convince him. I didn't want him to acknowledge the child or anything like that. I was mostly worried I was going to lose my job over it. And the rest of the staff did scorn me for getting with child without a husband to show for it.'

'So you left?'

'No, I wish I had. But my aunt was still there. She'd gotten me the job, just like she did here.'

'Here?'

'Didn't you know?' Claire asked. 'Mrs Appleton, she's my aunt.'

Danny didn't know, and the two women bore no resemblance at all, so she wouldn't have guessed. But she was more interested in the girl's story and asked, 'What happened after the child was born?'

'His lordship's sisters came to see the baby. He'd mentioned it to them, you see, that I'd tried to pretend it was his. I don't know why he bothered to tell them.'

'Maybe he thought you'd go to them about it and he wanted to warn them not to believe you.'

'Possibly, though I wouldn't have. They weren't very nice ladies, either of them, so going to them about anything was unthinkable. Two bitter old maids was what they were. I avoided them whenever they visited.'

'But they came to see your son?'

'Oh, yes, and insisted he was the very image of their brother when he'd been a baby. His lordship was their younger brother, you see, much younger at that, so they'd both been around when he was born.'

'So they acknowledged him as family?'

'Yes.'

'But wasn't that a good thing?'

'Hell no. They insisted I had to give my son to them to raise. You see, their brother was getting past middle age and had never produced an heir. They'd been frantic that he never would. But I'd supplied the heir. They could stop worrying and nagging him about it.'

'So you just gave him up?'

The tears started again. 'They didn't give me any choice. They were going to claim I'd committed all sorts of crimes and get me imprisoned if I didn't turn the boy over to them and agree to never see him again.

'Could they really do that?'

'Oh, yes, very easily. Who'd believe a lowly kitchen maid against two ladies and a lord of the peerage, after all?'

'But why'd they insist you never see him again. You were his mother!'

'Because they didn't want him to know that. He's their heir. They're raising him to be an acceptable member of the ton.'

'Without a mother? Produced him out o' thin air, did they?'

'Oh, his lordship has a wife. I didn't know that, or I never would have – well, you know. But I wasn't the only one who didn't know. Don't think most of the staff did, either, she'd moved out so long ago. I assume they didn't get along well, so she refused to live with him. The sisters had mentioned she'd run crying back to her family.'

'Why didn't she just divorce him?'

'The gentry don't do that.'

'But they're going to claim the child is hers? She agreed to that?'

'The sisters can be very convincing.' And then Claire leaned forward to whisper, 'They were going to tell her that their brother would come to live with her again. I gathered she'd agree to anything to avoid that.'

'They *told* you that?' Danny asked incredulously.

'No, but they discussed it in front of me, how they were going to handle it, as if I weren't there and hearing every word.'

The invisible phenomenon again. Absolutely amazing, how that worked.

'I take it you weren't allowed to work there anymore, after that?'

Claire's lips started trembling again. 'No, I had to leave that very day and also swear that I'd never come back or try to see my baby again. He's going to have a good life, though, the best schooling, the best of everything that money can buy.'

'And to go by what you've said, a despicable family as well.'

Claire sighed. 'No, actually, they dote on him.'

'How do you know if you never went back?'

'My aunt stayed there a while more, just to see how they treated him. They didn't know she was my aunt, so she didn't have to leave when I did. She said they adore the boy, that they're completely different when they're around him, like *nice* people. Even his lordship took to fatherhood well.'

Danny began to understand that 'unselfish' remark now. 'So you think he's better off with them?'

'I know he is. What can I offer him, after all, other than the stigma of a bastard?'

Danny knew that stigma wasn't so bad, at least if one of the parents was noble. Jeremy was proof of that.

'Love?' she suggested.

'He's getting that aplenty. No, he's much better off with them. I just – just miss him. The sisters didn't show up until nearly two months after he was born. I got to have him that long and – and I wish now that I didn't. It would have been much easier giving him up if I'd never held him, or suckled him, or—'

The tears started in earnest again. Danny felt some of her own gathering. She did hug Claire this time. And she wasn't pushed away.

After their emotions settled down a little, Danny asked, 'Have you thought of doing something different for work? You don't seem to be too happy with kitchen chores.'

'I don't mind it so much. I'm just always thinking about my boy.'

'Then have you thought of having more children? That might make it easier to bear.'

'More bastards you mean?'

'No, I was thinking of marriage first.'

298

Claire snorted. 'And who'd have me?'

Danny rolled her eyes. 'No one with the way you look and act now. But you have a pretty face, Claire. There's no need to be hiding it. I've a mirror in my room that doesn't get much use. Why don't we go and see if we can't do something with your hair? It's very ugly the way you wear it in that bun. And is there something wrong with your back that makes you slouch like that?'

Claire blushed and whispered, 'No, I just have very large breasts that drew the wrong sort of attention.'

Danny burst out laughing. 'I see I'm not the only one who needs some correcting. That sort of attention doesn't have to be wrong if you handle it right. If your goal is to have more babies, then your priority is to get yourself a husband first, so do yourself up as bait and catch one.'

'I don't see you taking that approach.'

'I need to better myself before I start looking for a decent husband. I'm doing that here.'

'I wouldn't call dallying with Malory an improvement, especially if you intend to find a husband for yourself.'

'That's true, but Malory is a prime exception to anything, if you know what I mean. He's so bleedin' handsome it's purely sinful. I tried to resist him, I really did, but now that I've stopped resisting, I'm damned glad I did. He's the type of man a girl just has to enjoy if she gets the chance to, a once-in-a-lifetime type of man.'

'And it doesn't bother you that nothing will ever come of it?'

'When I have no expectation of anything other than a good time for a while? I'll be ending it m'self in a few months, if he doesn't end it first. I'll be sorry to see it end, sure, but as long as I know it does have to end sometime soon, I won't be falling on m'face with surprise when it does.'

'That's a rather open-minded way of looking at it. Most women would never see it that way, you know.'

Danny laughed. 'I ain't been a woman for that long, Claire, so how would I know, eh?'

'You're that young?'

'No, I just wore pants that long!'

34

Jeremy wasn't taking any chances where shackles of the matrimonial type were concerned. He rounded up seven actors and brought them all to his father's house that day. And he had a stroke of luck. On the way there, he caught sight of one of his old school friends passing by in an open carriage and chased him down.

Andrew, or Andy as his friends called him, Whittleby, Viscount Marlslow, had actually shared a room with Jeremy at one of the colleges he'd attended and had been his cohort in many of the antics that had gotten Jeremy suspended a time or two and, finally, kicked out of yet another school. Andy had proven back then that he could be trusted to keep his mouth shut. That was the main reason Jeremy had lasted longer at that school than the others. Andy had frequently covered for him. He was a good sort, always willing to help a friend out of a muddle.

Of medium height, blond-haired, brown-eyed,

Andrew would be considered a Corinthian if he were a little taller. A handsome chap, he was still a bachelor. He'd retired to the estate that came with his title when he finished his schooling, so Jeremy hadn't seen him since then. He preferred a hands-on approach to managing his property, loved the outdoors, to go by his deep tan. And he was due to inherit a lot more property as well as titles when his father passed on, but that wouldn't be for many years. So he *was* a prime catch. Too bad Emily hadn't clapped eyes on him first.

After Jeremy explained the situation, Andrew agreed to be one of the liars. Jeremy had had no doubt that he would, splendid sport that he was. He'd even met Emily just a few nights ago and had thought about courting her himself until he'd heard the rumors that Jeremy was.

'Didn't think I'd stand a chance against you, Jeremy. 'Deed not, so I put those thoughts away. Regrettably, though. She's a damned fine-looking gel.'

'You're welcome to her, if you don't mind that she's scheming, spoiled, and an adept liar who will apparently resort to any measures to get her way. She decided I was going to be her husband, and when I didn't pay her the least bit of attention, she began her campaign of rumors that were mild to begin with, but progressed to this latest farce that she's having my baby, when I've barely even spoken to her, much less touched her!'

Andrew seemed amused and explained why, 'My

mum used to be like that – well, not quite like that, but something of the sort. She'd spin the most entertaining tales for our neighbors, get them aghast, alarmed, on pins and needles, and be sitting back laughing to herself over their gullibility. And they never caught on. She just loved spinning tales.'

'Not quite as damaging, but . . . I suppose being forewarned would make all the difference. So, you're still interested in Emily?'

'Oh, most definitely. I'll wed her if she'll have me, so I think I can be most convincing in that regard. Think her father will insist I marry her when *I* insist the babe she's carrying is mine?'

'Now there's a thought and just deserts, since that was her plan for me. Mention it to my father. He'll be handling this particular performance.'

'Oh, I say, I finally get to meet your father? Splendid! Always wanted to, you know. Amazing reputation that man has, unparalleled in the ring, and in duels for that matter, and did you know . . .'

Jeremy listened with half an ear as they continued to his father's house. He wasn't hearing anything he didn't already know about his sire, and the amusing part was, Andrew didn't know the half of it.

And then he was met with another unexpected stroke of luck. Drew had also volunteered to be one of their liars, and he already had his story lined up. Ironically, it was no more than his usual approach where women were concerned, so for him, it was merely a matter of inserting Emily's name in the tale. So it merely remained for James to pick a third from one of the actors Jeremy had brought along.

Jeremy was looking forward to the performance that would take place at the Bascombs', but when he mentioned it, James told him flatly, 'You ain't going along, puppy. Your presence ain't required and would only give the chit an opportunity to test her own acting skills. The idea here is to surprise her enough that she blunders with her own story.'

Jeremy was forced to accept that, but bloody hell, it wasn't going to be easy waiting in the wings to find out if the plan would work. But at least Danny could take his mind off it. Indeed, when he was around her, he could barely think of anything else.

It still boggled his mind, the change in her. She enjoyed making love, no doubt about that. Once she got over her objections, it was as if she'd never had any. What bothered him was her approach to their relationship: no ties, no obligations, just mutual enjoyment. It was almost *manly* how she wanted it handled.

Bloody hell, come to think of it, it was almost identical to his own usual approach with the ladies. But for once, he didn't want it that way. He would have liked to have Danny a little more committed than she wanted to be – well, actually, a lot more. He would have liked to spend more time with her each day than she was willing to give him, and not just in bed. It was becoming damned frustrating that he couldn't, that he had to keep their relationship a secret to avoid alienating his other household servants. If she were his mistress, he could spend all the time he wanted with her, could dress her accordingly and take her out to the many places where mistresses were acceptable. But she wasn't the least bit interested in that, much to his chagrin.

But at least she was there, in his house, accessible, well, for the most part. She wasn't around though when he got home. And when he finally gave up waiting and went down to her room, he heard female laughter coming from inside telling him she wasn't alone. Bloody hell. So much for their celebrating tonight. Of course, celebrating *was* a bit premature, when he wasn't quite out of the muck yet.

35

The Bascomb town house was rather small, but then Lord Bascomb and his lovely wife came to London rarely, and many of the gentry these days were of the new opinion that letting a house sit staffed, but otherwise empty, was a waste of good servants. Of course they wouldn't admit it was a waste of good coin. That was merely an added bonus of not keeping a town residence. The new trend seemed to lean more toward renting a furnished flat if a trip to London was required, or merely staying in one of the grand hotels if the visit was brief.

Bascomb had business interests in town, which was probably why he kept a town house there. And they were putting it to good use for their daughter's come-out. And for all that it was small, it was grandly furnished with some exceptionally nice pieces and artwork. The Bascombs were rather rich, after all, just intelligently frugal.

James Malory paid his visit the next morning.

He'd sent word the day before that he was coming, so his being kept waiting, and in the small foyer no less, he found rather amusing – for a while.

Albert was at home. The butler had informed James, after letting his master know James had arrived, that Albert was quite busy, so James might wish to return at a more convenient time. James had merely sent the fellow back with the message that he wasn't leaving.

'Rather rude of him, don't you think?' Andrew remarked after twenty minutes had passed.

'Probably just an indication that this entire matter has upset him,' Drew suggested.

'I don't doubt he was upset,' James replied with some annoyance. 'Enough to hie off to Haverston and lay it all before my brother Jason.'

'Then perhaps he just feels it's already settled and would be a waste of time to discuss it further,' Andrew suggested. 'Which would again be rather rude of him not to at least say so.'

'Jason might have given him the impression that it was settled,' James allowed. 'But I highly doubt it. Jason is good at telling a man what he wants to hear, but not really telling him anything.'

Drew chuckled over that. 'Wish I could figure out how that's done.'

'With finesse, dear boy, a lot of finesse,' James replied. 'And you have figured it out, you just use it exclusively with women.'

'Ah, *that* sort of finesse.' Drew grinned.

Five minutes later James's patience ran thin and

he told the younger men, 'Come along, but wait outside the door until I call you.'

The butler, standing guard outside his master's study, thought to stop James from entering it. It was a brief thought. A good look at James and he decided to open the door instead and announce him.

Albert had been reading some document at his desk. He glanced up and then sighed at the sight of James entering the room. 'This really isn't a good time.'

'So I was informed, though I doubt any time will be a good time for this, distasteful subject that it is. But considering you took this matter to the wrong Malory, you'll make time, won't you.'

It wasn't a question by any means. Albert understood that and set his document aside. James had never met the chap before. He was rather distinguished looking, dark brown hair with lighter shades at the temples suggesting it would soon be gray. James was surprised it wasn't gray already with a daughter like Emily.

'There really isn't anything to discuss further, other than a date for the wedding,' Albert insisted. 'Have you come to supply that?'

James didn't answer. He pulled one of several chairs near Albert's desk to the side of it, so he'd have a good view of the performance when it began. It was a comfortable chair, which was a good thing. He had a feeling this wouldn't be a brief visit.

The silence unnerved the older man, enough for him to burst out, 'Now see here. I *know* your reputation and I refuse to be bullied.'

James raised a brow. 'Come now, old chap. Where d'ye get the idea that I bully? I either ignore or I – well, it won't come to that, I'm sure.'

A flush rose up Albert's cheeks. 'Then get to the point, Malory. What are you doing here?'

'Well, it's a strange thing about rumors. They tend to either titillate, amaze, or enrage, depending on one's perspective and involvement.'

'I'm aware there are rumors of a highly embarrassing nature. Whoever spread them should be shot. But unfortunately, they happen to be true.'

'I beg to differ. It's fortunate they aren't true a'tall.'

'So your son intends to deny his responsibility? That's rather cowardly—'

'You will refrain from slander, Bascomb,' James cut in. 'I tend to take that sort of thing personally.'

It was said in the mildest of tones and yet Albert still paled, but then blustered, 'This is *your* grandchild as well as mine that we are discussing.'

'If it were my grandchild, you can be sure we wouldn't be having this conversation.'

'The truth will come to light on its own,' Albert said confidently.

'Indeed it will, but it won't be the truth you're expecting, and it won't surface until it's too late. So I've brought you a few other truths to chew on.'

'Is this where you make threats and promise to kill me?' Albert demanded.

James burst out laughing, not because of the question but because it was asked so indignantly. 'I don't know what you've heard about me, Bascomb, but it was probably only half true, I do assure you. Another case of rumors not adding up, don't you know.'

'I doubt that,' Albert mumbled.

'Suit yourself. But as I was saying earlier, because of the rumors currently making the rounds, one of which has Jeremy all but married to your girl, my house was besieged this week by two outraged swains of your daughter's who weren't aware that Jeremy has his own residence now. They thought he could be found living with me. There was a third, but he *is* staying with me, unfortunately. Wife's relative. Hard to get rid of.'

There was a cough outside the door, but Albert didn't seem to notice. 'And?' he asked with a scowl.

'Well, imagine my surprise when they each insisted that they have more right to marry Emily than Jeremy does, since they got to her first.'

'Got to her? Just what are you implying?'

James lifted a brow again. 'Do I really need to get vulgar in my verbiage, Bascomb?'

The man flushed with anger, stood up, and leaned forward, his clenched fists turning white. 'If you think you can make these insinuations without the least bit of proof, Lord Malory—'

'And where is *your* proof?'

Albert flushed again, but this time because he got the point quite sharply. James let a moment pass for it to sink in more fully, that what Albert had instigated was based purely on the tale his daughter had spun.

James then said, 'I would suggest you get your daughter down here to see what she has to say for herself. Actually, I insist.'

'You insist? This subject is unthinkable for a girl of her tender years—'

'Rubbish. The subject is hers, created by her supposed indiscretion. Did you really think you could force my son to marry her and *not* have her tell her side of the tale to us? And I've brought my proof with me, all three gentlemen who claim to know her – very well.'

'And you didn't bring your son? Why not? If Emily must be subjected to this embarrassment, then I'll hear what your boy has to say as well.'

'He'll merely tell you he don't know the chit a'tall. So what is the point of hearing him say it? You are the one making demands here, Bascomb, not my family. Do keep that in mind.'

Rigidly, Albert marched to the door to tell his man to fetch Emily. Seeing the three strangers there as well, he said curtly, 'Come in. I'd prefer to hear what you have to say before my daughter arrives.'

The three filed into the room. Only Drew made himself comfortable in the remaining chair by the desk. Andrew stood stiffly to the side, while the third moved over to one of the windows for better light. Actors always worried about the lighting.

Andrew didn't appear nervous, merely anxious. James had been surprised to hear that he still wanted the chit for himself. He would have wished him luck in the matter, but luck as he saw it would be that the lad wouldn't get the conniving chit.

The actor, William Shakes – James was amused every time he said the stage name to himself – was eager to perform. He saw this as an opportunity to test his acting skills on a more personal level. The Bascombs might have seen him perform, however, and recognize him as an actor. Which was why he wasn't going to lie about who he was.

It was pushing the limit, using the chap. Rather tawdry that a lady of Emily's stature would consort with a man out of her class. But then Emily Bascomb had deliberately tarnished her reputation beyond repair, so what was one more slip here or there?

36

'Before these two coxcombs give their accounts, Lord Bascomb,' Andrew began the proceedings, 'allow me to assure you that I adore Emily and would dearly like to marry her with your approval.'

'And who are you, sir?' Albert asked.

Andrew offered an assortment of titles and connections. Albert was impressed. Even James was impressed since he hadn't heard them all himself.

Albert admitted when Andrew was done, 'Know your father. Good man.'

'Now see here,' William began his performance with a disgruntled tone. 'All those titles don't change the fact that the child could be mine. You might not find me as suitable for your daughter, m'lord, but I assure you she found me quite suitable.'

'And who are you?'

'William Shakes, at your service. I'm an actor, sir, and a damn fine one. One of my recent performances was so sterling, in fact, that I was actually invited to attend a ball several weeks ago, which is where I met Emily. We hit it off splendidly, I don't mind saying. And we managed to find an empty room upstairs to, well, I'm sure I don't need to go into details.'

Albert wasn't just embarrassed now, he was understandably furious. 'My daughter consorting with an *actor*? Utterly preposterous!'

William ignored the rage, merely shrugged and remarked, 'Hero of the moment and all that. She was determined to make my acquaintance *and* make my day, I might add,' he said with a roguish wink. 'I'll even marry her, if the child is mine. Would rather not get married just yet if it isn't. That's assuming, of course, that you'd accept me into your family. Know there are quite a few nobles who would consider me not quite up to stuff.'

'At least you understand why you shouldn't even be here,' Andrew said, glaring at William. 'She'd never agree to marry you. Her father would likely disown her if she even hinted at it.'

'But what if the child *is* mine,' William countered. 'You can't just ignore that fact.'

'Which of us sired it is rather irrelevant since it might not ever come to light,' Andrew insisted.

'How's that?'

'It could take after its mother entirely. But I'm willing to marry her and raise the child, whether it turns out to be mine or not.'

'Now that's too bloody noble even for a noble,' William sneered.

'Not a'tall,' Andrew disagreed. 'I simply want her for my wife.'

Andrew's statement had a calming influence on Albert. The older man regained some of his composure, now that the options weren't sounding so completely abhorrent. But then he caught sight of Drew, sitting there so relaxed and even grinning, and he stiffened again.

'You find this all amusing, do you?' Albert demanded of Drew.

'All this?' Drew said, shaking his head. 'No indeed. That these two fellows have been at each other's throats since they found out that Emily favored them both, well, yes, I do see some humor in that.'

'And just who are you?'

'Drew Anderson. I don't think Emily realized that I'm a member of Jeremy's family, when she batted those pretty eyes at me. Not many know that my sister married Jeremy's father. We're Americans, after all, and ship's captains, my brothers and I, so we don't get to London often. I'd just docked a few days prior to meeting Emily, so I hadn't heard the rumors yet either, that she and Jeremy – well—'

'Get to the point, man.'

'Certainly. I travel a lot, and I'm not one to turn down a pretty wench when her intentions are so obvious. I take my pleasures where I can find them, you understand. Always have, probably always will.'

315

'I suppose you're claiming the child as well?' Albert demanded.

'Hell no!'

Albert frowned. 'Then what are you doing here?'

'I'm here because although I didn't actually make love to the girl, it was damn close. We'd gone for a stroll in the garden at some party my sister drug me to and found a nice secluded spot. Another minute or so and I'd be forced to admit the child could have been mine. But we were interrupted just as I was about to . . . well, anyway, we dressed quickly and got back to the party. She promised to meet me later to finish what we started. I showed up at the rendezvous, but Emily didn't. Waited a damned hour, too,' Drew added with some disgruntlement. 'She would have been worth it. And then the next day I hear she's to have Jeremy's baby. Hate to say it, Bascomb, but I don't doubt she is with child, with the way she's spread herself around.'

Albert was red-faced with fury again by the time Drew finished. James couldn't blame him. He would never have put it quite so bluntly, whether it was true or not. Typical of Americans to be so bloody blunt.

And that was when Emily Bascomb walked into the study. She'd entered with a smile, expecting only her father to be there. Such an exceptionally pretty girl. It was too bad she was so spoiled she believed she could have anything she wanted – at any cost.

Her smile vanished at the sight of her father's rage. But when she noticed James there, her eyes flared briefly with alarm before she assumed an inscrutable look. James sighed to himself. This might not be as easy as he'd thought, if she could conceal her emotions that easily.

'I wasn't aware we had guests, father.'

'We don't. I would not by any means call these gentlemen guests.'

Andrew flushed over that remark, which caught Emily's eye. She must have decided to play the gracious lady for the moment, because she said to him, 'Lord Whittleby, how pleasant to see you again.'

'The pleasure is all mine, m'dear,' Andrew replied with an adoring look and a flourishing bow, causing the girl to give him a brilliant smile.

'So you *do* know him?' Albert demanded.

Emily frowned over her father's sharp tone. 'Well, certainly. We were introduced last week at a soiree, then again a few nights ago. I wasn't sure he would remember me,' she added coyly.

'Oh, he remembers you,' Albert said in a derogatory tone. 'And wants to marry you, thank God.'

'I'm flattered,' she began, then went very still when the rest of her father's remark sunk in. 'What d'you mean "thank God"?'

Andrew was quick to reply first, 'Whatever happens here, Emily, please be assured that I would consider it an honor to marry you.'

'Again I'm flattered, sir, but—'

'You are fresh out of "buts," Emily,' her father interrupted sharply. 'Jeremy Malory doesn't want you and denies ever touching you.'

She sighed. A bit overdone, in James's opinion. Too much dejection.

'I warned you that he would deny it, irresponsible rake that he is.' And then she turned toward James and with an owlish look, as if she'd only just noticed him there, 'Oh, I beg your pardon, Lord Malory. But then everyone knows *where* Jeremy got his habits from.'

James burst out laughing over that remark. She was on the defensive already. She'd have to be dense not to realize something had gone wrong with her plan, with her father's anger so obvious.

'Yes, I'm damned proud of the lad, particularly of the fact that he doesn't lie.'

'To *you*, maybe,' she sneered. 'But he's lied about this matter—'

'Enough, Emily,' Albert interrupted. 'Do you or do you not know these men gathered here?'

Her back stiffened again. James had a feeling that she wasn't used to having her father angry with her, that that alone was disturbing her the most. She probably didn't know how to handle it, at least, not with others present.

She glanced about the room, admitted, 'I know most of them, yes.'

'The American here?' Her father wanted confirmation.

'Well, yes, I do recall meeting him. It's hard to forget a man as tall as he is.'

'And handsome,' Drew added with a roguish grin and a wink for her.

'Fie, sir, don't be so full of yourself,' she took a moment to rejoin in the typical form of flirtation.

'And this one?' Albert asked, pointing at William.

'No, I don't believe I've ever seen him before,' Emily said mildly.

William assumed an angry pose himself. 'I like that,' he said indignantly. 'It was fine and dandy to dally with me, as long as your father never found out about it, eh? Now you're going to deny it?'

'Deny what? I don't *know* you. What else is there to deny?'

'Good God, d'you really not remember? You were a little foxed at that ball, but I've never heard of a woman not remembering something like this. Or have you slept with so many men that you can't keep track of them all?'

Emily gasped in outrage, her face flaming. William had overdone it. Getting vulgar was guaranteed to offend, true or not, so her reaction couldn't be judged merely on the statement implied.

And she turned her offended outrage on her father. 'Is this what has you upset? A stranger comes here and tells you the most outlandish lies and you believe him! And I've never been foxed in my life – well, that one time at Mama's birthday

319

party last year, but you already know about that, and no men were around.'

'Your drinking habits aren't an issue, sweetheart,' Drew put in. 'I'm not here to claim your baby is mine, though you'll have to admit it was a close thing.'

She swung around with another gasp to face Drew. 'My God, you, too? What is this, a conspiracy cooked up by the Malorys?' And then she turned to her father again, her expression imploring. 'Papa, I swear they're lying!'

'All three of them?' Albert said in a tired voice as he sat down behind his desk. 'One I could have doubted, even two, but all three?'

Emily glanced at Andrew, gave him a hurt look. 'Surely not you, too?'

He flinched at her portrayed disppointment. There was a distinct possibility that he might break down and confess all. He did still want to marry her, after all. And since *she* knew he was lying, he'd have a bloody hard time working around that if he got his wish and Albert did give her to him. However, he must have recalled that this little scenario was exactly what she'd planned for Jeremy, that they were merely throwing the same lies she'd started back at her, so she was hardly in a position to carry a grudge.

'My main concern is the child,' Andrew told her. 'Which could be my heir.'

'We *both* know it's not yours!' she snapped. 'So stop this nonsense.'

'We know nothing of the sort. I understand your need to make denials. But don't forget that I still want to marry you. I'm willing to raise the child, whether it's mine or not, and willing to overlook your' – he paused to glance at the other men – 'many indiscretions.'

Again her face flushed severely, but no embarrassment was left, only pure rage, and she turned it back on her father. 'You have subjected me to these horrible accusations, none of which are even remotely true. Can't you see what they're doing here? This is a complete farce, a conspiracy contrived by Lord Malory there, I don't doubt just to get his son out—'

'Enough!' Albert snapped. 'Don't make me any more ashamed of you, girl, than I already am.'

That had to hurt. She did draw in her breath before she said, 'So you're going to believe them instead of me?'

She managed to get some tears rolling and to look utterly devastated. Drew's expression wavered. He was sucker for tears. Andrew turned around so he'd be less affected. William rolled his eyes, recognizing a fellow performer.

Fortunately, Albert knew his daughter well and her tactics. 'I know you're capable of lying, Emily. It's a bad habit you got into growing up. And I know you do it very well. I just never dreamed you could lie about something like this that has such irreparable consequences.'

She stiffened. The anger was back so quickly, it

321

was apparent it had never left, had merely been briefly concealed for her moment of melodrama. She chose to direct that anger at James now, having decided he was responsible for ruining her plans.

'I know you instigated this, Lord Malory. But you didn't give it much thought, did you?' she said scathingly. 'I can't imagine how you thought you could pull this off, when I can prove they're all lying.'

James lifted a sardonic brow. 'And how would you do that, m'dear, when it's your word against theirs, three to one as it were – no, make that four to one, since Jeremy has also branded you a liar?'

'Jeremy be damned, I can prove it because I'm still a—'

She realized what she'd been about to say and cut herself off, but James pounced on the opening she'd supplied. 'A virgin?'

James stood up. Emily took a step back, realizing belatedly just whom she'd verbally assaulted. But James was no longer interested in the chit. She'd done exactly what he'd hoped she would.

'My apologies, Lord Bascomb, that this visit was necessary,' James said.

Albert nodded stiffly. His expression was self-explanatory. He was embarrassed over the whole affair, now that he realized to what lengths his daughter had gone to entrap a husband.

'By the by,' James added, 'in case it hasn't occurred to you yet, she's the one who started the rumors and escalated them. I wouldn't recommend shooting her, but I would recommend some discipline. The girl can't go around deciding other people's futures on a whim. My family is done with yours. See that it stays that way. After you, gentlemen,' he said to his companions.

Drew and William filed out of the room. Andrew didn't move. 'Go ahead, m'lord. I believe Lord Bascomb and I still have much to discuss. Emily's reputation still needs salvaging, after all.'

'I'll salvage my own reputation, thank you very much,' Emily snarled, and marched out of the room herself.

James lifted a brow at Andrew. The smile he got in return said Andrew was still staying. The boy must be in love, to still want the girl after witnessing her theatrics and temper firsthand.

37

Back at Jeremy's town house, Danny was upstairs dusting that morning when the screaming and shouting started. She thought there was a brawl out in the street at first, it was that kind of noise, some cheering, some shrieking. When she realized the noise was coming from directly below her, she rushed downstairs to find out what was wrong.

The commotion led her to the kitchen. Claire was there. She was holding a pot in her hand, as if it were a weapon. Carlton was there. He had a broom hefted over his shoulder. Danny would have guessed that those two were having a rather serious fight, except they weren't facing each other. Mrs Appleton was there, too, but she was ignoring the uproar, just standing at the stove adding some spices to the stew she was cooking for lunch.

Carlton was bending over, looking under the cupboard. Claire's eyes were moving wildly about the room, searching for something.

'What's wrong?' Danny asked, wondering if she should pick up a weapon, too.

'A rat got in,' Claire said. 'I found it in the pantry. It ran in here.'

'A rat? In a neighborhood like this?' Danny said doubtfully.

'Not unheard of, m'dear,' Mrs Appleton remarked with a glance over her shoulder. 'They'll go where there's food, and we have a well-stocked house.'

'And the aroma o' yer food, lass, would lure 'em all the way from the docks,' Artie, the butler, said cheerfully as he came in behind Danny.

That got a blush out of the cook. Danny was marveling over that when Claire shouted again, 'There! It's behind the dry sink.'

Carlton leapt in that direction and thrust his broom under the long piece of kitchen furniture to flush the rat out. It worked. The rodent dashed for the next nearest place to hide, the big cast-iron stove that Mrs Appleton was standing in front of. She still didn't move, was just stirring her pot of stew, which made it difficult, but not impossible, for Carlton to get his broom underneath the stove.

'Stop it,' Danny said, but no one was listening to her at the moment.

Claire was shouting suggestions and warning Carlton not to miss again – he'd gotten in one swipe of the broom when the rodent had dashed for the stove. Artie was laughing quite loudly over the footman's antics.

Danny started to give another warning, but the stove wasn't close enough to the floor for the rodent to feel safe under it, particularly with the broom swishing toward it. It ran out in the open this time. Carlton straightened and raised the broom over his head for a good whack, and Danny dove straight at Carlton, knocking them both to the floor.

'You missed the rat, Danny,' Artie snickered.

'Weren't aiming for it,' she snarled, and sat on top of Carlton's chest to keep him supine long enough for him to listen. 'He's m'pet,' she told the incredulous footman. 'You try to mill him again and I'll be coming after you with that broom, see if I don't.'

He looked up at her wide-eyed, more amazed that she was sitting on him than that she kept rats for pets. 'Didn't know he was yours,' Carlton offered.

She nodded, accepting that, was about to get off him when Jeremy walked in, having been drawn by the noise as well, and said, 'You're fired, Carlton.'

Danny glanced toward the door to see that Jeremy wasn't smiling. In fact, his expression indicated he was dead serious. 'What's he fired for?'

'For trespassing.'

That was an odd way to put it, but she understood what he was getting at. Carlton did, too, because he dropped his head back on the floor with a groan.

Danny tsked at Jeremy. 'He wasn't. I knocked him on his arse because he was trying to kill my pet.'

'Then he's fired for that, too,' Jeremy said.

Carlton groaned again. 'You ain't fired, man, so stop with the groaning,' Danny snapped as she got to her feet. She spared a glare for Artie as well, who was back to laughing his arse off.

'You actually keep a rat for a pet, Danny?' Claire finally got around to asking.

And Jeremy said now, 'Oh, good God, a rat? Carlton, you're no longer fired.'

Danny was getting quite irritated by that point. 'He ain't a rat, he's a mouse.'

'Danny, that thing was huge!' Claire disagreed. 'It can't possibly be a mouse.'

'So he's a little fat. I feed him good is all. But he's not a rat.'

'Do you even know the difference between a mouse and a rat?' Claire asked.

Danny thought about that for a moment and had to admit, 'Probably not. He's still my pet, whatever he is.' She bent down so the large pocket on her apron opened against the floor. 'Come here, Twitch.'

She hadn't seen where he went to hide this time, so it took a moment for her to see him poking his head out from under the dough box. She didn't have to call him again. The moment he saw her looking directly at him, he scurried across the floor and went straight into her pocket.

'I'll be damned,' Artie said. 'Ayep, that's definitely 'er pet.'

'Didn't know a rat could be tamed,' Claire added in amazement.

'Mouse,' Danny mumbled.

Claire chuckled. It was a rich sound. Most of them had never heard it before.

All three men were staring at Claire now. Jeremy raised a questioning brow. 'What'd you do to yourself, lass? You look – softer.'

'She's a raving beauty now, ain't she,' Carlton added. He might actually have thought so, or he might merely have been making an effort to further relieve Jeremy's jealousy.

Claire didn't blush though, probably because she didn't believe him. But she grinned and told him, 'Don't be filling my head with nonsense.'

The change in the girl really was startling, but then confidence was an amazing thing. For Claire it softened all her rough edges, allowed her to flirt and tease and not take it seriously. She'd stopped slouching, too, and she really *did* have big breasts, which was the first thing Carlton had clapped eyes on this morning when he'd seen the 'new' Claire. Getting her hair out of her face, dressing her in some of her prettier blouses and skirts that she'd buried in the bottom of her trunks, just those simple changes made her look so different, she was barely recognizable.

But confidence had finished off the new package, was responsible for the smiles, the laughter, both of which altered her expressions and showed off a pretty face. She wasn't a raving beauty by any means, was a bit on the plump side, but all in all, she was a pretty girl who would have no trouble attracting men now.

Danny was mostly responsible for cracking Claire's shell, and she was right proud of that. They'd spent hours together last night in her room, then in Claire's room, talking and laughing while they changed the way Claire looked. They'd formed a bond. Danny felt she had a close friend now and she'd realized just how much she'd missed having one since she'd left home. Someone to talk to about things that mattered. Someone to share triumphs and failures with.

'You children need to get back to work,' Mrs Appleton said, mindful that the master of the house was still there. 'You can play with Danny's pet some other time.'

Danny rolled her eyes and headed to her room to put Twitch back in his box. He must have gotten comfortable with his new surroundings, to make him go exploring farther than her room, timid as he was.

She didn't expect Jeremy to follow her, with everyone watching. She did expect to talk to him later about his burst of jealousy. That was really too bad of him, making it so bleeding obvious to the others that he was her lover. Not that any of them hadn't guessed – well, maybe Mrs Appleton hadn't – but still, he'd as much as said to Carlton, 'Get your hands off her, she's mine.'

That had been quite annoying at the time, but in retrospect, she was rather thrilled by Jeremy's display of possessiveness. Maybe he cared about her a bit more than his natural sensuality implied. Then again, maybe he got jealous over all his women.

Unfortunately, that was probably more like it. Most men did fly off the handle, after all, if another man made obvious overtures to a woman they were currently sleeping with. She'd be a fool to make more of it than what it was, just a natural male instinct.

'You don't have any other pets in here, d'you? Snakes? Spiders? More rats?'

Danny swung around to find Jeremy leaning against her open door, arms crossed, ankles crossed. So he *had* followed her. And *that* was too bad of him, too.

As for his question, she snorted at him. 'He's not a rat, just a very fat mouse.'

'If you say so, m'dear.'

'And he's a coward.'

'I believe all rats are cowards when things one hundred times their size swing brooms at them.'

She grinned. 'You're probably right.'

He moved away from the door. Danny gasped. His relaxed pose had been deceptive. She saw it now, the heat in his eyes, the intensity. She had a feeling he hadn't recovered yet from that burst of jealousy. And the hard grip of his hands as he clasped her head just before he kissed her lent proof to it.

He wasn't hurting her, far from it. He was overwhelming her though with his passion, his tongue ravaging her mouth, his hands moving down to lift her up against him so she could feel his arousal. It was almost intimidating, his aggression, but thrilling, too, that he wanted her this much. It sparked an equal boldness in her that made her press one hand against the back of his dark head while the other slid down his back, barely reaching the curve of his buttocks to press him even closer.

With a groan of pleasure, he yanked her skirt up, and somehow got his hand inside the back of her drawers, curving it under her till he could reach her moist warmth. Oh, God, his fingers thrust inside her, again, again, in and out, his wrist pressed firmly between her cheeks, his arousal grinding against her from the front. She was so overwhelmed with erotic sensations that she cried out and climaxed within seconds. If he weren't still holding her so tightly to him, she would have crumbled at his feet.

His mouth slid across her cheek to her ear, his tongue delving there as well before he said, 'I want to feed you cheese in bed. Your mouse is welcome to share. I want to pour champagne over your naked breasts and lick them until one of us is drunk. I want to drape you in fine silks and pretty baubles. I want more time with you, Danny.' He leaned back, and that possessiveness was there in his eyes now. 'Be my mistress. I promise you won't regret it.'

She couldn't think at the moment, so wasn't about to reply to something that important. But she wasn't about to send him away either, despite everyone's knowing he'd followed her here. She was too inflamed herself . . .

'You might want to close the door,' she suggested in a husky tone.

He turned to do just that, only to have Artie appear. 'Yer pa is here, and yer uncle. Don't know if they've got good news for ye. They're at each other's throat as usual, so it were hard to tell if they're bringing good tidings or not.'

Jeremy sighed, not over Artie's remark, but because he hadn't gotten the door closed soon enough on intruders. Danny's sigh was even louder. She needed to sit down. She needed a cold bath.

Jeremy didn't take that into account when he said, 'Come along, Danny. You might as well hear firsthand how your idea panned out.'

38

'And how would you have helped the situation?' James was asking his brother as Jeremy and Danny arrived in the parlor. 'You're a married man, or have you been in the doghouse so long you've forgotten that fact?'

'Ain't in the doghouse,' Anthony replied. 'And I'd never forget that I'm married to the most beautiful woman under creation.'

'Have to disagree, old chap,' James remarked. 'George is much prettier.'

'George is an American,' Anthony rejoined, as if that didn't count.

James sighed. '*Some* things have to be forgiven, don't you know.'

'Besides' – Anthony got back to the subject they'd been bickering over – 'you missed the bloody point like you *always* do. Think you do it on purpose, don't you?'

'Me? Deliberately try to annoy you? Wherever would you get that idea?'

Anthony hooted with derision. '*As* I was saying, I wasn't suggesting I should have been on hand for the performance, since, as you so aptly pointed out, that wouldn't have helped a'tall. What I was getting at was I should have been consulted before the performance.'

'Why?'

'Because he's my nephew. Because I *am* known to have moments of genius and might have contributed nicely to resolving the issue.'

James rolled his eyes. 'If we had still been stymied on a course of action, you probably would have been consulted – eventually. But we had a splendid plan, so it wasn't necessary to gather more suggestions. And *genius* my arse,' he added for good measure.

Jeremy decided that was a good opportunity to interrupt their typical bickering: '*Splendid* as in *successful* I hope?'

James glanced at his son and even smiled. 'Indeed, lad. It went very well.'

'Despite the fact that I wasn't consulted,' Anthony mumbled.

'So Emily admitted she was lying all along?' Jeremy asked his father.

'Better than that, she admitted she's still a virgin. Slip of the tongue, as it were, but then that *was* what we were hoping for. It was close though, since she did accuse us of a conspiracy against her on your behalf. *She* knew it was exactly that, but at least her father didn't, and we were able to plant the seed firmly in his mind of her lack of maidenly morals, before she arrived to deny it. We also had the added bonus that he was already aware of her tendency to lie, since she'd been doing it from childhood, apparently.'

'I can't believe it went so well,' Jeremy said, beaming with relief.

'It might not have,' James was forced to admit. 'I think your friend Andy was the deciding factor.'

'How so?'

'If he hadn't assured her father right up front that he still wanted to marry Emily, then Bascomb might not have been so easily swayed to doubt her. And had her father stood with her on the matter, then she might not have lost her temper to allow the slip.'

'Even though it was three to one?'

'Could have been ten to one at that point. As soon as she tossed "conspiracy" on the table, that put a new wrinkle in it. But the odds *were* mentioned, and that was when it got out of hand for her. So three to one was sufficient. And we know who you can thank for that.'

Danny started blushing immediately when all three pairs of eyes turned toward her. She was thrilled that her idea had worked, that Jeremy wouldn't have to marry a woman he didn't want to marry. Actually, she was thrilled because that still left him a bachelor whom she could enjoy for a bit longer. But she hated being the center of attention as she'd just become, was completely embarrassed by it.

'It weren't nothing,' she mumbled.

'Wasn't,' Jeremy whispered beside her.

She stepped on his foot. 'That, too.'

He said to his father, 'Indeed, and I'm going to buy her a kitten as a token of my appreciation.'

'You call that an appropriate gift?' Anthony hooted, turning to his brother to add, 'What *have* you been teaching the lad?'

'Actually' – Jeremy frowned thoughtfully, changing his mind – 'cats don't like rats, do they? Think I better make it a puppy instead.'

Danny stepped on his foot again, much, much harder this time. 'Don't you dare mention my pet to them,' she hissed at him.

But his father wanted to know, 'What the deuce do rats have to do with it? And for once my brother is right. A pretty trinket would be a more appropriate token, don't you think? Always worked for me.'

'Did I hear that correctly?' Anthony jumped on James's remark. 'You said I was right?'

'Put a lid on it,' James mumbled.

But Jeremy explained, after he moved away from Danny to protect his feet, 'She'd throw trinkets back at me. The wench won't accept gifts.'

'So it's like that, is it?' James said, staring at Danny. Then he said to Jeremy, 'That why she's still wearing an apron, too?'

Danny's embarrassment twisted the spike at that and she replied hotly, 'My choices are mine to make, mates. Don't be trying to tack the title *mistress* to me. I ain't one and won't ever be one. I pay my own way and will take my pleasures on my own terms.'

'Hear, hear!' Anthony cheered. 'Good God, I wish more women thought like that. They don't, you know. Come to think of it, only a man would.'

The hot blush was firmly back in place. Danny threw up her hands in disgust and stalked out of the room, snarling, 'Bleedin' nabobs.'

'Well, damn me, didn't mean to insult the chit,' Anthony said.

'You didn't,' Jeremy replied. 'She just don't like being reminded that she spent the last fifteen years or so living *and* thinking like a boy.'

'So James wasn't pulling my leg for once?' Anthony asked curiously. 'She really did pass herself off as a lad for most of her life?'

'By choice. It kept her out of a whore's shanty, is my guess.'

'Ah, so that's why.' Anthony nodded. 'Smart girl. But it must be deuced hard dealing with her, if she thinks the way you do.'

Jeremy burst out laughing. 'You don't know the half of it, Uncle Tony.'

39

Teasing Danny was sometimes detrimental to his health, so Jeremy decided to wait until the afternoon before he approached her again. Besides, that gave him time to locate a gift for her that she'd have a hard time refusing. He also had a plan to give them some time alone together, and the time of day played a part in it.

So later that day he tracked her down and found her changing the bed in one of the guest rooms. God, it was hard being near her with a bed at hand, it really was. Hot desire shot through him every bloody time. Of course, it really didn't matter if a bed was at hand or not. Danny simply had that effect on him no matter where they were.

He stood in the doorway and cleared his throat to draw her attention. She glanced at him and frowned. She was obviously still annoyed with him for bringing up their relationship in front of his relatives, had probably been saving up a good chiding for him, but whatever she'd been about to say was forgotten when she caught sight of what he was holding – in each hand.

'Oh, you didn't,' she said as she approached him and grabbed the snow-white kitten from his left hand. 'I'm not keeping it,' she added as she put the kitten to her cheek to cuddle.

'Didn't think you would' was all Jeremy said, and managed not to smile.

With her eye on the tiny puppy in his right hand, she stressed, 'I'm not keeping him either,' as she held out her other hand to take the puppy from him.

'Course not,' Jeremy agreed.

She moved back to the bed to set them both down on it. They sniffed at each other for a moment, then the puppy curled into a ball to sleep, while the kitten sat next to it and started licking a paw. They were nearly identical in size, probably no more than a few weeks old.

'I've heard they'll get along splendidly, if raised together,' Jeremy remarked, coming to stand behind her to observe the small creatures.

'You think?'

'Should work with rats, too.'

She groaned and complained, 'You're a wicked man, Jeremy Malory.'

'Thank you. I do try.'

She glanced back at him. 'Can you just say you bought them for yourself?'

'But I did!'

'Very well, then you won't mind if I take care of them for you?'

'Wouldn't mind a'tall, luv.'

She beamed at him and sat on the bed to pull the kitten into her lap to gently pet it. 'They are adorable, aren't they?'

The only thing he found adorable these days was her. Come to think of it, he hadn't even glanced at another woman since he'd clapped eyes on Danny. But to keep the mood light, since he still had his other plans to introduce to her, he merely nodded.

'As much as I'd like to dress you up for a night on the town,' he mentioned casually, 'it occurred to me that we'd need a chaperone, which wasn't part of the plan. So I settled on a nice picnic.'

'It's past lunchtime, if you ain't noticed.'

'But not past dinner, is it? And who says picnics are only for lunch? I was thinking an early dinner picnic, next to a nice pond, flowers scenting the air. Now tell me that don't sound like a nice way to celebrate? And you *do* owe me a celebration. You were single-handedly responsible for extracting me from the depths of hell. Now while you might not think that is cause for celebration, I do, and I'd much rather do it with you. So how's a picnic sound?'

'Sounds pretty nice, actually. I've never been on one. There's a pond in the city?'

'I was thinking of something a bit more secluded, where we won't be interrupted by people who recognize me. And I know of a nice spot just outside London, not far a'tall. I've already ordered the carriage brought round, and Mrs Appleton has

340

agreed to keep an eye on the babies in the kitchen till you're back. She's also got the basket of food prepared. So grab your jacket and we'll be off.'

He left the room before she could think up some reason why she shouldn't accompany him. And thirty minutes later they were leaving London behind. He'd only lied a little bit about the distance they'd be traveling. The pond he had in mind was near an inn more than an hour away. His father usually stayed the night there on his way back from Haverston if he got a late start. And having an inn nearby was crucial to Jeremy's plans, since he hoped to be spending the night in it with her.

But she didn't really notice the time it was taking them to get there, since she'd never ridden up on the driver's perch of a carriage before and was enjoying the unobstructed view. He also kept up a steady stream of light conversation, telling her how he'd gone through hell and back trying to find those two pets for her, when in fact the kitten was from a litter at Reggie's house, and the puppy from a litter at Kelsey's house, the ladies having mentioned them when they'd taken him furniture shopping.

The pond really was a beautiful setting at that time of the year, flowers in a myriad of colors dotting the landscape around it, several ducks floating about in it, one with a small train of three ducklings following it. And Mrs Appleton had outdone herself on such short notice: the food was varied and delicious, with several bottles of wine included.

They ate, they laughed, they even had some meaningful conversation. Despite Jeremy's wanting to keep the mood light, goals somehow got mentioned, and Danny grew serious when she admitted, 'I had a goal many years ago, one that was unrealistic though, since I had no way to accomplish it.'

'What?'

She was lying on the blanket they'd spread out near the water, her head resting on his thigh. In one hand she had the stem of a daisy that she was lazily twirling about, her wineglass in the other.

'I wanted to get the younguns into a more stable environment.'

'The ones who lived with you?' he asked, his fingers casually moving through her curls.

'Yes. I had sorely felt my lack of schooling, so I figured the other children did, too. I wanted to get them that, get them supplied with a steady flow of food, too, so they wouldn't have to steal anymore.'

'Sounds like you wanted to set up a real orphanage for them.'

His fingers moved down to her cheek, and then on to her earlobe and her neck, his touch still casual. He noticed her shiver though and drop the daisy without noticing. And it took a moment for her to answer him.

'Well, I was too young at the time to have figured

that out. It was just a goal I had for a year or two,'
she ended with a shrug.

Jeremy was hesitant to mention it, but did anyway. 'Would you let me set something like that up
for you?'

She frowned. 'You mean you'd pay for it?'

'Something like that.'

'That'd be a gift, wouldn't it? With a really big
"beholden" factor. No, it ain't your goal. It was
mine, but even now, I still don't see how I could
accomplish it, not on a maid's wages.'

He coughed and said, 'I *could* raise your wages.'

She laughed at that point. 'Not unless you're
going to raise everyone's wages, you won't. You
snuck in one gift on me, mate. I'm going to let it
pass, but don't be doing it again, eh?'

He reached for her empty hand, brought it up to
his mouth so he could nibble on her fingers.

'You make it deuced hard, luv. You see, I have
this overwhelming urge to give you things.' He
drew one of her fingers into his mouth and sucked
on it for a moment. 'I don't know why. Never been
plagued with such an urge before.' He bit the pad
of her second finger. 'And it's rather frustrating –
no, actually, *very* frustrating, come to think of it.'

She was looking up at him now, said a bit
breathlessly, 'You've got nothing o' the sort.'

'And how would you know, when you've
probably never had such an urge before?'

'Actually I have,' she admitted. 'Every time I
used to see something I wanted, I always thought

to m'self, Lucy would probably like that, too. Of course, that was because I care about her. She has been like a mother, a sister, and a best friend to me. So what you're trying to tell me in your odd nabob way is that you care about me?'

'Oh, good God, if you haven't figured that out yet, I think I'll throttle you. Better yet . . .'

He dragged her up until she was lying in the crook of his arm and lowered his mouth to hers, tasting her deeply, thoroughly, with a passionate urgency he could not control. He loved tasting her, loved touching her, feeling her trembling in his arms as she was now. He began unfastening her blouse, but his finesse and his patience were deserting him, and he cupped her breast through the cloth instead. She put her hand on his cheek. That inflamed him further, but her groan . . .

Using every ounce of willpower he possessed, Jeremy pulled his mouth away from hers. 'Damn! If it weren't for the promise of a comfortable bed at the inn near here, I'd make love to you right here on the grass. I think it's time to leave, luv, I really do.'

40

It was nearly fully dark by the time they packed up the remnants of their picnic and got back into Jeremy's carriage. What little remained of the setting sun was hidden behind a thick bank of clouds and the trees along the road. If it weren't for those trees, which acted as a kind of fence, they might not have stayed on the road, since the carriage wasn't designed for country jaunts, at least not at night.

The well-lit inn was a beacon though, off in the distance, and when they finally reached it, Jeremy relaxed again. He didn't mention what *could* have happened out on the road, where highwaymen prevailed at night, where the slightest wrong turn could have ended them in a ditch. Sleeping in an open carriage alongside the road would have been a rotten way to end a most enjoyable day.

Arm in arm, they went upstairs to their room. Danny hadn't questioned why they would be staying at an inn instead of returning to London.

Nor did she question why he'd ordered just one room for them both. She probably understood about the dangers of the road, but as for the single room, either she was as eager for some lovemaking as he was, or she figured it wouldn't matter out here in the country where no one knew them.

Which wasn't exactly the case. The innkeeper recognized Jeremy and called him by name. He had been a guest there enough times over the years for the man to remember him. One of the other guests in the common room recognized him as well, or seemed to. Actually, the fellow was staring at Danny, and with an expression that indicated he was seeing an angel – or a ghost.

But the couple didn't notice, and again Jeremy's finesse went right out the door the moment he closed it behind them. Lighting the lamps could wait. Undressing fully could wait. Jeremy fairly tossed Danny on the bed and was kissing her so deeply, she wouldn't have been able to get in a word of protest. But she wasn't protesting in the least. In fact, he wasn't sure which of them was the more heated with desire.

Danny found Jeremy's lack of control incredibly erotic. He tore out of his coat and tossed it. She'd been carrying hers and dropped it when he tossed her on the bed. He ripped open the cuffs of his shirt and merely pulled it over his head. She quickly unfastened her blouse, afraid he'd rip that open next if she didn't. Her chemise he merely pulled down, then he gripped both her breasts and buried his head between them with a groan, suckling one until she cried out for mercy. His mouth, so hot, trailed up to her neck and kissed and sucked her there as well. Then he moved to her ear, where he rasped out, 'Touch me. I love it when you touch me.'

He rolled over and sat her on his loins to give her better access to him. Her hands moved over his chest, pinching his nipples lightly. He groaned when she bent down to lick one and became so aroused that he nearly unseated her. Yanking her skirt up out of the way, he slipped his hands inside her drawers and gripped her derriere, grinding her loins against his. But it wasn't enough for her, it was a mere tease. She wanted him inside her, hard and hot and buried deep. She couldn't wait any longer.

Her mewling said so. His hand gripped her hair, leading her mouth back to his as he rolled them over again, his other hand taking her drawers off as he did. And then she had her wish, he was inside her, such heat, driving hard to her depths, and she exploded around him, sucking him in even deeper, her cries of pleasure lost beneath his lips, continuing as he thrust again and again, until his own cry ripped through the room.

Jeremy's heart was still pounding hard. Without a doubt, that had been the most spectacular climax of his life. So that's what happened when anticipation built for hours upon hours?

No, he'd experienced anticipation before. It had

347

never been like this. It was Danny. For some reason, she was affecting him like no woman ever had before. And it wasn't just the lovemaking. This wanting to be with her, every minute of the day, when he knew bloody well he couldn't, was such a keen frustration, he wasn't sure how to deal with it.

Jeremy was loath to move away from her even for a moment, but he finally finished undressing. He even got up and lit some lamps since the hour was still early and he wasn't the least bit tired yet.

'We didn't bring anything to sleep in,' Danny pointed out as he rejoined her on the bed.

'Yes, we did,' he said, pulling her close to him again. 'I don't know about you, but I'm sleeping in your arms. You're welcome to try sleeping in mine.'

'If you think that will work, I suppose I'll trust your judgment.' She curled into him to get comfortable. 'It feels odd, being at an inn when I'm not here to rob the guests.'

He chuckled. 'I don't need to lock you in, do I? You can restrain yourself for the duration?'

'I'm considering it. Guests get noisy, after all, when they find out they've been robbed. Don't think I'd care to be awakened by the commotion.'

She said no more. He waited nearly a minute before he lifted his head to see if she was grinning. She wasn't, not even a little.

'You *were* joking, weren't you?'

'Course I was, mate,' she assured him. 'But

348

while we're on the subject of restraint, you need to be practicing some of your own.'

'Bite your tongue. You hold me off enough as it is. Any more and I will go quite insane.'

She snorted. 'No, you won't, and I didn't mean that kind of o' restraint. I meant your jealousy.'

'Jealousy!' he exclaimed, then added indignantly, 'I've never been jealous in m'life.'

'Then what'd you fire Carlton for this morning, eh?'

'Oh, that,' he said with a shrug. 'That was – well, that was, hmmm, I'm not sure what the bloody hell that was, but it certainly wasn't—'

'It was. *And* it was silly. You didn't even pause to find out why I was sitting on him before you fired the poor man. You might as well trust me, Jeremy, because the only way this works for us is for it to *only* work for us. See my point?'

'Not in the bloody least.'

She released a long sigh. 'I've made an exception for you. If I start making love to every Tom, Dick, and Harry, then I'll have turned into what I swore I'd never be. So there won't *be* any other man for me. When we're done, I'll wait for marriage to some bloke, but I won't be testing the waters first, if you catch my drift.'

He pulled her closer. 'Danny, luv, I seriously doubt "we'll" ever be done.'

She didn't reply immediately. He found himself holding his breath until she said, 'Unless I get offered a better job.'

He sat up. She pushed him back down. 'I was joking, mate. Cor, learn the difference, eh?'

He frowned. 'I believe I know the difference, and you weren't joking in the least. What job would tempt you away from me?'

Again, it didn't seem as if she was going to answer him, but finally she sighed and said, 'Wife and mother. I've made no bones about it. I want my own family. You've already got a family, a large one, so you have no hankering for a new one. But I'll be moving on eventually to accomplish my goals.'

He held her to him, tighter than necessary. He didn't like being reminded of her goals, but her 'eventually' could be years off, might never even arrive, so he wasn't going to worry about it now, while their affair was progressing nicely.

A while later he confessed, 'I'm not sure how I'm containing how happy I am just now.'

Danny had been drowsing off, but hearing that definitely woke her up. She leaned up to stare at him. 'Are you really?'

'Wouldn't have said it if I wasn't. But I do wish you'd start sharing my bed at home. It's not as if the staff doesn't know I've staked a claim. I made that perfectly clear this morning, didn't I?'

Her eyes narrowed on him. 'If you tell me that silliness was deliberate, I may just pinch you – hard.'

'Well, no, not deliberate a'tall.' And then he grinned. 'But it worked out rather well, don't you think?'

'I think we better leave things as they are. You keep trying to turn me into a mistress. Stop it. I've told you my terms. Equal all the way.'

'Yes, but what's that got to do with sleeping together nightly? *Sleeping*, Danny. I truly do love just holding you in my arms.'

She smiled at him and snuggled back down. 'This is kind o' nice, ain't it? I'll have to give it some thought.' And then as she drifted off to sleep a bit later, she mumbled, 'You make a nice nightgown, mate, 'deed you do.'

41

An inn wasn't a good place to do it. Tyrus came to that conclusion when midnight rolled around but the lights were still on in the girl's room. He still couldn't believe he'd found her again, after he'd lost hope that he would. He'd been so confident, after visiting the nabob, that he'd get the job finished this time. Then to find she wasn't where he'd thought she'd be, where he'd seen her go the day he'd followed her. She'd been kicked out and they didn't know where she'd gone. And London was too bloody big to just hope he might run into her again, so he'd given up.

He hadn't gone back to tell the lord though, didn't want to own up that he'd failed yet again. But he'd found her again! And he wasn't going to lose her this time; he was going to finish the job tonight.

He'd figured he'd have a few hours' wait, so he'd swiped a bottle of rum out of the innkeeper's stock to take up to his room. He hadn't figured the couple wasn't there to sleep. He should have though. The girl had turned into a prime piece, just like her mother. And the gent she was with had had his hands all over her.

Still, they had to sleep sometime. He doubted they'd head back to wherever they came from in the middle of the night. So he waited, and waited. Every ten minutes or so he'd open his door just enough to see if the light was still coming from the crack under hers.

It was too bad the girl was with a Malory. That family was so notorious, even he'd heard of them. That they were all bloody lords wasn't the problem, but rather that they weren't men to cross. Prime shots, he'd heard, masters at dueling, masters at fisticuffs – masters at evening scores. So he'd try not to hurt the bloke, just hit him enough to knock him out.

With his rotten luck, he'd probably kill Malory, too. But not if he killed the girl first. As soon as she was dead, he'd have his luck back.

Danny had the dream that night, the bad one. She shouldn't have. It had only ever plagued her when she was nervous about something, frightened, or just plain uneasy, none of which applied that night. But it woke her, as it usually did, when the club swung toward her head.

After a single shiver to shake the dream off, she turned to move closer to Jeremy. For once, she had someone to gain comfort from. Not that she thought to wake him. Just being near him, touching him, was comfort enough.

But she was awake enough now to have no trouble hearing the soft rap on the door and the woman's voice asking, 'Jeremy, are you there?'

Danny stiffened. A number of things ran through her mind, none of them nice. And she was none too gentle in shaking Jeremy awake to hear about it.

'What?' He sat up immediately.

'There's a wench at the door calling for you,' Danny fairly snarled.

'The devil there is. Were you dreaming?'

And outside the door again: 'Jeremy, I hear you in there. Are you decent enough for me to come in?'

'Oh, good God,' he said now in surprise. 'Amy?'

'So you *do* know her, eh?'

Danny's tone was angry enough that he guessed, 'It's not what you're thinking. That's my cousin.'

'Sure it is,' Danny said as she put both feet to his backside and kicked him out of the bed.

'Blister it,' he said, gaining his balance before he landed on the floor. 'It really is.'

He flicked a match to relight the lamp by the bed. Danny's gasp drew his eyes back to her, and then to the man she was staring at. He looked just middle-aged, though his hair was pure gray and long, clubbed back with straw. Straw? He was tall, skinny, and dressed like a beggar, his clothes threadbare and riddled with holes.

The man had frozen where he stood when the

match flared to life, several feet away from the edge of Danny's side of the bed, looking as amazed as they were. He had a club in one hand and a pillow in the other, which he had probably intended to use to stuff their belongings into. He had liquor fumes coming off him, an indication that he wasn't thinking clearly.

'Amy!' Jeremy called out. 'Get back from the door, because I'm about to throw something through it – unless you have a gun, in which case you can come in and use it.'

'I don't carry guns,' the woman called back. 'Warren does, though. He's putting our horses in the stable. He'll be here in a moment.'

Jeremy was already on his way around the foot of the bed to get to the intruder. The mention of guns had put some panic in the man's eyes and had him leaping across the bed to get to the door and out of there. Danny caught hold of one of his feet as he shot over her. She lost her grip though, with the momentum he'd gained. It did cause him to tumble headfirst to the floor on the other side of the bed, but he didn't stay there. Fast for his age, he scrambled to his feet again and ran out the door.

Jeremy charged after him, with no thought for his nakedness. Danny quickly got her skirt and blouse on so she could follow. The door was still wide open. The woman in the hall didn't try to peek in through it. If she really was Jeremy's cousin, then she was probably standing out there with her back turned.

Jeremy came back just as Danny finished dressing. He looked nothing but disgruntled, which started her laughing.

'What the deuce are you laughing at?' he asked, his tone as annoyed as his expression.

It was such a comedy of errors, on everyone's part, she couldn't help it and said, 'You just chased that thief down the hall buck naked.'

'And scandalized me!' Amy called out in an indignant tone from the hall.

'He would have been gone if I'd grabbed my pants first,' Jeremy pointed out logically.

'So chasing him naked helped?' Danny asked. 'You caught him?'

'No,' Jeremy mumbled. 'He took the quick way down the stairs, tumbled the lot of them, and damned if he didn't get right up and keep on running. I draw the line at scampering about the countryside naked, thank you very much, particularly without my boots on.'

'Never mind boots, have you got your pants on yet?' Amy asked.

Jeremy rolled his eyes and reached for the pants Danny was holding out to him. A few moments later he said toward the door, 'Get your arse in here, puss, and tell me what the devil you think you're doing, banging on my door in the middle of the night?'

Amy poked her head around the opening now, and seeing that he was at least halfway decent with his pants in place, she came in and said huffily, 'I didn't bang. I was very quiet about it, I'll have you know.'

'She was, too,' Danny added, sure now that the woman was his cousin.

It was the tone he'd used, and what he'd called her, that had convinced Danny. But seeing the woman now left no doubt whatsoever. She bore the same midnight black hair as Jeremy, the same deep cobalt blue eyes with the slightly exotic slant to them. She was stunningly beautiful, too. Was their entire family like that?

'What are you doing here, Amy?' Jeremy wanted to know. 'For that matter, when did you and Warren get back to England?'

'We sailed in this afternoon, or rather, yesterday afternoon. And I got this feeling—'

'Good God, never mind,' Jeremy cut in with a groan. 'Forget I asked. I don't want to hear about it.'

'Oh, be quiet,' Amy said as she got comfortable in one of the upholstered chairs the room offered.

Jeremy looked about the room for his shirt, since he'd sent it flying when he'd taken it off. He was trying his best to ignore his cousin. Danny sat down on the bed, having a feeling she wouldn't be getting back to sleep anytime soon.

'We docked this afternoon, or rather, we rowed in. Warren's ship is probably *still* waiting for docking permission. But as soon as my feet touched the dock, I got the strangest feeling that you were in some sort of trouble. So we went straight to Uncle

James's house, only to find out you'd acquired your own residence while we were gone, so you weren't there. By the by, how are you liking that?'

'Splendidly, thanks. You didn't tell my father about your feeling, did you?'

'No, no, I managed not to. But then we expected to find you at your new town house. Was quite annoyed to hear you'd gone off for the day. But at least you had the presence of mind to tell your housekeeper where you were going, in case you were needed.'

'What sort of trouble, Amy?'

'Nothing specific, and actually, it leaned more toward danger than trouble. You weren't planning on tackling anything of that sort, were you?'

'Anything dangerous? No, nothing like that on the agenda this week.'

She gave him a sour look for the dry reply. 'Don't scoff at this. You know my feelings are *never* wrong. I wouldn't have dragged Warren out here when we'd only *just* got home if it were just a mild feeling—'

'Course you would have.'

She tsked over his interruption and continued, 'But this was a strong feeling. She's not planning on killing you or anything like that, is she?'

Danny blinked, since the woman was looking directly at her as she said it, and quite suspiciously at that. Jeremy started laughing.

'She kills me with pleasure, but other than that, no,' he got out between chuckles. 'This is my –

friend, Danny. Danny, meet my imp of a cousin, Amy.'

'Is that what they're calling it these days?' Amy said, rolling her eyes.

'I wasn't painting it up nicely,' Jeremy insisted. 'She refuses to be my mistress, refuses to be my lover, for that matter. She'll only be my friend. Well, and my maid. Insists she earns her own keep.'

Amy smiled at Danny, 'How refreshing. A servant who doesn't jump at the chance to laze about. Nice to meet you, Danny.'

Danny nodded curtly. She didn't like being discussed in such frank terms. And it was the first time *she'd* heard that Jeremy considered her a 'friend.' She wouldn't exactly call him that, but then, what would she call him, when he was much more than just her employer? Partner in love-making? Cohort in pleasure? Was there even a name for their particular relationship?

'Nothing is amiss, puss, other than your arrival interrupted our getting robbed,' Jeremy went on to assure his cousin.

'So that's what that was about?'

'Yes. Not exactly a dangerous occurrence, since the chap was only carrying a club. But you *did* interrupt it, so I'll wager that's what your feeling was about.'

Amy looked doubtful for a moment, but then conceded, 'I suppose he might have awakened you, there could have been a scuffle, which you could

359

have gotten hurt in. Yes, I suppose that could have been it.'

'Does that mean we can get some sleep now?' Warren said as he came through the doorway.

'Welcome home, old man,' Jeremy said, giving his cousin by marriage a jaunty smile. And to Danny, he explained, 'This is the second Anderson to have married into the family, the first being his sister, George—'

'Georgina,' Warren corrected by habit.

'Who married m'father,' Jeremy continued. 'Warren used to be the most bitter man alive, now he's one of the happiest, thanks to my cousin here.'

Amy stood up and made a flourishing bow. 'I do take all the credit.'

Warren was extremely tall. Danny didn't see much of his brother Drew in him, except for the height and the golden brown hair the men had in common. Warren's eyes were a lime green and filled with warmth when he glanced at his wife.

'This is my friend Danny,' Jeremy introduced again.

'Another male name?' Warren replied with a shake of his head. 'What is it with you Malorys and your propensity for giving your women manly nick-names?'

'This one wasn't my doing.' Jeremy grinned. 'It's her actual name, though *I* think it's short for Danielle.'

'It ain't,' Danny mumbled.

'And how would you know when you can't remember?' Jeremy countered.

'I just know,' she insisted.

Her terse tone prompted Warren to say, 'I believe we could all do with some sleep.'

'You got us a room?' Amy asked.

'Across the hall.'

'Splendid,' Amy said, and to Jeremy: 'We'll see you in the morning then. We can ride back to the city together. And I want to hear everything that's been happening while I've been gone.'

Warren pulled his wife out the door before she could think of anything else to say and closed it behind them. Jeremy joined Danny on the bed again.

'Are you all right?' he asked carefully.

'Why wouldn't I be?'

'Well, I assume you aren't used to being on this end of getting robbed. Not all that pleasant, is it?'

'Don't be censuring me on what I was forced to do all these years. I never liked stealing. I hated it.'

'But you did it anyway.'

'I come from the slums, mate. D'you realize how few choices women who can't read or write, who can't even talk proper, have?'

'I see why you have such an aversion to that "word,"' he replied, careful not to say it.

'Well, that *is* what most of them end up doing, whoring or stealing.'

He put his arm around her shoulders. 'That's not what has you upset at the moment. Admit it.

361

Being the victim has you realizing how all your victims must have felt.'

She rolled her eyes at him. 'Not even close, mate. And we didn't get robbed, nor would we have. I was awake. I would've heard that bungler tiptoeing about the room if I didn't hear the knock on the door first, or I would've smelled him. He reeked of rum, if you didn't notice. He was doomed to fail. A good thief knows better than to steal when he's foxed.'

'Very well, I give up guessing.' He sighed. 'What turned you sour?'

'I ain't sour. I just realized, listening to you, that we have no definition, you and me. You called me your friend, but you paused before you said it. You don't really think of me that way, now do you?'

'Well, if you consider the definition of *that* word, then, yes, I do. What is a friend if not someone you feel close to, someone you like being with, someone you can confide in and share pleasures with.' He grinned wickedly. 'Of course, not the sort of pleasures *we* share, but you get the idea. Now we ain't best friends – yet. But we're getting there.'

She was surprised, asked him, 'You ain't pulling my leg, are you?'

He pushed her back on the bed so he could lean over her. 'I will never joke about *us*, Danny. Now, I haven't done much confiding, other than things you could have heard from anyone. So here's a little tidbit for you. Amy *is* my best friend, and you'll be seeing a lot of her, since she visits often –

when Warren isn't dragging her off to America. I'd like you to get to know her better. You'll like her. Actually, you can't help but like her. She's a sweetheart. Just never bet with her, over anything.'

'Why?'

'Because she never loses.'

'She's that lucky?'

'No, she's that gifted. It's those "feelings" she gets. She's never wrong about them. So consider yourself warned in advance. If she wants to bet with you about something, run the other way.'

42

Jeremy had been right about Amy Anderson. It was impossible not to like her. She was vivacious, refreshingly frank, funny, and capable of an endless stream of chatter. Danny sat in the carriage next to Amy while Jeremy drove them back to London, and Warren rode his horse alongside. Somehow, Amy had managed to get Danny's entire life story out of her, all that she could remember anyway, including her goals. And Amy hadn't been surprised in the least, merely interested. Amy did cast a few glances at Jeremy's back, and Danny had to wonder if he was listening. But he never joined the conversation, so she doubted it.

They were approaching the outskirts of London when Amy suddenly said, 'We're being followed.'

Jeremy stopped the carriage immediately, proving he had been listening all the while, though Danny hadn't said anything he didn't already know about.

'Who?' Jeremy asked his cousin, then realizing

she couldn't possibly know that, he asked instead, 'They mean us harm?'

Danny was about to point out Amy couldn't know that either when the lady replied, 'Most definitely.'

Danny became distinctly uncomfortable at that point, as Warren rode off to see if he could ferret out anyone behind them, or hiding alongside the road. She'd had the same feeling, that someone was following, but she'd discounted it, since she'd felt it more than once since moving uptown, and nothing had ever come of it. But with Amy having the same feeling, and since her family certainly didn't doubt her, Danny wondered if she should mention that this wasn't the first time.

She held her tongue. It simply couldn't be related. The two times she'd felt she'd been followed in the city had no doubt been due to that thug Lucy had told her about, the one who'd been trying to find her. Whoever was following them now would have nothing to do with her, was probably just some highwayman who'd missed his chance to stop them before they got too close to the city.

Sure enough, Warren came back shaking his head, having found no one. And Amy relaxed again, announcing, 'The danger has passed. I do believe you scared them off, Warren, whoever they were.'

They continued on their way as if nothing out of the ordinary had happened. Danny was amused.

The two men took Amy's pronouncements as gospel. She said they were no longer in danger and so they thought nothing else about it.

Jeremy merely dropped Danny off at home before he took Amy home. He mentioned that he probably would be late getting back, since he had some business to attend to, something about carpenters he had to hire for one of his uncle's properties that needed renovations.

Danny got right back into her cleaning routine as if she hadn't spent the night out with the master of the house. The house hadn't picked up much dust while she was gone though, so she finished her work before dinner. Jeremy returned about that time and interrupted her dinner with a summons to the dining room where he was having his.

'Have a seat, luv. Have you eaten yet?'

'I was eating.'

'Fetch your plate then and join me.'

She'd sat down next to him. She wasn't getting back up. 'You know that ain't proper.'

He sighed. 'I won't keep you then. Just wanted to let you know I'll be gone for the weekend.'

She sighed now. 'You know you don't have to keep me apprised of your schedule.'

'Why are you throwing up a wall between us again? I thought we agreed we were friends. And friends do tell each other what they're up to.'

She looked down to avoid his gaze. Was she doing that? Trying to put more space between them in preparation of her leaving? Probably. It

366

wasn't going to be easy to walk away from Jeremy Malory. But the sooner she did so, the less it would hurt.

To put off that unpleasant thought, she said, 'So what are you up to, mate?'

'Aside from the Crandle house party, I'm up for anything *you* have in mind.'

'Crandle? Ain't that where Percy got fleeced?'

Jeremy didn't answer. He stood up, came around behind her chair, and drew her to her feet as well. And before she knew what he was going to do, he was kissing her so deeply her toes curled. She didn't know how long he continued to do so. Every single thought went right out of her mind as it usually did when she tasted him.

She wrapped her arms around his neck and kissed him back. And then he was setting her back from him, and she didn't have to guess that he was angry.

She hadn't sensed it in the kiss, but it was definitely there in his expression as well as his tone when he warned, 'That's going to happen every time you play at indifference with me. Don't do it again. I bloody well don't like it.'

She hadn't been pretending indifference about his plans for the weekend, she'd been desperately trying to ignore what he made her feel every time she got near him. Which was pretty pointless. She should have realized that by now.

Annoyed with herself *and* with him now, for the way he chose to get his point across, she stabbed a finger in his chest. 'I wasn't pretending anything. I was trying to keep from pouncing on you and dragging you off to your room. I thought you'd want to finish your dinner first.'

He blinked at her, then burst out laughing. 'God, no, you can pounce on me anytime you like, dear girl.'

She snorted. 'Sit down, mate. The impulse has passed. And you can tell me why you're going to a party where Lord Heddings is likely to be.'

He tsked, but took his seat again. 'Because he *is* likely to be there, of course.'

She frowned. 'You're going to try to catch him stealing, aren't you?'

'Certainly. Aside from what he did to Percy, the man stole from my family. If I don't see to his apprehension, then m'father is going to step in and kill him. In the end, I'm sure Heddings would prefer my approach.'

She rolled her eyes at him, *hoping* he was just exaggerating about his father. 'Did it occur to you that he might not work alone? That he might employ others to do the stealing for him?'

'You're thinking like a thief, m'dear. Think like a lord instead—'

'Exactly. Would a lord really risk doing the dirty work himself when he could hire others to do it and just sit back and rake in the spoils? I mean, the man employs servants who walk around with pistols in the middle of the night. That should tell you something.'

'That was deuced odd, wasn't it?'

'More like a normal butler used to blokes of the nasty sort showing up at all hours of the night – ourselves excluded, of course,' she thought it prudent to add.

'Naturally. But I hope not. I'd prefer to catch him red-handed. Much more satisfying.'

She sighed. 'You'll be careful?'

'Aha!' he pounced immediately. 'Finally going to admit you worry about me, eh?'

'Not a chance, mate,' she grumbled. 'It's my wages I worry about.' Then she teased, 'Maybe you should pay me before you leave for your weekend party.'

'No, but I'll make *you* pay for that remark.'

He did, too, most pleasantly.

43

Danny had left the lamp in her room burning low for the pets. She'd taken them to bed with her, but didn't expect them to sleep the night through with her, so she wanted them to have a little light if they wanted to play a bit before settling down again.

It was the kitten's tail, swishing against her cheek, that woke her from the dream, though not soon enough. She relived it once again, the club falling toward her head, then the burst of pain. It hurt. She'd never had pain in her dream before, just the memory of it . . . oh, God, she wasn't dreaming.

He swung the club again. She saw him clearly, a middle-aged man, gray, straggly hair, and then she saw another image of him, younger, black-haired, with the same dark eyes filled with deadly intent. He was the man who'd hurt her before, the one who'd disrupted her life and stolen her memories. She hadn't recognized him at the inn, but it was so clear to her now that he was the man from her past. And he was still trying to kill her . . .

She couldn't move far with the covers hampering her, but she got out of the way of that second swing of the club, heard it slam against the pillow next to her head. She fought with the covers to get her feet loose, didn't think she could avoid the next swing unless she rolled out of the bed. But she was afraid she'd be even more tangled then, helpless, so her only real chance would be to fight him and wrest the club away from him.

She turned back to try to intercept the next swing, but Jeremy was suddenly there and tackling the man to the floor. He punched him, again and again. She'd never seen Jeremy like that. He seemed determined to kill the man with his bare fists.

'I don't think he feels that anymore,' she said.

Jeremy glanced back at her. He'd been holding the man off the floor by his collar, so each blow would land squarely on his face. He let him fall now and came to her side. He lifted her face, examining it intensely.

His voice held a frantic note as he demanded, 'Where'd he hit you?'

'My head, but I think I deflected the worst of the blow with my arm when I raised it to move the kitten away from my cheek.'

He inspected her head now, found the small lump forming. She winced as he touched it, but said nothing. It was starting to throb, though not extremely. Her forearm actually hurt more.

'The skin didn't break,' he told her. 'You'll probably have a bit of a headache though for a day or two. We should have some ice in the house to put on that. I'll have Artie fetch some after he gets rid of the trash.'

He went to the door to shout for their butler, but came right back to the bed and finally sat down next to her so he could gather her in his arms.

'I don't believe what just happened,' he said. 'You're all right, though, right? Tell me you're all right.'

'I'm fine. But how did you know he was here?'

'I didn't. Some noise woke me, probably him robbing the rooms upstairs. But once I was awake, I thought of you all warm and cozy in your bed and decided my bed was rather lonely. Amy must have been right. He followed us from the inn.'

'He followed *me*,' Danny corrected. 'If he was upstairs, it was to find me. He's the same man who tried to kill me when I was a child, the same one who killed my parents.'

He stared at her incredulous. 'You didn't know that when you saw him at the inn?'

'No, I didn't recognize him at all then, not until I saw him with that club raised over his head tonight. I should have known, though, that he wasn't there to rob us that night. I'd had the feeling I'd been followed recently, since I came uptown, but I managed to lose him.'

'Until he found you again at the inn and followed us back?'

'It looks that way.'

'You think he was just tidying up loose ends, because he knew you could recognize him?'

'But I couldn't. I didn't remember him at all until tonight.'

'But he wouldn't have known that, would he?'

'No. Look out!' she screamed as the man loomed up behind Jeremy's back.

Jeremy swung around, but her warning must have changed the man's mind about attacking them, because he bolted out the door instead – and ran into Artie by the sounds of the butler's complaint. Jeremy hurried to the door, told Artie to apprehend the fellow, then came back to Danny.

He wasn't leaving her alone with a madman in the house. 'Artie will catch him. He can be quite ruthless when warranted.'

Danny felt that Jeremy's confidence was a bit misplaced until the butler came back and announced, 'He's dead.'

'Blister it, Artie,' Jeremy complained, 'I wanted to question him, not bury him.'

'I didn't kill 'im,' Artie said with a shrug. ''E dove back out that window 'e broke to get in the 'ouse and landed on a sharp piece of glass.'

Danny started to cry. She was silent about it and turned her head aside so the men wouldn't notice, and fortunately, Jeremy left with Artie to see to the body and to summon the authorities, so she had time to get her emotions under control. But she couldn't manage it, the tears kept pouring, because she'd realized too late that that fellow could have told her who she really was. But now he couldn't.

44

'You're coming with me and that's final,' Jeremy said.

'You get really silly when you're worried, mate,' Danny replied. 'That chap was a loner. No one else is going to break in here and try to kill me.'

'You don't know that for certain, or have you remembered more?'

They were in his bedroom. Jeremy was packing for the weekend trip to the Crandle house party. He'd almost talked himself out of going that morning, he was still so worried about her. But he'd mentioned that Crandle wasn't known to throw a great many parties, just a few per season, so it might be a long time before he had such a prime opportunity again to observe Heddings and hopefully catch him at some wrongdoing. Danny had to convince Jeremy once again that she was fine, that he shouldn't change his plans on her account.

She thought she'd succeeded. He'd agreed. But apparently not completely, since he'd just summoned her to his room to inform her that she would be accompanying him.

'I've remembered nothing else,' she told him, answering his question.

But she was still quite amazed that she'd remembered her name, not all of it, just the first name. It had come to her that morning just after they awoke in each other's arms, and she'd blurted it out, 'My name is Danette,' and then she'd laughed. 'A far cry from Danielle, eh? And don't be calling me that. It sounds too foreign for my liking.'

'I think it's rather pretty,' he'd said.

'Too bad. It's mine and I choose to forget it again.'

But she wasn't going to forget it. And she had hope now that more memories would come back to her. Because she'd taken another blow to her head? Or because she'd come face-to-face with her worst nightmare? Whatever the reason, she had confidence now that she *would* remember more.

'You're still coming with me,' he insisted. 'Or do you prefer cleaning house to going to parties?'

She snorted at his logic. 'I'd prefer being realistic, if you don't mind. I don't belong at such parties and you know it. Look at the fuss you made about my attending that ball.'

'But you did splendidly there.'

'So? What's that got to do with another party? I don't have the clothes for it either. I have that one ball gown—'

'Which will do just fine.'

'For both days? You gentry wouldn't be caught dead wearing the same clothes two days in a row, mate.'

'It will have been in the only trunk that was salvaged when they all got dumped in the river. Quite understandable.'

She stared at him, then laughed. 'Who would believe that whopper?'

'Anyone I mention it to. You don't think the gentry suffer simple difficulties like having baggage come loose from its strapping and roll down a hill into the river? I assure you, the same mishaps that bedevil the general populace can bedevil the upper crust, too.'

He got his way, the scoundrel. Despite all her objections, he was able to talk circles around her, cajole, tease, and otherwise browbeat her in his nabob way.

Her last warning was, 'You know, mate, if you don't stop making me pretend to be a lady, I might like it and work on getting m'self a lordly husband, rather than just a respectable one.'

But that didn't work either, merely had him replying in a casual tone, 'I haven't shot anyone lately. I suppose I'm overdue.'

That shut her up quickly. He was joking, of course, but she still hadn't liked the sound of that, which reminded her too much of his father. He *was* James Malory's son, after all, and although he was mostly just a lovable scoundrel as his cousin had termed him, there could be another side to Jeremy that he didn't allow her to see.

'I never thought I'd see the day, Jeremy,' Amy said, 'that you'd fall in love.'

Amy and Warren had come with Jeremy and Danny to Lord Crandle's party. That had been decided when Jeremy stopped by to borrow their coach and he'd been reminded that 'Danielle' should have a chaperone.

'Bite your tongue, Cousin,' Jeremy replied. 'You ain't seen it yet.'

Amy raised a brow at him. 'Don't tell me you're going to be the last to know?'

She started laughing then, causing him to grit his teeth. They were dancing, the first opportunity they'd had to talk alone since she'd returned to England. A trio of musicians had started playing after dinner, and with Warren keeping Danny occupied teaching her to play cards, Jeremy had let Amy drag him onto the dance floor.

Lord Heddings hadn't made an appearance yet, and he might not show at all. Amy had agreed to pose as the 'temptation', wearing some of her best jewelry for the duration of the visit. Fat lot of good that was going to do if the thief didn't show up.

'You see, you can't even keep your eyes off her for two minutes,' Amy said triumphantly, as if she'd just made her point.

Jeremy snorted. 'She's a raving beauty. Of course

I'm going to stare at her every chance I get. I'd have to be blind not to want to.'

'It's all right to love her, you know. She comes from good family.'

'*If* I were going to love her, I wouldn't give a bloody damn where she came from, and how the devil do you know about her family? No, never mind. Forget I asked.'

'Don't worry, it's not one of my "feelings." You just have to watch her, listen to her, to know she's got good breeding in her background.'

He gave a hoot of laughter and said, 'You wouldn't be saying that, puss, if you could have heard her talking just a few weeks ago. Right out of the gutter she sounded, and was, for that matter.'

'Exactly,' Amy said triumphantly. 'You don't really think someone like that could learn to speak so well in just a few weeks, do you? Unless it was how she used to speak. She said as much, that her friend Lucy taught her to talk like a guttersnipe. Did you never wonder where she came from before she got adopted by that riffraff?'

'Course I have, but that's all I can do, when she can't even remember her full name. And she's sure her parents were killed by that bastard who tried to kill her. They'd have searched high and low for her otherwise. So even if her memories do return, she has no one to go back to.'

'Don't sound so hopeful,' Amy huffed. 'She could have distant relatives other than those *you've* created for her. And even if she doesn't, that does *not* mean you're going to get to keep her as your maid forever. The girl has goals, Jeremy, if you didn't know, and you've only supplied one of them in giving her a job.'

'I know about her damned goals,' he grumbled. 'Bloody hell, did she tell you her whole life story on the way back to London that day?'

Amy grinned at him. 'You know I have a way of getting people to open up. There's no prevaricating when you're around me.'

'More's the pity.'

'I don't know why you're protesting what is so patently obvious, scamp. And you *could* supply her other two goals, though come to think of it, you don't really fall under the heading of *respectable*, do you?' Amy feigned a sigh. 'Forget I mentioned it.'

Jeremy scowled. He hated when Amy got in a teasing mood. Like her two more notorious uncles, she went for blood.

Fortunately, a change of subject walked in the door. 'Ah, there he is finally.'

Amy followed his gaze. 'Lord Heddings?'

'Yes, and why don't you go introduce yourself, puss, and let him get a good look at all those baubles you're wearing. You and Warren *were* given a room of your own, right? I doubt he'll take the chance of sneaking into a room if it's being shared.'

'Yes, we have our own room. Crandle has a standing arrangement with his two closest neighbors to help him with any extra guests when he runs out of rooms. It's fortunate we arrived early, or we probably would be staying elsewhere. I take it you'll be sharing a room yourself?'

'Of course. With a half dozen other bachelors at last count. And Danny was put in with the single young misses. Hadn't considered that when I dragged her along,' he added with a frown.

'Don't worry, she'll do fine.'

He was glancing about the room now, having noticed that Danny was no longer where he'd left her at the card tables with Warren, was nowhere in sight. Heddings was heading to the card tables, though.

'Intercept him before he settles in at one of the tables. He's known to spend all night gambling. I'll go see where Danny's gone off to.'

She'd gone to bed, according to Warren. This early? She'd mentioned a headache, which made Jeremy feel like the worst cad, for having forgotten the knock on the head she'd taken. She'd said she was fine, but the wench was probably as good at lying as she was at stealing.

He bounded upstairs to check on her. This early in the evening, the room she was sharing was likely to have only her in it. He knocked. She opened the door, was still dressed, had probably just gotten up there herself.

'Why didn't you tell me your head was still hurting?' he admonished rather sharply.

'Because it wasn't. It was trying to concentrate on the cards that brought the headache on.'

He gave her a suspicious frown. 'You wouldn't lie to me, would you?'

'Of course I would. Thieves are good at that, you know.'

His scowl got worse. She chuckled. 'I was joking, mate. Cor, you're touchy lately.'

He sighed and leaned against the doorframe. 'Crandle has a very nice garden, I was told. I was hoping to show it to you later.'

She raised her brow at him. 'That'd be better suited to the daytime, wouldn't it? So I could actually see what you're showing me?'

'Well, no, you don't have to see anything for this.'

He'd no sooner said it than his arm snaked out and pulled her body flush with his, and his mouth covered hers. He wanted to devour her, but he restrained himself, just barely. The kiss was sensual, God, he loved the taste of her. She kissed with her whole body, not just her mouth, pressing into him.

He broke off abruptly before he lost all sense and carried her to bed, a bed that wouldn't be private for long. He stepped back. He was actually trembling!

'I'm sorry,' he said. 'I shouldn't have done that.'

'No, you shouldn't have,' she replied breathlessly.

He groaned inwardly, almost grabbed her back. He stuffed his hands in his pockets rather quickly instead and got the subject off kisses and how much he wanted to make love to her right now.

'Heddings showed up finally,' he said.

'Well, that worked out rather well, didn't it?'

'How so?'

'If he doesn't know I'm here, he won't know to look for me in the morning. He'll be doing a head count before he tries sneaking into any of these rooms. *If* he's going to try it.'

'You still don't think he will?'

'I think he's too smart to do the stealing himself,' she reasoned.

'I disagree. I don't think he can resist the temptation.'

'But look what he risks if he's caught.'

'Exactly. Some men would find the danger of that exciting. But I'll allow we could both be right. He might not take the risk often. However, with Amy's jewels as the bait, he's more likely to try it. She travels too much these days, being married to a ship's captain. So if he wants her baubles, he'll need to grab them while he has the chance.'

'But how would he know she's not often in England?'

'Because she's going to tell him, dear girl. Amy is quite as good as Reggie at setting up a plot. She's going to mention that although she and Warren only just returned home, they're going to be leaving again in a few days. She's even going to hint that they might not return this time, that Warren's been talking about a new trade route that would bypass England. And she's going to leave the baubles in her room tomorrrow. So it will be now or never.'

Danny shrugged, conceding, 'Well, if he's that stupid, as I said, it's a good thing then that I came upstairs before he noticed me. I'll just remain up here in the morning and keep an ear open for him to make his move. If he's going to do it, it will be after he's assured himself that all the guests are accounted for downstairs.'

Jeremy shook his head at her. 'You aren't going to be doing the catching here, m'dear, I am. If or when he comes upstairs in the morning, I'll give him a few minutes and then follow—'

'And miss him in Amy's room if he's quick? Finding him in the hall here or in his own room won't prove a bleeding thing, now will it? Your timing would have to be too perfect.'

'Her jewels being missing will be proof enough.'

'Not if he hides them somewhere up here. He could even toss them out the window there at the end of the hall to one of his accomplices waiting below for just that. She's going to miss them, after all, which means a search will ensue. So he won't keep them on his person.'

'Bloody hell, you're coming up with too many variables. *Must* you think like a thief?'

She grinned at him. 'You can do the catching as you planned to. I'll just be up here to point you in the right direction.'

384

'And miss the rest of the party yourself?'

'I didn't want to be here in the first place, mate. But, no. If he doesn't make his move before noon, I'll be coming down for some lunch. I'm not going to starve myself to catch your thief.'

45

Danny would have regretted her decision to wait upstairs the next morning, since she got hungry not long after waking. But she'd gone to sleep early, so was awake before any of the other young ladies she was sharing the room with, and likely the other guests as well. So she took the chance to slip downstairs for a bite to eat and got back in her room without running into anyone other than the servants.

She used the same excuse of a headache to remain behind in the room when the other girls started waking each other to go down for breakfast. They hadn't brought their maids with them, were apparently used to helping each other dress at weekend gatherings like this one. And they were all envious of Danny, having heard the rumors that Jeremy Malory was courting her, and thinking them confirmed since she'd arrived with him and his relatives.

She'd had to listen to each of them gushing

about how handsome he was, how he was the most eligible bachelor in all of England. She'd managed to refrain from laughing. Bachelor, yes. Eligible, not a chance.

Alone again, she got comfortable near the door so she could listen to the comings and goings in the hall as the rest of the guests headed downstairs for the day. She wasn't about to lie on the floor to watch the feet passing as she'd done in Heddings's house, since one of the young ladies might return for something and end up banging the door against her head. But she felt safe in cracking the door open just a smidgen and leaving it like that. With Amy's room just across the way, the crack gave her a clear view of the only room that mattered.

And she didn't have long to wait. A well-dressed gentleman in his middle years came into her line of vision. Tall, distinguished looking, with black hair turning silver at his temples. He stopped at Amy's door, glanced both ways down the hall, then tried the doorknob. Finding it unlocked, he quickly slipped inside.

Danny was amazed. She hadn't really thought he'd be that stupid, but Jeremy had been right. Unless that hadn't been Lord Heddings. But who else could it have been? She'd met most of the other guests last evening at dinner, and that man hadn't been one of them. He was also dressed too fine to be a servant. And his caution before entering the room spoke clearly that he was up to no good.

She listened closely to hear Jeremy coming up the stairs, but no other sound came from the hall. She hoped he didn't give Heddings too much time. She wasn't sure what she should do if the lord left Amy's room before Jeremy arrived. And what if he hadn't even seen the man come upstairs? Heddings was going to get away with it if Jeremy didn't hurry. She could accuse him. After all, she'd witnessed him enter Amy's room. But fat lot of good that would do if he disposed of the jewels first.

The door opened again across the way so silently, she wouldn't have heard it. He didn't leave the room immediately either; he was looking down the hall first, then he poked his head around to look down the other way. Finding no one about, he fairly flew out of that room and closed the door again, leaving it as he'd found it, then hurried farther down the hall, out of Danny's view.

Danny had mere seconds to decide what to do. Maybe she could just detain him long enough for Jeremy to arrive.

She stepped out into the hall and said, 'Wait up, Lord Heddings.'

He turned around to face her. She was looking to see if anything was in the hall that he could have put the jewels in temporarily. There wasn't, not even a vase. And the window at the end of the hall was still a long ways off, so he had to have the jewels still on him.

But then she noticed that he was staring at

her quite incredulously. So he was going to play the innocent, was he? She snorted to herself. He should have waited until she actually accused him.

She did that now, warned him, 'Give it up, m'lord. I know what you did.'

'So he failed again to get rid of you?' Heddings replied, his tone filled with disgust. 'Still as incompetent as he was fifteen years ago? But whatever he told you, you can't prove it.'

Danny felt poleaxed. She couldn't breathe. He wasn't talking about the theft he'd just committed. He was talking about the man who'd tried to kill her, twice, and his own involvement in it.

And then she really couldn't breathe, because his hands were suddenly around her neck, squeezing, and she heard him snarl, 'I'll finish this myself.'

She fought with his fingers, tried to pry them loose, but too quickly her own were tingling, losing strength. A haze was clouding her eyes. The last thing she saw was the hate in his . . .

Jeremy came around the corner at the top of the stairs. He sighed to himself when he saw Danny standing there in the corridor in front of Heddings, her back to him. He'd warned her to stay out of this. It would be nice, it really would, if she'd pay attention to him occasionally.

He'd almost reached them when Danny slumped to the floor at Heddings's feet. 'What the hell?'

'She fainted,' Lord Heddings told him. 'Mentioned she hadn't eaten yet today and not much yesterday. I'll fetch some smelling salts.'

Jeremy knelt down to pick Danny up and get her to a bed, but he couldn't help seeing the red surrounding her neck with the low cut of her gown. So much emotion welled up in his chest he couldn't breathe for a moment, then it released in a keening cry. He gathered her limp body to his chest. He rocked with her. Pain was ripping him to pieces. He hadn't felt such loss since his mother died.

'Jeremy?' Warren said hesitantly, putting a hand on his shoulder.

Jeremy looked up. He couldn't see Warren clearly through the moisture in his eyes. 'He killed her,' he said simply, his voice choked.

Warren bent down, tried to take Danny from him, but Jeremy wasn't letting go of her, continued to rock with her in his arms. Again Warren said hesitantly, 'Jeremy, I don't think she's dead. She's still warm.'

Jeremy went still. He looked down at her chest, but it wasn't moving. He put his ear to her mouth, heard the barest rasp of breath.

'Oh, God!' he cried, and squeezed her even tighter in his relief.

Warren wasn't hesitant at all this time, said sharply, 'For God's sake, Jeremy, you're giving her no room to breathe. Let her go.'

That snapped Jeremy out of it. And a new emotion took over, one so primitive it was all-consuming. 'Take care of her for me,' he said, handing Danny to Warren. 'I'll take care of him.'

'You've caught him, and for more than stealing. Let the authorities handle—'

Warren didn't bother to finish since Jeremy wasn't there any longer to listen. He ran down the hall to the only room with an open door. Heddings was just climbing out the window. Jeremy charged toward him, yanked the man back inside so forcefully, he was tossed across the room. Instead of getting right up, though, Heddings scrambled to get the pistol out of his pocket that he'd fetched from one of his bags, the reason he hadn't escaped immediately.

Jeremy didn't notice the gun, he was too busy getting to Heddings again. He heard the shot fly past him. Couldn't miss that. But he ignored it, too, that primitive rage still in complete control of him.

He reached him, kicked the pistol out of his hand, and started pounding him. He wanted to hurt him, not knock him out, not kill him, though he didn't care at that moment if that was the result. The man had to pay for hurting Danny, that was the only thing in Jeremy's mind.

He had to be pulled off him. Warren was probably the only man there who could have managed it, as enraged as Jeremy still was. Others were present though, having been drawn by the pistol shot. And he hadn't killed Heddings. He'd broken a good many of his bones though and damaged his face badly enough that it would never look the same.

Jeremy left Warren there to explain to the other

391

guests what had happened and went to find Danny. Warren had placed her in his own room. Amy was there, sitting next to her on the bed. And Danny was sitting up, rubbing her neck. Sure now that she was going to be all right, he directed some of the rage still riding him at her.

'You accused him, didn't you?' he said angrily.

'Well, yes, but he thought I was accusing him of something else.'

'What do you mean?'

Before she could answer him, Amy stood up and shoved Jeremy back. 'Now isn't the time to be questioning her. Open your ears, Jeremy. Can't you hear how faint and scratchy her voice is?'

He stared at Danny. The redness on her throat was fading, but bruises would probably appear there in a few hours. He felt immediately contrite, knelt down next to her, took her hand in his to bring it to his lips.

'I'm sorry. Amy's right. You need to rest your throat. Don't talk for now.'

'I'll talk if I want to, mate.'

Jeremy threw up his hands over that stubborn remark. But Amy said reasonably, 'We should leave her alone so she can rest.'

Jeremy didn't want to leave her alone for a second, wanted to get her back home where he could care for her himself. But he nodded at his cousin. And he still had to talk to the magistrate himself, to make sure Heddings got charged with more than just theft.

But Danny had too many questions of her own to watch them leave without getting answers. 'Wait a minute. What happened with Heddings?'

Jeremy summed it up nicely, or tried to, so she wouldn't have to ask any other questions. 'He's unconscious at the moment. And he won't be trying to escape out any more windows. I believe he broke at least one of his hands when he tried to block one of my punches.'

'You knocked him out?'

'Something like that. The magistrate has already been sent for. He'll probably want to question you as well, but I'll make sure he keeps it brief.'

'He was going to kill me,' Danny whispered. 'And not because I caught him stealing. He knows who I am. He knows that other man who attacked me, too. I think he's the one who sent him.'

'So you recognized him?'

'No, not at all. There's nothing about him even vaguely familiar to me. But he knew me as soon as he saw me. He can tell me who I am.'

'*If* he will. I doubt he'll be very accommodating under the circumstances, luv.'

46

At Danny's behest, Jeremy confronted Heddings before he was escorted away. After the local magistrate had congratulated Jeremy, the fellow confessed that they'd been onto Lord Heddings for quite some time now, but had never been able to prove anything against him. He did work with others, as Danny had guessed. Apparently, he'd spot the jewelry at the parties he went to, get the owners' addresses, then send his men to steal the items. He didn't usually try to take the jewels himself.

He'd come under suspicion when he got greedy for more than just money. Most of the jewels he merely sold off, but those from prominent people, he'd wait a few months, then approach the owner of the bauble, say he'd heard of their loss and happened to have come across a piece that looked like it in a pawn shop, so he bought it on the chance that it might be the piece. These he gave back without charge, earning favors instead, favors that wouldn't do him a bit of good now.

Amy's jewelry was removed from Heddings's pockets before he regained consciousness, and with enough witnesses that the lord wouldn't be talking his way out of the crime. He was well and truly caught, and furious about it when he did wake. The rage probably kept him from feeling the worst of his injuries. It also kept his mouth shut on the subject of Danny.

'You tried to kill her. Why?'

'So she's not dead? Too bad.'

Jeremy had to be pulled back again, was going to slam his fist in the man's face once more. Heddings laughed at him, confident that the three constables waiting to drag him away would keep Jeremy off him.

'Why do you hate her?' Jeremy demanded.

'I don't hate her. I don't even know her.'

'So you just try to kill pretty young girls for the hell of it?'

Heddings snorted. 'It's who she is, Malory, that matters.'

'Who is she then?'

Heddings seemed surprised. 'She didn't tell you?'

'She doesn't know.'

Heddings started laughing again. 'Now that's rich. Almost makes this worth it, to know that.'

'*Who is she?*'

'If I knew, do you really think I'd tell you?'

Heddings sneered. 'Not a chance. That information would go with me to the grave *if* I knew, recompense, as it were.'

'You're lying.'

'No, I'm done talking to you.' And to the constables, Heddings said, 'Get me out of here, or get him out of here. I really don't care which.'

Jeremy considered trying to talk his way into a few minutes alone with Heddings, but he didn't think it would work at that point. And besides, he was sure now that no matter what he said or did to Heddings, the man wouldn't cooperate.

He was forced to return to Danny with the bad news. She'd been ordered to stay in bed the rest of the day. One of the guests was a doctor. He'd packed her neck with cold cloths and given her a balm to soothe her throat. A maid was there to change the cloths as they warmed. Jeremy sent her out of the room, closing the door after her.

Danny sat up, asked hopefully, 'What did he say?'

Jeremy sat on the bed next to her, cupped her cheek with his hand. 'Does it really matter who you are, luv? You've gone through life this long without knowing.'

She slumped back on her pillow. 'You're right, it's not important.'

'I didn't say that—'

'No, really, you're right. It's not like I have family or anybody waiting on me to come home. If I did, they would have looked for me, wouldn't they? Or Miss Jane would have mentioned taking me home, but she never said anything about going back, which would indicate there was nothing to go back to. So he wouldn't tell you who I am?'

'No.'

'But he knows! I know he knows. I saw it in his eyes, his expression. It fairly bowled him over to see me standing there in the hall.'

'I don't doubt he does know, but he's decided it's a fitting revenge to keep it to himself. After all, we were personally responsible for his downfall. He's going to prison because of us.'

'What if you promised to get the charges dismissed for him?'

He smiled gently. 'It's too late for that. There's a house full of witnesses here who know he tried to kill you, several of them who've been robbed in the past and are sure now that he was responsible, after Amy's jewelry was found on him. Besides, he was already under suspicion, has been for many years now. There'd just been no proof to charge him with. We supplied the proof.'

Jeremy would be trying again though, he just didn't want to get Danny's hopes up, in case he failed. But he'd give Heddings a few weeks to realize just how much trouble he was in, then dangle the offer of reduced charges in exchange for the information he wanted.

She sighed. 'Well, at least you accomplished what you came here for.'

'And nearly got you killed.'

She flinched at the admonishing tone. 'I was only going to detain him. You were taking too long to get up here,' she admonished right back. 'He could have dumped the jewels, and then where would you be?'

'I'd be fine. And you'd be without bruises around your neck.'

She frowned at him. 'How was I to know he'd recognize me and attack me for something that had nothing to do with the jewels he'd just stolen? What were the bleeding odds of that, eh?'

He grinned. 'Nothing I would have bet on. Now get some rest. We'll go home in the morning.'

'I'd rather go home now. I'm fine. Don't I sound fine? Just a few little bruises to show for my folly. I'd rather get back to work than lie here and dwell on what I could have learned today.'

Put that way, he had to agree.

47

Danny waited four more days, long enough for the last of the tenderness to leave her neck. She didn't want any discomforts slowing her down. She was also waiting for Jeremy to be gone from the house for more than just a few hours, and Percy helped her out there. He came by that week to invite Jeremy to some horse races that were taking place a good hour's drive away from London. She didn't *really* think he would try to stop her from leaving, but she wasn't taking any chances, which was why she didn't want him to know about it until she was long gone.

As soon as Jeremy left the house that morning for the races, Danny went to her room to gather up her few belongings. It didn't take her long. She would have left the ball gown, since it was too bulky to lug about the city for very long, but Mrs Robertson's seamstress wasn't that far away and she figured she could get a few extra coppers for it from her, maybe even a few pounds. Every little bit was going to be needed until she got a new job.

She didn't think it would take long this time, though, finding a job. She had experience now, and her speech had improved so much, she didn't even slip anymore when she was nervous. She could probably get another maid's job in this part of town, but that would be too close to Jeremy. The middle-class area of the city would do her just fine and be the easier place to find a husband, too, maybe even a gentleman, at least a man who wasn't so lordly it'd be unthinkable for him to marry a servant.

She wished she could write Jeremy a note. She didn't want to go without leaving him an explanation. That was going to be a new goal for her. As soon as she could afford it, she was going to find herself a tutor to at least teach her to read and write. As an alternative, she dragged Claire to her room for a few minutes to leave a message with her.

'It's time for me to move on,' she told her friend. 'I'll be spending a few nights at my old home, if they'll let me, while I look for a new job. Or I'll rent a flat.'

'Why must you go?' Claire complained. 'We'd only just got to be friends.'

'That won't end with my going. I'll keep in touch. I might even come visit from time to time.' Danny wouldn't, couldn't afford to risk seeing Jeremy again after she was gone. 'Or better yet, you can come visit me. I'll let you know where I get settled.'

Claire sighed, but then asked suspiciously, 'You're not pregnant, are you?'

Danny shook her head. 'No, I was lucky in that regard. But that would become an issue if I stayed longer. And although I don't think he'd try to take the baby from me, I'd have an even harder time leaving with one.'

'So why leave at all?'

'Because I've fallen in love with the man, Claire, and he's tempting me to put my goals aside for him.'

'He doesn't know you're leaving, does he?'

'Of course not. He'd have no trouble talking me out of it. He's good at that, talking circles around me. So don't be telling him where I'm going. But I do want to leave him a message, if you wouldn't mind.'

'Certainly.'

'Tell him for me that I said thank you for improving my lot, that I'm much more confident now that my goals will be realized.'

Claire raised a brow. 'You really think he's going to want to hear that? Or doesn't he know what your goals are?'

'You're right, scratch that second part. Tell him instead that I'll miss him, but I have to get on with my life. And tell him—' She had to pause, was feeling her throat close up. 'Tell him I don't regret being his friend.'

'Eh?'

'He'll understand. Now I have to go. Watch over my pets for me?'

'You're not taking them?'

'Only Twitch. The other two, he shouldn't have given to me in the first place.' Danny hugged Claire. 'I'll miss you. I'll miss all of you.'

'Bloody hell, I think I'm going to cry. Go on then, if you're going. And good luck.'

Danny ran upstairs one last time before she left. Jeremy had warned her never to touch it again, but too bad, she was taking her old hat with her. Not to wear. It would look silly with her skirts. But it was hers, and she wasn't leaving anything behind.

She paused in his room to give it one last look. She touched his bed, his pillow. The tears started.

She didn't want to leave. She'd said it to Claire, but that was the first time she'd put it into words. She loved Jeremy Malory. It wasn't supposed to happen. She thought she'd be able to leave before it did. But it was too late. She wanted to spend the rest of her life with Jeremy. He could fulfill all her dreams – if he would. And, dear God, what if he would? How could she leave without finding out?

It would mean confronting him and spilling her guts, and risking what she'd feared, that he'd try to talk her out of going. He couldn't. Her resolve was firm now. But it would rip her up if he tried, make it that much harder . . .

Danny waited, went through an agony of indecision. But in the end, that tiny hope that Jeremy loved her, too, enough to defy convention and marry her, kept her there until he got home.

She let Claire know that she wouldn't have to give him any messages for her after all, and why. 'You've got more courage than I would have under the same circumstances,' Claire said. 'Good luck, Danny.'

She didn't need luck, she needed her one small hope to be realized.

Jeremy returned in time for lunch. Percy was with him. They were laughing as they entered the house. Danny savored the image from where she stood in the doorway to the parlor. She wasn't holding her sack; it was on the floor just inside the doorway where she could grab it quickly.

It must have been her expression, though, that made Jeremy's expression turn serious and tell Percy, 'Run along to the kitchen and let them know you're hungry, old man. I'll be along shortly.' He approached Danny then, put his hand on her cheek. 'What's wrong, luv?'

She stepped away from him, moving back into the parlor. She wasn't going to be able to say what she had to if he was touching her. He followed her into the room. He was going to reach for her again. She put up a hand to stop him.

'I'm leaving, Jeremy.'

'I just got home. Where are you off to?'

She realized he'd been drinking, for him to mistake her meaning like that. But he wasn't foxed. Jeremy Malory was incapable of getting drunk.

'I'm not going out on an errand. I'm leaving for good.'

'The devil you are. It's too soon.'

'Actually, I shouldn't have stayed this long. But don't misunderstand. I don't regret my time here with you, not a'tall. I – I'll miss you.' She had to pause, was feeling her throat close up. 'But I have to get on with my life.'

'Don't do this, Danny.'

'Then give me a reason to stay! Living my life sharing only half of yours isn't what I want for myself. I want a real family, and children who aren't bastards. I won't get either here unless you marry me.'

There, she'd said it, put her heart on the table.

And he said nothing.

Even his expression was inscrutable for once. For a man with such telling eyes? That *was* his answer. He wasn't going to remind her that marriage wasn't for him. He was sparing her that. God, what a fool she'd been, to grasp and cling to such a small hope!

She wasn't sure how she got out of there without bursting into tears in front of him. But no sooner was she out of the house than the tears began in earnest. Thinking about leaving just wasn't the same as walking out the door and realizing she'd never see Jeremy Malory again.

48

It took Danny a few extra hours to find where Dagger had moved the pack to. She knew the right people to ask. Back in the old neighborhoods, it was amazing how many people didn't recognize her at first. A few did and were dumbfounded, but most didn't recognize her at all, had to be reminded, and she'd known these people most of her life!

Had she changed that much? Probably. And it wasn't just the female attire. She was walking boldly into the most crime-ridden area of the city, confident that she could deal with any trouble that came her way.

Dagger was home. So was Lucy, who squealed in delight when she saw Danny walk in the door. A few of the children were also there and demanded an equal share of her attention. It was a good ten minutes before she thought to look at Dagger to judge his reaction.

He'd said nothing yet. And he was just staring at

her, as if he didn't recognize her either. But he *knew* she was a woman now, so he was probably trying to figure out how he'd missed that fact all these years.

Finally he said in a gruff voice, 'Ye can't stay 'ere. There's a dangerous fellow looking for ye in these neighborhoods who means ye 'arm.'

'Yes, I know.' Danny moved to join him at the same old kitchen table where he could usually be found. That table always traveled with him. And she realized now that he treated it like his office, or his throne. He gave all his orders there, dictated his rules. He should have an office, a real one.

She said as much. 'You should have an office, Dagger. Why did you never turn one of the bedrooms into one?'

He snorted. 'Like we ever 'ave spare bedrooms. And don't be changing the subject.'

She noticed his nose was a little off-center and nodded toward it. 'Did it hurt a lot?'

'Bleedin' right it did. It were that fellow looking for ye who broke it.'

'Yes, Lucy told me.'

Dagger spared a moment to glare at Lucy, who shrugged as she joined them at the table, too. 'So I knew where she were working. It's a good thing ye didn't, or ye would've spilled yer guts to that thug.'

'It doesn't matter,' Danny interjected. 'He found me anyway. He's dead, though, so you don't have to worry about him anymore.'

'*Ye* killed him?'

Danny shook her head, explained, 'He did that on his own when he got caught trying to kill me and ran. And the lord who hired him, he's off to jail himself, so he won't be doing any more hiring.'

'A lord?' Dagger exclaimed. 'Wot the devil 'ave ye been getting yerself into, Danny?'

'Nothing. It was my past catching up to me. That lord, he knows who I really am. He wouldn't say though, the bastard, and I still can't remember. But I think he's the one who killed my family. I was supposed to die with them, but my nurse protected me and escaped with me. Then Lucy found me.'

Dagger turned an incredulous look on Lucy. 'Ye brought home a *nabob*!'

'I don't think I'm one of them,' Danny was quick to deny. 'That lord, he's as crooked as they get, a thief himself. If my family was associated with him back then, maybe they weren't so upstanding themselves. He did want us all dead, after all. To wipe out a whole family sounds like revenge no matter how you look at it.'

Lucy snorted now. 'She were a nabob. Dressed like it, spoke like it. And lords kill each other all the time for all sorts of silly reasons that don't bother us down this side o' town.'

Danny rolled her eyes, was about to mention that not only nabobs talked like that, that even upper-crust servants did, but Dagger demanded of Lucy, 'Then why'd ye bring 'er 'ome, eh? You bleedin' well knew better.'

'Because she 'ad no one, and no memories, and

was barely five years old. If ye think I'm that cold 'earted that I'd leave 'er in an alley to fend for 'erself, then I'm thinking ye need yer nose broke again.'

'But ye 'id wot she was, not just that she were gentry, but that she were a female. Why'd ye do that?'

'Because ye were going through one o' yer desperate-for-money periods and were about to force me to whore for coins. I was furious wi' ye, Dagger, over that. And I didn't want to see the same thing 'appen to Danny. I wanted 'er to 'ave choices, and men get more choices.'

He was blushing by the time Lucy finished. ''Ow many times do I 'ave to apologize for that, eh?'

'Oh, shut up, Dagger. I made a good whore as it 'appens. But I'm thinking o' retiring. I've met a man who wants to keep me exclusively to 'imself.'

Danny grinned and guessed, 'That hack driver?'

Lucy chuckled. 'Aye, 'e's sweet on me, 'e truly is. Wants to get married! Who would've ever thought, eh?'

'So I'm going to lose ye, too?' Dagger said, looking crushed.

Danny thought that might be a good time to introduce one of her old wishes. 'Dagger, have you ever thought of turning this into a real orphanage? We could get real jobs to support it, hire a teacher for the children, get them real beds. Lucy would probably help, too.'

He was staring at her as if she'd lost her mind.

'D'ye 'ave any idea wot kind o' money yer talking about, to run an orphanage? Teachers ain't cheap, are bleedin' expensive. And beds!'

'It *could* be done, Dagger. Think on it.'

'Bah, where would I be finding a real job, eh? Ye didn't, did ye?'

'I did,' she said, her tone turning defensive.

'Then wot are ye doing back 'ere?' he demanded. 'Got fired already?'

'No, I left of my own accord. It was a good job, I really liked it. But I was getting too attached to my employer, so I thought it best to leave.'

The moisture started gathering in her eyes again. She stood up, turned away from the table. Lucy was suddenly beside her, putting an arm around her shoulder all the while she was glaring at Dagger.

'I'm not here to stay, Dagger,' Danny continued when she got control of her emotions again. 'I'm just here to leave my things with Lucy for a few days while I look for another job. And I missed you all, and the children. I know you told me not to come back, but—'

'Hush, luv,' Lucy cut in. 'Ye can visit for as long as ye like. Ain't that right, Dagger?'

It was said in such a threatening tone that Dagger merely mumbled something under his breath, grabbed his hat, and left, probably to find the nearest tavern. But as soon as he was gone, Lucy turned Danny toward her, studied her tear-reddened eyes for a moment, then hugged her close.

'Ye poor lass, yer not pregnant, are ye?'

'No, at least, I don't think so.'

'Then ye let yer 'eart get broken?'

'There was no stopping that. I thought if I left sooner rather than later, then it wouldn't be so bad, but I – I didn't think it would hurt this much.'

'There's no chance for the two o' ye?'

'No, I told him I was leaving and why. He didn't try to stop me.'

'Because he's upper-crust gentry?'

Danny shook her head. 'He might have a huge family full of titled lords and ladies, but there's members of it who buck convention, even his own father. He just doesn't want to get married. He's one of those confirmed rakehell bachelors. All he wanted to do was make me his mistress for a while.'

'I take it ye were 'aving none o' that?'

'None a'tall.'

'Even though some men keep their mistresses for as long as they do their wives?'

Danny snorted. 'He's not *that* type. Lucy, I swear he's so handsome he could melt butter with a smile. He's got women scheming and plotting to lure him to the altar by any means, while he'll go to any lengths to avoid it. But it doesn't matter. I want a family of my own. Jeremy Malory can't give me that.'

49

'I'm not surprised,' Anthony was saying as the coach meandered through traffic late the next afternoon. 'Saw it in the bone structure.'

James snorted at his brother. 'You saw nothing of the sort.'

'Beg to differ, old man. Just because *you* didn't see it doesn't mean someone with a more discerning eye wouldn't. Maybe you need glasses in your old age?'

'Maybe you need an invite to Knighton's after we finish with this mess.'

Anthony chuckled. Knighton's Hall was a sporting establishment that specialized in exercise of the brutal sort. Both brothers had been known to spend many an hour there in the ring perfecting their skills at fisticuffs.

'Be glad to take you on anytime,' Anthony replied. 'But fess up. You're just annoyed because *you* didn't see this coming.'

'And how was it even a remote possibility that

Jason would remember an obscure meeting that took place over twenty years ago? He'd only met the chit once back then.'

Anthony laughed. 'Because it annoyed him. He felt he should know her, so he bloody well wasn't going to stop thinking about it until he recalled why she looked familiar to him. I'm not surprised either that he hied himself back to London just to blister your ears over the matter.'

'It wasn't my ears he was after. He went straight to Jeremy's house, but my lad wasn't home. Impatient as our brother is, I then became his second target.'

'Don't envy you. Wouldn't want to have to tell *my* son that he has to give up such a prime piece.'

James snorted. 'You don't have a son. And I ain't telling mine any such thing. The youngun's a man now, he can make his own decisions on what to do about this mess. 'Sides, just because Jason says so? Not a chance.'

Anthony grinned. 'I've been having devilish good luck lately, to have been on hand for his tirade. I know bloody well you wouldn't have told me about it after the fact.'

'Course I would have. Misery loves company, don't you know.'

They didn't find Jeremy at home either, but unlike Jason, James knew whom to ask for his whereabouts.

''E's gone to find the wench,' Artie informed James. 'She abandoned ship.'

'They had a fight?'

'Don't think so. She's gone off to get a new job, according to the kitchen wench.'

'In what direction did you send him?' James asked mildly.

'Didn't. The kitchen wench did, though. She told 'im the lass was going 'ome first, before she looked for a new job.'

'And in which direction are you pointing me?'

'Ain't,' Artie surprised them by saying stubbornly. 'Unless ye bring me along to watch yer back.'

'Certainly. Wouldn't have it any other way. Now where's he gone looking for her?'

'Worse part o' town ye can imagine. The slums of the slums.'

'Have you thought about an orphanage, Dagger?'

'No,' he mumbled. 'Did ye even think it through? Wot 'appens if yer idea falls apart, eh? Ye give these younguns 'ope of a better life, then it gets taken away from them when we can't meet all the costs. Then ye've got a lot o' discontented younguns worse off than they were before. At least now they don't expect better, so they're 'appy enough as they are.'

So he *had* thought about it. And she hadn't considered that aspect of failing. But he was being too negative. With that attitude, of course they'd fail.

'I found a good job this morning, first one I applied for, too.'

'Wot's yer point?'

'The pay is better uptown. If you could get a job in the same area, we could start the orphanage there. It's a nice area of town, no gentry, mostly tradespeople.'

'Forget it,' he said angrily now. 'I've never 'eld a real job.'

'You have. You're an organizer, a manager, a foreman, and a host of other things you've been doing right here for years.'

'I know wot I know and I don't try to reach for wot ain't possible. Be gone with ye. Yer goals are too fancy for 'ere. The only way ye'll get an orphanage is with government support or private support.'

'If I could get the private support, would you be willing to run the orphanage?'

'Sure, ye set it up, I'll run it for ye.' But then the sneering tone was back as he added, 'So ye've rich friends now, do ye?'

He said that only because he didn't think she had a chance in hell of pulling it off. And maybe she didn't. But it wasn't something she was going to give up on.

'She does, actually.'

Danny swung around and gasped at the sight of Jeremy filling the doorway. He was staring at her as if he wanted to grab her and shake her – or hug her. In fact, so much emotion was in his eyes she simply couldn't decipher exactly what he was feeling. But he finally tore his eyes off her to glance behind him

414

at the pack of children who had gathered to ogle at a nabob in their part of town.

He tossed one a coin, said, 'Be a good lad and watch the carriage for me. If it's still there when I come out, there'll be another coin for you. If it's not, I'll help you dig your grave before I put you in it.'

That brought Danny out of her daze. She rushed to the door. 'He didn't mean that,' she told the boy who was standing there with his mouth dropped open. 'Just sit in the carriage and give a yell if anyone tries to take it.'

Then she moved away from Jeremy again before she swung around to demand stiffly, 'How did you find me?'

'I had to beat that tavern behemoth to the ground and threaten to rip out his heart before he told me where your cohorts in crime were located.'

'You tangled with *him*?'

'Well, no, sounded good though, didn't it?' Jeremy said with a cheeky grin.

Danny didn't find that amusing, but Dagger certainly did. He burst out laughing. Jeremy continued, 'As it happens, money loosened his tongue without any coercion a'tall. Loyal bunch you have around here,' he added dryly.

Dagger's laughter had drawn Lucy out of her room. She stared at Jeremy agape before turning an even more incredulous look on Danny. 'Ye left *'im*? Cor, Danny, 'ave ye lost yer flippin' mind?'

Danny started blushing, but Jeremy flashed Lucy

415

a smile and said, 'You must be Lucy. I owe you a debt of gratitude, 'deed I do.'

Lucy blinked. 'Ye do? For wot?'

'For protecting the chit all these years until I could find her. Thank you. And you as well,' he added to Dagger. 'For giving her the boot out of here so she could find me.'

Danny rolled her eyes. Dagger coughed. Lucy said, 'Dagger, let's go admire the bloke's carriage for a bit, eh, and give these two a moment alone.'

'Only a moment,' Danny insisted, but they were already heading out the door. She then glared at Jeremy. 'Why are you here?'

'I've come for my hat, of course. Warned you not to steal it.'

That wasn't what she expected to hear, and even though she recognized he was teasing, she angrily marched into Lucy's room, dug the hat out of her sack, and came back to throw it at him. He picked it up, approached her, and handed it back.

'There. Now I've given it to you and you can keep it this time.' He no sooner said it than he yanked her into his arms, whispering, 'But I'm keeping you. God, Danny, don't ever put me through such hell again.'

He was squeezing her so tight she couldn't breathe, but for a moment, she didn't care, just savored the feeling of being surrounded by him. But then reason returned and she pushed away. He let go, but he didn't let her move so far away that he couldn't grab her back in an instant.

'You shouldn't have come here,' she told him.

'I shouldn't have had to. And I would have been here sooner, but the people around here thought it amusing to misdirect me for half the day.'

'I wouldn't have been here anyway. I only just got back m'self to get my things to take to my new job.'

'You can forget about any new job. You're coming home with me where you belong.'

Danny groaned inwardly. She'd never heard anything so nice. *Where you belong*. Good God, she'd known this would be too hard, if he tried to talk her out of her resolve.

She turned around, had to force the words out. 'I'm not changing my mind, Jeremy. I want more for myself than you're willing to give me.'

'If you hadn't run off so quick—'

She gasped, swung back around to cut in, 'I didn't run off. I told you what would keep me there, but you ignored it. You let me go!'

He tsked at her. 'Bowled me over, dear girl, is what you did, proposing like that. You really need to remember that you aren't wearing pants anymore. I was bloody well in shock if you must know.'

'The devil you were. You knew it was going to happen. It's not as if I hadn't warned you previously what my goals were *and* that I'd be leaving soon to accomplish them.'

'But your "soon" was years off in my mind.'

She snorted. 'Then maybe *you* need a dictionary.'

'Perhaps, but all I really need is you. Come home—'

'Don't!' she choked out, tears welling up in her eyes. 'Just go, Jeremy. You didn't miss an opportunity to talk me into staying, if that's why you're here. It wasn't going to happen and still isn't. So just go.'

'I'm here to apologize and to discuss marriage.'

'To whom?'

'To me, of course, you silly girl.'

She took a swing at him, aiming for his eye. She was furious. But he ducked, exclaiming, 'Bloody hell, what'd you do that for?'

'That's nothing to joke about, Jeremy Malory. That was so bleedin' cruel, I can't believe you said that. Get out. And don't come looking for me again.'

Instead of complying, he yanked her to him again, hard. And his arms wrapped around her completely so she couldn't do any more swinging, the scoundrel. Nor was he the least bit repentant.

He said in a jaunty tone, 'Was that a yes?'

She squirmed to get at his eye again. He chuckled. 'Bear with me, luv. I'd never planned to propose marriage to anyone, so of course I was destined to muck it up. But you should know me well enough to know this is one subject I would *never* joke about.'

She went very still. He was right, he'd never joke

418

about that. But she still couldn't believe he was serious, had to ask, 'Why? I know you don't want to get married, ever. You've made that very clear. So why would you consider it now?'

'Because you're stubborn. Because it's what you want and I want to make you happy. Because I love you. Because the thought of going on without you rends me to pieces and I'd rather not experience that again, thank you. Because I want to wake up with you every morning, not just when I get lucky. Because you're everything I could want in a woman, Danny, so why wouldn't I want to marry you? Well, that's what I asked myself, and now we both have the answer. I didn't *know* I was in love with you until I thought I'd lost you. I would have figured it out eventually, but I'm rather glad to know it now rather than later. So will you marry me and let me be your family?'

She leaned back, staring at him in wonder. 'You really mean it? You love me?'

'More than I can possibly express in mere words.'

Anthony's voice intruded behind them as he and James walked through the door. 'They told you not to interrupt them. Deuced embarrassing to hear that mush, ain't it?'

Jeremy turned, grinned at his father and uncle. 'Congratulate me. She's agreed to marry me.' But he whispered to Danny, 'You will, right?'

'Yes,' she whispered back, nearly bursting with the most profound happiness. 'Most definitely.'

'Well, I'll be damned,' James said. 'Don't think that even remotely occurred to Jason while he was having his tirade. It does solve the dilemma, however.'

'What dilemma?'

'Jason knows who she is, lad.'

'That she comes from here?'

'No, who she *really* is.'

50

Late-summer wildflowers filled the fields along the road through Somerset. It was far from London, a full day of riding plus half the next morning. Danny didn't notice most of the journey. She was in such a daze, her emotions ripped asunder.

There was the happiness. She'd never experienced anything like it. Jeremy loved her. He was going to marry her. He was going to fulfill all her dreams. It was almost more than she could bear, might have been, if the fear didn't counter those emotions. But the fear was overriding everything else.

She was afraid it wasn't true, that Jason Malory was mistaken. She was afraid if it was true, that her mother wouldn't still be alive. She'd last been known to be living in Somerset on her grandmother's estate, but no one had seen her since she'd retired there fifteen years ago. She could be dead, they could be making this journey for nothing. But Danny was also afraid that if Evelyn

Hilary *was* still alive, she wouldn't accept Danny as her daughter. There was no proof, other than some vague resemblance. Why would a great lady, the daughter of an earl, the widow of a baron, accept some street waif as her own blood?

James Malory had come with them. He'd insisted. The chit requires chaperoning, now that you know who she is,' he'd told his son.

Jeremy hadn't liked hearing that, and Danny would have snorted herself if she weren't in such an emotional daze. They didn't know for certain who she was yet, they were only guessing. Just because the tragedy associated with Evelyn Hilary closely matched her own meant nothing. It could merely be coincidence.

'The lady wasn't there when her husband, Robert, was murdered. They had come to London for a brief visit, but she was called back to Somerset. Her grandmother had taken a fall, or something like that. The murders made all the papers, were assumed to have been committed by a madman who broke into their London house and went on a rampage of killing. Her husband, Robert, and several servants were killed. Their daughter and her nurse were never seen again, but the blood left behind suggested they'd both been killed as well and dragged off. That those bodies had been disposed of, yet the others left behind, was what prompted the madman conclusion. There was simply no rhyme or reason for such slaughter.'

'Why is it you didn't recognize her?' Jeremy had

asked his father. 'Weren't you in London during that time?'

'Well, it was rather romantic actually,' James said. 'I recall being disappointed that I never got to meet Lady Evelyn. But as it happens, she had the shortest season on record, attended all of one party, which was where Jason happened to meet her. Apparently Robert Hilary was already acquainted with her and followed her to London to propose. She accepted and returned home the very next day. And they settled down on his country estate in Hampshire, where they had one daughter. Occasionally they visited London, but they didn't actually socialize when they were in town, which is why so few people remember Lady Evelyn.'

Danny heard all of this with only half an ear. It sank in, but she couldn't really relate it to herself, not yet. The fear wouldn't let her.

Jeremy offered her comfort just by his presence, but more, he kept an arm around her for the entire journey. Without that, Danny would probably have fallen to pieces. The closer they got to Somerset, the more tightly the fear choked her. If she had been thinking clearly, she would have been running in the opposite direction.

The estate they finally arrived at was magnificent, three stories tall originally in the main block, with shorter wings off to the sides, dark gray stone covered with ivy. It spread out over immaculate lawns dotted with stately old oaks. It shot Danny's fear up a dozen notches. She'd never seen a building so big that someone actually lived in.

They weren't going to be let inside. Danny was glad when she heard that, that Lady Hilary didn't receive visitors, for any reason. The butler was quite adamant. The name Malory meant nothing to him.

The door was about to be closed in their faces when Jeremy got annoyed and dragged Danny around in front of him – she'd been hiding behind his back. 'I believe the lady will want to see her daughter,' he told the man.

The butler, a rigid fellow, paled by slow degrees as he stared at Danny. Finally he said in a shaky voice, 'Come inside. My lady is in the garden behind the house. I'll direct you—'

'Just point the way,' James said, still irritated with the fellow.

She wasn't in the garden. One of the workers there pointed them to the skating pond just beyond a stand of trees, saying the lady often walked there.

Danny was holding back and had to be dragged along by the hand. She finally dug in her feet altogether. Jeremy stopped, lifted her face to his, saw how pale she was, and put his arms around her.

'I can't do this. Take me home,' she pleaded with him.

'What are you afraid of?'

'She's going to hate me. She isn't going to want

someone like me for a daughter. It's too late for her and me to be a family.'

'You know that isn't true, but you'll never know for sure unless you face her.' And then he added in a tender tone, 'And if it is true – you still have me.'

She melted against him. Her happiness, lingering beneath the fear, pushed forward again, surrounding her, giving her back some of her courage.

She let him lead her through the narrow stand of trees to the other side, where James had stopped to wait for them. Jeremy made an attempt to distract her, asking, 'You don't recognize this estate?'

'No, none of it. It seems too big for someone to live in it.'

'Actually, it's rather small.'

'Liar.'

'Really, nice and cozy.'

She snorted at him, but then she caught her breath. A field of flowers spread out before the pond, and in the field walked a lady with white-gold hair.

'Oh my God, it's my dream, Jeremy. I *have* been here – with her.'

He had to drag her forward again, her feet simply wouldn't move of their own accord. James preceded them. Neither of them were going to let her avoid this.

The lady was walking slowly through the flowers, her back to them. She was so deep in thought, she didn't hear or see them approaching.

James's first words startled a gasp from her, and she swung around. 'Lady Evelyn, allow me to introduce myself. James Malory, at your service. You met my older brother Jason many years ago.'

'I don't recall, but more to the point, I don't receive visitors. Please go away, sir. You are intruding on my privacy.'

She turned away and walked on. She'd barely glanced at James, didn't glance at Jeremy at all, nor notice Danny hiding behind his back. She was serious about not receiving and didn't inquire why they were there or how they had gotten past her butler.

'Can we leave now?' Danny whispered in a trembling voice.

James heard her. 'Bloody hell,' he swore softly, then called after the departing lady, 'We didn't come all the way from London to be dismissed out of hand. Ignore me as you will, but you might want to take a gander at my future daughter-in-law. She bears a striking resemblance – to you.'

The lady turned around again. She didn't appear at all surprised by James's remark. Instead she appeared quite furious now.

'Don't take me for a fool, sir. I assure you I am not so gullible anymore. Do you think you are the first to come here to try and foist a daughter on me, in an effort to lay claim to my husband's estate? The first instance devastated me. The second attempt I was wary, but still willing to believe I'd found my daughter. After the third attempt, I lost all hope. Do you know what it's like to lose all hope?'

'Can't say that I do. But we aren't here to convince you of anything. There's no need. The wench is soon to be a member of my family. We take care of our own, so she needs nothing from you.'

'Then what *do* you want?'

James shrugged. 'I imagine she wanted her mother back. I'm beginning to think she'll do better without one.'

The lady stiffened. Danny snarled at James, 'Don't be assuming things for me, mate. And don't be insulting her either.'

James raised a brow at her, said dryly, 'Lost your fear of me at last, have you?'

Danny blushed, then hid her face in Jeremy's back again. That 'We take care of our own' had endeared James Malory to her for all time. She really wasn't afraid of him anymore. But she still didn't have the nerve to face her mother.

Evelyn had heard her though, and although she couldn't see any more of Danny than her skirt behind Jeremy's legs, she gave him her full attention and demanded, 'Why is she hiding?'

'Because she's terrified that you won't want her,' Jeremy replied. 'She lost her memory all those years ago. She's only just getting some of it back.'

'Spare me, please,' Evelyn said derisively. 'That excuse has been used before as well.'

Jeremy didn't reply to that. He turned around

and lifted Danny's chin. 'You're making this worse, you know. She's going to regret everything she's said.'

'Or tell us to get lost again.'

'So she does. Then we go home, get married, start making babies.' He grinned at her. 'If that's what she's going to say, luv, then let's get it over with. Delaying isn't going to change it one way or the other.'

Danny groaned. He was right, of course. She was just prolonging her fears, and getting more and more sick to her stomach because of it. She stepped away from him, saw her mother's angry expression. It felt as if her heart just dropped on the ground.

But Evelyn had been expecting disappointment again, was still furious with them all for trying to dupe her. It took her a moment to look at Danny, really look at her, and then she was so shocked she couldn't speak. She was seeing herself twenty years ago, nearly identical, and the child she'd thought she'd never see again.

Danny had turned away, her worst fears realized. She put her arms around Jeremy and buried her face in his chest.

Her throat had closed off, she could barely get out, 'Take me home.'

She wasn't going to cry. She refused to cry there in front of Evelyn Hilary. Later –

'Danny!'

She looked back. Her mother was extending a

hand to her. Her shock was evident now. She'd paled a ghostly white.

'Oh, God, Danny, it's really you?'

The tears started. Danny took a step toward her, then another, then ran the last few, was sobbing openly by then and even more when her mother's arms went around her, crushing her with her own emotion. The smell she recognized, the softness, it was coming back to her, how much she'd been loved here. She was home.

51

It was a large parlor, utilitarian, cleaned as needed, but rarely used. They sat in it, Evelyn and Danny on the sofa, Jeremy in a chair across from them. James stood off to the side, by the empty fireplace, merely observing and remarking as needed – or not.

Evelyn held Danny's hand. She hadn't let go of it once since she'd first taken it to lead them back to the house. She was still crying off and on, every time she looked at Danny, actually, so she tried to keep her eyes on Jeremy instead. Danny was still crying off and on as well, and it didn't take much to set her off again. She had her mother back. She had her identity back, her real life back. She was still waiting to wake up, was still so incredulous that everything that she'd ever hoped for had come true.

She'd already explained what had happened to her on the way back to the house. Evelyn had asked that almost immediately, wanting the whole story. She hadn't seemed that surprised when she heard it. It explained why she'd never been able to find Danny herself. She'd never thought to look in the worst of the slums.

'I thought you were dead,' Evelyn was saying now. 'After years of searching, I'd finally given up all hope. And then those impostors began showing up. They had your eyes, all three of them. They bore no other resemblance. Hair color might change over the years, appearance might change as well, but eyes don't. They'd had tutoring, obviously, from someone who knew my family very well.'

'How many were there?' Jeremy asked.

'Three. The first girl was ten, she fooled me the longest. Five years passed before the second attempt. Then another two years before the last. I had the feeling that Robert's cousin was finding these girls and training them in what to say. He wanted Robert's estate and title. After he tried to have Danette declared dead and failed, I think he resorted to creating a new Danny, one that he would have control of, or dispose of, to have substantial proof that she was dead.'

'I was wondering about that,' Jeremy admitted. 'After fifteen years, she should have been legally pronounced dead.'

'He did try and was furious when his petition got thrown out. My grandmother was still alive then, and she was close friends with the judge.'

'This was your husband's only surviving relative?' James asked.

'Yes. He was a third cousin, though, and illegitimate, which was why the title would have passed through to Danny's childen before it would go to him. But he could have gotten it if he could have had her declared dead before she started having children of her own. Do you have any?' she turned to ask Danny.

Danny blushed. 'No, none yet.'

'Soon though,' Jeremy added with a grin.

Evelyn sighed. 'I don't suppose I could prevent this marriage? I've only just found her and already I'm going to lose her?'

'No, but you can come to London and live with us if you'd like,' Jeremy offered.

'That's very generous of you,' Evelyn replied. 'But I couldn't intrude on newlyweds. I will however move back to London, if that's where you're going to settle, so I can see Danny often. I had our old house there torn down to the ground and never rebuilt. Knowing what happened there—' She paused to shudder. 'But I could rebuild now. I still own the land.'

'I have no memory of that house,' Danny said.

'That isn't surprising. It was your first trip to London. We'd only been there a few days, which were mostly spent shopping or in the park, where your nurse took you to play. So we weren't in that house very long before the night the murders occurred. I would have died that night as well, I have little doubt, if my grandmother hadn't broken her leg. We were very close, she and I, and she was all I had left. My own parents had died when I was young, and my grandmother raised me after that. So I couldn't rest until I saw for myself that she was all right.'

'So you were here when it happened?'

'I hadn't even gotten here yet, I'd left London that afternoon. The news did come to me here though. I was destroyed. I nearly lost my mind. Robert was the love of my life. I'd known him since I was a child. His family estate is near here. I only went to London for a season to force his hand. We were already in love. It just took him longer to realize it. The possibility that Danny had escaped the mayhem was the only thing that sustained me during that time. But not knowing what happened to her was anguish in itself.'

'I don't doubt that Miss Jane would have returned me to you, if she hadn't died herself,' Danny said.

'Oh, I know she would have. She was a good woman. Which made it hard for me to keep up my hope. I finally suspected something had happened to her to prevent it. And you were too young yourself to find your way home. I never dreamed you had lost your memories completely.'

'They've been coming back to me slowly, since I met Jeremy. I remembered that park I had played in. I remembered my first name, though I didn't like it very much.'

Evelyn laughed. 'Neither did we. It was Robert's mother's name, though, so we were obliged to give it to you. But even he didn't care for it and was the first to call you Danny instead.'

Danny smiled, but continued hesitantly, 'And I recognized the man who did the killing that night, when he found me and tried to kill me again.'

Evelyn paled. 'When was this?'

'Just recently. He died himself in the attempt though, so we didn't find out who he was.'

Evelyn sighed. 'I'd always suspected it was Robert's cousin. He was the only one who stood to gain by Robert's death. And he'd always hated Robert. But there was no way to prove it. And he wasn't even in London when it happened.'

'His name wouldn't happen to be Lord John Heddings, would it?'

'John Heddings, yes, but he's no lord. How did you know? You'd never met him. He never visited us after you were born, hating Robert as he did, and we never mentioned his name. I'd only met him a few times myself, before we were married. You could sense his animosity when he was around Robert. He never tried to hide it.'

Jeremy explained, 'He's been living in a grand house not far from London, and pawning himself off as a lord. Obviously, no one has bothered to check his background. But he's been a gambler and jewel thief for quite a few years, which is how he's been supporting himself in such high style.'

'And he tried to kill me as well,' Danny added. 'We were trying to catch him stealing, because we knew he was a thief. But when he saw me, he recognized me, or rather, recognized you in me, so he knew who I was. He mentioned that other man, that he'd failed again to get rid of me, that he was just as incompetent as he'd been fifteen years ago. And he said he'd finish it himself, just before he tried to kill me. Jeremy showed up in time to stop him. I knew then that he was the man who'd sent that other one all those years ago to kill me. We couldn't prove it, though, and weren't aware that he had a motive.'

'My God, so I was right,' Evelyn said. 'I'll have him prosecuted!'

'You'll have to get in line,' James remarked. 'The younguns have already had him arrested for theft as well as attempted murder.'

'Then I'll make sure the charge is changed to murder. He's not going to get away with this, now that I know for certain he paid to have my Robert killed.'

'Be assured his days are numbered, Lady Evelyn,' James said. 'My family also has a vested interest in this now, since Danny will soon be one of us.'

'Ah, yes, another reminder that I'm soon to lose her. But until the wedding, she'll be staying with me. I don't suppose you'd agree to postpone the wedding?'

Jeremy was already groaning over that 'she'll be staying with me' remark. To his future mother-in-law, he now said, 'Not bloody likely.'

Evelyn tsked at him. Danny grinned at him,

though, before she told her mother, 'I was about to say not bleeding likely m'self.'

'So you love him then?' Evelyn asked softly.

'Oh, yes, with all my heart.'

James rolled his eyes, said dryly, 'Let's not get mushy before dinnertime, children. And do keep in mind it will be separate bedrooms for the duration. Have to take this chaperoning business seriously, don't you know.'

Which had Jeremy groaning again quite loudly.

52

They were married in late August. The banns had been posted in Evelyn's shire, as well as in London, shocking the ton. It might have been rumored that Jeremy was courting the Langton beauty, but no one had thought he was *really* going to put the shackles on.

Danny learned that Regina Eden often came to the rescue when tricky situations arose, and explaining why Danny had been introduced to the ton as a relative of Kelsey Langton's, but was now Evelyn Hilary's daughter, definitely fell under tricky. But Reggie smoothly let it be known that she'd merely forgotten to mention that the Langtons had adopted Danny and raised her as their own since it had at the time appeared she had no family.

It was a magnificent wedding. After thinking for so many years that she wouldn't have the opportunity to arrange her daughter's wedding, now that Evelyn had the opportunity again, she outdid herself.

Danny was offered a new gown, in any design of her choosing, or the gown Evelyn had been married in. Never having thought that far ahead, and actually, thinking she wouldn't need a real wedding dress to get married in, since her marriage aspirations hadn't been that high, she chose her mother's dress. It was too beautiful to pass up, ice-blue satin and lace that was so soft it felt like silk. And it fit her perfectly! It had taken her a while to notice, during their reunion, that her mother was exactly as tall as she was. That was one of the reasons that Evelyn hadn't wanted a season in London, and why she'd left immediately after Robert had proposed. She'd always been self-conscious about her unusual height. Robert, actually, had been no taller, so Danny got all her height from her mother.

It was odd how their relationship developed over those weeks before the wedding. It was almost as if they'd never been separated. The warmth was there, the love was there, there was no hesitation in giving it. And Evelyn wanted to know every single aspect of the years she'd been denied. They talked endlessly together, sometimes into the wee hours. They laughed, they cried. More and more memories were recalled, of those first years Danny had spent with her parents. God, it was so nice to have her mother again.

While she was so happy she felt she'd burst with it, Jeremy wasn't. He'd all but been asked to leave. Told he would just be underfoot, told he would have Danny the rest of his life, that he could wait

438

just a few more weeks, no, he wasn't happy in the least. But he sent letters to her each day, completely forgetting that she couldn't read them. Actually, she was to find out later that the fellow who had delivered the first one was supposed to tell her to save them, that Jeremy would read them to her after they were married, but the chap had been so dazzled by Danny's smile he hadn't mentioned that part. So Danny had her mother read the letters to her each day, and if Evelyn did a lot of blushing over those readings, Danny was too engrossed and thrilled by the depth of Jeremy's passion to notice.

He loved her, really, really loved her. She wondered if she would ever stop being incredulous over that. And he was miserable over their short separation, said he even got foxed for the first time in his life. Well, actually, he said he was doubtful he did, but that his father, two uncles, and Percy all claimed he'd done exactly that, so he had to allow it might have happened.

Evelyn surprised Danny by sending for Dagger and Lucy, as well as all the children. She'd sent three coaches to collect them all and wasn't going to let them return to London. She'd decided to take up Danny's cause and support an orphanage herself. Robert had had two properties nearby, both of which belonged to Danny now, and one of them would be a perfect environment for children to be raised in. Dagger would run it, but under Evelyn's supervision.

They didn't get along well at first. He didn't like

the thought of working with a grand lady. She resented that he'd gotten to raise her daughter. They did a lot of snapping at each other, but it calmed down after they finally got used to each other and worked out the details.

Jeremy's servants were also invited to the wedding. They were friends of Danny's, after all. Danny had decided to offer Claire the chance to change jobs, thought she might be happier working with children. And she'd been right. Claire jumped at the opportunity, and *she* and Dagger hit it off right from their first meeting. Dagger usually took getting used to, but Claire had too much confidence these days to be intimidated by him.

Dagger, in a fine suit for the wedding, had undergone a remarkable transformation. He'd shaved for the occasion as well and was humbled by his own appearance. Danny was reminded why she'd thought of him as 'family' for so many years. She'd already forgiven him for kicking her out, especially since she would probably never have seen Jeremy again if he hadn't. And she'd amazed him by asking him to escort her down the flower-strewn path to the altar, to give her away.

Lucy, in fancy new togs as well, cried like a banshee during the ceremony. So did Evelyn. Danny shed a few tears under her lovely veil, too, but only because she was bursting with joy as she said the vows that joined her to Jeremy Malory. She might not have gotten the respectable husband she'd had in mind when she'd first determined to get one, but she'd landed one who was so much more than that, the most sought-after man in all of London, and he was all hers now.

He hadn't gotten to see her before the wedding. He'd arrived the night before, but she'd been sent to bed early and had been busy all morning getting ready. When she'd joined him at the altar was the first time she'd seen him in several weeks, so it was little wonder the kiss he gave her after they were pronounced man and wife was a bit prolonged and had to be broken up with numerous coughs that didn't work, and finally his father slamming a hand on his back to congratulate him. Bleeding well nearly knocked them both over.

Every single Malory had shown up for the wedding, so Danny got to meet those she hadn't met yet, including the children, since she'd requested that they be allowed to attend. The Malory family really was much larger than she'd thought, and she was one of them now, which was another wish of hers granted, to have a big family. In fact, between her mother and Jeremy, all of her hopes and dreams had been fulfilled, with just one exception, which she mentioned to Jeremy that night as they lay in the huge master bed in *her* house, her father's ancestral home, which was hers now until she had a son old enough to claim it and the title, baron, that went with it.

They'd just spent several hours making up for missing each other. The bedcovers were in disarray. She was lying against Jeremy's chest, his arms firmly around her. She wasn't the least bit tired yet. Neither was he.

'We'll have to air out this place a bit more. It's still a bit musty,' Jeremy was saying.

Danny agreed. 'It was only recently cleaned, had been closed down all these years.' Then she thought to ask, 'Did you want to live here?'

'No,' he replied, then asked after a long pause, 'Did you?'

'No, I rather like your house better. It's much easier to clean.'

He sat up abruptly and frowned down at her. 'Don't even *think* of still cleaning that house, Danny. I mean it. Your days of wielding a duster are over.'

She chuckled at him, pulling him back down so she could get comfortable again. 'I was just teasing. I'm quite aware of my elevated circumstance.'

He mumbled, 'It's a bloody good thing I wasn't aware of it before I asked you to marry me, or I probably wouldn't have asked.'

Now she sat up abruptly and demanded, 'Why not?'

'Because, m'dear, your mother wouldn't have let me anywhere near you, so I wouldn't have gotten to know you, wouldn't have fallen in love, would still be going about my merry way blissfully unaware that I'd be miserable without you.'

She thought about that for a moment and then laughed. 'She would have welcomed you once she got to know you.'

'Don't count on it, luv. She would have sized me up and decided a scoundrel like me wasn't good enough for her daughter. You *could* have aspired to a lofty title, you know, and *that's* the way mothers think.'

'I'd like to be one to find out.'

'One what?'

'A mother.' Then she whispered, 'I want a baby, Jeremy, your baby.'

He groaned, pulled her back into his arms, said huskily just before he kissed her, 'It's going to be my absolute pleasure to grant that wish, Danny, I do assure you.'

'Since it's going to be my pleasure, too, can we work on it a little bit more tonight?'

'Tonight, tomorrow, every single day until you're puking your guts out, dear girl.'

'I'm not going to have morning sickness. My mother said she didn't, nor her mother.'

'Don't run in the family, eh? Well, that's one thing I'll thank your mother for.'

'*Doesn't*,' Danny said.

'Eh?'

'*Doesn't* run in the family.' She beamed at him. 'Now that was rather nice, correcting you for a change.' Then she mimicked him, ''Deed it was.'

Jeremy burst out laughing.

THE END

THE PRESENT
by Johanna Lindsey

The mysterious present was hard to miss. Wrapped in gold cloth, banded with a red velvet ribbon and bow, there was no indication of who it was from, nor who it was for . . .

It is Christmas time, and all is not well with the Malorys. As the family gathers for its traditional Christmas at Haverston, there are underlying tensions between black sheep James and his wife Georgina, while Jason Malory, Marquess of Haverston, remains unable to convince Molly, the love of his life and mother of his only son, to marry him. And in the midst of the turmoil, a mysterious present arrives that will dramatically affect the lives of the whole Malory clan.

The gift is an old journal – a tender and tempestuous account of the love affair between Christopher, the second marquess, and an enigmatic dark beauty named Anastasia. The story confirms a long-held family suspicion that their grandmother was, indeed, a gypsy. And as the magical snow adorns the landscape and festive spirits soar, there is a miraculous blossoming of romance which echoes the passion of that long-ago love affair, in this season of peace and giving and love.

0 552 14737 0

CORGI BOOKS

JOINING
by Johanna Lindsey

Seldom have two people about to join together in
holy matrimony have been so ill-disposed towards
each other. Milisant Crispin's beauty is exceeded
only by her boldness – hardly an endearing quality to
the handsome, arrogant Wulfric de Thorpe, the
future Earl of Shefford, who would prefer a more
biddable wife.

When Wulfric arrives at Dunburgh Castle to claim
his bride, he expects her to be the wild, impudent
young girl he knew in his youth. But instead he finds
a stunning beauty, possessed of a passionate fire that
could consume any man close enough to feel its
warmth. Her father has decreed that Milisant should
have a month to get to know the future Earl before
the marriage takes place, and as the time goes by
Milisant desperately searches for a way out. Yet
even as she resists, she cannot deny the strange
attraction she feels – just as Wulfric finds himself
falling under the spell of his proud bride.

0 552 14781 8

CORGI BOOKS

THE HEIR
by Johanna Lindsey

Has anyone in London ever taken part in the coming-out season with less enthusiasm than Sabrina? She is young, lovely, and possesses a sparkling wit – but she is a simple country girl, whose grandfather just happens to have been a nobleman. Luckily Ophelia, the daughter of a family friend, has been chosen to usher Sabrina through the pitfalls and perils of this all-important first season – and what better guide than this sophisticated blonde beauty who is the most sought-after lady in the city?

Even less keen to be in London is Duncan McTavish. Having lived all of his twenty-one years in the Scottish Highlands, he has recently learned that he is the sole heir to an English Marquess and is now required to assume his grandfather's titles and estates. Worse still, a betrothal has already been arranged, without his consent, to the ravishing, viper-tongued Ophelia. But then the dashing highlander meets the enchanting Sabrina, a woman for whom Duncan would willingly abandon his beloved Scotland – a kindred spirit whose wit delights him, and whose essence is the exquisite stuff of dreams. But a secret dwells in her past which theatens their romance, and Duncan is in any case promised to another. A match that should be, a passion that *must* be, looks impossible – unless true love can somehow, miraculously, find a way.

0 552 14847 4

CORGI BOOKS

HEART OF A WARRIOR
by Johanna Lindsey

A love that is written in the stars . . .

Brittany is proud and strong, a modern woman who vows that no man will ever plumb the depths of her soul. Then one day, Dalden walks into her life. She sees him across the lawn, where he immediately entices her with his tremendous strength and physical presence. Dalden is a warrior, powerful and brave, a man who fearlessly fights for what he wants.
And he wants Brittany . . .

He begs her to help him in his quest. It is a quest which will take Brittany to strange new worlds – and the depths of her own heart.

'First-rate romance'
New York Daily News

0 552 14912 8

CORGI BOOKS

A SELECTED LIST OF FINE NOVELS AVAILABLE FROM CORGI BOOKS

THE PRICES SHOWN BELOW WERE CORRECT AT THE TIME OF GOING TO PRESS. HOWEVER TRANSWORLD PUBLISHERS RESERVE THE RIGHT TO SHOW NET RETAIL PRICES ON COVERS WHICH MAY DIFFER FROM THOSE PREVIOUSLY ADVERTISED IN THE TEXT OR ELSEWHERE.

14972 1	DROP DEAD GORGEOUS	Katie Agnew	£6.99
14060 0	MERSEY BLUES	Lyn Andrews	£6.99
15059 2	SCORE!	Jilly Cooper	£6.99
15034 7	THE ROWAN TREE	Iris Gower	£5.99
14895 4	NOT ALL TARTS ARE APPLE	Pip Granger	£6.99
14538 6	A TIME TO DANCE	Kathryn Haig	£5.99
15033 9	CHANDLERS GREEN	Ruth Hamilton	£5.99
13872 X	LEGACY OF LOVE	Caroline Harvey	£6.99
13917 3	A SECOND LEGACY	Caroline Harvey	£5.99
14220 4	CAPEL BELLS	Joan Hessayon	£4.99
14603 X	THE SHADOW CHILD	Judith Lennox	£5.99
14737 0	THE PRESENT	Johanna Lindsey	£5.99
14781 8	JOINING	Johanna Lindsey	£5.99
14847 4	THE HEIR	Johanna Lindsey	£5.99
14912 8	HEART OF A WARRIOR	Johanna Lindsey	£5.99
15048 7	THE PURSUIT	Johanna Lindsey	£5.99
15130 0	A MAN TO CALL MY OWN	Johanna Lindsey	£5.99
15045 2	THOSE IN PERIL	Margaret Mayhew	£6.99
13569 0	A KINGDOM OF DREAMS	Judith McNaught	£6.99
13252 7	ONCE AND ALWAYS	Judith McNaught	
13826 6	ALMOST HEAVEN	Judith McNaught	
14354 5	UNTIL YOU	Judith McNaught	£
15152 1	THE SHADOW CATCHER	Michelle Paver	£6.99
08930 3	STORY OF O	Pauline Reage	£6.99
15163 7	HOW WAS IT FOR YOU?	Carmen Reid	£6.99
15141 6	THE APPLE TREE	Elvi Rhodes	£6.99
15017 7	LYDIA FIELDING	Susan Sallis	£5.99
15138 6	FAMILY FORTUNES	Mary Jane Staples	£5.99
14135 6	THE WEDDING	Danielle Steel	£6.99
15032 0	FAR FROM HOME	Valerie Wood	£5.99

All Transworld titles are available by post from:
Bookpost, PO Box 29, Douglas, Isle of Man IM99 1BQ
Credit cards accepted. Please telephone +44(0)1624 836000, fax +44(0)1624 837033
Internet http://www.bookpost.co.uk or
e-mail: bookshop@enterprise.net for details.
Free postage and packing in the UK.
Overseas customers allow £2 per book (paperbacks) and £3 per book (hardbacks).